HOT-WALKER

Life on the Fast Track

Mallory Neeve Wilkins

Sports Crime Romance Novel

Mallory Neeve Wilkins

2

Hot-Walker Life on the Fast Track
Mallory Neeve Wilkins

Library and Archives Canada Cataloging in Publication

ISBN: 9781770843523 (ebook)
ISBN: 9780986903526 (print)

Dedicated to
LAW
MJW
DW

PART I

'The Way We Were'

Chapter 1
Toronto - 1976

A magnificent rainbow reflects its brilliance onto the city's large glass and concrete structures as Peter Edwards maneuvers the red, 1967 Dino Ferrari from the airport to 590 Jarvis Street, Homicide Department.

Together, we continue into the old neglected building where we wait outside the office for Detective Riley. When he arrives, we shake hands and he welcomes me back to Toronto.

"Please, step inside so we can talk in private, but first I'll get us some coffee. How do you take it?" The detective, a man in his mid-fifties, wears dark framed glasses and has a receding hairline.

Sitting on opposite sides of the rustic wooden table, Peter and I wait until his return. Less than a week has passed since my best friend Susan Edwards, Peter's cousin, and I sat in the Fountain Abbey Pub, a local watering hole for St. Mary's Hospital staff, discussing Detective Riley's call. Because I lived in London, he explained they would not subpoena me, but I needed to return to Canada as a classified material witness.

The detective returns with a tray of coffees. "Miss Harrison, it's been awhile since we last met. You look different from what I remember," he remarks while he opens a paint blistered window allowing a fresh breeze to enter. Feeling nervous, I clear my throat and clasp my hands together.

"That happened several years ago when I was recuperating in the hospital." A vivid memory flashes before me, a day of horrific bloodshed when my fiancé was brutally murdered. I inhale deeply.

"How do you enjoy living in London?"

"Very much, thank you."

"Ah-h...," he reminisces, "Great life. I worked with Scotland Yard for a couple of years, back in my youth before I emigrated to Canada and I now think of Toronto as my home."

Riley retrieves a thick binder of paper, which he places on the table in front of me, and then sits next to Peter. He explains the *brief,* prepared by Homicide for the Crown, contains a description of the murder scene and the witness's statements. He takes a few minutes to update us on the latest happenings.

"Miss Harrison, we have one eyewitness that can identify the murderer." He hesitates. "And that would be you." Peter nods, agreeing, while sitting straight in his chair, still wearing his racetrack clothes, muddy boots and has a cigarette tucked behind his ear. The detective continues.

"Last spring, on a Friday night at Fort Erie Racetrack, a brawl took place in the stable area when an argument started and one thing led to another. Two witnesses testified that one of them reached into a wooden tack-box full of brushes and rags and pulled a gun on the other fella who tried to jump him in an effort to wrestle the weapon away. The man who initially reached for the gun dropped with a bullet in his shoulder. Police were called. Our forensic scientist identified the surgically removed shell as coming from the same gun that killed your fiancé, John Mencini." Riley looks at me but says nothing. He opens a file containing three photographs, and then sets them on the table in front of us.

Peter and I place the first faded photo to one side. We examine the second picture. "Isn't that the guy who used to sell racing forms in the backstretch? I can't remember his name; do you know it, Pete?"

"Sure. Everyone used to call him 'Smoocher.' He peddled everything from dope to watches for a buck. He was a real 'kiss-ass' and would do just about anything for money." Peter downs the dregs of his coffee.

"Correct." Detective Riley picks up the file, places it under the brief and continues. "While we had this scruffy character in recovery, police charged him with having an unregistered firearm for the purpose of endangering the public peace, giving us an opportunity to recheck the Mencini file."

Riley halts briefly to take a cigarette from his jacket pocket and light it. As Peter passes the ashtray from the far end of the table, Riley blows smoke arrogantly into the air.

"Let me take a few minutes and review a few things. Your statement given regarding the June 3rd, 1969 murder, Miss Harrison, cited a bald man firing a weapon, and then leaving the crime scene from the stable area parking lot at Woodbine Racetrack. He was driving a station wagon. A statement received from the security guard who heard the shot, also reported seeing a station wagon pull away, squealing tires. He identified it as a late sixties, dark red GM model with woodgrain siding. After this recent incident, we checked again with racetrack owners, trainers and grooms to see if they remembered this person, Smoocher, owning such a vehicle, but no one did. We thought we were at another dead-end." He goes on to say that a few weeks later he and Constable Warner visited the track kitchen for a sandwich when one of the cooks overheard them talking. She revealed Smoocher had borrowed her car on occasion, as they had been friends for years. However, one day, he didn't return it. Shortly afterward, he bought her another. No one knew this woman owned a car because she would bus to work. This was their only lead. Eventually, the car was found near the Buffalo border crossing and identified as the one belonging to this woman by tracing the registration numbers and ownership papers.

"Detective Riley, are you are telling us that you have a matching bullet and the getaway car?" Peter inquires.

Barely comprehending what he's saying, I watch Riley pick up the file to show us the pictures of a man wearing an old denim hat with a few weeks chin growth. Unable to recognize any familiar detail from that terrifying day of the murder, Peter takes an even closer look.

"Here is another photograph of the same man when booked on the possession charge." The detective drops the photo on the table in front of me. I jump up from my seat, shaking.

"That's him! That's the guy I saw in the station wagon pulling the gun back through the car window. He is the killer!" Walking away from the table, I pace the floor trying to focus on what Detective Riley is telling us. "I don't get this. You are telling us that Smoocher's gun also fired the bullet that killed John and that he had driven some woman's car that matched the description of the one the security guard and I saw. But really, look at him in this picture here. There is no likeness to the other one."

"Sit down, Frannie," Peter pleads. Organizing the two photos, the detective places them side by side. Peter shakes his head, and then speaks as placidly as possible. "The eyes. Yes, the eyes. They are a match." I also note the similarities.

"Miss Harrison, the bald man in this picture you pointed to **is** Smoocher. They took his photograph when discharged from the hospital without his disguise of hat and beard. It doesn't take much to change one's appearance, a pair of glasses, a mustache, different hair color. But, I am telling you, the killer is Alexander 'Smoocher' Newman."

The information overwhelms me. Several silent moments pass while I carefully re-examine the pictures; the recognition is vague, but it's there.

Walking nervously across the room to compose myself, thoughts rush through my mind about the evening when John and I returned to Woodbine Racetrack to check the horses when the dreadful incident occurred.

The door to the office opens and two men join us. One I recognize. Riley makes introductions.

"Miss Harrison, Peter Edwards, I'd like you to meet the Sergeant, who works on this case with me, Constable Warner." We shake hands. "And, James Whittmore is the Crown Attorney, Miss Harrison." He is a stern-faced man who grasps my hand firmly. "He will be handling the Mencini trial." Certain coldness shows in his expression and I feel a definite uneasiness. Whittmore's powerful presence dominates the room.

"You were about to say something, Miss Harrison?" Riley asks.

"I don't understand why he would kill John? What was his motive? What in the world triggered such a horrible killing?"

Peter quickly replies, under his breath, "Drugs."

"Pardon?"

"Come on, Frannie, you knew John had pushed that stuff around the track and everyone knew Smoocher was his contact. Whatever the jockeys, trainers, or grooms needed, it didn't matter if it was for the horses or for themselves, he would find it." I could sense the lawyer watching my reaction.

"Pete, you often said how relieved you were that he quit or am I out-to-lunch on that, too?"

"Frannie," Peter whispers, touching my knee. Placing my hands on my hips, I stand up and stare right into Whittmore's eyes. He's sitting with legs crossed and arms folded behind his head.

"Well, I'll tell you something, I don't buy it." Frozen in my stance, I wait.

"Miss Harrison, please sit down," Detective Riley requests. "Do you now believe that this man in the photo killed your fiancé?"

"Of course I believe it, but I'm telling you the motive stinks." I inhale deeply, trying to control my voice. "Perhaps, Smoocher got stiffed. You know, a bad deal where the stuff he peddled from the street wasn't any good, and in turn, he took revenge thinking it was from John." There is no response. I add, "I just don't buy it!"

"Listen, Frannie," Peter interrupts for a third time, "For God's sake, you have to be reasonable. You know as well as I do that John had bad connections."

"Look, did Newman tell you this was his motive?" I turn to face Riley.

"He's pleading *not guilty*," the Sergeant states flatly.

"Well, I knew John and he wouldn't have done anything that would have been worthy of murder," I explain.

"Miss Harrison, you obviously don't want to see your fiancé for whom he really was," Whittmore announces.

"Boy, you are a hard-nosed bastard," I stammer.

"Frannie!" Peter interrupts. "Look, this is the brief and it's full of statements."

"Yes, Miss Harrison," Whittmore continues, in an unmoving manner. "It is full of character witnesses regarding John Mencini, the American draft dodger who made his fortune by peddling drugs to juveniles and dope to trainers to get as much money as he could. You are a naive young woman who still does not want to face reality."

Silence prevails as several moments pass before I respond. Taking a deep breath, I make amends.

"I can accept John for who he was. I know of his involvement in several bad dealings, even rigging races and several other misdeeds. I apologize for speaking out of turn." I am feeling overwhelmed at this point.

The Sergeant places a notepad on the table and opens it to where he scribbles several notes. My emotions are beginning to overtake me. I excuse myself. Peter stands to open the door for me; I whisper, "That Crown is something else. He thinks he's hot shit. I can tell."

"Well, Frannie, he is the best criminal attorney going for the Crown."

"Doesn't say much for the Crown. I don't like him." I leave the room.

"That's obvious," Peter replies, and then returns to his seat.

Wishing I stayed in London, I begin to feel heartsick as I remember the good life I made for myself there, but deep down inside, I know that I will never be truly free until these tragedies from my past are resolved. Peter was John's best friend; we had known each other since high school and his cousin Susan and me had been childhood friends.

After I return, the men decide to break for lunch and meet back in the office at two o'clock. Peter leads the way back out onto Jarvis Street where he explains that he needs to drive to Woodbine racetrack to check the entries for the next day's racing card. It has been many years since I worked the stable area.

Together, we enter the barn area where the familiar smells take me by surprise. Mixtures of liniment, hay and leather saddle soap linger and it all seems as if it happened yesterday. A voice from the overhead speakers calls the horses for the first race of the day. This causes an overwhelming sense of loss, as I catch a glimpse of the red Ferrari in the parking lot. As I view the car from a distance, the shock of John's presence touches me, momentarily. The car wasn't just a vehicle; it had been a big part of John's identity and had remained parked for a long time before I could ride in it, let alone drive it.

Shaking away the image, I step up to the Larson Stable that appears more prosperous than I remember. Bridles hang neatly on the stall doors waiting for the horses racing later in the afternoon. The grooms are busy cleaning, washing down the area. The atmosphere reminds me of my earlier life, one like no other.

Peter returns carrying sandwiches and drinks as I remark on the impressive stable that trainer Bob Sharp maintains. He explains Bob as the leading trainer at Hialeah in Florida, and at Greenwood, the old Woodbine racetrack. Last year, his stable finished second at Blue Bonnets Raceway in Montreal and he won a few *stake* races when he shipped his better horses down to Aqueduct and Santa Anita in the States. He now sits on the board of the Ontario Jockey Club, as well as a dozen giant corporations.

"Too bad he couldn't have shared it all with his family," I add.

"That's why he is so successful. He had all the time in the world to devote and develop his fortune. You would not believe his place in Caledon. There are hundreds of fenced acres, which contain one of the finest breeding farms on the continent with indoor heated training tracks. Shit, you couldn't imagine his setup." Peter wipes his brow with the back of his hand.

"Who lives there with him?" I ask, sipping on my Pepsi.

"Oh, hell, there's no shortage of guests, that's for sure. The place crawls with high rollers all the time; out-of-towners, breeders, industrialists, veterinarians or developers. A few years back, he donated a small fortune to build a surgical clinic in Freelton for experimental operations on thoroughbreds. I'm telling you, Frannie, this guy is in another world now. I heard through the grapevine that he cooperated with the police during their investigation by giving them a few good leads."

"Has he helped you along the way?"

"Well, our relationship isn't anything like the one he had with John. No one could take his place. We are strictly business. Now that I have my trainer's license for my own horses, I assist and saddle for him whenever he is out-of-town. In turn, I board SnoMann at his farm and have breeding privileges." Brushing crumbs from his lap, he tosses his wrappers into a nearby bin. "Hey, come on over here. Wait until you see this colt. He's a two-year-old that will race next week for the first time."

Peter walks me down the dusty shed-row, stopping at stall 33. "What do you think?"

Chirping to get the horse's attention, it turns, and I can see a strong resemblance to the horse that brought us much glory and heartache all in one day.

"My Lord, does he ever look like SnoMann! Tell me, what did you name him?"

"After you … remember what Bob used to call you?"

"Little Britches?"

"Yup." I reach out to the bay animal with a small star and a narrow strip of white hair down his nose. I notice the four white socks similar to his sires and stroke his head while he munches away on clover hay.

"It's a long time ago, isn't it, Fran?" I sense a sentimental tone.

"Boy is it ever! I would love to see SnoMann again. I still have three distorted toenails to show for my time as a hot-walker."

Peter chuckles at my recollection. He confesses his own sorrow at having to return to the racetrack right after John's death. "Man, it was so hard. Someone still had to care for the stable. After SnoMann's big win, he was in high demand. The papers haunted me with questions and so did the cops. Glad I was busy because I missed John." I nod, understanding. Recognizing a tall, well-groomed man approach Peter, I try to recall his name. They speak for a few minutes before I remember he used to bet on many of Sharp's horses. Frankie, Frank Bressan, one of the biggest gamblers back in the 1960s.

My glance turns to a gray Coupe de Ville that pulls up alongside the stable. A fair-haired man climbs out of the back seat and holds his hand out for an attractive middle-aged couple. I stare for a moment.

"That's Bob, talking with some new owners." Peter points out.

"But, he used to have red hair," I recall.

"Yeah, a little gray now, and it looks kind of blond. Want to go and say hello?"

I shake my head, "Nah, I'm not up to it. Another time." Making an effort to leave, we approach the Ferrari.

"Frannie, if you hadn't met John, where do you think you would be today?" Peter asks, opening the passenger door where the leather interior looks and feels like new.

"Boy, things sure would be a lot different. He was the main figure in both our lives. I hope to hell they get the guy who did him in." Peter starts the powerful engine and pulls slowly along the roadway.

Sitting solemnly, I ask, "You know, Pete, I want to get all this behind me, but aren't you worried about Whittmore? He is obnoxious."

"Frannie, I don't understand you. He is the best. I mean it. He's not just going to sit there and let a murder trial involving drugs, the track, fixed races and whatever else, just go by. This is huge. He is a perfectionist. Many defense lawyers don't like him. They say he's a bit of a rebel. Honest, don't worry. The guy is good. You just have to relax and wait 'til you get some sleep and recover from jet lag. Everything will look differently."

Returning downtown to the station, I follow the group of men into the small room where we previously met. Detective Riley speaks, but his tone has changed as he explains that he has some disturbing news. Apparently, Newman's lawyer approached the sergeant. After reading his copy of the brief, he wants to change his plea. He is willing to tell the Crown the name of the guy who hired him to do the killing, that is *if* the Crown will allow Newman to plead guilty to a lesser charge.

Aware of my surprise, he pauses. "Miss Harrison, I can see your confusion. Let me explain. Newman or Smoocher as you refer to him, apparently realized he would be found guilty of first-degree murder and sentenced. Consequently, he decided the only way to avoid a life sentence was to confess to his lawyer that it had been a *contract* killing. Newman will name the person who put out the contract *if* it could get him a lighter sentence. It's called *plea bargaining*. He's hopeful of a charge of manslaughter with a jail term and some hope of parole down the line. He knows we have enough evidence to put him away for life, unless... " Riley stops mid-sentence when he sees the expression on my face.

Peter places his hand on my shoulder to comfort. "You mean to tell us that Smoocher didn't kill John?" Riley wipes his forehead and draws a deep breath.

"No, Peter. He actually did do the shooting. He killed Mencini and should be charged with premeditated murder, but the question is whether the Crown will go along with this plea bargain."

"Well, why the hell wouldn't he? I mean if there is a chance to get to the bottom of this?" I bark, without thinking.

"Miss Harrison," Riley whispers, "You must realize that we have the person who pulled the trigger. He is the murderer. Whittmore feels there is no reason to justify a reduced sentence for someone who is the actual killer, giving him less punishment than he deserves."

"So, what happens now?"

"The Defense and the Crown met after lunch. We are now going over to Whittmore's office to see if they convinced him to go with the new plea. I wouldn't have a chance in hell of talking to Whittmore about a new charge, but the Defense feels otherwise; so he approached him directly."

"What makes him feel he can do better? What do they do - eat lunch together?" I persist.

"Frannie!" Peter exclaims, butting my elbow. "What are you... stuck in some negative energy field? It's time to move on, get past this."

Once again, we leave the station as the sun's strong reflection bounces off the new office building windows, momentarily blinding. We pass the impressive new Eaton's Center and spot the recently completed CN Tower feeling the city has changed drastically in six years.

Peter wheels the Ferrari down the City Hall parking ramp, following Detective Riley.

We enter through the grand marble foyer of the 1966 courthouse where a sign indicates Toronto firm of Marani, Rountwaite and Dick as the Architects.

The sergeant leads the way to the Crown Attorney's offices. Riley approaches the desk to make the necessary inquiries when Whittmore appears in his black gown. We enter his office confirming that Newman is pleading guilty to second-degree murder and that his lawyer will bring application to the Supreme Court to have him released on bail while he awaits trial. Newman will then help them get a confession from this other person who hired him to do the killing. Suddenly, I feel Whittmore look deep into my eyes.

"There is something else that we will need from both of you."

"What's that?" Peter asks.

"Your help."

"In what way?"

"We want Newman to put out a call to his partner in the contract and get him to put up bail. Then, when released, the police will fit Newman with a body pack so he'll get a verbal confession on tape to many of the charges."

"I still don't see; what do we have to do with any of this?" I ask calmly.

"Miss Harrison, Newman's contact is someone whom you both may recognize and we feel that with your help, we can arrange things more exactly." Looking back at me, Peter agrees, realizing that this case is all of a sudden getting complicated.

"Why would this person put up bail?" I ask.

"Because Newman will tell this guy that he 'owes him' and if he doesn't, he'll squeal."

"So, who's the real culprit behind all this? Who wanted John out-of-the-way so badly that he had to hire someone to...?"

"A man obsessed beyond restraint."

14

Chapter 2

Legal Procedures

Peter unlocks the front entrance door of his townhouse, walks into the kitchen and grabs a cold beer from the fridge. Stunned by the day's events, knowing the information is strictly confidential until the police get a statement, Peter swiftly slams his fist against a stack of books in a rage.

"Frannie, some mother-fuckin' bastard took us all in. Can't you see? Whoever it is, did a huge snow job on all of us, but poor ol' John was the one who paid for this whole friggin' mess." He swears, falling on the sofa, a long day for both of us.

"I'm feeling sort of sick," I announce. Peter apologizes and suggests I get some rest. He carries my luggage to his guest room as he accounts for many possibilities concerning the murderer; a gambler, a vet, a member of the mob or someone who felt cheated by John. Peter would do everything within his power to make up for John's unwarranted death.

Peter spends the weekend keeping busy while I catch up on my sleep, feeling no compulsion to leave the townhouse. I miss London, my job, my friends; Susan, Matthew and especially Bradley.

Late Monday afternoon, the telephone rings and I answer, hesitantly. James Whittmore explains he just returned from the preliminary hearing and would like to see me right away. Blindly replacing the receiver, I pick up my jacket, feeling surprise and confusion.

Less than half an hour later, I park at a street meter on University Avenue and enter the building looking for the familiar markings that lead to the Crown Attorney's office.

Trailing students, lawyers, and police officers down the marble hallway, I recognize Whittmore speaking with another gowned attorney. We enter his office to talk in private. His rugged features show no expression as he eyes me, his prospective witness.

"Miss Harrison. I want to thank you for coming so promptly," he declares, as a matter of etiquette. "We have a few updates for you and new facts. Newman had his preliminary hearing before a Provincial Court Judge and committed to trial by agreement on a charge of second-degree murder."

The news is unmoving as my real concern isn't Smoocher. I want to know the next step. He explains how they presented the judge with an *Information Document* laying out the charges. Sergeant Warner testified, satisfying the Judge that our case has enough evidence to justify a trial on that charge. He notes my sudden uneasiness.

"The Defense will now apply for bail which will probably be around $40,000. Then, the police will get Newman to put out a call to his contact to provide bail threatening to finger him to the police if he doesn't comply."

"What is the date set for the trial?" I ask.

"That will be decided in a few weeks."

"Is it a long procedure?"

"Yes." Whittmore glances impatiently at his watch.

"I would like to speak with you further on this, but I have to drop this brief at the sergeant's desk and then prepare in polished form my summations for another jury trial tomorrow. I wonder if you would join me for a bite to eat, and then we can talk. I am sure you will appreciate a more relaxing atmosphere." He smiles for the first time.

I straighten my coat as he politely opens the door to find the officer awaiting the brief, and they exchange comments on the case.

Leaving the Courthouse, we walk toward the Four Seasons Hotel where he orders a white wine for me and a double Black Velvet for himself. I thank him, extending my glass to wish him a successful trial.

"Well, it will take some work on your part, Miss Harrison, or may I call you Francine?"

"Of course," I return.

"What I have heard, from different sources, is that you once worked on the racetrack for the trainer, Robert Sharp, some years back. Also, you lived with his daughter, Karen? By the way, I saw her wedding pictures in the Globe and Mail the other morning. She is a beautiful woman."

"Yes, she definitely is. A famous supermodel, now." For a split second, my thoughts drift to Montreal and the time we spent at Expo in 1967 when we raced at Blue Bonnets Raceway.

"From my understanding you were close to the family, traveling with them to different racetracks where you became good friends."

"Yes, I suppose you could say that. Karen and I spent quite a bit of time working together."

"Have you seen or spoken to any of them since your return last week?"

"No. No one." I answer, hastily.

"Good. I want you to keep it that way. Stay away from the racetrack, and keep out of sight for the time being. I want to talk with you later this week. I need to know a lot more about your past."

"Sure, but why?"

"When Detective Riley fills you in on his specific plans and what part you will play in all this, we want you as part of the meeting with Newman's contact. We need to know he will turn up, unsuspecting. This way, Newman will be under protective custody until we turn him loose in a place that he would not likely appear." I want to know the suspect's name, but at the right moment they will tell me. One slip of the tongue and their case is ruined.

"Wow. This is really going to be...."

"Complicated," he adds.

I sip my wine watching his expression change.

"You will have lots of time to prepare yourself emotionally for this encounter and I hope that you will cooperate."

"No problem. I'll gladly help out." I want this case resolved as too many years have passed.

After awhile, I drive the Ferrari into the garage of Peter's townhouse, noticing his truck parked in its usual spot on the street.

He greets me at the basement door. "Well, where were you? You never leave this place, and then you're gone without leaving me a note." He is still wearing his track clothes, holding a cigarette in his hand.

"Sorry about that. Whittmore called to see me." As I explain my afternoon, Peter falls clumsily onto the sofa.

"I don't believe it! You actually had lunch with Whittmore? You must be kidding." Laughing at my initial reaction, he throws up his arms.

Peter describes his talk with Bob at the racetrack earlier the same day. While Bob was busy showing clients around his stable, his 'betting friend' Frank Bressan and his partner arrived. They chatted with Peter about the week's prospects, and then went for coffee together. Bob mentioned he thought he saw me in the stable area the previous week, but when Peter didn't respond, he dropped the subject.

"You know, I was also at Homicide today." Peter leans forward in his seat, and then continues. "I told Riley that while scrounging around one of the tackrooms yesterday, I stumbled across an envelope with some papers inside. I tossed it aside, but then I felt this odd sensation, so I went back and found a list of drugs, veterinarians and trainers names scribbled out. I took it downtown, and they said the vet's names could help Newman's testimony about connections with the inside trafficking of narcotics. An expert from Forensic will analyze the handwriting."

"Great intuition! We have to listen to that little voice inside us more often. What do you think that was all about?"

"You see, once in a while, some of Sharp's friends or gamblers, like Frankie and his pals, wanted to be touted onto a sure thing when placing their bets. When it looked like a *boat race,* which means there was a good chance to get a horse on the board, one of the trainers and a vet would pump a little extra insurance into a horse's jugular. Many times, they would say it was a shot of vitamin B12. However, other times a trainer would also be in on the hit. A vet would cover by switching urine samples after the race before they went into the testing lab. It was their extra guarantee. I remember once in Montreal when a vet, Jean St. Hilaire, and Bob tried some heroin on this big bay gelding we were running that had never got closer than sixth in his life. The damn thing went berserk. When the gates opened, it took off like a shot out of hell and ran right down the backstretch and through the fence towards Decarie Boulevard. Boy, I thought the Stewards were going to blow the roof sky-high, but with a decent bribe, it never hit the papers." Peter points a finger, changing the subject. "Can I get you something?" he offers.

"Got any Scotch?"

"Scotch? Francine Harrison wants Scotch?" Peter laughs.

"Single malt. Glenfiddich."

"No lady, we don't serve that brand in this bar. Perhaps you. . ."

"Never mind, just a DuBonnet with lemon." I smile.

"No problem. Be right back."

Peter returns with our drinks and continues with his thoughts. He flops down on the carpeted floor amongst a few cushions and week-old newspapers, and then asks if I have heard anything from my brother Leonard, who lived in Europe, since I returned to Toronto. Shaking my head, he pauses, knowing he would want updates on what was happening. Peter changes the subject.

"Yeah, like I was saying, the cops are making up a long list of charges. Man, I just cannot believe all this happened right under my nose. It's got to be one of the gangsters."

"I know what you mean, but did you ever think it would get this involved? I thought I would be heading back to London by the end of the month. This could drag on for months, and I miss Bradley, Susan and Matthew so much. Bradley will have to get someone in the office to replace me while all this is going on."

Peter taps my foot with his. "Hey, you don't have to worry about that guy. He is the salt of the earth. Just make sure you keep him up-to-date with all the details."

"I suppose so. I'm not to call him until tomorrow. Right now, he is busy with the design of the Mallett Community Center and the construction deadline. It will be a miracle if he gets away at all."

"Hey, not to worry. It's Brad. He will make it happen." Peter is right. Bradley has been his friend since childhood. We all went to school together and Peter has great respect for him, as I do.

"By the way, did you get a chance to read the whole article about Karen Sharp's wedding in the gossip column? Never thought I'd see the day when they would marry." Peter switches positions, stretching out his legs.

"Whittmore saw the paper, too, which made it sound glamorous. Karen found her man, and they make a good couple."

"Yeah, and that's something you should know." Peter winks.

He reminds me that I need to divulge the details about Karen and I reuniting in London and how she met her husband, but I doze off before finishing our conversation to the tunes of Mike Oldfield and Tubular Bells.

The confinement of the townhouse is like an imprisonment as I miss the buzz of London. The days are long as we wait for information regarding the upcoming case.

Suddenly, I am feeling the urge to get out. I slip on a pair of sunglasses, take a Madras golf hat from Peter's closet, and take a drive.

Traveling from one end of the city to the other, the afternoon slips by and I end up near Wilket Creek where I notice a large group gathering on a hill near the hotel, Inn on the Park, that catches my eye. Curious, I wheel the sports car up the steep incline into the parking lot where several polished classic and antique automobiles were judged on restoration. As I stroll through the exhibit, hearing the names of the winning vehicles over the speakers, I enjoy viewing the best from each category until sunset. Walking toward the exit, someone taps my shoulder, unexpectedly.

"Francine, I wasn't sure if that was you under there. What would you be doing in a place like this all by yourself?" I turn in the direction of the familiar voice.

"What brings you out of the halls of justice?" I reply. The informally dressed Mr. Whittmore is standing beside a teenage boy carrying an armful of Vintage Car magazines.

"Now, Francine, I hope you don't think I am completely all business. This is my hobby. My son and I have a car here that we are showing." The young man steps aside to chat with friends, dropping from the conversation.

"Really? How interesting. I would never have guessed that you had time for any such hobby, let alone one so involved."

He scratched his head; a smile dimpled his rugged features. "Anyway, I am pleased we ran into one another. There is some new information. Would you join me in the Hotel?"

His unexpected offer takes me by surprise. I follow him to where we soon sit overlooking the gardens with our cocktails.

"Tell me, Mr. Whittmore, which one of those beauties belongs to you?"

"The 1939 Buick convertible; the maroon vehicle with the white top parked over by the trees."

"Oh, yes, as a matter of fact, I recall seeing it parked next to a '52 Jaguar that caught my eye as well. Yours is a real beauty. Do you drive it - or is it strictly for show?"

"Without a doubt, we drive it. I believe in using - not storing. The car is my son's pride and joy, which he drove to commencement this fall and had an absolute ball. It makes me feel proud that we can share something. We haven't done much together over the years."

"I can imagine. Not being at home much could be difficult."

He clears his throat. "…and your interest?"

"I collect cars, Morgan, Ferrari." I kid. The attorney's eyes widen.

"No, I'm only pulling your leg. I actually do own both those cars, but they come with a history. I'm just an interested fan of classic cars."

"Obviously," he remarks, taking a long pull on his drink. "Now, let me fill you in on the latest. The bail hearing went through. Newman put out a call to his contact the other day. However, nothing happened. Then today, this unknown person showed up and put up the bail for him. We assume it was an undercover person. Newman is now free but kept under wraps for the time being. We wouldn't want his contact suspicious of his turning up as if it was planned."

"Well, I'm sure glad to hear that news. I guess it's time for our meeting soon."

"Yes, we need to talk, right away, and then you will meet with Sergeant Warner, who will give you the details for arranging a meeting." I agree, feeling more confident in one way, and anxious in another.

"I want to stress the importance of being very cautious with whom you speak about the trial. The charges include not only murder but trafficking in narcotics, illegal betting, conspiracy to defraud the public, bribery of jockeys to pull horses in some races, cruelty to animals involving drugs, falsifying documents with intent to defraud,,, and so forth."

"God! I don't believe it!" I stammer, thinking it's a vet or an insider.

"Listen, young woman, there's a great deal more. However, I suppose that's enough for now. What is important is for you to realize we are supporting you. If there is anything you want to know or you don't understand…" He removes a card from his pocket and scribbles his private number on the back.

"This case will be very emotional for you, Francine. Remember, we want to put this person away because he has gone free far too long. In addition, Francine, we *will* convict him. Don't ever think that he will get himself a sharp defense attorney to get him off on some technicality because he won't, not so long as I am handling the case." I blush at the man's self-assurance. "Beware of the press. Once the case begins, they will hound you. In fact, do not talk to them at all. We have to be careful what we say, even to the police." He points to himself.

"I think you have enough confidence for both of us," I grin.

"I work hard at it."

I raise my glass. "How long have you been a Crown Attorney?" I query, changing the subject.

"Some days, too long! No, a little over twenty years." Whittmore relaxes back in his chair. He looks directly at me.

"The Crown's position can be complicated because we are under a lot of strain. We do have significant resources, the police, and criminal investigators who obtain the evidence. They are the makings that give me the experience to be able to spot and find the underlying cause of the real crime. Remember, it's the Crown who has to prove its case *guilty beyond a reasonable doubt* - not the Defense." I nod understanding.

He continues, explaining his training and practice at law school never taught how to deal with people like myself or others, only the practical mechanics of the court. Yet, it's all part of his function. Most people lack an understanding of the system and the courts. Sometimes, a witness forgets all the facts so thoroughly discussed in pre-trial examinations when he steps up into the witness box. When confronted by the Defense Counsel, a witness suddenly begins to shake, becomes scared, even panics and freezes.

"I'm not saying it'll happen, but for the life of me, one of the hardest points to tell a person is not to be afraid and to remain calm. They are facing something they do not understand, especially in a criminal trial dealing with a death. The T.V. reporters, the press, and other news media twist and confuse matters. Once the case reaches the papers, everyone wants to take center stage. Please, don't get me wrong. You may be able to handle this easily, but I want you to be aware that a murder trial is like no other. In preparation, we advise every witness to act and dress to impress the jury. The press will blow this case out of proportion. Remember, you are just as important a witness as Alexander Newman is. Even Peter knows a great deal about many people around the racetrack because he worked with John on the circuit for many years. The police and I must gather every detail of incriminating evidence to nail this case shut." I listen intently, knowing that my part is critical to the success of the procedure, hopeful my memory is storing this information.

"Well, I've just about talked myself dry for the moment, Francine. I had better get back to my son and help him close up for the evening." We make our way to the exit, where the young man meets us.

"The cars are pulling out now, Dad. Thought you might want to see them."

"Yes, I would." Whittmore's arm wraps around his shoulders. "Francine, this is my son, Reagan, and Reagan, this is Francine Harrison." We shake hands. "He's my class-A auto mechanic and he has done considerable restoration on the Buick with me," the lawyer beams.

While walking back to the parking lot, to the amazement of the eighteen-year-old, several interested spectators surround the Ferrari.

"You mean this machine is yours? Wow! What a beauty!" gasps Reagan. "It's a Dino, right?"

"Sure is! Do you like it?"

"Like it? Love it!" he cries, looking through the windshield and examining every contour and feature of the shiny sports car. I smile, tapping on the hood for his attention. He looks up. I toss him the keys, and he hesitates.

"Here, I'll let you take it for a short spin." The young man's face shows his excitement. He glances at his father for approval.

"Jeez, why I don't ... I mean ... sure! Thanks." Reagan unlocks the door and slides down into the driver's seat. He proudly turns the key and feels the powerful engine turn over. Slowly, he backs the car and drives down the hill.

"You know, Francine, it bothers me to think of you involved with a bunch of trackers. You! A hot-walker? For the life of me, I cannot figure where or how you fit in, or what you were doing with those guys. You know, a thoroughbred is the result of fine breeding and you, my dear, I would like to think of as one fine thoroughbred. Whatever led you to that life, I'll never really understand. I hope this ordeal won't pull you back there because it seems that you are now on the right track. And, that's not a pun! Just be sure to stay there." He smiles. Whittmore's sudden interest and change of attitude makes me believe he is searching for specific information.

"No problem. I am here to clear up this mess and I hope I may be of some help."

"You surely will be." Whittmore agrees. We watch the classics leave the parking area.

"By the way, if you ever come across an old Packard convertible, I'd be interested in knowing about it," I confess.

"What year?"

"1937 and yellow."

"That will be a chore, but I will put the word out. It will be expensive because that was a rare car and a pretty fancy one, too." Whittmore ponders, almost thinking aloud.

"Yeah, I suppose."

"Any special reason for that particular year?"

"It was my Mom's engagement gift from my Dad. They are both dead now, and I thought after seeing all these beauties that it might be a great one to add to my collection."

Nodding his head, he acknowledges some friends as they pass by. The roar of an engine sounds as Reagan pulls up next to us. I open the door for him.

"That was the greatest, Miss. Boy, what a fantastic machine! That thing can move and those carbs really open up." He offers his hand in appreciation.

"You're welcome, Reagan. You can try it again at another show someday." I say without realizing the consequences.

"Super, we'll remember, eh Dad?" He turns to join his friends. Bidding farewell, I head back to Peter's townhouse, satisfied by my outing.

I often wonder about these kinds of days, serendipity. My premonition was to get out of the townhouse, and then somehow I ended up in the right place. There were things I needed to hear, things I needed to face. Running into Whittmore was more than a coincidence and I marvel when these things happen, all part of the journey. It's my destiny.

Nevertheless, now it is time for me to reminisce - to recollect the facts of my mundane past as a hot-walker. A past that I had hoped I would never have to recall ... in detail.

Chapter 3
Reliving the Past – 1960s

The sixties rolled into North Toronto filling local high school parking lots with '55 Chevys. We listened to Beatles music at Friday night dances and going steady was the 'in' thing. Cafeteria conversations consistently buzzed from... who was hot-rodding their mother's car, to the latest 'backcombing' hairstyles.

Toronto had turned into a draft dodger haven and Yorkville was their Mecca. Young men were forsaking canteens, bunkers, ditches and planes in Vietnam to sleep on the floor of some vermin-filled overcrowded, condemned building.

One of these young men, John Roberts by name, became popular in that area of Toronto, not because of his illegal entry from Ohio, but for the merchandise he handled, small amounts of dope and hash. His brother, President of a local plastic manufacturing firm located in the suburbs, provided him entrance into Canada on a phony working visa. Many followed by other means and soon the village of Yorkville became a drop-in center for unemployed youths. Parents warned us about the changes.

Peter Edwards quit school and I remember when he left home to venture out with no particular course in mind. He eventually teamed with a car crew at Mosport and camped, worked in the pits and hung around the track following friends to Watkins Glen. Hard work, long hours and lack of money only brought him back home despondent, but full of experience. His father tried to 'straighten out' Peter only to have him leave for another kind of track, one more to his needs - Greenwood. He would become successful betting the horses.

Making money and friends all via the alcohol, sex and drug route, Peter's racetrack acquaintances steered him to John Roberts, who promptly became a close friend. Together they spent days at the track and nights in the village of Yorkville. Occasionally, Peter's school friend, BJ Nichols, came to rescue him from some bind. BJ was our high school hero who thrived in sports with hopes of playing Junior A hockey with the London Knights. A group of us spent many summers at his family cottage.

In the spring of 1965, BJ competed for his high school track and field events at the Georgian Bay Finals in Aurora. Success could lead to the Toronto Track Meet at the Canadian National Exhibition and on to the Ontario Championships qualifying him for a tryout at the Olympic Field Events. However, that dream would never happen for him. It was a day I would never forget.

Track and field was my specialty during those years, but I struggled to win the girls senior championship that spring. Peter and I had not seen one another for over a year when he and his friend turned up at the event to see BJ and his cousin Susan compete in their races.

Later that afternoon, we met up together. During our conversation, Peter recalled the days we danced at Teen Town before my mother died and I moved in with my Aunt. We enjoyed the sunshine as we reminisced, as this was also the day he introduced me to John Roberts.

Running in the last event of the day, BJ needed the win to finish in first place. We stood close by as the eight muscular competitors stood along a chalked starting line, digging in their toes, rocking back and forth on their markers. I noticed BJ rub one eye hurriedly, shaking his head before placing himself into position. A shot rang out and the cinders flew in all directions as the runners left their mark together. The tightened muscles in their thighs flexed and their arms reached forward as they raced past spectators towards the first hurdle. Long strides and lanky bodies stretched along the track, and the pack separated as they covered the second hurdle, reaching for the next. The crowd screamed. BJ passed another, narrowing his distance. Approaching the fourth jump, he caught up with the leader in the second lane, but another was closing fast in the fifth lane beside him. Startled, he ducked, and then hit the hurdle with his toe. Falling into the cross rail, he knocked the other knee against it with such force that it made an audible snap. He tumbled to the ground and lay motionless as the race finished in another's glory.

Students swarmed onto the track. "Don't touch him, anyone," called one of the teachers. "Someone phone an ambulance, immediately." The badly damaged leg could not move. That event was the beginning of the end for BJ and his dreams of becoming a professional athlete.

That same evening, we heard there were complications when the hospital nurse explained that the shattered kneecap needed an operation, which happened the following day. He would be in a cast, out of action and doing therapy for several months.

Peter could not comprehend the incident and wondered what made BJ take a dive. We watched him race several times over the years.

A day later, we learned that his doctor noticed BJ complaining about double vision. Mr. Nichols said he thought it started at the end of the hockey season in March. We remembered attending a game where BJ was cross-checked into the boards. Dr. Carter, an ophthalmologist, gave him a thorough eye examination, learning he had Diplopia, an eye imbalance caused from when he hit the boards so hard that his helmet cracked. This incident was the cause of his accident when he ducked from the approaching runner. His doctor prescribed corrective lenses to balance the vision of each eye by pulling the muscles back into place. It appeared no different to us than a lazy eye, turning inward.

All through high school, Peter and Susan thought BJ as the one students who would succeed and make it big in sports, but it was not meant to be. We grew up together, more or less, all through our school years. BJ and Peter spent years together camping, hiking, learning to drive, tasting the forbidden fruits of alcohol, smoking weed and sharing tales of their first love until Peter left school for a different life. One with more adventure.

Things began to change for the four of us that summer, things that would alter the direction of our lives.

Yorkville Village

During the hot Ontario summer months, Peter, John, Susan and I saw a great deal of each other as we spent weekends at BJ's family cottage in the Muskoka Lake district with other school friends. We hung out together going to concerts, drive-in movies and canoeing. .

Susan submitted applications to a couple of community colleges that offered courses in interior design. Her boyfriend at that time, Kenny Gligowski, stayed in school to finish grade 13 so he could go on to university while BJ remained in hospital doing therapy until he moved up to the cottage. Eventually, he would skate again, but never to play hockey professionally. The calcium chips that remained lodged in his knee would be too painful to bear the constant pressure that skating would put on his leg and he needed to decide on a different future. Mr. Nichols suggested several options, such as sports medicine or business, which only led to unnecessary arguing and damaged their relationship.

Peter was back in his family's good books once again, but on his own terms. This presented a few problems. They disliked his living in Yorkville, which received bad press as American draft dodgers moved in. Many drug pushers began to leave and John gradually withdrew from the drug scene, spending more time with Peter at the racetrack. They started working early hours with the horses in hopes of 'claiming' one to race.

I had my own uncertainty - finances. Dissatisfied staying with relatives in a prosperous neighborhood where I lived since my Mom died, I listened as Peter and John tried to persuade me to move in with them. It would have been different if Leonard, my brother, had not moved away – I missed him being around, but he was a few years older and felt the need to leave the city. John and I began seeing more of each other through the winter months.

After weeks of cold rainy March weather, I felt overwhelmed by depression. Making my decision, I packed my bags and left security, comfort and suburban living for the unknown. I moved downtown into the welcoming arms of my two friends at the Bloor subway station.

As I passed through the subway's glass swinging doors, the filth from the garbage-strewn streets made me pause a moment. The Yorkville I remembered visiting with my mother as a child, wearing my funny little white gloves and smocked dresses, no longer existed. The view of hundreds of kids, not unlike me, walked the littered streets of the old Victorian village. I took it all in.

The sidewalks filled with colorful flowers and drawings, painted fire hydrants marred with ice cream or urine stains, and windows of the tall gingerbread houses marked with soda pop spray. Some Rochdale kids carried protest signs while others had flowers pinned to their vests or wore British army uniforms. Flower children wore buttons 'Make Love Not War' while unusual characters displayed strings of love beads and headbands. Love poems covered the old brick walls along the side streets. Flashing lights of police cruisers and the honking horns disoriented me, and I found myself bumping into people. The paint-blistered windows in the old houses showed neglect, but others painted in psychedelic pinks and greens held unfamiliar flags. It was another Haight Ashbury.

Following John closely, we walked along Cumberland Street, passing discotheques with go-go girls in glass cages, hearing guitar-strumming melodies drifting from those sitting on stairways sipping coffee. The distinctive smell of marijuana permeated the air as we heard acid rock coming from the basement of a dilapidated building.

Only a few original storeowners remained in the village. Most had moved away, unable to get insurance. This once prosperous area now sat in ruins, yet it filled with a new generation unlike any other.

The dress code was loose with ill-fitting vests and long hair on both sexes. Through open doorways, I could see unmade mattresses without springs or headboards, boxes of ragged clothes tossed on the floor and nude bodies at a third-floor window calling to others below.

Amidst the grime was an immaculate senior citizen home where the elderly rocked peacefully on the verandah and watched the gardeners carefully manicuring their grounds, which appeared to be the only piece of sanity left.

Tables, set up café-style, blocked the sidewalks. Tiny shops offered pottery, peasant type garments, special herbs and spices, candles and beads. We passed through an alley where several couples, eager for a little bit of *speed*, stopped to greet John, which made me uneasy to see how popular he was. Passing through the battered doorway of an old red brick house, we sat down on the badly cracked steps. Moments had passed before anyone spoke.

"John, I don't know what I want to do; just need to start living and I suppose this is as good a place to begin as the next." Peter laughed, quietly. Everyone in the village was looking for a new direction. In that sense, I was no different.

Days turned into long nights, and even longer weeks. My new environment filled with young hippies wearing long straight hair and ragged torn clothes, which contrasted with my curly style and daily habit of bathing and wearing clean clothes. The different types I rapped with all had their own stories, but none seemed to hold my interest. Unable to find regular work, I shared a common trait – unemployment – with the others.

Many days I walked up and down Yonge and Dundas Streets applying for jobs in boutiques and small offices, but no one was hiring. My appearance slowly deteriorated to reflect my neighborhood and the shopkeepers didn't want anything to do with kids from Yorkville. Since I lacked experience, only the bigger department stores, Eaton's and Simpsons, hired part-time and only if I trained for three weeks and worked evenings. I needed pocket money, so over the winter, I began training and working on billing machines until Peter and John teased me about it. By March, they made their point known.

"God, Frannie. You're making peanuts and working late hours. What will you bring home, perhaps $50 a week, eh?" Peter asked defiantly as he took a swig from his beer can, and then stretched out across the dirt-filled hallway.

"Look at it this way, Frannie." John offered. "You're hanging around the Village here all day and working evenings when you should have a good time. Plus, you are working Saturdays. Why don't you reconsider and join us at the racetrack." He paused, hearing me sigh. "It sure as hell isn't that hard, and I'm telling you, Frannie, you will be making big bucks in no time. We can get you a job walking *hots*, and at $5.00 a head, you will be able to walk ten horses in a morning and do just fine pulling in almost $300.00 a week. That will pay for entertainment and nice clothes, or whatever it is you fancy," he persisted. He sat cross-legged on the floor beside me. "Come on..."

"Get off it, guys. I've never ridden a horse in my life, and I'll be damned if I want to be near some high-strung animal that will probably sense that I'm scared to death of it and stomp on my feet. I have no idea what you mean when you say 'walking hots,' for crying out loud. How the hell would I fool anyone trying to get a job doing that?"

Peter leaped in surprise, having awakened my interest. He set his beer aside, rubbed his hands briskly, and leaned forward, smiling.

"Fran, we can help you. Come on; say you will try it. Go with us and we will show you around, fill you in on what it's all about. This will be so much fun." I didn't reply.

Sitting there on the floor, John stretched, leaned over and whispered, "Frannie, listen. Walking *hots* is simply cooling out a hot racehorse after he has had a workout so he doesn't get a chill. A groom will take a horse that has just come off the track from his morning *breeze*, gallop, or whatever, and remove the tack and replace it with a halter. He will probably hose the horse down before giving it to you to cool out – that is, to simply walk it around the shed-row. Every so often, you take the horse to its bucket, which hang outside its stall, and then you let him drink, just a little. Now, does that sound so hard?" John waited.

"The groom will clip the shank onto the halter, and if you want, when you're done, he will walk the horse back into its stall."

I asked, genuinely puzzled, "Shank?"

"Yeah, shank. It's a six-foot strap of leather with about eighteen inches of heavy chain attached to one end. It hooks under the halter, or some trainers wrap it around the horse's nose for better control, so you have a lead to walk it with. You just hold on, and go." Moseying across the room, I picked up a beer from the paint-chipped table that sat beneath the broken window. All the cans were empty.

"Anyone got a beer?" I changed the subject. "I'm hungry. How about a sandwich?" I reached under the rollaway and pulled out a box. Lifting out a loaf of stale Wonder bread and a jar of peanut butter, I offered them some. Disappointed in the change of subject, they ate.

The environment was unlike anything I had imagined. Feeling like a stranger in a strange land, I struggled daily to fit in with the Yorkville crowd and their private clubs. Many youths wandered the streets sharing a joint while others sat on splintered doorsteps listening to rock on their radios. The strong aroma of incense drifted from a rowdy house party where the only invites were those who took to *coke*. It became apparent that the racetrack boys, known for selling joints, offered other pleasures as well. Private gatherings and clubs tucked into dark alleys. To enter, it was by invite only.

While strolling down the littered roadway, a tall, dark-skinned teenager approached John and whispered something. She wore a loosely fitted woven Mexican top, which revealed her bare breasts when the wind blew. On her hip, she carried a load of books, which identified the University she attended. She was searching for a little party action with some *nose candy*. Peter supplied her needs, and the two disappeared arm-in-arm. John grasped my hand and we roamed the streets, passing Queens Park, to where we drank espresso in the Purple Onion. John talked about the racetrack as we listened to melancholy folk music when a popular old-timer poetically spoke about the area as he strummed his guitar. The singer described Toronto's oldest adjoining village, Yorkville, as founded in 1830 by entrepreneur Joseph Bloore, as a residential suburb. The village grew enough to be connected by an omnibus service in 1849 to Toronto. His music explained how the cost, of delivering services to the large population of Yorkville, was beyond the Village's ability, so it petitioned the City of Toronto and annexed in 1883. The character of the suburb did not change and its Victorian-style homes, quiet residential streets, and picturesque gardens survived into the 20th century. He sang about our generation of alternative lifestyles as one from all walks of life arriving in the early 1960s when Yorkville flourished as Toronto's counter-cultural Mecca and we were all a part of it.

Close to midnight, we returned to the house where we noticed an older woman in torn denims leaning out the door of the upper-level room, as a loud party echoed through the halls.

"Ah-h Johnny, my boy," the partially dressed, intoxicated woman called. "We have a message for you to call your brother. He has some good news for you - eh?" Then, touching her lips, she backed into the room locking the door.

I was halfway up the stairs when John called that he would return the call and be right up. Wearily, I opened the door and was confronted by a shocking sight; two guys lying nude on the bed about to do something I'd rather not witness.

"Hold it, assholes!" I called out, surprising the hell out of them. Both were under the influence of something, barely focusing on me. "Did you not hear me? Move it! And I mean now!" I screamed as they stumbled from the room. I stood at the door feeling sick. Calming my shakiness, I entered the room and took my sleeping bag from the corner, unrolled it, covering the soiled mattress. Without a pillow or any other covers, I flopped down on my stomach, crossed my arms under my head and rested until John arrived. He watched for a moment and then closed the door behind him. Feeling his presence, we laid side by side. John being few years older gave me a sense of security as his arm stretched across my back, and one leg twisted over mine, we dozed off, blocking out all the noise and loud music.

The morning sun poured through the open window. I noticed two sparrows land on a nearby ledge and peck away at scattered crumbs. John stretched, rolling over. We kissed softly. He tucked in beside me, squeezing my thigh and pressing his lips against mine. Our eagerness caused me to giggle as I responded to his warmth. Pressing down on my body, not waiting for approval, we locked hands whispering impious expressions and passionately kissed, lingering as tongues touched and our damp clothes clung from perspiration. Our eyes met, we removed one another's shirts and he caressed my breasts, enhancing the sensation of warm skin touching.

A loud knock sounded on the door. "John, are you in there? We're late! I've been looking for you for half an hour. Frannie, have you seen John?" Peter disturbed our private moment.

"To be continued," I teased, as John reached for the door.

"Yeah, I'm here. And would you keep it down." Peter peered around the corner to see me, lying on my back, partially covered by the sleeping bag.

"Oh, did I come at a bad moment?" He grinned. "But listen John, we've got to go and I mean now."

Picking up John's jacket, Peter tapped him on the shoulder. "Shall we?" Leading the way down the hall, John shrugged, throwing me a kiss with his fingers.

Just after sunrise, they reached the ten-year-old Dodge, a gift from my Aunt when I moved to the city, parked on the street a block away from our house. Peter gazed over the roof and apologized for his interruption.

"Well," John replied as he pulled onto Bay Street, "I think we're ok, now. She's settling in a bit more. I don't care that she's not part of the Yorkville scene - she's unique. Really stubborn and sure has a mind of her own. I thought she would have come with us today after our talk ... about the track.

"When we got back to the house last night, I got a message that my brother called. You remember Mike, he owns United Plastics Company in Scarborough. In the past, he used to give me leads on when a good shipment of powder arrived. Anyway, I told him I was not interested this time that it's been months since I pushed that shit around here. I am becoming too familiar with the locals. Anyway, listen to this. Mike says that if I brought up the 50 grams, it would be worth thirty thousand to me!"

"What? What is it - gold?" Peter gasped, putting out his cigarette.

"That's what he said. I was only getting a grand before - but the demand is high now, with more kids getting into the stuff. So they're making a killing. I said I'd let him know, but that was no good. He wanted an answer right away. At first I told him no – but then, I thought about the idea of getting our own horse. This way we could claim a twelve thousand dollar horse, and use the rest of the money to cash in on a good size bet.

What do you think? Anyway, I gave him the ok. Now, I have to get someone to help me."

"Holy shit! Thirty thousand dollars! That's a lot of bread for selling shit." John laughed as he edged into the morning rush hour traffic.

"You can practically buy a house for that kind of dough. I don't know. I always get cold feet messing with that stuff."

They discussed the matter in some detail as temptation was knocking at their door.

Chapter 4
Lessons in Thoroughbred Racing

Greenwood Racetrack

The old Dodge stopped at the lights at Woodbine Avenue, just before reaching Greenwood Racetrack where John signaled to make a right turn. Startled by a figure that darted out in front of the car, Peter jumped. John slammed on the brakes, barely missing the person. To their surprise, they turned and saw that it was me, giving them the thumb.

"What the hell?" yelled Peter.

"Goddamn, I don't believe it! Look..." added John, rolling down the window.

"Hey, dummy, want a lift before we have to carry you? You almost got yourself killed." I jumped into the back seat.

"Well, guys, here I am."

"Yeah, so we see. How did you get here?"

"Hitchhiked."

"You? You hitchhiked?" hollered John.

"Yes. What of it?" I returned, watching Peter shake his head.

Driving into the stable area at Greenwood Racetrack, John slowed down so the guard could see their pass on the windshield.

Amazed by the tremendous activity around the grounds at 6:15 am, John parked the old car and the three of us walked toward a freshly painted barn. The stall doors displayed green and gold wooden plaques identifying the trainer's emblem. I followed rather tentatively, carefully watching several grooms do their chores. Numerous horses walked along the roadway with their trainers, blocking our way, as several grooms brushed the animals with currycombs standing on the lawns next to the road. A long tractor-trailer van delivered hay, and parking behind it was another van unloading horses to one side. A smaller red pick-up truck parked next to it, which made for a lot of confusion. Someone climbed down from the feed truck and hollered out harshly....

"Damn crap, Sam. I didn't ask for timothy. I wanted mixed hay and you know that means with alfalfa or clover. This is not worth a buck a bale. I'll be damned if I'm gonna pay that for this stuff. Now, what's going on here? Tell me - am I going to get mixed or not?" The heavyset man bellowed, making me feel uncomfortable. I glanced at Peter.

John marched ahead of us toward another stable where he assisted with the morning training. A husky man walked in his direction leading a saddled chestnut mare, which gleamed in the morning sun. John led the thoroughbred over to an exercise boy wearing a hard-hat and carrying a riding crop. With a helping hand, the kid climbed up and grabbed the reins just as the spirited horse spooked. His strength controlled the rearing animal as I heard a raspy voice yell, "I told you to put full cup blinkers on that colt!" I drew a deep breath, cringing.

"Hey, Peter, how are you doing? And who do we have here?" asked a handsome red-haired man in his forties. I forced a smile, nervously.

"Bob, this is my good friend, Frannie Harrison. Frannie, this is trainer Bob Sharp," introduced Peter. "I wanted to ask if you would know of anyone short a hot-walker. She wants to do some morning work, eh Frannie?" he coaxed.

"Yes, I would like to try," I added, shyly.

"To be honest, Pete, I'm a bit short myself today. With school break over, I've lost most of my help. Have you ever been around horses, young lady?" he inquired, giving me the once over.

"Never. However, I'm sure I can learn and will work hard and do as you say and not get in anyone's way. Just give me a try," my voice squeaked.

The trainer glanced at Peter, smiled, and said that he would offer me an opportunity, provided I could guarantee getting Peter down to the track before six, and none of this six-thirty stuff. He liked chores finished before nine as he had several horses.

"Oh, sure can. Promise!" I added without hesitation.

"Well, now, you can come with me. Pete, I want you to gallop the two-year-old for about three miles, and let her look around at the starting-gate to get used to the sound of the bell ringing. Familiarize her with the setup, ok?" Bob rested the palm of his hand on my shoulder as we walked around his stable.

"Let's start at the beginning." Bob pointed to the stall doors marked with Larson Farms plaques. "These are my twelve thoroughbreds. I have a farm in Caledon where I graze twenty more that also race here. I ship them back and forth to make sure they all get a good rest during the long racing season, which starts when the snow is still on the ground in spring and runs right through into the winter. Each horse has its own stall so if one has a cold, it won't pass through the whole stable. Each has its own feed tub and water bucket." Bob Sharp casually rested his foot upon a bale of straw found lying in the way, pulling a long strand up to his mouth to chew. "These animals are worth a great deal of money. I train about half of them for other people and the rest are mine." My attention deepened.

Peter approached with the bay filly heading toward the training track. Wishing me luck, he waved as he left the barn area and trotted down the road.

"I'd like to watch this filly and check how she handles the going. I will leave you here for a few minutes and won't be long.

"Hey, Karen, come over here for a minute." Still chewing on his piece of straw, Bob motioned to an attractive red-haired young woman walking down the shed, dragging a rake. She carried herself well, displaying a unique beauty, a definite polish, appearing too feminine for the racetrack.

"Hi, what can I do for you, Dad?" She smiled, leaning against the railing, appraising my apparent innocence.

"Listen, Karen, I want you to meet Frannie Harrison. She will be helping in the mornings from now on. That is, if she works out." I smiled, nervously.

"I'm just going over to the backstretch to watch Misty, so would you please do a little clean up on the feed tubs? I'm sure they've finished eating oats by now, and Karen, Frannie hasn't been around the track or horses at all, so please be careful. We don't want any accidents. By the way, Wicked Willy is running in the fourth. Make sure you clean the stall out, no water, straw, anything left, ok?"

"Sure Dad, we'll get right on it." Karen motioned for me to follow her down the shed, passing enormous, terrifying animals as their heads bobbed out the top half of the stall doors. Some snorted, sniffed, while others nibbled at my shoulders. I ducked, nervously, jumping out of their reach causing Karen to chuckle. "Just relax, Frannie," she advised. Reaching the end of the familiar colored door plaques, Karen ducked beneath the webbing that crossed the front of the open stall door and stroked the horse's neck before retrieving the feed tub from the corner wall. We removed all twelve containers to one side of the yard where there was more space to work. Karen connected a hose, finding some powdered soap and brushes; we scrubbed the hardened food from the sides and rinsed them clean before setting them to dry in the early morning sun. The environment was definitely new and I needed to pay close attention.

"Tell me, Frannie, what brings you to work on the track?" Karen inquired.

I explained my situation and need for money.

"Right, I know what you mean about needing money. This is a great place to pull in a couple-of-hundred bucks a week freelancing, but the trainers will try to get hold of you and pay some measly fifty dollars a week. If you go from barn to barn, you can pick up five dollars a head, cooling out." She noticed my interest. "Dad pays ok, but he's the same as the rest. I help in the mornings if he is short; otherwise, I work for other stables. I'm also taking modeling classes and the courses are so expensive it takes all I have to keep well dressed, finance my photo shoots and pay the bills. I'm not living at home, either, and that's a big expense, too."

"Like your Dad said, I've never even been on a horse, let alone worked with any, so I'll appreciate any advice you want to give." We finished cleaning the feed tubs when Karen left me to clean out the stall of the horse that was racing that afternoon. All the brightly painted feed containers had numbers inscribed matching those on the door plaques. I returned each one, hanging them outside the stall, fearing to enter. In the distance, I noticed an automatic walking-ring with five horses cooling out, each connected by a long rope. This appeared more logical than walking around a stable interfering with grooms doing chores. Later, she explained that walking-rings were not practical for the high-strung racehorse that could spook at the slightest disruption causing the others to rear and possibly endanger their legs. The walking-ring was more suitable for the ponies that accompany the racehorse during workouts.

Karen carried her last basket of dirty straw over to a large manure wagon located in the middle of the roadway between the barns, where all the stables tossed their manure. I found myself a rake, not wasting time standing around.

"Why do you do that?" I queried as Karen finished with the stall.

"Dad feels the horses should not eat or drink a lot after their morning feed if they are going to race the same day. That is the purpose of cleaning out every last bit of straw or leftover hay, making sure they are empty and drawn up tight, so to speak, when they race. Take ol' Wicked Willy here. He is a gelding, a stud that's fixed. You know, like a steer instead of a bull, if you know what I mean," she laughed. I nodded.

"A thoroughbred knows the moment the stall is cleaned out that he'll be racing and will start to weave back and forth in anticipation. He'll whinny and turn his lip up, a real showoff, if you ever saw one." We both stepped out of the way of a passing hot-walker leading two horses, one behind the other.

"I would think one horse would be hard enough to handle, let alone two. What happens if one horse gets excited and rears, or tries to pull away?"

"Well, it's not a good idea, but you will see a few of the guys do it. You are right; sometimes one horse will break away or do something to scare the other. Then it becomes a horror show as the whole stable area turns into a wild ruckus of high-strung horses trying to break loose."

At that moment, Peter returned from the track followed closely by Bob. Karen rushed to retrieve the horse, leading it away from the busy stable. Peter jumped down, removed the bridle and exercise saddle as she tossed them aside, and then slipped the halter on as the shank dropped to the ground. The filly's sweat created white foam on her stomach where the girth rubbed. My attention to detail went unnoticed, but I knew nothing was overlooked.

Exhausted from the workout, the two-year-old stood unbelievably still. Bob held her while Karen took a bucket of warm water, a large sponge and began washing her down. The filly behaved well. Karen removed the water from her coat with long sweeps from a metal scraper, which looked much like a curved-edge ruler. Peter continued with his exaggerated pace heading to another stall to saddle up.

"Well, Frannie, are you doing ok?" he whispered as he passed.

"Yeah, I think so." He motioned for me to follow.

"What?" My glance dropped as he handed me the horse. Feeling uneasy, I held on tightly to the shank while Peter ducked under the webbing to saddle. Karen grinned, approvingly, to her father as they watched.

Within the hour, and with coaxing from everyone, I was walking 'hots' around the shed with the other grooms. My fears lessened as I became more determined. A swift pat on the ass from Peter brought me into pace taking a strong grip on the leather shank.

The coffee truck arrived and pulled up alongside the stable, which suggested it was close to 9:00 and break time. Surprised at how fast the time had passed and with only two bruised toes and a slight limp, I joined the others for a bite.

"Well, what do you think now, Frannie? Going to come back tomorrow after today's introduction?" Bob inquired, devouring warm Danish and sipping black coffee as I sat next to Peter on a bale of hay.

"To tell the truth, I'm enjoying myself, Mr. Sharp, but boy, do I ever have a lot to learn. Karen asked me for a ring-bit and I didn't even know that was a type of bridle. In fact, I don't even know if I'm sitting on straw or a bale of hay." I paused, watching them smile. "When I heard Karen's comment about picking up buns, I sure didn't get the connection that she was referring to, well … turds." My naive comments prompted a healthy round of laughter.

"Yes, I would say you have a lot to learn," agreed Karen. "But everything is important. If a groom was not informed and happened to reach for a bridle and put a D-bit on a horse that raced with a ring-bit, it could cost the trainer the race. That would be horrendous if it was a *stake* race for a $50,000 purse. If you are as keen as you appear, by the end of the week, I'll take you up to see the farm and show you the life of a thoroughbred from the time it's foaled up to the time it comes to the track. Then, you'll have a better understanding of what it's all about."

"Thanks. I'd like that."

"Peter, would you be able to help out this afternoon? I need a pony to accompany Wicked Willy to the post in the fourth. Do you think you can make it?" Bob asked.

"Sure, that would be about two o'clock that we should get ready?" Bob nodded.

"I would let Karen walk him to the paddock, but he's fussing a lot lately and the last time he reared up on the jockey when he was galloping before the race. That calls for some assistance. We need to keep him under wraps so he can loosen up before the race, but not too much. I think he will be easy enough to handle. You've ponied with him many times in the morning." Peter nodded; assuring Bob there would be no problem.

Suddenly aware of the quiet, I gazed around the barn area; most of the heavy morning training completed. Grooms and trainers were heading toward the track kitchen for breakfast and a look at the daily racing form. The speakers echoed loudly as Peter explained about *ponying* a horse.

"Bob is particular about making sure that each horse gets to the track every day, whether to pony, gallop or have a workout. He says thoroughbreds are bred to race and standing in a stall more than eighteen hours is not restful, but causes joints to stiffen. Others don't always do this. Each trainer has his own way of preparing his horses. Some days, you may walk a horse for a half hour or longer, usually the day after he has raced. It's all about learning the routine and learning it well. You'll do just fine."

The next day's racing card, which names each horse and its post-position, announced over the loudspeakers. Bob noted that a race for *'three and four-year-olds; non-winners of three during the year - going six furlongs'* had not mentioned the horse he entered.

"I suppose there weren't enough horses to make the race split and she missed the draw. I'll check the Condition book again to see if there's something for her on Friday, for fillies only. I would like to get her out soon. I feel she is ready, not to win, but maybe a 'show' would be an improvement. That's all I want to see. If she doesn't, I'll drop her down to run for seventy-five hundred."

Peter respected my puzzled look.

"Frannie, there are mainly two types of races. A 'Claiming' race means a horse runs for a set figure, say twelve thousand dollars. Anyone could have a trainer put in a claim, by putting the money in the 'claim box' before the race, to buy it. The other types of races are Allowance and Stake races, which mean no purchase made. So what Bob is saying, if she doesn't run well for ten thousand then he'll drop her down to seventy-five hundred. The horses would be of an easier class, running slower, or they are sore, or just plain not good enough to compete with anything better. If the filly could run third in a race for seventy-five hundred, then she should win eventually. It also means that someone watching her form and sees her drop down in value might claim her thinking he could improve the horse. Nevertheless, the rules say that once you claim a horse, then it would have to race for higher value. A trainer wants to win as many races as he can because it costs money to enter a horse. There are the jockey fees, hot-walkers, grooms, feed and vet bills, transportation, etc. To have a horse never make the board - that is to run 1, 2, 3, or 4 - is financially not acceptable. There are huge expenses."

"I see, now." I nodded, relieved to receive an explanation.

Karen stood up, attracting attention as she brushed off her skin-tight soiled jeans and announced she would be leaving. "Do you want me to feed at noon hour, Dad? I have to drive down to Bloor Street for a class."

"Nah, it's ok. I'll be around. See you tomorrow." Bob replied, showing his approval by rubbing her shoulder. Watching closely, we noticed her aloofness that warned men, 'hands off.' Bob's love for his daughter went without saying as his admiring eyes followed her.

"Must say, this work will do her good. Just think how easy it will be to stay in shape without having to do boring gym exercises," Bob reported, looking down at my own thin frame. He chuckled. "Right, Little Britches?" Pete laughed, agreeing.

John finished his chores and joined us with juice and donuts. Patiently listening to our idle conversation, he announced time to go. Tired and dirty, we bid farewell leaving the quiet stable area as one of the track veterinarians approached Bob. Watching them closely, I thought how generous and kind Bob was that morning, taking me under his wing and patiently guiding me through the tiniest of details. *The sport of kings* had a lot more going on behind the scenes than what the general public saw when sitting in the grandstand, and he was the first to clearly clarify any confusion. Bob was a master at his profession, a patient man with great respect for his employees and a thoughtful caring father who often spoke of his wife, Mollie. It was easy to see why people liked working for him.

On the way to the car, John stopped to speak to a rough-looking character selling racing forms, keeping Peter and me waiting. Unlocking the door, John explained the person they called *Smoocher* had given him a hot tip on the third race. He suddenly paused, turning to look at Peter, who sat beside him in the front seat. "Did you think any more about what we were talking about earlier?"

"A little, but the whole thing worries me."

"What's this about?" I asked curiously, leaning my chin on the back of the front seat, yawning. No explanations offered. Fifteen minutes later, we arrived back in the village where summer debris had gathered, I wondered which smelled worse, the track or the housing in Yorkville. I longed for a shower and sleep. The job would be just fine, for now.

Chapter 5
The Hurtful Truth

A few hours' drive north of Toronto, in another part of the province, pouring rain and cooler temperatures drenched the lavish green lands of the Muskoka Lakes. BJ's family had their summer cottage on Lake Rosseau.

The last of the hot summer sun scorched the small remaining patches of water left on the worn cedar deck. The grounds saturated by heavy night rains required substantial sun and wind to restore the dry grass in time for the closing picnics, which Peter, Susan and I had attended regularly during our high school Labor Day weekends. Now, our busy racetrack schedule made it almost impossible to get away, but Susan and Kenny continued to make the three-hour drive.

The large Viceroy cottage had been a place of firsts for us. We met a different group of kids each year from other parts of the province at beach parties and dances. We learned to water ski; we swam in cold waters while jumping off the 'cliff' near Skeleton Bay; enjoyed barbeques with roasted chicken, burgers and corn on the cob. We lounged on the raft, situated mid-point in the bay, diving and playing with their family dog, tossing sticks until exhausted. We survived on coke and fries at the local restaurant in Port Carling and tasted our first beer under the moonlight at a neighbor's bachelor party. It was the place to be during the summer months and Peter, Kenny and BJ spent most of their youth there.

For BJ, it was not one of his most productive years. He didn't work his usual job at the nearby resort in Port Sandfield, and so time dragged since his track injury. While his leg mended slowly, his eyesight improved when he wore glasses. Most of his cottage friends returned to the city before attending out-of-town universities, but his injured leg required continued therapy. He felt lost without knowing his future.

BJ's parents made several unsuccessful attempts to reach out, eventually deciding to move ahead with their own life and make changes. They previously hired a tutor for his grade 13 subjects, but by the end of the year, he came up short with the necessary requirements for university which they had pinned their hopes. BJ lacked interest and lost his initiative, enjoying the beach parties instead.

There had been problems in the past for the Nichols family concerning his sister Nancy, who had a number of misadventures during her high school years, including an unwanted pregnancy. Her flirtatious ways brought about many late night discussions as her parents searched for professional help.

BJ knew he disappointed his parents and it hurt him deeply. Understanding his depression ever since leaving the hospital, his father's encouragement helped in his successful recovery, but nothing BJ could take credit for. He and his sister lingered in making any decisions regarding their own future.

Time arrived when they announced their news to BJ and Nancy, just after the October Thanksgiving long weekend. The information of an upcoming move came as a shock to both of them. Their house listed for sale, Mr. Nichols sold his business and dissolved the original consulting firm. He explained his plans to reopen under the name Nichols, Patterson and Sons Ltd. when they moved overseas to form a new partnership with BJ's Uncle William, a quantity surveyor in Birmingham, England. Getting together before Christmas, they would finalize their plans.

Devastated by the news, Nancy and BJ realized they had been so absorbed in their personal traumas that they never detected any changes within the home. Neither working nor in school and without any thought for their future, the once close-knit family would soon go their separate ways.

Stella Nichols felt her husband's anguish when she confessed she had finished nagging, secretly wishing the family would move together. She believed it was time to let go and offered financial assistance to continue their education, if needed.

They discussed the details, but there was no need for debate. When the conversation ended, BJ's parents left the cottage and walked along the lakeshore.

Sounds of laughter wafted across the bay and the crickets chirped as evening settled in with a cooling breeze. BJ missed this display. He was there only bodily as he sat in the back of the well used outboard. His mind drifted in thought over years past, forcing himself to do something he hadn't wanted to think about and couldn't comprehend, but he understood that this phase of his life was over. He had to move onward and upward if he was going to move at all; take hold and be responsible.

Times were changing, and like the rest of us, BJ was blind to what lay ahead for him.

While Peter, John and I were on a different path, Susan ventured out on her own journey as the five of us would go our separate ways, each creating new relationships while searching our destiny.

A new generation of alternative lifestyles was in the making.

Chapter 6
Indecision

Solemnly, I sat behind the steering wheel of my car, watching patients enter the medical clinic. I had just finished my consults with Dr. Boursin's office where he had delicately explained my sexual problems as Candace Syndrome. I was frigid!

For the better part of the afternoon, he searched deep into my childhood awakening memories that might have horrified others while trying to resolve my difficulty in making love to the man I lived with. Explaining that by taking the birth control pill before ever having had intercourse made me feel very uncomfortable, for it decreased the volume of natural fluid secreted by the vagina. All my tightness was not due to fear. He listened to my confusion and understood my anxieties as I recalled an incident when an older man had paid me to touch and arouse him when I was seven years old. Stressing that environment could affect my problems, he suggested that I leave Yorkville and the racetrack, and go off the pill. Urging me to take one-step at a time and not panic, he assured that I was medically fine. He also surmised that I suffered from FAS, (Fetal Alcohol Syndrome). Children with FAS are often naïve, lack judgment and decision-making skills. Sometimes, they find themselves facing abuse and difficulties in later life. Abnormal behavior, such as a short attention span, hyperactivity, extreme nervousness and anxiety are other symptoms. Needless to say, this information didn't help my self-esteem as I found much of the information true. I was a mess!

Perhaps my mental attitude needed healing. Reasoning that my love for John would come naturally when I relaxed and understood my past, Dr. Boursin advised me to accept the way things were, and try to handle one thing at a time. His best suggestion was to get out of Yorkville and into a better circle of friends because change would be good when surrounded by positive energy. He had me take Kava-Kava and recommended that I take DHEA as I matured in my later years.

Slowly backing out of the parking lot, edging into the line of traffic already bumper-to-bumper at rush hour, I drove north on Mount Pleasant Avenue, unconsciously turning into the cemetery to escape the crawl.

A couple of years had passed since Moms burial, I wondered if I could locate the grave as I drove through the winding roads of the 300 acres making it difficult for even the groundskeeper to navigate.

Angled shadows had foretold dusk before I spotted the familiar place where an oversize willow tree cascaded the landscape. Lazily, I wandered through the plots, accidentally stumbling and overturning a basket of withered flowers. Setting it upright, I spied my mother's stone hidden in the grass cuttings. I sat cross-legged beside it watching the sky darken, dulling my vision as I softly confessed my sorrows and loneliness, asking for guidance from whatever sacred spirit existed.

My whole life lay ahead of me. I needed to get my priorities straight, but did not know what I wanted; never did. Brushing some twigs from the gravestone, identifying the spot where my mother lay, I realized how people dominated and manipulated her. Somehow, I would learn how to find strength and courage. My brother Leonard moved to Quebec soon after she died; I lost contact. We had been close, but Mom's life with Dad messed our lives up. Why? Why did she ever start drinking again?

Unaware of passing time lost in my thoughts, I remembered my father. Todd Harrison, the big shooter, the high roller. They had it all; youth, good looks, health, and all that money. But, for whatever reasons, they ended up destroying one another... alcohol, smoking, partying, all in the name of the social life.

When I left the cemetery, I whispered, "Maybe I don't know what I want, but I sure as hell know what I don't want and that's a good enough start for me, right now."

Instead of returning to the village, I drove to my Aunt's home north of the city where I had lived after my mother died. I stayed for several days before deciding to visit Susan to see what she was up to.

The driveway of Susan's parents' modest home had a new coat of asphalt and the house appeared freshly painted. Mr. Edwards was house-proud and kept things up-to-date. Chatting with her mother as we sipped tea, I learned Humber College had accepted Susan into the Interior Design program.

Within the hour, Susan arrived home from school, pleased to see me, reporting that Peter had kept her somewhat updated, but she was eager to know more about why I left Yorkville the previous week.

We relaxed in her recreation room enjoying a couple of soft drinks. Curled up in the comfortable red leather sofa, I accounted for the latest happenings regarding John and I renting a flat on St. Clair Avenue. We had decided to move in on the weekend as we both agreed to leave Yorkville.

Relating my consults with Dr. Boursin, Susan expressed her opinion; it was time to consider my future plans. She knew I had none.

Susan and her boyfriend Kenny Gligowski, who she had met at the track meet the spring of BJ Nichols accident, had no plans to live together. She thought it was cheaper to live at home, plus she didn't have a job.

Gazing out the window for a brief moment, I recognized a cardinal perched on a spruce tree. Their well-manicured yard, bordered by rare flowers Susan's mother prized, made me realize how much I missed not having a home and family. Susan pushed for more racetrack news as several women were now working on the racetrack. A few trainers from the States preferred the gentle nature of women around their high-strung horses. My different lifestyle was nothing like Susan had ever experienced and sometimes I wondered how I ended up there, but it got harder to turn away from the money in a profession and a place I knew nothing about. There were creepy characters around the racetrack that would eat shoe polish for alcohol and screw the animals, like the goats that stayed in the horses stall as companions, but not everyone was disgusting.

"Pretty bad, eh?" Susan queried.

"You said it, just a different life. One day, Bob had two horses shipped in from the States somewhere. While they were unloading, everybody was busy rushing around. John handed me a double shank and said walk them back to the barn. It happened so fast. John positioned one horse behind the other and I started on my way when one of the three-year-olds, a little rambunctious from the long van ride, spooked. The horse reared up on his front and kicked out with his hind. He nailed me right between the legs, sending me flying. I mean right through the air, and guess where I landed? Yes, right in the middle of a manure wagon full of shit! It knocked me out cold. Only this time, the horses ran off through the stable area and I laid there crippled up waiting for help. I could not move a muscle. A groom named Otto called an ambulance that drove me to the

48

hospital where they kept me for days checking for blood clots. However, the funny part of it all happened when admitted. The nurse gently unfolded my legs from the fetal position. When they tried to remove my jeans for an examination - this will kill you - they wondered if they had the wrong sex. For some stupid reason, it had been one of those crazy rushed mornings and I couldn't find clean clothes, so I quickly put on a pair of John's jockeys. And this is what they found me wearing." Susan howled with laughter, tears rolling down her cheeks. "Here I was in Emerge - and they were in hysterics, thinking, *Like what is it we have here?* I'm not too sure about this type of life."

Once calmed, Susan wanted to know about the seriousness of the injury. Explaining the doctor's warning of severe complications, I would not be able to have kids. The bruising lasted several months as well as the brutal pain. John knew I had no experience, so why he gave me two horses to walk, I will never know. Maybe, deep inside it was his anger or frustration with me that came out.

Susan asked about Yorkville and the rowdy battles that had broken out in the streets over some bad dope as the village turned into a dangerous place.

"What the devil would you guys do?"

"Nothing, just watched out the window at everyone rushing around, doing their own thing."

"Well, Frannie, that's big-time negative energy. You really amaze me. Remember how we used to talk, and believed that we were nothing but a reflection of our environment. You're living and working in a bad space. I hope that you'll keep your head on your shoulders. I'm sorry, but I have to agree with Dr. Boursin - it is time for a change of scenery, right now. If I could afford an apartment, I would say, 'let's get together', but don't and can't. All I have to say is, you must really love John to be staying there living that kind of life." Susan appeared disgusted. "I can smell Mom's lasagna cooking. Let's go upstairs and crack open a bottle of wine, how about it?"

After dinner, we finished washing up when their doorbell rang. It was Peter.

"Am I not even going to get a hello, let alone an explanation?" he complained. "You should have let John know what you were up to. I mean, I thought the two of you were moving into your own place, and so did he.

Then, you bugger off. Just what's going on?" His voice raised; his temper shortened.

"Hold it!" Susan interrupted, hastily. "Now listen here, cousin, don't come in here and start harassing Frannie. She has her reasons."

"Well, whatever the hell they are, she better straighten up and get her act together. Listen to me, Frannie. I am here to tell you Bob is taking a dozen of his horses to Montreal next week, to race at Blue Bonnets. John and I are leaving tomorrow to go too. Now, are you coming or not?"

This unexpected news took me by surprise. Susan and I exchanged looks.

"Huh? When was all this decided, and why? Were you caught with some of that white powder in your possession, or were the cops putting the heat on?" My outburst caught him off guard, took him by surprise.

"I, ah...I told you. We are going with Bob. John and I thought the change would be good for us all. Why the accusations?"

"I think I know you both well enough to see this sudden change. What happened? Did you get another bad batch?"

"Frannie!" Peter jumped, flushed by this charge, dropping his pack of cigarettes. With his plaid flannel shirt unbuttoned, he tucked them back into the pocket. "You are way off base, I'm telling you. If you think you are so high and mighty, just forget the whole damn thing. John would be better off without you anyway. You're so screwed up that you have him doing anything you want. He's still waiting for you and really does care, you know. So forget about me and think about him for a minute."

I had about as much intention of going to Montreal as I did of going back to school. However, unexpectedly, I remembered my brother Leonard was living there. The offer suddenly became very tempting. Could I find Leonard in Montreal? Susan knew what I was thinking.

"Pete, how about some coffee? I think we could all use some." Susan eagerly led me by the arm through the dining room into the kitchen. Without a word, we filled the electric percolator and set up a tray. I could sense Susan's penetrating eyes as she took three mugs from the cupboard. She shrugged. "Don't go, Francine!"

"But Sue, Leonard could be in Montreal. Maybe I can locate him. Perhaps that's all I need, to talk to my brother," I said, in a low pleading voice. Susan frowned, admitting that if anyone could help me, it would be

Leonard. One step at a time; at least I would be moving away from Yorkville.

Susan showed her disappointment as she brewed the coffee. "You know, Frannie, I often thought your attachment to John was because Leonard left and no longer in your life. After your mom died, maybe you were looking for someone… to replace him." I set the mugs down on the table, and then looked at her, seriously.

The three of us drank our coffee and chatted about the latest concerts in the city and the most recent news from BJ and Kenny.

Returning to my Aunt's house later that same evening, I spoke about my visit with Susan. Unable to decide my next move, my Aunt advised me to follow my intuition.

Could it be my chattering mind or my heart that wanted to go to Montreal? My gut feeling was to find my brother.

Chapter 7
Blue Bonnets Raceway

Montreal – 1967

The crowded twelve-horse van didn't allow for extra movement. Flakes of hay hung in rope nets directly in front of the horses' heads swaying back and forth in narrow stalls as the van shifted along Highway 401 on its way to Decarie Boulevard, Montreal. Each thoroughbred's space was less than forty inches allowing for little ruckus. Even though the tranquilized horses remained calm, there was always the possibility that one high-strung animal might flip.

Karen stood next to Little Octopus, a two-year-old filly on her first long trip, which took six-and-a-half hours to reach Blue Bonnets Raceway. Peter wondered why Karen had not stayed back to finish modeling school. She explained that Bob needed her to help for a week or two until he got things set up and under control. Peter discussed his plans to claim a horse with John.

The red and yellow Ehrlick horse van turned off the boulevard and wound its way around to the stable area. Peter noticed the small racetrack, which appeared more like a fairground in comparison to the size and grandeur of the Toronto circuit.

The van's large metal doors heaved open when unbolted and the impatient, weary thoroughbreds whinnied at the sight of daylight as the driver assisted the grooms. While Karen and Peter carefully began to undo the webbings and back the animals down the ramp, they searched for the Larson stable stalls.

Bob and I were waiting at his barn, which faced the backstretch near the walkway that took the horses to the paddock area, which made for a great location. Peter commented on the unfamiliar pavement in the stable area, as the lack of grass and mud created an unusually clean appearance not seen in the Ontario racetracks.

Around 10:00 pm Bob invited me to join him and Karen at the motel, Ruby Foos, directly across the road from the racetrack where Karen and I shared her suite. Bob's wife Mollie expected to arrive sometime on the weekend.

The magnificent motel displayed an Asian décor in the rooms. Even the coffee shop decorated with potted plants and plush carpet was elaborate. Everything coordinated and I thought of Susan, who would have appreciated these details.

Having a few days to spare before the meet began, Bob cautioned that we would be busy with preparations and expected our full support, even with Expo open. The world event would attract thousands of travelers, adding a new excitement to the French metropolis.

One morning at break, when everyone gathered on scattered bales of hay for a coffee, John and Bob discussed the dividing-up of his stable, giving John three horses to train. This would be in effect until they both felt John was ready to write the exams for his trainer's license.

At this time, Karen expressed her interest in staying on for the whole racing meet to take in the sites and Expo. Checking his watch, Peter announced he was heading to the Secretaries' Office to pick up a few copies of the Condition book, waving to Karen to join him.

In the distance, Bob noticed another trainer from Toronto unloading horses and went to speak with him while the grooms and I set-up the stable.

John placed his coffee cup in the nearby bin. Our eyes met briefly when he walked toward me. I thought how he differed from the other men, almost too smooth to be recognized as one of the workers around the track. His skin tanned easily and his thick dark hair, worn brushed to the side from his forehead, framed his chiseled features. His walk was never rushed but self-assured and he always held his head high, but never appeared arrogant. John stood six inches taller than me, medium build and his deep-set blue eyes held patches of gold that somehow enhanced his full lips, which smiled kindly.

He sat down, leaning cautiously toward me. He extended his hands and placed them on my knees. A dimple on his left cheek appeared when he spoke.

"Are you alright, Frannie?" He asked in a concerned tone. "I've been really worried even though I knew you would work things out."

Bob called from across the driveway, waving to John. "Do you know any trainers from Ohio?" He asked as he approached.

"No, Bob, not personally."

"I was talking with this guy from Ohio who pulled in with a stable that he raced at Wheeling Downs, West Virginia before it burned. He's interested in selling off a few. I saw them unload. They are a good size – at least sixteen hands. A couple of grays caught my interest and if my guess is right, they could belong to Santo's stable. He's known for picking up Cuban grays banned from racing in the States and then bringing them into Canada to run. There could be some good stock. Come on over and take a look." Bob's voice trailed off as they walked away. John called back to me.

"See you after chores tonight. We'll go to dinner, say about six, ok?" I nodded, agreeing.

Moments later, Karen and Peter returned with a handful of Condition books from which trainers select the type of race they want to run their horses in.

"Well now, girls, I am going to leave you two alone, and go check out the tackrooms, and then I'll set myself up a room as my 'den of iniquity'. I must unroll my bed and carpets and hang my Rembrandts. So, if you will excuse me…" and Peter bowed formally, disappearing around the side of the barn.

"Hey - nice guy. He merely leaves us unescorted for the riff-raff to check out." Karen commented on his quick exit.

We chatted briefly about my need to locate my brother, Leonard, who I suspected lived somewhere in Montreal. Karen explained we would have the use of her Dad's pick-up to get around, as her mother would be bringing the *Benz* when she came.

As we talked, I learned about the name 'Larson Farms.' Karen explained its history; they never had a name for the Stud Farm in Caledon. When her brother died in a motorcycle accident a few years back, Bob decided to name the stable after him - Larson. "I'm sorry. I never knew you had a brother," I suddenly felt embarrassed.

"Larson was a loner and didn't socialize much. Somehow, he ended up with Satan's Choice when he dropped out of grade eleven. A bunch of them had decided that our farm was a good place to unload their sleeping bags and hang out. Mom and Dad put their foot down after a year, knowing that he would leave. Dad had been pretty liberal with him but when he started shooting up, doing acid and doping the horses for laughs, things got out of hand. So, down the road he went. Mom and Dad were upset. They kept praying he would come back to his senses and dump his gang.

"No such luck. We heard he went to the west coast, and then the bike accident happened when he was in California, somewhere near Oakland. He was totally spaced out, apparently. Mom was a wreck for many months. Dad flew down and had his body sent home for the funeral. Mom could not face it. She didn't go, so I helped Dad deal with the arrangements. She is pretty well recovered now. Lars had made up his own mind and went to live his own life. There was nothing she or Dad could do or say to change it. I used to feel like something happened to him. It was as if some evil spirit got a hold of him, or he walked through a negative field. He just changed overnight. To be honest, the two of us did not get along. We were almost like twins; only ten and a half months between us; however, we were never close. He always gave into peer pressure." Karen suddenly dropped the subject.

Going on with our day, taking in the afternoon sun, we acquainted ourselves with Montreal and its many one-way streets. We began our search for Leonard, not finding his name listed in any of the district phone directories. The telephone operator had no listing for him. I decided I would write my Aunt who mentioned that Leonard was in Quebec and had settled in Montreal, hoping she would now have a new address for him. Karen sensed my urgency to locate him.

We swam in Ruby Foos pool, and then headed back to the track to do chores. While fooling around to the music playing on the radio, Karen became playful, dancing around.

"You're too much," I kidded, noticing her pressed denims and sixty-dollar Givenchy designer shirt. Always coordinated, she wore a sweater tied around her neck or waist. Somehow, her polished boots always stayed that way and her perfectly applied make-up, nail polish and hair were done according to the latest style. Perfection! This was just her way.

Bob stopped by and asked us to join John and him for dinner. We accepted, promising to be ready by seven.

The taxi driver dropped us off at Joe's Steak House where a strong whiff of garlic permeated the air. Comparing French drivers to those in Mexico held the conversation until our superb 'Alberta beef' steak dinner and two bottles of wine arrived. Eventually, the talk turned back to the track. Karen quizzed John about his idea of claiming a horse at the meet.

His financial situation was a delicate subject and he chose his words carefully.

"Well, Pete and I have been planning and saving for this opportunity. We want to pick up a strong long distance runner that we can try to improve upon. I'll get my trainer's license soon. I've still got a good deal of reading to do, along with the practical experience before I would even consider applying, but I'd like to begin as soon as possible."

"What price tag are you looking at?"

"Around the $12-15,000. range."

I wondered about the source of the money, knowing that it costs thousands to support a horse's training and transportation fees.

"I'm giving John the three and four year olds to train, and I'll watch how he does. You know, he grew up with horses in the States." Bob explained, turning to face John. "The bay gelding is having problems with wandering and not concentrating during the race. This causes him to knick his ankles and throws his head. Every horse has its peculiarities. This will be one problem for you to handle, especially on a bullring like this track. Since the other two horses haven't won a race this year and Kosta is still a maiden, these will be good challenges" Bob finishes the last bite of his dessert. "I'll spend time advising you on any animal you want to consider at claiming."

I listened, reluctant to comment as we finished our meal.

The evening passed and before we knew it, it was ten-thirty, time to retire for an early rise. John and I walked toward the pool area of the motel where we sat, feeling the chill of the evening breeze. He lightly rubbed his hands along my bare arms to warm me, and then offered his sweater.

Silent and still, I waited until John spoke.

"I suppose after what's happened over the past few weeks you have changed your mind about moving in together, but I want you to know that I haven't changed and feel even stronger about the idea. When you didn't return to the racetrack or the village, I knew you were uneasy about the situation, but I wanted you. I felt hurt and afraid that you were changing your mind and wanted out. So, Peter and I talked it over, and decided to join Bob in a whole new scene. That is why we came here with his stable. You heard us talk about claiming a horse a long time ago, and knew we were planning on it as soon as we could get the bread to do so. Frannie. I really do love you."

John caressed my cheek, and then we kissed. Stirred by his warmth and desire, we held each other close. I felt myself withdraw in a strange inexplicable way as something was missing, still not right.

"Johnny, there's something else. I don't mean to say you've lied to me, but I just don't feel good about this whole relationship. Somehow, I just cannot figure out, for the life of me, how you got that money put together. I know you got dough in the village pushing weed that you brought up from the States. I thought you stopped all that when we started getting serious. You know how I feel about that stuff, a cop-out. I know you were not into getting stoned. I didn't even know how much you were taking while we were together, but you got involved feeding it to those innocent kids. I know that you were not the only one peddling it and did have connections. In fact, to me, that's worse." I said it the way I saw it.

"Johnny, I know Peter never had enough gumption to do anything like that on his own. When he told me he had the money to go in with you on claiming a horse, well, I knew for sure he was connected, somehow, in bringing another shipment across the border. I don't want to hear any crap about how you wanted the money to do things for me. This has nothing to do with your love for me either. It's your greed!" I snapped. His passive expression hardened. "So level with me now. What are you up to?" Folding my arms, glaring back at him, I knew my words came across strong.

His thick hair blew gently in the breeze; he brushed it back into place with his open hand while standing with one leg resting on the outdoor furniture.

"Ok, Frannie. It's like this. You won't like it, but if that's what it takes to make or break this relationship." He inhaled deeply.

"My name is not John Roberts. It's Mencini. John Mencini. I dodged the draft a few years ago, arriving in Toronto from out west. My brother had set up a company about the same time. He talked me into going back down south to bring the drugs back for him for a pretty good dollar. That was my contact. We never had to use passports, so no suspicion crossing the borders. Besides me, four or five other guys peddled the stuff in the village. This went on for some time, then, like you said, I never participated after we were together." He paused. "I got a call. Remember, your first day at the track? It was my brother. He told me of a great deal that would bring me an easy thirty thousand, so, Pete and I went south and got the stuff. No sweat. But, then they raided the village, as you know, and finally someone squealed and police started investigating. A lot of the guys took off or got thrown in the slammer. When Peter found this out, we left and that's why we're here now. We both wanted to use the money to claim a horse and cash in a big bet, one day, which will make us enough money to get us off the track and into something else. If we find such a horse that looks bad on paper, Pete and I would put in the claim or buy it. We would make improvements and then give it a few races, running it on the big track and placing a huge bet. We will gamble enough to quit the track for good and start out on our own. We could open a business or take on some kind of a franchise. That's the whole truth, and that's the way it is."

Stepping in front of me, blocking my view, I detected a slight tremble. A deep pain attacked my chest as my true love conflicted with my morals. I realized that there was no changing him, not now, not ever. He knew what he wanted; I didn't.

John touched my head, and then turned to leave. The lights over the pool dimmed and the night air felt cold, but still I sat, motionless, until the early hours of the morning.

***

Another month of hard work passed. Karen and I became close friends, enjoying the sights of Montreal and visiting Expo during our free time, viewing as many events as we could, which was an amazing experience. Montreal was magical, so cosmopolitan. We became part of the mass of humanity that flocked into the incredible, vibrant city. The country's dual language policy changed making it difficult for most companies. Many people explained they felt driven out of the French city due to new requirements. All signage, literature and packaging required the French language printed beside the English version causing a huge expense, especially for those working and manufacturing in the province of Quebec, as well as restaurants and retailers.

My high school French came in handy as we conversed with the locals while the rest of the country remained English. We thought it would take many years for the province to recover from the loss of big business that relocated.

John spent his spare time studying the Condition book and racing rules, and his evenings at the races examining the horses as they entered the paddock, watching their forms. Nothing had interested him so far. The time to make his claim drew near as he concentrated on training one particular horse for its race. He tried blinkers and a shadow roll to keep its head from gawking around; he persisted with the difficult task and finally succeeded. The horse's running time decreased by several seconds. This change pleased Bob, who knew that a thoroughbred ran approximately five lengths a second.

The 'maiden' Kosta, who had never won a race in her life, was John's to train. He decided to use her as a 'pony' to accompany the other thoroughbreds when galloping in the morning… for a total of fifteen miles a day, to ensure its fitness. He entered Kosta into race for three and four-year-olds, non-winners of the year, instead of a *maiden race* that was shorter distance. The odds before race time were 30 to 1. Kosta would run against accomplished horses that had already won, but not during the current year. Karen and I disliked the maiden but still decided to place a small bet on it and hope for a long shot. Besides, we felt we should support one of our stable-mates.

John requested I walk Kosta to the paddock. I felt he wanted me by his side. The mare appeared tight, in excellent condition and well drawn after all the workouts. Karen referred to her jokingly as the 'pig' of the stable, but the truth was that the horse just wanted to run, not race.

As I retrieved a clean D-bit bridle from the tackroom, a distinctively French voice called the horses for the fourth race. I gave Kosta one last dusting before accompanying her to the paddock. John remarked, disgustedly, that she was the soundest horse in the barn and with no wonder because she never ran hard enough to hurt herself.

The men drove back to the grandstand in Bob's truck; parking in the owners' designated spots outside the entrance. Hurrying into the paddock, they waited for the horses' arrival dazzling the avid spectators in front of them. Ten stalls lined the back of the paddock where the horses waited for the valets to saddle them. The trainers spoke privately with their jockeys giving them last minute instructions and discussing track conditions before mounting-up.

With a firm grip on the four-year-old that plowed along, I followed behind the other seven contenders. The jockeys marched out in their colorful silks after I led Kosta into the stall marked '3', which was the post position that corresponded with that in the program for those making a wager.

Holding her head steady with both hands on the bridle, John rubbed Kosta's neck commenting on her lack of vitality. The jockey arrived, sporting the Larson Farms green and yellow silks, with a large overlapping L on the back of the shirt.

"Hey, Roger, how's it going? You rode a nice race in the second half of the double earlier." John complimented jockey Roger Belle with a handshake.

"Thanks, John. I was a little anxious using the stick, but she sulked on me. I think I lost a few lengths trying to recuperate and hand-ride her down the stretch. Luckily, she had it in her to finish so good. What about this ol' gal, how'd you like her to run?" he asked, casting a sidelong glance at me.

John explained in some detail, "Try to have them load her in order, or she will never prepare herself... gallop her before the race a good three furlongs, then walk the rest of the way. Like I said, do your best to get her out of the gate. Her form shows she is last out every time. If you can accomplish this, we will have a chance. She has one speed, that's it, so try to lay close, and then when the front speed dies, she will still hang in there. If only they had a two-mile race, she'd last all day." The bugle sounded announcing the horses onto the track. John gave Roger a leg up, wishing him luck. Bob came forward.

"Take her away Fran," and I led them from the paddock onto the track, and then joined John and Karen standing by the railing next to the finish line.

"Look at those odds, I don't believe it." I gasped as they had jumped from 10-1 to 18-1, and continued up to 30-1 by the time the race was about to begin.

"Boy, she's a real dog. Look at her. No life in her at all," mumbled John, placing his hand into the front pockets of his jeans, as if he'd washed-his-hands of her.

In a very self-assured tone, I sarcastically announced, "Why, John! Oh, what was it?... Mencini? I thought for sure you would have a bundle bet on her. I mean, look, here's your chance to cash in on a little of that pot of gold you and Pete are so anxious to get." He frowned down at me.

"Frannie, not now, ok?" He turned to walk off, but I followed closely. He met Peter, chewing on a half pack of gum, and then we joined Bob and his wife, Mollie, now standing with Karen as the horses were loading into the starting gate. Mollie and Karen showed a strong resemblance, but I felt her personality was more like her father, Bob.

I glanced at Karen's program and ran to the five dollar wicket, just in time to put my money on a 'place' bet for number three. You gotta follow your intuition.

The loudspeakers cracked as the announcer called the race in both French and English, making it difficult to follow the positions. I missed Kosta as they raced by the finish line for the first time. The horses bunched tightly, hiding the over-classed maiden in the middle of the pack. Bob commented on Belle's excellent break from the gate, making all the difference in her race. Lots of practice had helped.

As they headed around the turn into the backstretch, passing the halfway mark, Kosta was in fifth position, but almost ten lengths behind the leader. I started hollering at Belle to get into her and ride the bitch. I didn't usually show this kind of enthusiasm as my interest in the race caught the others' attention. My screams encouraged their cheers as the maiden made a strong effort along the inside rail as the early speed dropped back, and they headed into the final stretch. Thousands of fans gasped, and then roared with frantic encouragement. I leaped upon John's back, hollering for all I was worth, trying to see over the crowd, taking him completely by surprise.

"Go Kosta! Go Kosta! Come on Belle, ride her! Ride the hell out of her." John amazed at the mare's strong finish as the jockey dropped low in the saddle, keeping the reins high on her neck. He whipped at her backside, then to her shoulders as she kept close to the rail, saving ground. "She's coming. She's coming!"

"Go Belle! Run ... run, Kosta!" The big-boned chestnut mare, displaying the green and yellow colors, covered ground passing tired sprinters and unfit geldings, and then made a strong rush. Pulling herself into contention as the leader weakened, her large bony legs stretched over the sandy track below as they neared the finish line. The pack squeezed into only four lengths of the leader with Kosta closing.

They crossed the finish line with the first four only a 'head' apart, calling for a photo finish to decide the positions before the final call could be posted. The fans cheered in anticipation, holding their tickets as John and I embraced, overcome by the excitement. I seemed like the only one who suspected such a vibrant and gallant race to the finish. Bob grasped

John's shoulder as they waited for the horses to return. We walked with Bob to the track while talking a wild-stream-a-minute.

"I know she was right there. I could see." Convincingly, "In a split second, I bet she makes the board." They could hardly keep from laughing at my constant chatter.

The horses galloped around toward the backstretch before they pulled up and began their way back to the winner's circle. By the time they reached their trainers, and the jockeys dismounted, the flashing 'photo finish' light was off and the numbers posted on the board accordingly, and announced. "Number seven, Willow Tree was first, followed by number three, Kosta and..." John's face beamed with delight. As he was about to dismount, Belle cautioned John to hold on a moment, and then we heard the announcer call...

"There has been a *foul* claim against the winner number seven, Willow Tree, by the fourth place horse, number eight, 'Just in Time'! Hold on to all tickets, please."

Bob clarified that in case of a possible disqualification, they would take photos of the first two horses in the winners' circle. The Sharp family followed the others into the designated area. The thrill of the race exhausted us all as John proved himself worthy.

The two horses went to an area where all the winners cooled-out and urine samples taken, testing for drugs or steroids. While I strolled alongside the sweaty, snorting animal, the others returned to the grandstand to wait for the results. One groom from Bob's stable arrived with a cotton blanket, halter and shank for me to change. My heart pounded as I anticipated a win for the mare that was so disliked in the stable of twelve.

Several minutes later, I began hot-walking and the groom returned to bed down the stall and prepare Kosta's feed. I walked briskly, impatient to hear the results. Finally, I heard the screams roar from the crowd at the grandstand.

"The results are posted. The stewards have ruled the objection and fourth-place 'number eight' foul claim against the winner, 'number seven' for '*interference down the backstretch*' has been allowed. The order of finish is number three, Kosta; place is number one, Bart-a-bull; show is number eight, Lucky Lucy; with number seven, Willow Tree, now in fourth position." Seconds later the payoffs flashed across the board.

I shattered the silence with ecstatic shouts, talking to everyone at once. After an unusually long cooling, Sam, the man who took the urine samples called me to place the horse into a specific stall, and then closed the door. I waited, hearing the sound of his whistling in an effort to encourage the horse to void. Five minutes later, he came out asking me to continue walking, giving the horse more to drink before he would try again. This went on, and on, and on. I could lead her to water but couldn't make her drink. Another hour passed and still Kosta would not cooperate. My excitement was slowly fading.

The winner from the seventh race arrived, sweating and snorting vigorously. Catching sight of John speaking with Sam, I walked over to their side. Sam led the horse into the stall. Kostas awkwardness, oversized features, and clumsy manner warranted her being called 'mare' when she wouldn't be one until she turned five.

John's request for running water came from a nearby tap, and again the familiar whistling. Within moments, they returned with a sterilized half-full bottle. I drew a sigh of relief. As an afterthought, I handed John my winning ticket, unaware of his surprise.

Once back at the stable, I joined Karen and Peter in the tackroom where Karen showed off her handful of cash.

"Frannie that old nag paid sixty-seven dollars to win, forty-two to place and thirty-five to show. She was a hell of a long shot. Thanks for the tip. Fantastic, eh?"

"I was so excited with the ol' pig, I almost got laryngitis from all the yelling," I broadcasted.

"We noticed," offered Peter. "What was the problem with Kosta over at the paddock cooling out?" He lit up a fresh cigarette.

"I don't know, she wouldn't urinate and Sam tried her four or five times. Anyway, John finally showed up and solved the dilemma."

Peter recalled a time when he had to wait over three-and-a-half hours.

"And to think I was under the impression that they always went within fifteen minutes,"

Karen offered to buy us a late dinner with her winnings. We decided on Chinese food.

"… and take it back to your room?" Peter flirted, smiling. I kicked out hitting his shins with my boot. He had been smitten with Karen from the beginning.

"Boy, you just can't be satisfied with a lady's offer, can you?" I smiled as he retaliated with a flick of his wet fingers, dripping with water from a nearby pail. I responded by tossing a handful of water back and raced out of his reach, around the corner, charging straight into John. I tumbled to the wet ground.

"Well, well. This is the nicest offer you've made in months," John said in a sarcastic manner, holding me down. Rolling me over, he attempted a kiss as I scrambled from his grip. Karen and Peter quickly appeared watching the struggle, which turned into a solemn moment.

"You better start being a good girl or I won't give you the hundred dollars," he teased.

"What?" Peter cried, inquisitively.

"Oh, you mean she didn't tell you either?" John queried, looking up at the two standing with their hands resting on their hips.

"Well, I... you know, the last second before the race, I just had this funny feeling and well, I ran to the only wicket free for a five dollar place." I blushed.

"Another hundred dollars!" repeated Karen and Peter in unison.

"Yeah, can you imagine Miss Little Britches cashing in like that?"

"I think they ought to wine and dine us in style at the Bonaventure or the Queen Elizabeth. How about it, girls?" Peter coaxed, nodding to John.

"Definitely," John added, "I'll make us a reservation for tomorrow. We're going first class and you two are paying!" John released his clasp, pulling me up onto my feet. With an open hand, he pushed me on my way.

Chapter 8
Wine & Dine

Frantically racing against the clock, Karen and I quickly cleaned up, replacing track clothes with perfume and knee-length cocktail dresses. She had spent the afternoon with Mollie shopping in Cote des Neige and was now wearing the latest fashions.

Karen abruptly stopped in the middle of drying her hair. "With all the excitement of dinner, I forgot to tell you there is a letter on the night table. I believe it's from your Aunt."

Only half-dressed, I began reading the folded pages aloud.

' ... *I had written Leonard to congratulate him on his engagement, but I never heard back from him. All I can do, dear, is give his old address to you, and perhaps a forwarding address was left so you...* '

"Oh Fran," Karen whispered. "I'm sorry, but at least we have a starting point, right?"

"Yeah, sure," I replied, tossing the letter aside.

Karen slipped out ahead of me, saying we should meet in the lobby.

Within no time, I walked to the front of the building, but no one was in sight. Frustrated, I paced up and down the walkway. A brilliant red two-seater sports car pulled alongside. The driver gave the horn a light honk.

"Excuse me, but would you be looking for a lift?" A familiar voice called out. The driver's door opened and out stepped my handsome man, immaculately dressed, displaying his brightest smile with his thick hair slicked back.

"No, it can't be!" I murmured. John extended his hand, awaiting my approval. The navy three-piece suit hung magnificently over the clean lines of his broad-shouldered body. He held the passenger door as I carefully eased into the plush ivory-leather bucket seat, taking in the modern well-equipped dashboard. I glimpsed the word 'Ferrari' etched into the wood-grain of the glove compartment. I was impressed.

John pulled the car out of the parking lot, where a few admiring teenagers stood whistling, onto Decarie Boulevard and headed downtown to the 'Queen Elizabeth' for dinner.

Before I knew it, we had arrived. He tossed his keys to the valet. John placed his hand affectionately on my shoulder as we entered the grand hotel to find Peter and Karen waiting.

The maitre'd seated us at a black-linen covered table where the pewter vases held fresh red roses. He departed quickly replaced by younger waiters filling our water goblets. Peter settled into place, about to light up a cigarette, when a third waiter approached, offering him a light, which surprised him. Karen assessed the French menu, describing a few dishes that she found appealing.

The evening was memorable. We began our meal with champagne, bubbly and dry, followed by chilled zucchini salad. The entrees served varied from duck a l'orange to sole amandine with a well prepared fillet somewhere in the middle for Peter. A mellow Nuit St. George accompanied our meal. We lingered over our delicious dinner until midnight, ending with a parfait Grand Marnier and coffee. We chatted, laughed, danced and ate too much. John held me close and whispered that he wanted us together again. The wine was working its spell as John talked of his love as we kissed tenderly. We danced long after Karen and Peter left until the lights dimmed.

Gathering our belongings, John took my arm and walked through the lobby to the elevator where we traveled up to the observation level. Viewing the magnificent Montreal on a perfectly clear night, as the stars glistened and the lights from the buildings slowly faded, we kissed passionately. I sensed the need to reach out and surrender.

Descending a couple of floors, the elevator doors opened to two businessmen observing our passionate embrace. We smiled as we parted, heading down the dimly lit corridor. Entering the elaborate suite, I stood in awe. The windows draped in luxurious aqua velvet fabric, a French provincial bed held a matching quilted spread, and a white satin brocaded loveseat sat in the far corner, complemented by a small fruitwood coordinating dresser. Next to the silver ice bucket sat a bottle of Chablis, two Waterford crystal goblets and a plate of Belgian chocolates. A substantial bouquet of white roses offered a welcoming fragrance.

Placing my shawl and purse on a nearby chair, I waltzed through the room, gracefully sitting on the loveseat, looking out from the twenty-seventh-floor aerie. John loosened his tie, reached for the wine as the room filled with mystique. Withdrawing the cork, he sniffed its aroma before half-filling the slim stemmed glasses, and then he offered a toast.

"Frannie, let's make a toast to us, my love." Grasping the stems, we tipped in unison. He slipped off his jacket slowly and casually laid it across a chair, eyeing me in his wolfish manner.

"Happy?"

"Oh yes. I really am." I beamed.

"You surprised us yesterday with your little bet. I'm sorry you had to stay so long cooling out Kosta. Bob introduced me to some people at the grandstand and I couldn't get away sooner."

"There were no problems and no need to apologize. I, too, must compliment you on such an excellent job of preparing Kosta, getting her to break her Maiden, which means she has finally won her first race." I sipped the wine. "When do you plan on writing your trainer's exams?"

"As a matter of fact, I wrote them today and do the oral section tomorrow afternoon. I feel things are going well, thanks to our trainer, Mr. Robert Sharp. He took every opportunity to teach and guide me and was more help than I ever expected," John praised, downing the remains of his glass.

"I'm glad to hear you say so." I set my drink down and sashayed around the room.

"That car of yours tonight? That is something else," I remarked, taking my comb and whisking it briskly through my tangled hair. I could sense his hesitation.

"Yes, it is. I rather liked it and hoped you would too."

"Where did it come from?"

"You mean you don't believe it is mine? Now Frannie, why wouldn't you think that I could afford a little gem like a Ferrari? It's a Dino Ferrari, that's all." John smiled shyly. Setting down my comb, I returned to the loveseat thinking he truly must have cashed in on the race. "Well, Mr. John Mencini, I wouldn't put it past you to arrive on the scene with a Bentley if you fancied it."

Placing his empty glass on the table alongside mine, he touched the dial on the stereo filling the room with romantic classical melodies. John pulled me closer and slowly took the zipper and slid it down my back. Our moist lips met, and then softly parted as we embraced 'a la Françoise'. He slipped my dress past my elbows, exposing my waist and withdrew his hold. Glancing down, he caressed my breasts, and then rubbed my back as my dress fell to the floor. Kissing my neck, he whispered in my ear.

"My beautiful Frannie, I love you." Without further hesitation, we carefully kept the mood by slowly undressing one another. I held him in my arms as we relaxed side by side along the cool, satin sheets. His embrace strengthened, and our lustful kisses grew frantic. Our desire fulfilled a ravenous yearning as my inhibitions were far from my mind. Our bodies wrapped together, encouraging our completeness with tenderness as we both were willing final commitment.

"Johnny. Now ... love me," I whispered in a throaty voice, fingering his hair and tracing his lips as we combined into one. Filling with desire, I clung tightly, breathing slowly and moving in a rhythmic motion as he penetrated. Our warm bodies united, craving the passion as strong vibrations exploded within and filled us with ecstasy. We were perfect together, every nerve in my body quivered, every cell fused as we became one and swayed to the sounds of background melodies, which will linger in my memory forever.

We eased together intimately, motionless. Our exhilaration subsided, and I felt a tightness and soreness within. At last, I experienced complete passion and love at twenty. I smiled, wholeheartedly.

"What was that all about?" he kissed my brow and held me close.

"Oh, I was just wondering why it took me so long, when I realize now how beautiful and fantastic it feels." Convinced of my desire, what else could there be? At least I knew I was no longer frigid. I just had a lot of hang-ups, but not anymore.

We dozed, waking to the morning vibrant pink skies enfolding the horizon, and once again, we enjoyed magical lovemaking, feeling a new sense of contentment.

John dialed room service for eggs, French toast, coffee and juice to satisfy our ravenous appetites.

Showering beneath the refreshing spray of the warm water, we playfully scrubbed one another with tiny soaps. My long hair fell below my shoulders when John wrapped around me kissing and exploring new intimacies, which vibrated throughout my whole body.

Lingering over breakfast, I held onto the moment as long as I could. We took a final look, and then I tucked a souvenir postcard into my bag and left the beautiful room, transformed.

Driving past the entrance to Blue Bonnets Raceway toward the stable area, we passed a familiar red and yellow Ehrlick van leaving the grounds, which usually meant horses arrived or left. We parked John's shiny showpiece outside the gate and walked through, flashing our passes for the security guard. It was almost noon and all was quiet except for a few grooms cleaning or feeding.

Three horses crossed the road well ahead of us, coming from the direction of the training track.

Drawing a little closer, I commented, "Wow! Check it out! Take a good look! That's the horse I'd suggest you look at; the big bay stud marked with a white star and narrow strip on his head. He has the red cottons on his tendons. He is gorgeous!" My intuition took charge, once again.

John examined the animal carefully. He stood seventeen hands high and his tight drawn-up stomach indicated his fitness. He bowed his powerful neck as he trotted along. With the outline of an Arabian head and wide-set eyes, he was one of the most outstanding thoroughbreds John had ever laid eyes on. He waved at the groom leading the dynamic thoroughbred toward the barns.

"Hey! Could you tell me what stable you are with?"

"All these horses belong to the Levesque Stable."

I thought 'big bucks here'.

"Where are they coming from?"

"These horses were just released from quarantine at Dorval. They flew in from Argentina a couple of weeks ago."

"Do you know anything about them? Who owns them, or how old?"

"Nope. Nothing." The groom walked on ahead.

It wasn't hard to see that John was impressed and agreed with my first impression that the foreign imports needed investigation. "Outstanding, eh?" I commented, excitedly.

We reached the Larson Stables to find Bob and his wife, Mollie, sitting in their lawn chairs on a patch of grass skirting the tackroom walls.

Bob explained they needed to stay close to the stable because of a rumor that someone was getting to the horses lately - either by injection or by putting drugs into their feed. Peter had also picked up the rumor in the pool hall. John appeared surprised. I offered to stay around if they wanted to get a bite for lunch.

"That's kind of you, Frannie. I think Mollie and I will take you up on that offer. Emerald Isle is in the second race, and John's gelding Ed's Soldier is in the eighth, so it will be a long day for all of us. And you, my lad, have those orals at two o'clock, right?"

"Yes sir." He replied as I whispered in his ear.

"You know, John. You will need your own set of silks to register when you race. Have you given any thought to what you want, 'cause I have an idea." He ruffled my hair and laughed at my suggestion.

"I'm sure you have lots of ideas."

Bob approached John.

"Join us. I have a few things to discuss. Pete will be back in half-an-hour, Frannie, so watch the post until then." Bob winked, appreciative of my gesture, and then departed. Checking the stalls of the two running, I became aware that Emerald Isle moved into a different stall, as had Ed's Soldier. As a precaution, another chestnut horse was placed in his original stall, just in case the rumor was well founded. Switching horse stalls would become a regular practice.

Slouching into a nearby lawn chair, exposing my bare arms in the warm October sun, I dozed off, dreaming of my enchanted evening. Unexpectedly startled by an approaching stranger, I jumped up.

"Hey, you! Wake up!" I slowly focused on the heavy voice yelling at me from above. Slitting my eyes, I saw a scruffy old character with long whisker stubbles and a wrinkled face squinting back. His hat sat crooked and hair hung down touching his shoulder.

"Listen, girl, where can I find the Marshall Stable?" he demanded, roughly. Bobs warning about possible drug pushers flashed before me.

"Are you deaf, girly? Eh? Eh?" he snapped again.

"Well, I'm just trying to think - let me see - I believe it's around here somewhere." Caught off-guard, I stuttered for time. At that moment, Peter arrived.

"Hey. What's the matter, Smoocher - are you lost?"

"Uh? Oh, Pete. How are you? Yeah, I wants to take these here papers over to Marshall's place but can't find their barn. He must have moved his stock. Any idea where they are now?" he blurted between his wide-spaced gray teeth. He looked like a street person.

"Marshall moved his stable over there into the enclosed barns, near the trotters' stable." Peter pointed, responding to Smoocher. Feeling relieved, we watched him stumble along the road, on his way.

"It's ok, Frannie. He's been around racetracks for years. He helps at the racing secretary's' office delivering messages and doing other odd jobs. You have seen him before selling racing forms around the backstretch. No hassle. However, I'm glad to see you didn't offer any information. We must be careful with everyone." Peter patted my shoulder approvingly. "We really enjoyed last night. You're a good sport to treat us all to that fabulous meal. I have never had those escargot things before, and then you guys telling me they were snails! I thought you were kidding. Yuck!"

Karen, watched closely by Peter, jogged across the paved roadway toward us.

"Frannie! Frannie! You will not believe this, but I found him!" She hollered, waving a piece of paper.

"What's she saying?" questioned Peter.

"You found him? Where? When?" I jumped in frenzy, knowing she must be referring to Leonard.

Karen stopped, frantically catching her breath. "Frannie, wait 'til I tell you."

"Go ahead. Go ahead," I encouraged.

Karen's day off had given her time to snoop, making a few phone calls and visiting the address given by my Aunt. Finally learning that Leonard lived in Snowdon, staying in a small apartment with someone named Julie, she heard that he was working out of town for a few days expecting to return early in the week.

"Fantastic! I'm speechless." Hugging and laughing, we did a little celebration dance.

Peter laughed as he reached for a clean bridle from the tackroom and hung it on the door of the stall where he had been working. He liked to listen to our gossip.

The overhead speaker announced the calling for the next day's racing card. We recognized Bob's voice.

Out-of-the-blue, I changed the subject, almost as an afterthought. "Pete! I have found your horse! A great looking bay stallion arrived this morning. Do you know the Levesque Stable?"

"Of course, I do," Peter and Karen answered in unison. "They are the top winning stable at this meet. Why?"

"Well, go there and see if you can get a look at the bay with a white star and strip down his head. Tell us what you think. He is big, fit and great looking. Don't know a thing about him." Peter smiled at my enthusiasm, wondering what I found. He agreed to check it out when he took his break.

The nights in Montreal were wickedly cold so we took advantage of the afternoon sun's blissful rays. As we enjoyed the warmth, Karen quizzed me about my relationship with John. We talked for a while and then she wanted to know. "So, Frannie, tell me. What is it that you want from him... a proposal?" Karen took me by surprise.

"Marriage? I've never thought... considered it.... I mean. Wow!" I reflected on the dilemma put before me. All of a sudden, Karen made it sound like I faced the possibility of getting into something I was not prepared for. I didn't want to shack-up like a lot of the couples our age were doing, but I realized that I had to resolve this quandary before someone got hurt - mainly myself. I pondered the situation as she sat reading a fashion magazine.

Shortly after five o'clock, we finished feeding and mucking out stalls when John returned, reporting that his exams had gone well. We decided to grab a bite to eat at a local diner where Peter described his visit to the Levesque stable.

"I discovered that ol' Gordy from Toronto was working there and he filled me in. He told me that the horse was by *Snocat*, who is one of the Queen's stallions standing stud in Argentina, and out of a mare called *Romantic*, who had exceptional South American breeding. I don't recall his name, but I think it could have been Snow Romance or SnoMann or something. Apparently, he is a three-year-old and raced only three times in his life. His first race was a Stake Race, which he won handily. His next two starts were something else again. I never saw his papers, but Gordy told me three horses are for sale. When I tried to find out the price, he wouldn't say. By the sound of things, I imagine it could be high. I think we should keep a close eye on these three, especially during morning workouts, to see how they handle the going here. Gordy was telling me they've never started from a gate before, and raced in the opposite direction as well. They're bound to need a great deal of training; it will be like starting from scratch."

"Sounds interesting, all right," John admitted. The seed planted.

Our final weeks at the Blue Bonnets racing meet ended in great success with the Larson stables taking sixteen wins, eighteen seconds, and twenty-seven thirds. John qualified for his trainer's license, which pleased Bob who rewarded him with a substantial bonus for the training of the three horses. John would race under his own stable with new silks; white with red arms and a red maple leaf on the back to mimic the brand new Canadian flag. I told him it would take the American out of him.

Peter studied the Argentine threesome. The Levesque stable raced the stallion twice unsuccessfully in Allowance Races where claiming was not allowed. Peter approached the two owners, asking if they would consider an offer. The wealthy middle-aged women from New York were in no hurry to release the horses until their trainer advised them of suitable replacements.

John knew that it was rare for any racehorse owner to spend more than five consecutive minutes with their horses. They mostly patted them in the stables with grooms or trainers in attendance, or in the winner's circle, after a race. Owners never connected with the animal or sensed their energy creating a bond together. They were enthusiastic, but ignorant owners who put blind trust in the friendship, good faith and honesty of their trainer. They were just people, not riders themselves and had no fields of their own where the horses could graze. Horseracing was a hobby, an investment or just another commodity for most owners.

One of the vets John knew, Jean St. Hilaire, reported to him regarding the horse, SnoMann, who was good to go. His legs were cool; teeth were consistent; range of movement was normal; eyes were clear; his trot was sound; no damaged knees or bowed tendons.

The women owners named their bottom price of twenty thousand dollars. After days of lengthy discussions, indecision, and listening to Bobs cautioning words, John and Peter decided to make the deal binding. They offered fifteen thousand. The sale took place the day before closing but ended up selling for eighteen thousand dollars, a few thousand more than the Dino cost him. The magnificent muscular animal with the four white stockings came into the Larson Stables under trainer, John R. Mencini. He was now in business.

***

Earlier in the month, my first contact with my brother had been emotional leaving both of us teary-eyed. Five years had passed, but Leonard and his wife Julie welcomed me into their home, hopeful that I'd spend as much time as I could with them, which I did.

We experienced one strange weekend, just days before the racing meet ended, which influenced my life. Leonard and I faced a traumatic incident - one we knew would happen one day. Our father, Todd Harrison, requested us to return to Toronto, immediately. Neither of us had talked about him or wanted to see him again after our mother's death. Without explaining the details to anyone, except Julie, we decided to fly back on the Friday. Everyone at the track thought I was spending a few days with my brother and his wife.

As we stepped into a waiting airport limousine in Toronto, Leonard asked for Sunnybrook Hospital. Closing my eyes, I remembered the father who I had adored as a child, but eventually came to detest as a teenager. Leonard whispered his truth.

"We lived through hell. I'm just those few years older that allowed me to get out and play sports while you watched him abuse Mom, slowly drinking herself to death. It's a wonder you stayed sane, that you didn't hit the streets or get into the drug scene like some other kids." Leonard looked away. "You're a pretty sharp kid, Frannie." He smiled. There was a moment's silence.

"It takes two. Mom should have left him years ago." I replied, but knew divorce was not accepted then. She was a teenager, not quite twenty, when they married in the 1930s.

We rode on in silence, remembering days and nights of years past. Our painful experiences needed healing as life's all about *how* we react to the good, the bad and the ugly.

One of the nurses on duty in the west wing directed us to his room. She described the extent of his poor health ... influenza, emphysema, poison in his system, cirrhosis of the liver, poor hearing, purple toes, fingers and nose and on and on. We believed this came about from all his

74

drinking and bad eating habits. Leonard held my hand as we entered his room.

Our father lay on his side with the hospital gown draped around his frail body. He weighed no more than a hundred and thirty pounds, if that. Except for the blue that tinged his skin, he was pasty white. Veins showed through his tissue-thin skin, and tubes inserted in his mouth and nose made him look a hundred years, but he was in his mid-sixties. His finger moved. One eye opened, and muffled sounds escaped through his dry cracked lips. I began to shake when I realized that he wanted me to step closer. I stood there frozen, feeling sick inside. The shock of seeing someone in that condition was overpowering. Leonard never moved a muscle. Minutes passed. Two pale gray-blue eyes stared over the starched white sheets and blinked only once.

Something moved within me and I suddenly stepped forward. I whispered. "Anyone, anyone on earth who looks like this has suffered enough." I touched his hand and he held mine in his for ten minutes, and then closed his eyes. Liquid dribbled from the corner of his mouth. He was gone.

Todd's mother, Martha, had outlived her son, only to bury him alone. Both Leonard and I returned to Montreal, never to mention the situation again. The echo of his belligerent voice drifted from our memory. We were at last free of his demands, and the guilt gradually lifted for both of us. Finally, we could let go of our anger knowing the evil spirit that dwelled within him was now gone.

Someone once told me that a negative energy field surrounded me, so maybe now, releasing the past with forgiveness, I would let loose the painful demons.

***

My days at Blue Bonnets Raceway came to an end with Leonard and Julie offering their place to live, urging me not to make any rash decisions. Karen returned to Toronto, hoping I'd share her spacious high-rise. At the same time, Peter and John busied themselves for the long haul south. They planned to winter at John's family farm in Ohio where they would begin to retrain SnoMann for the spring meet at Waterford Park in West Virginia, confident that the cheap track would build up bigger odds. Once again, my indecisiveness caused me the usual turmoil. I always left matters undecided until the last possible moment, creating an emotional upset for myself, always afraid of making the wrong choice.

On our last night in Montreal, I aimlessly walked past Shea's Bowling Alley, shuffling along the sidewalk on my way back to Ruby Foos. Lost in thought, I passed the motel. The sound of squealing tires caught my attention. The familiar flamboyant sports car pulled up alongside the curb. John waved.

"Frannie, by God, I'm not about to go into this again, but honey, here's a little gift for you." He stretched across the seat, handing me a package. I reached out touching his hand and held it. He smiled, knowing I did not want to see him go. "Take care, eh? Whatever you decide, I'll always be waiting... there will never be anyone else for me, ever."

John shifted gears as he pulled the powerful machine into the line of heavy traffic and out of sight. Tears blurred my vision when I opened the package to find a small book, *The Prophet*, by Kahlil Gibran. Holding it next to my heart, thoughts and memories streamed through me.

Oblivious to the changing streetlights, wistful snowflakes falling, and noisy traffic, I drifted into the shadows of the night.

Chapter 9
The Gathering

Toronto, Spring - 1969

The doorbell chimed a melody as the bathroom door opened and Susan stomped down the hallway with her hair wrapped in towels.

Peter was back in Toronto. In his usual clumsy manner, he dropped chunks of dry mud from his boots. Noticing her annoyance, he swiftly removed them as they exchanged warm greetings after his two-year absence. Susan offered him a drink and he explained that it would have to be white, as milk would soothe his active ulcer. Susan sipped on an orange crush giving Peter an up-to-date account of her current unemployment woe, namely, her interviews at Atwood's, Ridpath's and Shelagh's of Yorkville.

"Humm, that's not so great. What's up with your love life? Are you still dating Kenny?"

"Yes, but not as steadily as before. He's studying at Queens University in Kingston and working the summer months at Ontario Place again this year. As a matter of fact, I talked to him earlier this week and he's planning to meet BJ, who flew in from London on business. We decided to get together for dinner."

"No kidding! That would be great! I haven't seen BJ in a few years. Say, why don't you give Kenny a ring and see what's happening?"

Susan made the call from the kitchen. Peter could hear her leave a message.

He divulged information regarding SnoMann and the problems he had experienced. The previous summer, John and Peter returned to Montreal to 'turn him loose' but everything had gone wrong. The bull-ring track was too small with its sharp turns for the big stallion causing him to pull a tendon. Laid up for most of the meet recovering, they gave him a race to be sure he was sound during the last week of racing. The jockey kept him under wrap, but he finished third, which resulted in ruining his racing form. Peter thought they had entered him 'over his head'

Returning to the States, SnoMann ran at Liberty Bell in Philadelphia in the late fall, Florida at Gulfstream over the winter, and then spent seven weeks at John's family farm in Mechanicstown, Ohio, between Steubenville and Akron. SnoMann rested up as John acquired a few other horses to train for different owners, which gave them a small stable of six.

Susan joked at Peters relaxed manner, lying stretched out on the floor. "You two guys are something else! How does John get back and forth across the border?"

"Susan, don't be so naive. Paperwork. It's not that hard."

"Right. Should have figured that one out."

During their time traveling, I had stayed in Montreal after Expo until December when I visited for a few weeks over Christmas. While living with my brother and sister-in-law, I enrolled at a Secretarial College in Montreal. Peter liked to call my relationship 'the great romance without commitment.' When they returned to Blue Bonnets in late summer, John and I took a small apartment and stayed together for the thirteen weeks. When Christmas arrived, severe storms prevented Peter from flying back to Toronto for the holidays, so he stayed in Ohio.

Flying south after Boxing Day, I found the airports over crowded as several airlines were grounded. Upon arrival, John presented me with a black velvet box containing an engagement ring, saying we would be married as soon as he completed his plans with SnoMann in the spring. We had a wonderful holiday with his family.

Traveling into West Virginia to Waterford Park, they gave 'Sno' two races at the cheap track before arriving at Woodbine. John convinced jockey Raymond Cooper to join them in Toronto to ride because he wanted to have an unknown jockey ride in Canada, hoping to keep the odds down.

Peter rubbed his eyes, yawned and entered the kitchen where he replenished his glass of milk. He gazed out the window at the garden his Aunt Mae kept so immaculate. A sense of longing developed, maybe even a little homesickness. Susan watched him from the doorway. The ringing of the telephone brought them back into the moment. Kenny returned Susan's call and made arrangements for dinner in the Dickens Room at the Ports of Call where he and BJ would be waiting.

"Great!" Sitting at the kitchen table, Susan removed the towel from damp hair.

"Did I ever tell you about BJ's bon voyage party at the Old Mill in the west end? Nearly two hundred people came, including his hockey teammates, track and field friends, neighbors, school chums, relatives, etc. His sister Nancy arranged the party with a new Honda 350 motorcycle waiting for him at Heathrow. He was really upset about leaving."

"No kidding? Wish I had been there." Peter thought about his good friend from his youth for several minutes, and then began to fidget as he stood up to leave.

As the door closed behind him, Susan entered her room to finish dressing for her date with Kenny. Noticing a letter I had written sitting on her desk, she sat a moment to read it.

'*Hey Sue – How's it going? I owe you more than a quick note, but I am so busy lately I hardly find time to eat a half-decent meal anymore. I got the most terrific job with Regal Oil, all because Leonard convinced me to go back to school. I am the happiest I have ever been in my life, girl. My feet don't even touch the ground. I have almost finished my marketing courses, which in time could help me get into administrative work. That is my aim, anyway. I can't believe how everything is coming together, and it's incredible how good I feel about myself, finally. Take care - and I will see you in May when SnoMann runs for the money. Ciao for now. Love Fran*'

Susan and Kenny were the first to arrive at the Ports of Call Restaurant, where they checked their coats as Kenny described his lunch with BJ the previous day, finding him just his old self again. They had finished their first drink when Peter entered, dressed in bold check slacks, turtleneck and sports jacket, much to their surprise. His long hair slicked back, neatly combed.

A round of cocktails arrived when BJ appeared showing a British influence in his light wool trousers, tailored shirt, conservative tie and tweed sports jacket. He had acquired a look of maturity that belied his young years.

The group reacquainted as BJ ordered a Canadian lager and explained about his family's move to England, bringing everyone up to date. Susan remembered his farewell party at the Old Mill, wondering if he actually put his motorcycle to use. Smiling, he admitted it had become his primary means of transportation as British gas prices had hit the three dollars a gallon mark. He recalled his counseling year after high school, which had instilled a new interest in art and drafting. During the weeks he was organizing his new office in the Bull Ring complex in Birmingham, BJ talked with his Uncle William who was associated with the RIBA Journal.

"What's that?" Susan inquired. "The RIBA?"

"It stands for Royal Institute of British Architects. I talked with the RIBA board of education to find out where to apply. Their list consisted of five names; the University of South Wales, Liverpool, Manchester, Nottingham or Leeds Polytechnic. The first acceptance came from Nottingham University, and off I went, itching to get started."

"Well, I'll be damned!" exclaimed Peter, with a mouthful. "Our man Nichols... the Architect. Fan - tas - tic!"

"Well, I don't know about that, but I am putting everything into this. I've even signed up for the RIBA conference at Stirling University and a summer workshop at Portland Place. It's all or nothing, with me. According to my Dad, I'm making up for lost time." Ken asked about the company's expansion and BJ replied that they were hoping to open in London within three years.

"No girlfriend?" Ken asked. BJ shook his head.

"Haven't got time."

Settling back after the plates cleared, they finished their second bottle of Chianti before ordering desserts. "The never-ending meal," Peter remarked.

"What has anybody heard from Francine Harrison? The last time I saw her was in the hospital after that track meet in Aurora. I, ah, always liked Francine. She sure had her share of misfortunes. Pete, you told me she moved into Yorkville with you and your friend John, didn't you?"

Peter lit up a cigarette and pulled an empty ashtray within reach. He shed some light so BJ knew about our years on the racetrack, finding Leonard and my engagement. BJ became noticeably solemn as he removed his glasses and reached for his napkin. He gave them a cleaning, still without commenting. Susan glanced at Ken, puzzled.

"What's the look for, BJ?"

"I could never see those two getting together. They always seemed so different somehow and especially living in Yorkville, let alone working on the track." Susan nodded in agreement. "So, tell me Pete, is she happy?" Taken back by his comments, Peter reassured him and gave details about me living with my brother and going to school in Montreal.

BJ explained his plans to return to the U.K. the following day when Peter related the story of SnoMann's purchase, the lengthy training program, anticipating a big win. At that moment, Susan and Ken paid their tab and left the restaurant. Peter spelled out the scoop of their big gamble, which John hoped to collect half a million dollars from their bets. Peter asked BJ to stay longer to see the race.

"Yes, I'd like that; it would be fun. I'll see what I can arrange. In fact, I'd like to see Francine again before she becomes Mrs. John Roberts."

"Yeah, well, it won't be Roberts. It will be Francine Mencini." BJ's grin turned into a look of perplexity.

"What? I thought...?"

"Never mind, my friend," Peter interrupted, standing to leave. "It's another one of those long stories. Keep in touch, eh? And, try to stay over for another week or so, if possible. I'm staying up at the parents' place."

The following day, BJ entered 390 Bay Street to visit his father's lawyer to complete the procedures to disband the partnership his father once had. He then placed a call to Birmingham to his Uncle William, who promised to relay the message that he would be delaying his return for a few more days.

Hailing a cab, he drove to Woodbine racetrack hoping to find Peter before he left the grounds. The security guard at the stable entrance paged him, but there was no response. BJ waited several minutes before deciding to leave. A screech of tires came from behind as the Ferrari forced him to jump aside. The driver, whom he vaguely recognized, opened his door and peered over the roof and shouted, "Hey, Milty, can I pick up my pass here?"

The security guard raised his hand to shade his eyes.

"Well, if it isn't 'the wanderer.' How are you, John? Yes, I can give you a sticker, but you will have to pick up your passes at the Secretary's office. Where'd you come from this time?"

The older man tossed an envelope over to John, who tore it open and placed the sticky emblem on the windshield. BJ waved to get Johns attention and when there was no response, he called out.

"John... John Roberts? John Mencini," he corrected. When he got no reply, he tapped lightly on the passenger side window. John looked his way.

"Well, I'll be damned! If it isn't the athlete of the 60's. What the hell are you doing out here? Pete was telling me about your dinner last night."

Briefly explaining his recent visit, BJ accompanied John into the barn area. They parked the car alongside stable M, then walked down the dusty shed and inspected each stall until they found number twenty-six.

"Here's the ol' boy. Hey, Sno, get onto your feet and move over here. Don't you recognize your trainer anymore?" John puckered his lips, creating a kissing sound that attracted the animal's attention. The big bay stallion rose to his calling, stretching his legs and whinnied back to his owner's voice. SnoMann nuzzled against his shoulder until he got his head rubbed and heard more comforting words. It was obvious that a connection existed between the two.

"Wow! He is a big bugger. A real beauty, that's for sure," BJ commented, taking a good look at his form.

"Yeah. He sure is. Pete and I feel he is ready. This next race will be the big one." BJ explained the race was his reason for extending his visit.

"Yep. I'll have to get a race picked out for him. There is a suitable one tomorrow. I will enter and see if he gets in. If he does, he will run Friday. I guess Pete told you about Cooper?"

"Your jockey? Yeah. Did you bring any of your other horses with you this time, John?"

"Uh-huh. These three here are mine and there will be two more coming in soon. They should like the firm grass on the turf course here. Sno will improve too on these long stretches. This track is one of the best."

Continuing their conversation, they walked to the track kitchen where they grabbed lunch and shot a few games of pool until four o'clock when Peter arrived. Picking up some coffees, they left the smoky premise to relax in the sun on a patch of long grass next to their stable. Discussing the details of their plans for the week, Peter filled John in on SnoMann's latest workout.

"I had Cooper take Sno out today for a light breeze. He tried the *switch* on him and he really responded to the damn thing. If the word is right, he has the fastest workout of the morning. I hope that doesn't hit the papers. There are times those guys like to keep a little inside information to themselves."

Disappointed at the thought, John agreed.

"I want him to carry as light a weight as possible in the race and with the apprentice allowance that should help. Cooper rides at one hundred and twelve pounds. Just because SnoMann's a stud, he'll have to carry more weight and every pound counts. I'm strictly going with an Allowance … non-winners of the year. No stake race. No claimers. From all appearances, the public will read his racing form and conclude that he is running out of his class. Unless, of course, his morning workout time is printed - the half he ran in forty-six. He is strictly distance, and as long as he breaks from the starting gate without mishaps, all should go well."

"Why? Is there trouble loading him?" BJ asked.

"Yes, you could say that. The fact is, BJ, this horse is from Argentina and they don't use a starting gate there, just a wire. The horses also run in the reverse direction. When we got him, we had no choice but to start training him right from scratch." John related the procedure taken to reintroduce the horse to the ways of North American racing. While he was running in Philadelphia, an observant vet discovered the stallion's shortsightedness, which explained his bad behavior trying to load in the starting gate. The vision problem corrected with the addition of a pair of blinkers and by having SnoMann backed into the loading gate from the front. BJ nodded, understanding the complications.

Later that evening, the three of them drove to our Avenue Road stomping grounds. The formerly ratty buildings and garbage-filled streets were remarkably tidier. With only a few derelict homes left in Yorkville, a good number transformed into expensive boutiques, four-star restaurants and elegant antique shops, which changed the face of the historic homes.

They located our old two-story purple house, which now boasted a modern storefront window that displayed casual cotton gowns and shirts in rainbow hues. As they walked the newly paved avenues, John became excited about the prospect of constructing an ultra exclusive mall. He wanted to speculate all the available real estate, as the area slowly changed into an elite shopping area of the city. He enthusiastically explained his plans to form a syndicate with his proposed winnings. John's dream was to create a center from the remaining slum houses, making enough money from property dealings to take us away from the racetrack hassle.

"You know guys, there will be a time when not one of the original homes will remain here. This redevelopment is the future, I'm telling you."

They ventured further down the street and through the alleys onto Cumberland where tiny basements remodeled for bakeries, salons, furniture shops, second-hand stores and shoe boutiques.

"Look! A decorator's shop owned by Robert Dirnstein. Just mark my word, boys, he'll be world famous in less than five years," John boasted as the others rolled their eyes at his rambling. "And you know why he'll do that well? Because he started here. Just like us, Pete." Peter folded his arms, puffing on a fag that dangled from his lips.

BJ remarked on the new structures and collaborated with John. They discussed the possibilities and visualized the concept, talking about building codes, development conceptions, space planning, and height restrictions as BJ expressed architectural material restraints. John realized his need to research was about to commence.

While sipping coffee in one of the newly converted little restaurants, Peter renewed acquaintances with an old neighbor. She recounted how the changes had taken place.

"I suppose you could say it happened gradually as kids moved west to Vancouver or Haight Ashbury and the police raids grew more frequent," she explained. "Remember Baldy, the cop? What's his name?"

"You know, Hank, the cop that would hang out here all the time a few years back. What was his name?" she called to her husband working in the kitchen.

"Oh, you must mean Elwood," he returned. John became more attentive.

"Yeah, that's it. A few new couples drifted in to set up shop while others moved on. Anyway, Elwood really freaked out, a while back, when his youngest boy OD'd and they found him in the Don River. Elwood knew this place was where his son hung out. Poor guy, they put him away somewhere for a year 'til he'd settled down. The cops scared a number of kids, threw some in the slammer for smoking pot or trafficking drugs, while others moved south to Haight Ashbury, San Francisco as things got worse. In the end, a few artsy types began upgrading the village with trendy shops to bring in some money. That's what was really needed." Peter listened, intently, as they finished their coffees.

John's usual ebullient mood grew quiet as they drove to the north end of the city, wanting nothing more than a good night sleep.

Chapter 10
Woodbine Racetrack, Toronto

The intense humidity and the familiar manure odor lingered as everyone's pace slackened. Perspiration dripped from both man and beast as they followed their morning routines. To keep their bodies cool as well as their tempers, they hosed down the stable hands and thoroughbreds.

Peter leaned against the stall door, wiping his brow with the back of his hand. He finished his Pepsi and tossed the can into a nearby garbage bin.

"Man, am I glad we don't have anything running today! In this friggin' heat, I would be afraid of passing out. I don't ever remember this heat; it's even hard to breathe. The radio said it was 97 degrees."

John was in stall twenty-six grooming SnoMann. As he finished rubbing him down with a dust rag, he picked up one leg and cleaned out around the aluminum shoe with a hoof-pick. Then he rubbed his hand over the horse's tendon, feeling for any warmth.

"I'll take no chances this time, Pete. Better pick up some ice-packs at the tack shop and we'll freeze that tendon. In fact, put him in a whirlpool-tub this afternoon. He'll like that. There's no heat evident in the tendon but still, I want to make it as comfortable as possible - eh boy?"

John pointed in the direction of a female, decked out in jockey gear, approaching their stable.

"Hey there, Pete - John. It's good to see you guys back in town." Karen offered her hand to each. "I had no idea you guys were back until I saw the *Overnight* with SnoMann entered in the quinella. This is the big one, right? Will Dad ever be sorry. He's at the Keeneland sales in Kentucky for a couple of weeks."

John nodded knowingly, pleased to see her.

"Yeah, this should be the big one," Peter acknowledged.

"Listen, John, you're my most favorite trainer in the whole world. As you can see, I've changed my profession," she pointed to her clothes. "When I saw you hadn't named anyone on SnoMann ... well, I thought you could do us both a big favor and let me ride him. I'm a full-fledged jockey

85

now and could do you some real good. Like with long shots. Oh please, Johnny, say you will think about it. If I could ride SnoMann and win, it would do us both wonders. I'd pick up some really good stock to ride here. Oh, Johnny, you have to let me ride him. Please say you'll think about it, huh?"

Peter and John looked at one another, in shock.

"Oh, my God! Karen, what have you done? What are you asking?" Peter sputtered out.

"Come off it, Pete. Get with it. This is a new generation! You can't tell me for a moment that I'm not good around the horses. I've been riding them my whole life and have handled Dad's stable for years. You know that! Well, now it's time to try to make some real bucks at doing what I know best, and that's riding. I can ride with any of these jockeys. These little shrimps haven't the faintest idea how to handle a horse. Most of them fell into the profession because of their size. Do not try to tell me any different. I know SnoMann. I galloped him for two years in Montreal. I know how he gets all upset when he's loading in the gate. I don't see what the problem is. I have the right weight with apprentice allowance, no dead weight required, to speak of. There's no possible excuse you could give me that would make any sense. Well, John? Will you think about it? Huh?" Karen pleaded. She tucked her riding crop under her arm, in her distinctive and graceful manner.

John crossed his arms and tilted his head. He paused, rubbing his chin as if giving the idea a great deal of thought. Peter could not believe that John considered the idea.

"Oh, get off the pot, man! You can't actually be thinking about this! Karen is a super lady and a gorgeous one at that, but riding our horse? I don't think so. And, just remember that, man, it's OUR horse! And I say no way! We already have our jockey. You took two months convincing him to come up here for this one race, and don't forget that either. We're committed to him. Mencini, get off this kick! Damn it, man, think straight, will you?"

Karen gave Peter a push on the shoulder. "You! You can get off the pot! I'm telling you I can do better. If you thought about it, you'd know it's true, too. All I am asking is that you will talk it over." John raised both his hands for peace.

"Cool it, you two. Karen, Pete's right. We have already committed ourselves to this guy. I needed to trust someone, and so I got hold of him and he is riding SnoMann for us. I'll tell you what, I'll let you ride any mount next week. You have my word. You'll be named on whatever horse."

"Yeah, that's great. Nevertheless, I need SnoMann to make any difference, and then I won't have to ride all the dogs on the track. I'll never do any good unless I can get better stock. I don't mean to be ungrateful, Johnny. I'm sorry if I sound like it, but..."

"Well, you sure as hell sound like it to me," Peter butted in.

"Listen Karen, I can't. Cooper will ride SnoMann tomorrow and that's all I can say right now." John put his arm around her shoulder in comfort.

Disillusioned, Karen walked away. Peter remarked, "I can't believe that girl! What has Bob let his daughter get into anyway? I mean, look at her. Gorgeous! Beautiful! What the hell does she want to be riding horses for when she could be modeling? I just don't understand that one."

"Oh, I don't think she's trying to impress anyone. She honestly feels that she's capable and can make a go of it if someone gives her a break. You must admit, she handles the animals well. And has had years of experience." John turned around and slapped SnoMann on the shoulder with affection. The heat seemed even more oppressive as they finished their chores.

John asked Peter to get hold of the blacksmith. With several days of hot, dry weather, the track conditions would remain slow. "We'd better get him shod this afternoon. How have his ankles been while training here? Any signs of running down? I was checking earlier and everything looks good, no need for patches." John commented.

"No signs. He has been doing fine since you put the block-heels on behind. But, if you want, we can put patches on for extra insurance."

"Nah. They look fine."

"What time is Frannie flying in tomorrow? Are you going to be able to meet her at the airport?" Peter changed the subject, wiping his brow for the umpteenth time. John had suggested Susan pick me up at the airport.

A familiar call sounded from his jockey, Raymond Cooper. They chatted briefly, and then met up with the track vet.

After the blacksmith finished shoeing the horses, Peter heard SnoMann sneeze. Quickly retrieving a bottle of Vicks and placing two swoops in each nostril, he realized he had become edgy and overcautious. He had to laugh at himself; he was acting like an old woman, Cooper commented.

As the time grew closer to noon, Peter borrowed John's car to meet BJ for lunch. Afterward, they returned to Woodbine to make preparations on SnoMann where they found John. He chatted briefly with Frankie Bressan, one of Bob's gambling friends.

A slight breeze blew across the grounds as they finished chores shortly after five o'clock. SnoMann grazed upon the uncut grass across the pathway while they discussed the upcoming race. Peter and BJ enjoyed a cold beer whereas John sipped on a can of flat pop; he never was much of a drinker.

After snacking on take-out food, Peter gathered up dinner containers and was about to depart when John offered the Ferrari if he washed it, so he wouldn't have a dusty car when I arrived. Making a quick getaway, Peter grasped the keys and drove off with BJ.

Later that same evening, Susan telephoned Peter to say she was unable to pick me up at the airport as an unexpected interview came up, and she didn't want to miss an opportunity. BJ volunteered to help and received my flight number. Problem solved.

An early sunrise with overcast skies brought another day of heat and humidity. The temperature was well over ninety degrees Fahrenheit for the sixth day in a row.

BJ drove to the airport, enjoying the luxury of the imported sports car, to find the new Air Canada terminal under construction, which caused him some delay. Scanning the incoming passengers, BJ caught sight of my bright citrus-green T-shirt. My big hair was longer than he remembered and tied to the side in a single pigtail. I wore oversized sunglasses pushed above my forehead. Taking a second look, almost missing him altogether, I questioned, "BJ? BJ Nichols?"

"The one and only," he replied, taking my luggage.

"I don't believe this. Of all the unlikely places to run into you … what is …?"

"I'm doing John a favor. I have been staying in town a few days and I decided to postpone my departure to watch their horse race today. I wanted to see you again, too. Hope you don't mind the switcheroo."

"Not at all. In fact, I'm flattered. Boy, it's good to see you again. I mean it." I welcomed the unexpected and took his arm as we left the busy terminal. The short flight from Montreal went without hassle.

Outside the busy air-conditioned terminal, hot muggy air assaulted us as we chatted all the way to the car where he placed my bags in the jump-seat behind the familiar ivory leather bucket seats, and then we were off.

"Seems to me I've seen this car before," I giggled, taking a scarf from my purse.

"I know," he added, changing to his sunglasses as the brilliant rays penetrated the windshield. The day began with a nice surprise but was only the first of many unexpected events to follow.

When we sighted the stable, everything was in a state of turmoil. A substantial red van had pulled up and parked as horses were unloading from another nearby. Peter was scrambling in an attempt to locate a blacksmith because SnoMann had kicked the wall in the commotion and loosened his shoe. Standing to one side, John saw me out of the corner of his eye and rushed to my side, swinging me in playful circles.

"It's been too long, Babe. No more commuting. I missed you so much." His passionate kiss drew a round of applause from the observant grooms. "Come on, you two. Let's break for coffee and donuts in the kitchen. I've got to pick up today's form and see what SnoMann's up against." Peter led the way.

John gave details of the day's race as we walked into the track cafeteria. He read the entries for the fifth race. Entered was Starlight Girl, a mare who arrived from Aqueduct and once placed second to Damascus but this would only be her third race of the year. John read her form, which indicated she had some early speed and liked the mud aloud. Another contender was Hammer 'n Tongs, who set a track record in Fort Erie the previous year and earned over a hundred thousand dollars, thus far. Realizing SnoMann was in with tough competition, he studied the racing form carefully as he downed the last dregs of his coffee.

With little knowledge of the exciting event, BJ sensed the intoxicating atmosphere of the race. A young jockey appeared unexpectedly. John introduced Cooper and then took him aside to speak privately, arousing curiosity among the rest of us. We returned to the stable area.

John arrived sober-faced, yet irritable.

"What's up?" Peter asked anxiously, sensing some complications.

"Boy, we've got problems cut out for us now. Let me tell you."

"Why?" I butted in. "What's he say?"

"The big boys are in this race. They have Starlight Girl on the lead. They haven't approached him directly, but the word is out that she's to go all the way. Apparently she's been hurting pretty bad, but with the jockey's cooperation there should be no problem."

"What are you saying? You mean to tell me, out of all these goddamn races, we have to get in one with the bloody mafia. No!!" Peter blurted out, kicking the stall door in frustration. "Fuck this! I'm going to find Frankie and see if he knows about this."

"Sh -h! They're not necessarily mafia. These guys have got a good horse but when they are hurting they drop them down in class, and that's why she's racing here and not Aqueduct. The jockey is the one who is doing the *stiffing*. They probably won't even contact Cooper after seeing SnoMann's form. It is pitiful. Anyway, he is afraid and doesn't want to end up in some garbage field, dead. And that's what sometimes happens if you turn on them when a big gamble is on the line."

"So, what does he propose doing?"

"Well, he's worried. If he doesn't go along with their plans, goes ahead and lets Sno run, he could be in for one miserable time, to say the least. Remember, he is an outsider and has to go along with the rules. Their rules, that is! And if he doesn't, they'll ruin him."

"Just the same, what do you do?" Peter paced, nervously. "What the hell are we going to do?" His voice hardened and his face reddened.

"I don't know." John shook his head, disgustedly.

"The damn little bugger," I stomped.

"Frannie, honey, you know as well as I do that he didn't have to tell me. Remember, he knows what we are up to, so he decided to be a straight shooter. It's not his fault." He sighed, filled with anguish. "Most jockeys don't tell." A cool breeze suddenly brushed through the stable area. The energy was changing.

"Peter, did you pick up that ice pack for Sno?" He nodded a reply. John hesitated, and then proceeded to fetch a metal comb and braid SnoMann's mane. He mentioned to Peter that he had seen SnoMann's workout recorded in the racing form from the day before. John warned Peter to remain calm. Horses could sense our negative vibrations.

I listened carefully as they discussed the race and reviewed the other horses' forms in detail. John decided that SnoMann would have to lay no further back than fifth to have enough run left for the closing stretch. He felt that the distance of a mile and an eighth was in his favor and against the injured mare, even if she did outclass the rest of the field.

Anxiously, Peter reminded him, SnoMann needed a pony and he wanted to be there. They both agreed. There went my chance to walk SnoMann to the paddock.

I stood next to SnoMann rubbing his head while John continued to braid his mane. Sno was unusually patient, as if he could sense a shift in energy. His eyes were exceptionally bright and he stood remarkably still. John worked on his legs. I walked him around the shed several times while Peter refreshed his stall. I had the strong feeling that SnoMann seemed different somehow.

Shortly thereafter, the call came for the first race. Peter fetched a bucket of water, took the chemical freeze-pack out of its blue wrapper and began to soak it thoroughly. John applied it to the front right tendon. To hold his leg steady and prevent movement, Peter lifted the opposite leg as John bandaged it firmly in place.

I walked over to SnoMann, who dropped his head and searched for food. Stroking his neck for several minutes, speaking softly, I admired the magnificent animal and noticed a strange light in his eyes, which indicated a particular calmness at that moment. I whispered, "Love you, Sno. This is your day, you know that?" He had a funny way about himself where he would extend his tongue, rolling it up. I laughed, thinking, always the show-off.

BJ and I stood close by scanning the racing form as I showed him the proper way to read it, identifying the codes and short forms. Impatient and excited, we left for the grandstand when they called for the fourth race in the backstretch. It gave us enough time to place bets on the third race, which was already in the paddock. As we headed toward the stable gate, the speakers announced ... *John Mencini - please report to the racing secretary's' office immediately.* Shrugging his shoulders, John headed in that direction.

Peter watched closely. He wondered if SnoMann would be turned loose, and if so, how much money John was going to bet. They had notified a couple of bookies previously.

Within a few minutes, we reached the grandstand where BJ admired the stylish landscaped grounds as he placed his bets. Beginner's luck had brought him a profitable ninety dollars on the third and fourth races.

For the fifth race, we quickly approached the wickets to gamble on SnoMann, whether anyone liked it or not. We were hopeful. My stomach was churning, as I knew in my heart that John had been two years planning for this moment.

Scanning the grandstand, I watched the record crowd rumble across the hot pavement as the high temperatures finally cooled and bets placed. The Argentine horse liked the hot weather, which would be to his advantage. Colorful spring attire brightened the landscape as people viewed their programs with eager thoughts of collecting their fortune and fulfilling their dreams, when the favorite, Starlight Girl, made her appearance.

Proudly, I pointed out the dapper bay stallion to BJ as the horses paraded one behind the other into the paddock circle. Riding the gray dappled pony, Peter accompanied SnoMann, who arrogantly bowed his powerful neck and gnawed on the bit.

"Well, I wonder what's up now." I focused on the entrance to the clubhouse parking lot. John appeared, changed from his work clothes. I hurried over to his side while BJ stayed in the background waiting and watching my every move.

John continued into the enclosed paddock area and I returned to BJ. He knew something was wrong. In a loud whisper, I explained that our jockey, Raymond Cooper, wouldn't go along with the other jockey's game, and took a tumble as he was pulling up at the end of the second race. He had scratched from riding the rest of his mounts for the day. We stood there in disbelief.

"Maybe it is better this way. At least he is honest about it all."

"Probably, but that's not the half of it," I added, breathing heavily.

"Go on."

"Well, John had to name another jockey to ride SnoMann and you'll never guess who! Karen Sharp. That's who! Karen Sharp!" Dumbfounded, BJ gasped.

"The model? Frannie, he must be kidding, of course." I shook my head furiously. My expression sickened and my color faded. I looked over to the paddock and saw Peter's annoyance as John apparently had explained the changes. My heart sickened as I had bet all my savings.

They announced the results of the previous race. The race times were much slower indicating conditions had worsened and the track was now deep and slow. Numerous spectators had gathered nearby. I overheard the idle chatter and comments praising the well-marked SnoMann. He appeared sharp and alert. The favorite was Starlight Girl, which BJ thought looked pretty good on paper. Her chestnut coat gleamed and her belly drawn up tight, showing her class.

"She appears very calm," BJ commented. Nervously, I bit my thumbnail so hard that it snapped off. I watched John's every movement and began to take deep breaths.

"Well, Sno is ready and sharp. By the look of the filly's knee, she's frozen. See the hair and how it is not smooth but ruffled a bit," I rambled on. "But, what does it matter? We have Karen riding, an unknown female jockey. Not much good that will do us." I frowned, suddenly annoyed. "This is just not the best time... unless...?"

Voices from the crowd became louder as they made their selections. The horses entered their numbered stalls where they waited for the valets to arrive and saddle. A steward checked the tattoo on the horses' upper lip, which corresponded to their registration papers. Peter and John spoke as SnoMann displayed his magnificence, swishing his tail nervously.

I began to twitch, expectantly. "I heard they don't tattoo the horses' upper lip in England as in America. It makes it easier to run a ringer. Have you heard that?" I questioned BJ. He shook his head, admitting he knew nothing of racing. "What's a ringer?"

"It's known that a trainer would substitute a horse with the same markings in a race."

"Why?"

"Well, let's say an owner wants to see his horse run all the time. This is not really a good idea, especially if the horse is well bred and could be used for breeding. You want to have its racing history show lots of wins,

93

not lots of races, which can break an animal down. Therefore, to keep the horse sound, less is best. In addition, on the bad side and for gambling purposes, they switch horses. They tell the owners it is a winning race. They bet a bundle with a bookie who knows the ringer is racing and so he pockets the money, or splits it with the trainer instead of betting it. Now, they have the money ready to cash in themselves for when the real horse races.

"I don't believe it!"

"Believe it."

One after another, the jockeys marched out from their changing room, exhibiting the colorful silks of each owner's stable. The bright red maple leaf stood out among the group.

Amidst the jockeys, walked the slim figure of a female, our Karen, which created a surprising grumble from the many avid spectators. I held my breath waiting for the announcement. "A change of jockey" broadcasted over the loudspeakers for the bettors to mark their programs. "Number three, SnoMann, now ridden by Sharp." Everyone grew more intrigued with the race as boisterous chatter flowed. I gritted my teeth. This was only Karen's fourth mount. I heard and felt the change that spread through the crowd wondering if she was any connection with Trainer Robert Sharp. This substitute created an entirely new interest in the race.

The nine horses stood inside their stall for another moment before parading while the jockeys consulted with the trainers. Karen drew near when John motioned her to enter the center of the paddock. They met, and I suddenly wondered if somehow this was planned. Judging by the look on Peters face, he did not think so. Karen's confident smile indicated the other jockeys had not approached her. All was well. She knew nothing.

"Hi John. This is it! Are we going ahead?" Karen smile enhanced her perfectly applied make-up and feminine features.

He could sense the disapproval among the other trainers and jockeys as they talked and planned their own race. It showed in their expression and silent laughter, which didn't seem to bother Karen, bubbling with enthusiasm. John carefully looked over SnoMann seeing he was ready and had never looked better or sounder. Peter suddenly nodded to John, giving his approval.

"Relax, Johnny. It's all ok. No kidding," Karen reassured. "Look. I'm relaxed... no? I can handle it, I know this horse. Go bet your money. I did, so how's that for confidence, eh?"

"Karen! Look, first of all ..." he hesitated at the sound of the hecklers.

"John, piss on them. Now get with it, please," she snapped. He stared deep into her hazel eyes. She appeared focused and in control.

"Ok! All right! This is it!" He ran his sweaty palms along his hips.

"Have him under wraps when you go out onto the track. When he hears the roar, he's a real show-off and tries all sorts of tricks in front of the grandstand. Slowly, and I mean slowly, gallop him so he will loosen up, the whole time before loading into the gate. Then, as the other horses begin to load, make sure you have those guys load him last. Back him in from the front. You know how it's done. You were the one we worked with on this. So, no more about it. Just walk around, keep out of their way until he's loaded. They will break immediately after he's in, so be ready. You'll need to keep with the pack for the first furlong. The race is a mile and an eighth - so you'll have to make sure he's well placed. Starlight Girl will most likely go to the front and stay there, having trouble staying amongst the pack. They will want her to keep in front, not to get bumped, she's hurting. Try to lie about fourth or fifth; no farther back than twelve lengths, she'll be that much, or more, in front according to the form. Anyway, when you hit the half-mile pole, start to make your move. Get into him a little, drop low and make your rush around the final turn and then, flat as you can get, give him his head, and ride for all you're worth."

"Got it!"

The other trainers were assisting their jockeys into the saddle. John went to give her a leg up and whispered, "Listen, Karen. There's something else," he paused.

"Well?"

"Word has it, or perhaps rumor has it, that Starlight is on the lead, and you could find yourself trapped, unable to make your move. So stay prepared and watch out for the others. Don't let yourself get blocked in. Please. Fair warning." Taking her leg, he gave Karen a boost. She adjusted her hard-hat and tucked her crop under her arm. John straightened the cups on the horse's blinkers just before their exit. He gave SnoMann an affectionate slap on the shoulder and looked him in the eye.

Peter took hold of the reins, asked "Are we on?"

"Of course, you fool," Karen replied. Peter signaled John to confirm his bet, then followed the others down the chute onto the track as the bugle sounded, announcing their arrival. John followed by the wayside.

BJ and I walked through the grandstand, out onto the front landing and waited.

The odds board read Starlight Girl at eight-to-five; Hammer 'n Tongs at three-to-one; SnoMann at ninety-nine to one. John brushed my arm. "Here, I'll be right back." He discreetly handed a roll of one-hundred dollar bills to me and another roll of five hundred dollar bills to BJ. "Don't place these bets until they're loading the gate. I do not want a drop in odds to become apparent until the final moment so the public won't see the money posted until it is too late. Got it?" We nodded, tucking the money aside. Other monies were placed with bookies.

BJ and I approached the guardrail, and then pointed to the display board listing the *odds*. Beside each horse's number was the amount of monies bet. He looked at number three, SnoMann. Three hundred dollars listed under win, two thousand and sixty under place, and nine thousand and seventy-five under show, while Starlight Girl has over forty-five thousand bet on win alone. The actual 'real' betting would not start to show until after everyone had watched the horses enter the track, where they could see them move, gallop.

"How can he wait until this late?"

"He has other friends who have his money and will just wait until he confirms. He has to leave the track. No phones here. He has connections, don't ever think he doesn't." We watched Karen handle the striking bay stallion as he bowed his powerful thick neck and galloped along. Other jockeys were standing in the saddle, traveling at a faster pace down the center of the track. The sound of hecklers lashed out at Karen as she passed the grandstand; everything from 'good luck' to obscenities. Women were not a familiar face on the racing course.

Shaking my head, I whispered, "Karen's out of her mind. Nothing against her as my friend, but she is nuts if she thinks she'll make anything of this jockey career. I'm shocked. It's not that she hasn't the talent; it's her competition that won't allow it. I wish her well."

BJ watched carefully, "I don't understand it either. But, she definitely knows what she wants."

I reminded him about her earlier modeling career, and he replied "Something like you."

"Pardon?"

"Well, you once wanted to be a track star, and probably with the proper coaching and training, you could have made the Olympic team. Instead, you gave it all up and went to live in Yorkville. No one understood the reasoning there, either. So, I guess she's entitled to do her own thing, too." Having said his piece, BJ leaned against the railing, taking a piece of gum from his pocket. I was taken aback by his comments.

Peter followed alongside SnoMann on the pony, so that he stayed under control. As they were the last to approach the starting gate, the first horse was loaded. It was our cue for BJ and me to place the bets. We noticed Peter trot away from the starting gate, located to the left of the grandstand. This indicated that the horses would run past the grandstand twice to cover the distance of a mile and one-eighth. I thought about Montreal, where we had joked about this very day. There would be only one shot at it; every race was a gamble. Anything could happen over the short time it took to run the course - a bump, a tumble, a bad ride, a sulky horse, a rear, a head-bump or a poor break. I breathed deeply, knowing it was now out of our hands as we put our trust in Karen.

"All right?" John questioned as he wrapped his arm around my shoulder.

"Mission accomplished. I was surprised to see Karen up on SnoMann, didn't expect that. In fact, I wasn't aware she was even riding,"

"This is only her fourth race." My eyes widened. "I didn't know either, until yesterday, when she came up to me at the barn begging for the mount. She saw that I hadn't named Cooper on the *Overnight*. I just about died when I heard he took a tumble earlier today. I didn't know what to do when called in to name a replacement. I just blurted out her name without thinking. Something inside me, that unknown voice, I don't know where it came from - even the Racing Secretary commented, *are you sure?*"

"What are our chances?"

"50-50."

I remained silent, my stomach twitching as we watched one of the gatemen take SnoMann by the reins to load.

Karen called down that he should be backed in from the front, but he wouldn't listen, calling her 'dumb broad.' She persisted, and he smirked again. "Where in hell did you learn to ride?"

The starter hollered obscenities down at them, and the gateman tried to take SnoMann again. Finally, he went to the front side of the gate as the other horses began to fidget and the speakers rang out with *there seems to be trouble in the loading of number three, SnoMann'*. Another helper assisted by opening the latch and climbing across the bars in an effort to settle the other horses that had already loaded.

"Damn it!" cursed John. "I knew this was going to happen. Look at him. He's so shaken up he's sweating like a bugger." He paced back and forth looking through his binoculars.

The powerful bay stallion fought back, as two men tried backing him into position. Karen's comforting words put him somewhat at ease as the sweat dripped down his nose from behind his blinkers.

Finally, the latch locked and the men leaped out of the way, as the clang of the starting bell rang. The gate crashed open, and the horses broke.

"They're off!"

The pack rushed down the chute in a tightly knit group. Soon they broke the pattern, spreading out as they passed the grandstand. Karen was riding him to the rail as several bunched together passing the finish line for the first time.

The announcer called out their names as they constantly changed positions during the first half mile with Hammer 'n Tong and Starlight Girl running neck 'n neck ahead of the pack. It looked like an easy win for one or the other of the two *class* horses.

Opening up, as they came out of the first turn, Karen maintained her position just the way John wanted. Starlight Girl pulled into the lead and began pulling away from the pack with her early speed when they headed down the backstretch. John noticed a couple of jockeys try to crowd in and he began pacing furiously, swearing loudly above the screams of the spectators. His face reddened. His fierce language was not his usual way. Excited by the atmosphere, BJ stared, a bundle of nerves while I bit my nails in anguish.

Sweat rolled off the horses as they made their way around the turn with the filly over seven lengths out in front. Karen lowered into the saddle making her move as she encouraged SnoMann. A jockey swiped at her, then another. She got herself pinned against the rail and would have to pull wide. They trapped her opening, not allowing her through. One hit her a second time. She retaliated, fiercely, kicking out her long leg, hitting a rider, causing him to lose balance, and then she carried on.

Edging her way wide, into the open, Karen headed into the final furlongs with more than twelve lengths behind the leader.

She could hear jockeys cursing her as she fired-up with determination. The dirt flew back, stinging her as another lunged into her side knocking her off stride. Karen lowered her body and forced one mighty swipe with her crop along SnoMann's shoulders, then his back, bellowing encouragement. With his ears pinned back and gaining ground, SnoMann made his move. She sensed he was full of run.

With incredible strength and determination, SnoMann gained on Hammer 'n Tong. Each horse instinctively increased his stride as the real race for the money began. Pulling away from the rest of the field, running head 'n head, they came into the final stretch.

Karen flattened along his neck, calling out to him for all she was worth. Giving him his head, she slightly loosened her grip on the reins as SnoMann thrust ahead and overtook the liver-chestnut in second place. The distance between Starlight Girl narrowed quickly to six lengths.

The ecstatic roar of enthusiasm that erupted from the grandstand drove the stallion onward. His stride lengthened as he covered even more ground, and the gap began to close.

John was pounding the fence. Karen hit SnoMann one last time.

"I love you Sno" I screamed, "You can do it! You can do it!" My heart beat so hard from the excitement, I felt chest pains.

The announcer yelled, "…and that is SnoMann rapidly closing on the outside with two lengths…" he shouted. "One length… behind."

The crowd grew crazy as loud cheers and anxious screams ignited from the twenty thousand fans, rooting and raging in fury. Soaked with perspiration and with only half a length separating the two horses, they closed toward the finish line.

Every muscle tightened as Karen pushed forward, encouraging SnoMann with her knees tucked up high against his wither. Karen dropped his head, crossing the finish line, winning the race by a nose as waves of thunderous screams sounded throughout the grandstand. Eager spectators waited the flashing *photo finish* sign that officially announced the winner. The favorite of the day had been beaten.

Karen rose from the saddle, stiffening her legs, slowing SnoMann to a gallop. John leaped into the air, hugging everyone, crying out sounds of triumph as we all gathered in the winner's circle waiting for the hero to arrive for his photograph.

I was beyond cheering. I had lost my voice. The closing odds had dropped to forty-five to one, with all the money bet shown on the board. Karen returned from the backstretch, waving frantically to the crowd. She had remained calm, focused and made her mark.

Peter led the champions into the manicured enclosure for the picture taking as number *three* flashed across the board. Karen met my glance and winked.

"Look - $101.60! Wow!" I pointed out, taking John's arm. The announcer officially proclaimed a record-paying quinella for the year of number three and number five paying $7,348.00.... for a $2.00 ticket.

"Absolutely fantastic, Sharp! If that isn't what you wanted, you had better give up racing now. You rode a stupendous race. I'm so proud of you." John complemented.

Thousands of racing fans gathered around the rail to take a closer look at the unexpected winner who performed the surprising upset. John grabbed Karen's leg as she jumped down.

Taking the saddle to weigh-in, she headed toward the scales, and then returned to the change room. The astonished crowd cheered one of the first female jockeys ever to ride in North America.

Peter and John affectionately slapped the horse, and then led him away to the back paddock for the required urine testing. SnoMann turned to look at us standing behind; I applauded, knowing he knew we were proud of him. John and I walked arm in arm, embracing every possible moment. I'd never seen or felt him so excited.

A lot of money was lost in that race for many fans, but within moments, nine new horses passed the paddock for the next race. For me, it was an event that would change my life, and it took less than two minutes. *Fait accompli.*

Overwhelmed, BJ commented that he couldn't believe the preparation it took for a lousy few minutes of glory; the build-up of energy, the decisions and plans destroyed just because it rained, or the jockey got ill, or the horse had a stomach ache. He was worn-out just being a spectator.

John immediately launched into a monologue explaining his philosophy as we drove back to the stable area. We chatted tangentially while sitting on the grassy area beside the stable, relishing the resurrection of the past before SnoMann returned.

"The quinella - did you have it, John?" questioned BJ.

"As a matter of fact - several. I took Sno and wheeled him across the board more than fifty times."

Before he could offer further information regarding his bets, two reporters arrived, climbing down from a dusty pick-up, anxious to question John about the unexpected upset. He introduced me as his fiancée as they snapped a couple of pictures while waiting for the 'stars' to return.

Rechecking his stall, making absolutely sure that everything was in order, I retrieved a light flysheet to place over the winner's back after they hosed him down.

Unaware of the visiting reporters, Peter gave a mighty cry as he came around the corner riding the lead pony and escorting SnoMann. "Hal-le-lu-jah! The big boy made it look like duck soup." He stopped in his tracks. I gave him a swift reproachful glance as John took the sweaty stallion out onto the lawn to hose him down.

The reporters were quick to question Peter as if he were the stable hand. Several more pictures flashed as Peter and John were being particularly cautious in their remarks during interviews. The reporters got what they wanted.

Soon, the triumphant voice sounded, singing her praises. Karen arrived, immaculately groomed and skipped into the arms of Peter.

"Love me now? I think I deserve an apology, right? How about a big kiss?" she asked, boldly. Peter threw her back in his arms and planted a big one while we all watched. She disengaged herself from the embrace, laughing. "Wow. Pete, you never told me!" Karen teased.

BJ smiled as he stroked SnoMann, who munched on some well-deserved clover hay, turning his upper lip in foolishness. Such a show-off. John slapped his shoulder.

"The hero of the day. What do you say big boy?" He whinnied an appropriate reply.

Peter smiled, reluctantly. "Karen, I really do owe you an apology. I bad-mouthed you something fierce when I heard what John had done. I doubted your ability. You are so beautiful, how could you possibly be so damn talented, too?" he teased, tossing her a kiss through his fingers.

Karen and I watched SnoMann eat, swishing his tail and bobbing his head. He was king and he knew it. The win would be the first of many to follow.

The sun warmed our hearts as the five of us sat sipping champagne reminiscing the day when SnoMann came into our lives.

Later that evening, we celebrated with dinner at the Ascot, a restaurant across the road from the racetrack. Susan joined us in our celebrations. As we became boisterous reciting the day's events, the race results announced on the TV news. We spared no expense that night since our finances had vastly improved. Peter whispered across the table that he would make well over $300,000.00 when he cashed in. BJs modest winnings of $1,000.00 pleased him immensely.

Karen wished her father had been there to see her ride and was confident that he would be proud of her accomplishment. She explained that before she left the grounds, she had picked up three mounts for the next day's card because of her ride that afternoon. It was no secret, everybody wanted to be with a winner and she had proven herself. I don't know who wore the bigger smile, Karen or John as she thanked him repeatedly for his confidence in her.

Then, out-of-the-blue John announced to everyone, a toast. We raised our glasses as he toasted the 'Lady of the Day, Karen', and then me, naming June 7 as the day of our wedding. He officially named Peter as the new trainer for their stable, admitting that he was ready to pursue other interests. BJ looked my way. My cheeks flushed at John's unexpected announcement; I touched his hand. BJ would never understand our relationship.

The performance given by SnoMann was the talk of the racetrack, putting the name Mencini into a different bracket as an accomplished horseman.

The following morning, photos and stories filled the newspapers about the Argentine stallion that had raced gallantly to a courageous photo-finish victory, upsetting one of the better horses to race on the Toronto circuit. TV and radio sportscasters praised their terrific efforts. Ambitious owners flocked to the Mencini stable, seeking his talents, hoping that the same good fortune might befall their own thoroughbreds. It was not racetrack etiquette for owners to change trainers.

Reports rapidly spread within certain circles of John's great financial gain. The quinella's extravagant payoff that had sold less than one-hundred tickets gave rise to suspicion. Anxious trainers remained stone-faced when confronted with talk of the race. The money gambled and lost on Starlight Girl was huge, as she was to be the winner.

SnoMann's leg showed noticeable swelling and needed delicate treatment, even though he displayed little pain, the problem of the bowed tendon returned. Peter knew one of the track vets who did surgery at the Freelton Clinic. He reported a corrective surgery whereby the muscle was spaciously cut, drawing heat and blood into the injured area, thus facilitating a long slow recovery. John was eager to locate the vet for further consultation before deciding to retire SnoMann to stand stud, or to continue racing him.

Outside the area of the racetrack, Susan and I excitedly made arrangements for my upcoming wedding.

BJs extended stay proved financially worthwhile, but he knew he could not delay his departure any longer. I was disappointed to see him leave and wondered when we would meet again. John and I drove him to the airport, all squeezed into the small sports car.

The flight attendant unlatched the doors for the BOAC flight to Heathrow. I clasped BJ's hand warmly, feeling his tender squeeze. Brushing a loose piece of sun-streaked hair from my brow, I kissed him lightly on the lips and stared into his concerned eyes. He winked.

"Thanks, BJ. Thanks for extending your visit. I'm sorry you can't stay for our wedding, but I understand. I'm going to miss you."

"Goodbye, Frannie." With a firm handshake, John and BJ said their goodbyes. An unanticipated stir came from within as I gazed at the spot where he had just stood. I quickly turned, taking John's hand, mechanically walking alongside him out of the airport, returning to the Skyline Hotel where we had been staying.

We discussed wedding plans with the service held in a little chapel and all the preparations that Susan and I had completed. The news thrilled John's parents and Leonard who wondered if this was ever going to happen. I also phoned work in Montreal and inquired about my transfer to work in Toronto. We had no plans to race at Blue Bonnets again.

John finalized the paperwork for a small syndicate to purchase property in Yorkville as it became available. He had plans to start working right away thanks to BJs great ideas on how to proceed with the development.

"You know Frannie, you don't need to work. There is certainly no reason to," he said, rubbing his fingers lightly across my shoulders.

"Well, I would like to for awhile - unless you object."

"Oh, hell no. That's completely your decision, but we should take a couple of weeks for our honeymoon. We never did decide on where to go, we could have an adventure. Perhaps, Alaska?" We agreed.

I had not heard from Leonard since SnoMann's win when he announced they were moving overseas. Julie had given her notice at the hospital, as well, so I had no idea if they would be able to make it to our wedding. If they did move, we made the decision to visit for Christmas. I felt like a youngster who just had the bikes training wheels removed. No turning back.

A few more days of hot weather ensued as we finalized our plans for our big day. The time on the dashboard showed four o'clock, when John remembered he had promised Peter he would do chores. We were caught in rush hour traffic on the 3rd of June, with overcast skies. Slowing down at the entrance to the stable area, John parked the Ferrari next to a gray Lincoln. He reached for our sweaters in the back, and then we hurried toward the gate. Immediately after we flashed our passes, a rough voice calling from a distance startled us.

"Roberts, John Roberts!" We stopped in our tracks. John's face paled.

"Hey, Roberts! That's you! I know it! I saw your picture in the newspaper. You've gone and changed your name. Yeah - Mencini, that's it now," the unfamiliar voice hollered from afar.

I hesitated as I watched John turn to face the direction of the caller, when a powerful blast sounded across the parking lot. All of a sudden, blood exploded from John's neck, hitting my face and covering my shirt. I turned to see what the shot was. Screaming at the top of my lungs, "Oh, my God! Somebody help! H E L P !!" Horrific amounts of blood spilled onto the pavement, soaked my shirt, splattered my hands and covered John's lifeless body.

The guardsman on duty rushed out from his booth. Staring at the gory scene in front of him, he quickly ran back to call the track ambulance. John fell heavily to the ground. Tires screeched as the car took off. I dropped to the ground, breathing hard and trying not to shake as I desperately wrapped my sweater over the wound, hysterically calling out, "Please, for God's sake, somebody help him!" I cried again in utter desperation "PLEASE! SOMEONE! HELP ME!" My tears distorted my vision as I held John, who lay motionless in a puddle of his own blood. "HELP" I cried over and over again. Several grooms from nearby stables came running to assist, but they stood helplessly on the blood-spattered pavement. One tried to feel for a pulse.

"He's still alive!" The sound of the siren echoed through the cool evening air, as it reached us. The paramedics rushed from the vehicle, opened the door of the wagon, and pulled out the prepared stretcher. They leaned down, carefully picking up the injured limp body and slid it into place. With exact precision, they moved rapidly as I stood helpless by his side, and then climbed into the back of the ambulance. The siren alerted all and with rapid acceleration, drove onto Rexdale Boulevard, heading to the closest hospital.

The paramedic attended his wounds, checking his pulse while he made a covering. I mumbled, "This isn't real! It just can't be happening." John's eyes closed as the sirens sounded again, alerting others of our arrival.

When we reached the hospital's emergency entrance, the doors flew open and a staff of four rushed to our aid. I stumbled as I climbed down from the vehicle, nervously entering the building. Impatiently waiting outside the closed-off section as my heart pounded, I began shaking so badly my legs would not settle. My tears never stopped. I waited.

John was pronounced dead on arrival. I collapsed and went into shock. Several nurses assisted me into the emergency.

There was nothing the doctors could have done for him. They said the bullet had passed through his neck and blood had clogged his lungs. The attending doctor shook his head.

"How old could he be? Twenty-eight or nine, maybe? Take his wallet. Call the police, and have someone notify the next of kin. I'll go check the girl."

The white sheet covering John's body was drawn up over his face. The clock showed 6:39 pm Time stopped for John Mencini.

Chapter 11
Grief-Walker

Four days passed before the doctors allowed anyone to visit me as I had no energy. By the time news of the murder reached Montreal, Leonard was already halfway across the Atlantic, but Julie flew to Toronto.

Peter stood patiently beside my bed, the first person that I recognized. The door to my room opened and a nurse entered carrying a tray of medicine. Picking up the chart from the end of the bed, she smiled, and greeted us kindly, then left.

I suddenly felt the rush of tears, Peter turned away. He stared, unbelieving, out the window. The matter was beyond comprehension and he hurt deeply. The traffic still passed and the sun still shone, and time waited for no one. We didn't speak.

A couple of hours passed, and then Julie arrived to find Peter standing in the hallway. They went to the cafeteria where they talked over coffee, trying to comfort one another.

Peter described the night that the police contacted him. He had been out with friends and then gone back to the track to tend to the horses when he saw John's car parked outside the gate, a little after midnight. He walked into the stable area, passed the spot where the pavement had been blood splattered. When he arrived at the barn, he saw that the horses weren't fed. They were snorting, creating a ruckus. Confused, he fed and watered off and left their stalls until morning. Looking in the tackrooms, and then walking over to Sharp's Larson Farms stables, he found no sign of John. He searched the track kitchen, but nothing. Peter asked the security guard if he had seen John come through, but he was new and didn't recognize the name. Peter figured John had car trouble.

When Peter drove up the street and saw the cruiser parked in front of his parent's house, his heart started to pound. His mother came rushing out the door, crying. He couldn't understand and so he walked her back inside where everyone sat waiting, including Susan. Peter learned of John's death earlier that evening and that I had been with him during the shooting.

Distraught, Peter covered his face with his hands as he explained the details to Julie, who sat listening with eyes closed.

"I only hope and pray that Frannie can handle this. She must have seen something. Anything that can help locate this maniac. I can't believe this has happened. My God, he's gone! John's dead!" He broke into a prolonged sob. Julie went to his side to offer comfort. They sat together for almost an hour, going over the same things, repeatedly.

"Friday is the funeral, Julie. I was going to fly south to Ohio, but his parents phoned and asked that I stay with Frannie; that she was going to need me more here. A couple of days ago, his father flew up by private jet and made arrangements to have his body shipped home."

During their investigation, the police had gone through John's hotel room and found three different bankbooks with almost a million dollars recently deposited. They thought for sure he was connected to a crime ring. With all the publicity about the race, the media were having a field day with it. 'Trainer of SnoMann Shot' and another said 'Mencini Murder Uncovered $million', and so on. The stories they wrote distorted the whole incident. The police, media and officials talked to Karen, and everyone else around the racetrack to get information. But, it all came out the same, bad dealings! Misrepresentations!

Back in my hospital room, I had just finished some soup. Julie and Peter stood along either side of my bed.

"Julie, is Leonard here, too?"

"No, dear," she replied as she sat down beside me. "He'd already gone."

"Oh, too bad. I guess I have been kind of out of it for some time, eh?"

"How are you feeling, anyhow?" Peter asked.

"Real sluggish. Find it hard to think straight. What happened, anyway? Why am I here? I'm not bruised, so no car accident."

Peter looked toward Julie for an encouraging nod to give details.

"Well, you passed out, Frannie," Julie spoke the truth.

"Oh. Is that all? From the heat?" I relieved, but felt half-drugged and couldn't focus properly.

"Not exactly. However, it has been hot lately. You're right about that. Tell me, where's your engagement ring?"

"Ring? What ring?" I looked down at my hand, and then hesitated, trying to figure it out. I saw the slight indentation on my finger, the mark of having worn one. I rubbed the mark trying to concentrate.

"Oh. Yes, my engagement ring. Well, it must be here somewhere. Let me look in this drawer." And, there it lay, wrapped in a Kleenex, tucked to one side. As I opened it, and placed it on my finger, my expression darkened as I remembered the horrifying incident. No one spoke. My face grew pale, and I began to shake. My lips quivered, and tears spilled down my cheeks, but I didn't make a sound. Julie handed me some tissues from the bedside table and gave me a hug.

"Honey, slow down. We are right here with you. It's been several days now and we want you to know that you're not alone."

I sobbed uncontrollably. "No! No! Please tell me it didn't happen. Tell me Johnny's alive. Please, don't take him away from me. No! No!"

Shaken and suddenly subdued, I covered my face. Hearing the commotion, a nurse entered and requested that Julie and Peter leave. I insisted they stay.

"They can't go. No! Julie, don't leave me. Please stay." Julie explained her nursing profession and asked that she reconsider and allow her to stay.

I made an awkward apology, trying to control my emotions. I could never explain the pain I felt. It felt like my heart had ripped out.

The following day, Peter began asking if I could remember anything about the incident. My eyes focused on his, which showed red and terribly sad. Julie listened, sitting quietly.

"No, I can't. It was so sudden. All I can remember is seeing John fall. Nothing."

He held his hands up in protest. "Forget about that part, Frannie. Concentrate. Please, try. We have to find the underlying cause of all this. Now think, please. Was someone else with you?" He paused. "What exactly was said?"

I considered the question. "A call? Yes. Someone called 'John.' He yelled out his name when we were walking into the stable area."

"Yes, but what were the exact words? Frannie. Think. Real hard, please."

"Oh, I don't know," and I rubbed my eyes, dropping my head to the pillow. We sat still; the pain in my chest felt intense.

"Wait. Just a minute. I do remember something. He called out, John, yeah, John Roberts, at first. Then, he said something about he saw in the papers where he had changed his name to John Mencini. That's it. Those were his words." I sat up, bright-eyed. Peter beamed at my accomplishment. A sudden interrupting knock on the door brought a moment's silence when an older gray-haired man stuck his head around the corner.

"Miss Harrison? I'm from homicide. May I come in just for a very short time and speak with you? I'll stay but a moment, and then be on my way."

I hesitated, waiting for Peter to give approval. He sat motionless, letting me make up my own mind. I nodded.

"First, may I offer my condolences at this time of sorrow? I hate to have to come and question you. Honestly, I don't want to upset you. I am sure you are just as anxious to find this person as we are. Could you please, very briefly, explain where you were coming from on the evening of June 3rd?"

"Yes. The Skyline Hotel, where we were staying. John and I were going to the track to do chores around five o'clock."

"Now, what exactly happened?"

I briefly explained the situation.

"Did you see anything? Such as a car?"

"Well, I recall the squealing tires. Yes, now that you mention it, I did see someone in a dark station wagon. There was a man driving it. I remember! I do remember! It was a man ... in a station wagon!" I sat up, surprising myself as my memory cleared.

"Miss Harrison, what makes you so sure it was a man? Could it not have been a woman?"

"No. I know it was a man. I could see and it was definitely a male voice."

"Why are you so sure? Maybe it was a stout woman. A woman with short hair? Perhaps, it ..." The detective persisted to get identification that is more positive.

"No. I said it was a man, and it was! I remember; he was ... yes, he was balding," I said staring out the window. "That's right, he was bald." I was breathing rapidly and my heart was racing.

"Bald? Are you sure? Was he alone?"

"Yes, Frannie. Are you sure?" Peter asked, amazed at my sudden recollection.

"Uh-huh. I'm sure, and he was alone."

"Oh my God! No! Oh my God!"

"What is it?" they asked in unison.

Peter stood leaning against the wall for support. He looked as though he was going to faint. He went white and slid several inches down the wall, mumbling to himself.

"What is it?" the detective inquired again.

"First, tell me your name." Peter pleaded.

"Me? Detective Riley - Aaron Riley. I'm with the..." and he presented some police identification. "Well?"

"Do you know about that cop that used to patrol the Yorkville area? Named Elwood?"

"Yeah, but he left the force. He was pretty sick..."

"Well, he's bald, and..." Peter replied.

"Hold it. So, he's balding. That doesn't mean he goes around shooting people."

"Yes, but wait a minute. He went loony because his son OD'd on some bad dope. He got it in Yorkville."

"Well, what on earth has the Yorkville scene got to do with this racetrack murder? I really don't follow."

"Oh, no! I do!" I hysterically cried. Julie asked the two men to step outside my room and she called for the attending nurse. They promptly administered a sedative as I held onto Julie's hand, trying to explain between my unrelenting sobs, what I figured had happened.

Meanwhile, the detective had cornered Peter outside the room for further questioning.

"Listen, boy. What in hell are you driving at?" he asked as they walked down the quiet hallway.

"A few days ago, John, my friend BJ Nichols, and I were in Yorkville. John had big plans to use the money he had won to invest in some property there. You see, Detective Riley, all of us had lived there when the drug scene was at its worst. I mean, it was unreal!"

"Oh, you guys lived in that insanity. Are you trying to tell me something?"

"Damn it. Don't you understand? No, you wouldn't! You wouldn't." Peter shook his head.

"Well then, tell me, man. No more dilly-dallying around."

"John used the name John Roberts.

"What are you talking about?"

"Well," he paced the halls with squinting eyes, rubbing his hands together and flexing his fists.

"Come on, man. What is it?"

"When we moved out of Yorkville in 1967 and went to Montreal, rumor had it that there had been some bad stuff selling on the street in the village. Perhaps, that is where Elwood's son got it. Somehow, I'll bet he found out, and, in my personal opinion, he thought it came from John - and came after him once he knew where to find him. With all the recent publicity in the newspapers about SnoMann, he could have easily recognized John's face plastered all over the papers."

"Are you sure about all this?" Riley took Peter by the arm.

"As sure as my name is Peter Edwards."

"Well, I'm going to check into this. If your guess is right, I want to see you down at the station for a sworn statement. You and Miss Harrison, both. Don't leave town, Edwards. I want to see you again," and he abruptly left, using the stairwell. Julie joined Peter, who was beginning to show signs of exhaustion.

"Come on, let's go Julie. I think you would like to stay with me at my parents' place where there're loads of room." She followed, eager for some needed sleep.

Days drifted by slowly as I showed no sign of improvement. While Julie and Susan sat in a nearby restaurant with Peter, I took a turn for the worse. Before the lights dimmed, a nurse checking on her patients, found me flung across the floor beside my bed with a large open gash on my forehead. My face rested in a small pool of blood. She quickly called for assistance. They got me back into bed and prepared the dressing for the wound, which was not as serious as it originally appeared. Fearing that I might slip into a coma, a nurse sat at my side until I regained consciousness.

I had been trying to go to the washroom when I felt very dizzy and slipped. The doctor realized that I had a reaction to the medication. Fearing a blood clot, he withdrew all drugs leaving me to suffer the pain of the accident as well as the depression.

I slept sporadically. Waking before nine the following evening, I devoured a large meal. The nurse mentioned that Julie dropped in before returning to Montreal for a few days, but said she would be back.

I fretted, causing my depression to deepen.

The Friday before the August long weekend, the doctor notified me of my impending discharge. Fearing renewed loneliness and depression, they instructed me to have two consultations a week with my doctor, Dr. Boursin. I suffered anxiety attacks and spent the day staring at the door, realizing that I would have to walk out of the place on my own.

Susan and Julie arrived with a new outfit for me, hoping to cheer my spirits. Within an hour, Julie picked up the small luggage bag as we prepared to leave the hospital.

"I'm going to the airport this evening, Frannie. Is there anything I can do for you before I leave?"

"Please, give this letter to Leonard for me. I'd appreciate that." Julie tucked the envelope into her purse as a black BMW steered up to the front of the hospital. Peter's new car went unnoticed as Julie slipped her hand onto my knee. Peter steered towards the core of the city, without speaking. Susan sat next to him in the front seat, trying to make idle conversation. He approached the corner of Yonge and Eglinton Ave. where the traffic became congested. I gazed out the window as we drove.

"This is it. The next right turn, Pete." Susan pointed, speaking quietly.

The street sign read *Balmoral.* Three-story Victorian houses, a few undergoing extensive renovations, filled the roadway with large oak trees overhanging the sidewalks as we drove slowly looking for a particular number.

"Not much parking around," Peter muttered.

Inside the entrance of unit 3, a small tiled area showed brass coat-hooks on the linen white stucco walls. The gumwood trim and coved ceilings added character. A large living room opened into the small galley kitchen on the right, two tiny bedrooms to the left and a view of the colorful courtyard garden showed from the windows. Peter puttered around the flat while I followed close behind. No one pressed me for any decision. Susan revealed that she accepted a new position and offered to treat everyone to lunch. We decided to go to *Fran's,* a favorite restaurant on St. Clair Ave.

Susan described her new job working for the provincial government designing and decorating reception areas of the municipal buildings throughout the province. Her expense account would compensate the adequate salary. Susan wanted me to share her flat, but I was nervous about my finances. At this point, Peter offered to cover expenses until things settled and I started working again.

He explained that we all suffered a great loss that it was not only me. He spoke frankly of his own grief encouraging me to start making my own decisions now, and that he would be there for support.

It was decided that Susan and I would stay at her parents' home until we organized our move into the Balmoral apartment.

Not long ago, I thought I had things all worked out, and then another crossroad. Peter decided to speak with Bob Sharp about getting his trainer's license and go out on his own. He believed he was picking up where John left off. Karen stayed in contact and supported Peter, helping him out as her career took off.

***

Autumn arrived with the multi-colored changing of leaves, warm days and cold nights. Peter mingled well with the racetrack crowd, learning all he could, listening to the gossip, and studying the Condition book. He cooperated with the police in their investigation.

Detective Riley figured Peter's lead had no support, believing that there had to be some involvement with racketeers. He spent weeks talking with racetrack employees, prying into every possible clue.

Peter tried not to dwell upon John's death. SnoMann became his best friend, if that was possible, and he treated him with extra care and affection as he kept winning races. When Peter relaxed, he was too tired to think about the past, and most of his free time he spent with Susan and me at our new home. He chose to live on the racetrack in a converted tackroom, which he made comfortable for himself.

Meanwhile, Susan found her new job very demanding, but she loved the challenge of dealing with the engineers and architects when traveling throughout the province. Spending a week at a time working in Thunder Bay, Sarnia, or Ottawa, Susan's trips were more than she had ever anticipated. During these absences, she would fret about my spending endless hours staring at the ceiling. As the weeks slipped by, I became more depressed and distant. Sometimes, during dinner when complete silence fell upon me, my grip on my glass would suddenly loosen. Moments would pass as I looked at the mess on the floor before I made any effort to clean it up. Susan realized that the depression was beginning to take control.

One afternoon in late October, Susan spoke about the matter to her mother, who suggested that she go to my doctor and explain her concerns. She was certain it would help her daughter as well as me.

Susan explained another plan, which was to talk to Reverend McGee, the minister who was going to marry John and me, as he had helped me cope with the trauma of my mother's death. She felt desperate knowing I had lost both parents, my partner and my brother, who moved overseas.

Worried about the way I would drift off, unable to control my outbursts, Susan felt uncomfortable leaving me alone anymore. She took it upon herself to visit Dr. Boursin.

He appreciated her concerns when he said she had cause to be alarmed. She didn't know that I had missed most of my sessions during the summer making his efforts difficult when I wouldn't cooperate. The doctor feared that I could lapse into chronic depression, and admitted back into the hospital for treatment with the possibility of having to undergo electric shock treatment. Susan held back her tears, feeling helpless.

Returning to our flat later that same day, Susan cringed when she found me crying in the bathroom, among mounds of my long ginger hair that littered the floor. Only uneven stubbles remained. Susan stared, unbelieving. A heavy lump formed in her throat, tears trickled down her cheeks as she looked at me lying with my head buried in the chopped hair with the scissors still clutched in my hand, weeping quietly. Genuinely shocked, Susan whispered. "Sh-h sh-h, come on now Frannie. Everything is fine. You are all right. Let's get you up. Now that's it. That's a girl. Come on, you can do it. Give me the scissors."

She seized them, trying to lift me up ever so gently. Encouraging me back to my room, Susan witnessed stacks of clothes, papers, unpacked luggage strewn around, but still she managed to place me on the bed. Susan located my medication and returned with a glass of water to find me peering out the window, dazed and confused. I took the medicine and Susan threw a cover over me, and tiptoed from the room. Her immediate reaction was to clean the bathroom.

A short time later, Peter marched in dangling his key from his forefinger.

"Sh-h-h." Susan placed her finger to her lips and then pointed to my room. He passed by, retrieving a beer from the fridge, and then sat at a small pine table we used for dining. Susan brushed some crumbs from the hand-woven mats into the garbage bin and set out a plate of cheese and crackers.

"You look like hell. What's up?" Peter prompted.

"I love you, too." Susan gulped some of his beer, watching his smile that took the pinch out of the remark. Peter listened, compassionately, as she recounted the events of her day.

"Susie, what in God's name is happening to Frannie? How can she be slipping away like this? I do not understand any of it. Is there nothing anyone can do? This is nuts, as if she has been hypnotized."

"Well, she just can't cope. Anxiety. Depression. She's grieving and feels lonely."

Describing her hectic schedule for the next few days, Susan remarked she wanted to stay with me rather than attend a seminar. Peter took the liberty to peek into my bedroom. His expression was one of shock.

"Her hair! Susan, what the hell? Has Frannie gone wacko?"

On Saturday, Susan had a pot of soup simmering on the stove and sat across the table from me. She watched as I bit into a saltine and suddenly broke into a giggle when emotional tears filled my eyes.

"Susan, look at me. I'm so fucked up!" The tears fell, but I became hysterical with laughter. Sue grabbed my hand, holding it firmly.

"Stop it! Right now!" she snapped. I tried to, but ended up stuttering.

"What am I going to do? I can't get hold of myself anymore. I can't! I feel the sadness coming on, but I can't do anything about it."

"Come on over here," Susan beckoned. "Talk to me. Tell me what it is?" We walked into the living area where we sat down on the down-filled couch.

Placing her feet on the ottoman, Susan continued "Go on, talk to me."

"I don't know what to say. I feel so terribly sad. Sometimes, I am short of breath, overwhelmed and no energy. I try to go out and do something, or go somewhere and end up walking off in a daydream. I can't seem to get hold of a steady thought without drifting off. I try to shake out of it, but seem to have an overpowering feeling that drags me down. My stomach is tight and in knots and my chest feels heavy with pain and sometimes I can't swallow because of the lump in my throat. I'm full of grief. I shake all the time and cry; just cannot grab on to my senses. This must be what hell feels like. It is as if I am obsessed or under some foreign control. I take my meds, but feel drugged and have no power." Suddenly, I stopped rambling and looked straight ahead. "Why, I don't even ask about any of my friends and how they are doing!"

Susan brushed her hand along mine. "You haven't been going to your sessions with Dr. Boursin, have you?"

"How would you know that? Unless you've been checking up or he's been calling, trying to find me."

"Something like that."

"He questions and gives me these tests, like I was a mental case. I'm not!" I blurted. "At least not yet. I know I am sick and feel no hope. It's unbearable most times." I raised my voice and rubbed my head, forgetting the unsightly stubbles.

"Why did you do that? Cut your hair?"

"It all started out to be an innocent little trim. A piece of hair sticking out of place. Then all of a sudden, I got thinking about this and that and got myself all worked up, and then. .." I turned away and faced the window. "It's like ... this sounds stupid, but it is like there's another entity inside me that has taken control of my actions and thoughts. One minute I would be concerned with how I looked, and the next I was saying 'who in hell cares anyway, what's the use', as if I'm full of some kind of wicked demons. I can't explain it." Susan smiled at the comment.

"Frannie, doesn't that just prove that you do need help, just to be able to control your emotional outbursts? You only need to get a push in the right direction. You need to focus." The kettle screeched a whistle. I got up and prepared a pot of chamomile tea, bringing a tray into the living room when we heard a knock. Susan motioned me to answer the door. I wrapped a towel-turban over my head. It was Reverend McGee. I winced.

Susan invited him in for a cup of tea as he explained he had talked with her parents after church service hearing that the Susan and I had taken an apartment in the city together. Susan chatted for a few minutes, then excused herself and left to shop for something.

Rev. McGee relaxed, resting his arm along the back of the sofa. I apparently looked confused.

"Francine, how have you been keeping? Mrs. Edwards was telling me that Leonard moved to Holland last spring. So many changes! I never even knew he was in Montreal." He gave an approving glance around the room. "You must enjoy living here with Susan in this beautiful place." He continued the discussion eagerly.

"Yes. I couldn't ask for anything nicer, but I am missing Leonard. He was married. Did you know?"

"Yes. When we were preparing for your wedding, you mentioned that he married a nurse, Julie. I haven't seen you since visiting the hospital last spring." He paused, observing my expression.

"Francine, tell me, are you working?"

"Huh? Oh, no. I'm not at the moment."

"What kind of job are you looking for?"

"Well... I suppose I should apply to Regal Oil here in the city. I was working for the company in Montreal and applied for a transfer to Toronto last May, and..." I trailed off again.

"You haven't done so, as yet? It is November, which is six months."

"No."

He tasted some more of his drink, which had cooled. "To be honest, Francine, Mrs. Edwards wanted me to drop by and talk to you. What's happened? Tell me."

"I just can't pick myself back up. I feel sick inside and sad all the time."

"Francine, sometimes things occur that seem entirely wrong and unjust, and our hearts are filled with questions. 'Why?' we ask. 'Why did this unhappy event happen?' And sometimes we can find no answers. Sometimes, what is best is prayer. Pray for an understanding heart." He sensed my uneasiness and then hesitated, reaching for the pot, topping his half-filled cup. "There is always a new beginning after an ending, always.

As the old adage goes 'when one door closes, another opens'. It sounds trite, but it is true." I sat in utter silence.

"You are not bound by past decisions. You have the freedom to change; change your state of mind. Yes, incredible as it sounds, we have a choice, and the choice is all about what we will think, what we will hold in mind. Whatever mental state seems to have bound you to the old is now dissolved by the power of the Spirit in you. Through the power of three things - faith, prayer, and affirmation - you will be renewed, in ideas, and in attitude, and you'll find life, once again, fulfilling."

I nodded, concentrating on his every word.

"Reverend, I don't know if I can cope some days. I feel so sick and lonely."

"Naturally, child. But, even at such a time, we have more strength, more courage, and more faith, than we know. You must remember..." He walked to my side placing one hand on my shoulder. "You never, and I mean never, have to face anything alone. There is a loving spirit that is with you. Perhaps you could say, 'I trust in God completely' whenever you can't cope. Oh, Francine, I've seen you go through so much in your short life, and you've always been strong. Right now, you need help and I know you have faith. Remember this too - 'faith is the strength of the soul inside, lost is the man without it'. Your soul, that is what keeps on going, after the body stops. So, the stronger your faith, the stronger that soul of yours is going to be."

His words touched the very depths of me. Another long silence lingered before he spoke.

"If you're not working, why don't you come and volunteer with some others in need of help? You would be a marvelous influence as right now you have too much time on your hands. I believe you would feel better for doing this volunteer work, and would realize how bad some others out there have it."

Peter, as usual, arrived unannounced and came barging into the room wearing a ball hat, denim jacket and lighting up a cigarette.

"Oh! Oh, Reverend, why ... what? I mean, hello." Finding himself at a loss for words, he walked over extending his hand. I glowered at him. The Reverend gave a swift sidelong grin. I introduced Susan's cousin, who appeared more delinquent than those at the 'center' that the clergyman had referred to. He spoke of family resemblances, embarrassing Peter.

Within a few minutes, Susan returned with a brown bag of groceries. Fresh coffee was perked for Peter as we talked for the better part of an hour before Rev. McGee left, saying he hoped to see me again soon.

That very evening was the first of many pleasant ones to follow. We actually set some goals for me to follow, with one of them being to make a written list of my future plans. I had lived a life as a follower, now I needed to be a leader. It took a few days before I actually became enthused.

About a week passed when I was working on my list, a knock rattled the door. Dr. Boursin, sporting a pair of faded jeans, was my next visitor. I was embarrassed but welcomed him, wondering who else Susan had lined up for me to see, unannounced.

Wearing a winter coat and hat, we walked along Balliol Avenue, inspecting the renovations as we passed. Entering a small park at the corner of St. Clair and Avenue Road, we sat down on a bench next to a bronze statue of Peter Pan. This had always been one of my favorites as a child and I became entranced by it.

"Francine." The cold wind blew the leaves, and the late autumn dampness enveloped them. He paused as if addressing an audience. "You could never have done this terrible thing to yourself unless you were gravely depressed. I want you to come back into my office so I can do some tests. I'm going to tell you frankly that you have to pull out of this or you'll break. In that case, electric shock treatment would be next. People without a purpose are broken. You must understand, and realize it now that you cannot exist like this any longer. These types of nervous breakdowns are very real. Nothing can bring your parents or John back. Nothing at all. We are all born to die, some of us earlier than others do. I believe you were lost after your mother died, fighting between loneliness and the need to be part of something; something you thought John could give to you. And so you followed him blindly."

"But Dr. Boursin, I loved John. I loved him with all of my heart."

"Francine, of course, you did. I do not doubt your words, but every one of us has a first love that no other will ever touch. He was the first man in your life. He was your first love. However, at the time you met, you were lost, lonely and very vulnerable. Did you ever once take a good look at the situation? Have you been writing down your feelings over the past few months, as I told you to keep a journal?"

"For a while, I was."

"What happened?"

"I don't know. It all seemed useless, so I tore them up."

"In a rage? Why didn't you let me be the judge of that?" I gave an expressive shrug.

"I think I am beginning to put a few things together now. I spoke with Rev. McGee the other day, and some things started to sink in. I have tried to be more positive and thankful."

"Yes, I know you did. We are all concerned about you, Francine. You had undergone so much as a child and now you are dealing with these present horrors. We want to guide you back to where you can cope once again.

Standing, looking up at the statue, I thought of Peter Pan, who had no limits to his imagination. I struggled for the right words, still ashen, but I managed to control my composure. " I never thought I actually needed help." I turned around. "I know you are right. I'll start coming to your office on Monday and ..."

"That's better. Now, you are acting more like yourself. What about getting back to work?"

"Like this?"

"Sure. Buy yourself a wig, a couple of new outfits and get cracking. Don't waste another day. Let's take a walk down Yonge Street," he added firmly. We stopped at a coffee shop next to the cinema where we each ordered a soft drink. I was grateful he had spent this time with me, conscious that many people cared and I needed to be thankful. I knew nothing happens overnight. Staying in the moment and focusing would not be easy.

"Have you ever heard about Al-Anon, Francine? This active program in the States has a connection to AA, only it is for friends and relatives of an alcoholic. It helps them to share what they have lived through with others who have had the same or similar experiences. I do not believe these groups are in Toronto yet, but I will keep an ear open and let you know. Your past has become your present, and we don't want it to dominate your future."

A December snowfall left the roads slushy with a thin white blanket covering the ground. I shopped early for Leonard and Julie's Christmas gifts, wishing I could make the trip to visit them in Europe, but I lacked sufficient funds and the energy to do anything about it. I had not worked since May. Christmas with Susan's family was good for me and we all had a festive season.

My recovery was slow but going well as I started sending out applications for employment. Eventually, I heard back from Regal Oil.

Recapturing the courage and faith needed to pick up the pieces and make this New Year a new beginning, I experienced an unusual emotion, as if a resurrecting spirit unfolded within me. A different way of thinking commenced. I hesitated to wonder what would be coming up next for me. This path was just another part of my life's journey.

PART II
'Toxic Reaction'

Chapter 12
Character Reference

Preparation is in the making for when I come face to face with the man who contracted the Mencini killing.

Following two afternoons of prepping with Detective Riley and Crown Attorney James Whittmore, my emotions mix with anger and fear. They stress the importance of having a good plan and all we need to do now is carry it through to completion.

Peter and I retrace our racetrack history for Whittmore as we sense a mood change. Whittmore is of the opinion that something is missing. He wants more, as he puzzles over my part in the whole matter. We discuss and go through all the necessary details of the police's findings over the months since my return to Toronto from living in London. Whittmore still thinks information is being withheld or overlooked.

Spending the better part of the week discussing our involvement, we leave the courthouse *discovery room*. Whittmore takes a deep breath and goes into monologue as we stroll through the hallway.

"Francine, I believe you were either a scapegoat or part of a master plan. You just do not figure into this whole scenario. I believe John needed a cover. You and Peter were perfect, typical wholesome kids with clean backgrounds. I mean, look at you - from a good neighborhood, clean police record, no charges and you provided John with excellent camouflage so he could go unsuspected of any bad dealings. I am sorry, but I just don't see any other connection." He stops walking and looks deep into my eyes.

"I know this may sound a little unusual, Francine, but I think character references may be an important factor in this case. I need a clearer picture before we go to trial. I would like to know more about your early background. I'm sure you know you're the most important person in the plan we are preparing, and we are counting on you to make personal contact with the accused, but I need to see the bigger picture. You say you were living with an aunt when you met John and that you were still in school, is that correct?" I agree, nodding.

"I'd like to talk to her, if you don't mind, about your childhood years and your family. I believe this could be valuable information."

There is no reason not to, so I decide to make the arrangements. We leave the building. I am surprised that he walks with us, knowing he works on a tight schedule. Whittmore speaks in his deep lawyer voice.

"I look forward to chatting with your aunt. Please, have her call me." He takes a deep breath and slowly exhales, as if he is about to say something important, but hesitates and then returns inside.

A few days later, Whittmore relaxes quietly in his office contemplating the story my Aunt revealed, trying to digest and visualize the traumatic details about a young girl and her mother who lived within a suffering environment.

Toronto General Hospital - Autumn - 1947 -

A certain dullness took the color out of the bright fall mums, the glitter from store window reflections, and the gleam from passing vehicles - except one, a sleek, pale yellow convertible. It moved south on University Avenue toward the parking lot of Toronto General Hospital, turning the heads of men and women alike as it passed by.

The 1937 Packard displayed itself well despite its age. No rust dulled its gleaming exterior, and the chrome still glistened as if new. The distinguished driver entered the visitors' parking lot and pulled the classic vehicle to a halt. He lit his cigar, and then released the clutch and let the car out of gear. There he sat for a moment before climbing out.

He absent-mindedly touched the front fender and wiped away some imagined spot. The car, purchased ten years before as an engagement gift for his bride, Faye, seemed a symbol of their lives together; a symbol of so many things that never came to be. After he lit a cigar and inhaled vigorously, he dropped the match to the ground and nudged it with the toe of his polished brogue. He appeared tired. The strain of the last four days showed. Four days spent helplessly watching his wife labor to birth their second child. Four days of agony, that was his as much as hers. He squared his shoulders, straightened his white silk scarf around his neck, smoothed his overcoat and proceeded toward the main entrance of the hospital. He passed a young couple with their infant cradled in the husband's arms. They nodded.

Todd Harrison thought back to the previous evening when his child was born. The doctors repeatedly took his wife back and forth into the delivery room. He recalled his emotions and sweaty palms when he paced the floor, as he had done so many times before. It had seemed hours before the nurse came through the swinging doors of the 'fathers' waiting room to announce that his 'daughter' had had a baby girl and he was now permitted to visit her. His prematurely white hair had prompted the mistake, which she repeated, and then he barked that he was the husband, not the father.

He butted his cigar before proceeding, breathing heavily as he reached the second flight of stairs. He had always been proud of his fitness. Resting a moment, he regained his composure.

One of the nursing staff greeted him and directed Todd into the new hospital wing, a private room Dr. Cox had requested. He was in an area where he felt insulated from the buzz of hospital activity.

Todd observed the room, recently painted and the large bouquet of roses he had sent his wife Faye, who lay motionless with tubes connected to her arms. He signaled to the attending nurse, who entered and refilled the water jug.

Sitting down without taking his eyes off his wife, he recalled the young intern who had cornered Dr. Cox shortly after they admitted Faye. The conversation explained she was too intoxicated to take a painkiller for fear of a toxic reaction. Faye had already lost two babies through accidents or falls, all drunken mishaps, and the doctor had warned that next time her own life would be at stake.

Dr. Cox entered the room to visit his patient. He spoke to Todd regarding Faye's need for absolute rest and could not stress enough how very lucky she was to have made it through the ordeal.

The baby, Francine Mabelle Harrison, was born into a wealthy family, a gorgeous mother, Faye, and handsome flamboyant father, Todd, who flew his own airplane. He had grown up dominated by his own mother, eventually, turning to alcohol, becoming an arrogant and abusive husband.

Dr. Cox wanted Faye to stay put until she completely dried out and rid of the side effects, then he wanted to admit her to a medically assisted recovery clinic. The extensive treatment with Dr. Turner would require six to nine months. The idea took some doing, but in the end, Todd signed the required papers for admittance under the watchful eye of his domineering mother, Lillian, and father-in-law, Bob Reynolds.

Faye Harrison was thirty-three years old, a beautiful girl raised during the depression. Swept off her feet as a working teenager by a wealthy handsome young man seven years her senior, Faye's naivety and innocence led her to see only what she wanted to see. Faye married three weeks before her twentieth birthday. She had once worked in fashion, but no one would ever know it now. Her creative gifts were many; athletic in school, recognized fashion designer, an accomplished seamstress, decorator, cook, etc. Somehow, through the overwhelming personalities of her husband and in-laws, Faye lost her will to live. Following years of criticism and depression, which had brought her to this place, she could no longer compete with them. Faye had a son Leonard, and then finally birthed her baby girl, Francine, who she loved with all her heart.

Todd's continued ranting had disturbed Faye. Realizing he would not stop his drinking and change his ways for her, she observed that he fed off her weakness and insecurities. Alcohol developed her depression and became her addiction.

***

Only minutes after Todd left the hospital, a nurse hurried into Faye's room with some medication in search of Dr. Cox, waving for his attention. There had been an emergency in the nursery and it concerned the Harrison baby. Her digestive system appeared blocked.

By the time they reached the nursery, Francine was in intensive care, in an incubator with tubes connected to her small, mottled, almost lifeless body. Two doctors attended, one at each end of her little crib. Ben Cox prayed, for Faye's sake, that it would not be as serious as it appeared.

Shortly after midnight, Dr. Cox and the pediatrician talked for several minutes, when he realized he would have to repeat the story to the Harrison family. There had been several similar cases as Francine was born with an enlarged, thickened pyloric stenosis. The stomach filled dangerously because of this blockage and ballooned so that you would see the exaggerated contractions. An operation would restore the natural functioning of the pyloric valve, which regulated the flow of food from the stomach to the small intestine.

When Dr. Cox phoned Todd, he explained Francine's illness, which included signs of discomfort and pain; a condition called Hypertrophic Pyloric Stenosis and described the corrective surgery.

Three hours later, baby Francine released from intensive care to get watched over by attending nurses. Although the doctor pronounced the infant's operation successful, it would be days before her digestive system would be able to handle regular feeding, and, therefore, nourished intravenously. Francine had lost weight and her color was poor. The hospital staff felt it necessary to monitor her closely before discharging and transferring her to Sick Children's Hospital where the best care would be available. Confused by the trauma of the delivery and the ordeal of the infant's surgery, Faye could not think about her own situation.

Todd and Faye both lacked the ability to communicate. Her psychiatrist found her to be melancholy and obsessed with Francine's health and care. Faye's next step would be her most challenging. After her visit with Francine and Leonard, she would leave to contend with her own confinement and be out of contact with the outside world. The days had already been desperately long; how would she cope with months?

Finally, the day arrived when Faye left the hospital with Todd, visited Francine, and then began her own recovery. Deep within her heart, she knew that her 'will to live' waited for her return, under the care of her mother, Ruth Reynolds and her husband.

Chapter 13
Recovery

Surrounded with blossoms of yellow forsythia and iris, which bordered the long walkway of the Bell Clinic, a magnificent older home sat in a perfect location.

When Faye left the clinic, Ben Cox met with Dr. Turner, the psychiatrist, who explained Faye as a product of situation and environment. Medically, she was responding well to her medication but coping with Todd would be another story. Her liver damage would never heal completely, and if her drinking reoccurred, Faye would not make it back again. She needed to find something special for personal satisfaction, something to help her cope with the trivial tasks of each day. Love would be the answer to a successful recovery.

Dr. Turner reported that couples did not separate when they should and it was not acceptable to live in such trauma as five conditions underlie stress, depression and suicide. They were abuse, betrayal, rejection, abandonment and denial. He told Faye that regular visits were required.

The 1948 Oshawa-blue Oldsmobile pulled into the driveway of the stately Tudor home as Faye returned home. Ruth and Leonard sat in the back seat, chatting the whole time. Leonard told stories of his friends, his baby sister's playing with his toys, and how he could make his bicycle go as fast as her Packard. He wanted to know if he could paint his bike yellow so they would match. The clinic had allowed the children to visit her, but not nearly as often as Faye wanted. Her heart thumped excitedly when Leonard leaped from the car to run up to a large white English pram the nursemaid was pushing down the sidewalk.

"Frannie! Mommy's home! Mommy's home!"

Faye beamed with joy to hear him call his sisters name. In her excitement, she stumbled when she stepped from the car, bringing everyone to a halt. She regained her composure, smiled and walked cautiously up the walkway to the carriage.

Leonard whispered, "You ok, Mommy?"

"Yes, dear. I got a little excited and must remember to move slowly." Faye bent over, peered into the carriage, thrilled to see her daughter Francine break into the biggest smile she could have ever imagined. When her mouth opened, Faye saw one tooth breaking through the bottom gum as she leaned over to pick the tot up, and Francine responded with excited chatter. Tears welled up in Faye's eyes making it difficult to see. "Oh-h, Frannie. You're so precious with your big blue eyes and curly blond hair!" She squeezed her gently. Her children were her greatest joy.

"Isn't she nice, Mommy? You like her – eh?" bounced her five-year-old son standing at her side. She dropped her hand to ruffle his hair.

"Oh boy, I sure do. You have a beautiful sister, Leonard." Ruth and Todd entered the house as curious neighbors looked on. Faye was back home and back on track.

Many months passed while Leonard's time at school gave Faye a few hours alone with the misadventures of the new toddler. She enjoyed every minute of every day as she explained to her closest friend, a frequent visitor, Dr. Cox, when he would stop over for tea.

He noticed remarkable improvements in the house and the grounds from the loving hands of Faye and her helpers, which created a space envied by neighbors and friends. "You've done wonders again this year, Faye. No doubt, Dr. Turner has told you how thrilled we all are with your recovery. It's hard to visualize Todd actually co-operating with all these changes." As they conversed, chubby fingers and the curls of a smiling toddler appeared at the edge of the coffee table. Francine appeared out of nowhere, as she often did, startling her mother and the doctor.

"Hold on to your cup!" shouted Faye, jumping to support her child as she pulled herself to the table. "She's got spirit, and that smile of hers has given her too much spoiling. Now I shall pay," and once again, she took off, waddling awkwardly out into the hallway.

"Kookie, kookie..." she sputtered, which had been her first words.

Faye walked over to the fireplace and leaned against the mantle. Ben Cox caught a glimpse of her now fuller figure clinging to the knit dress, thinking, *'here is Eurydice returning from her underground hell'*.

Faye sighed, hesitating to respond to his questions regarding Todd. "Ben, he feels left out. I actually make a point of getting them off to bed early so that I do make time for 'us'."

"And?"

"Well, I listen to him talk about his work, and we eat together."

"Instead of drinking together?"

"Well, yes. I suppose so..."

"So, what's the discussion? Why don't you both eat with your children." He sensed her hesitation as they conversed, signifying something was bothering her. Faye's beautiful smile dulled, whenever discussing their relationship.

Dr. Turner would be consulted.

***

August 1955

A large dent showed on the left rear fender of a new two-toned coral and white Meteor that sat in the driveway of the Harrison home. Several of the neighborhood boys pointed at it from the sidewalk, laughing as they passed by on their way home from school. The front door had been left wide open and shrieks and sharp banging noises emanated from within. A petite well-dressed elderly woman walked swiftly into the home. Ruth Reynolds soon recognized the dreaded scent of alcohol. Leaving her purse on a cluttered hall table, she climbed the stairs to find her granddaughter in a frantic tantrum, smashing her hairbrush along a dresser's edge and firing books, magazines, and pillows at the walls. The screams from the eight-year-old ceased when she saw her grandmother, and Francine fell on the floor in hysterics, holding onto their black Labrador; there had been an altercation.

Leonard came out of nowhere, knelt beside them, wiping her tears. The three slowly left the bedroom for the kitchen. Ruth poured two tall glasses of milk and searched among the empty cupboards for something to eat. Dirty dishes and spilled, hardened food remained on the counters. She shrugged her shoulders at the meager contents of the refrigerator. Finally, she placed large pieces of sliced cheese and a plate of bread before them. They grabbed the food as if they had not eaten in awhile.

Ruth listened to the children tell of their mother's demise, and the sadness that affected them both, alcoholism.

They explained that Todd had started bringing cases of booze into the house, keeping it locked up in the basement. They saw that he was buying liquor by the case. He would arrive home from work and grunt some kind of hello, and then give them an argument about their bikes lying around, or whatever else he chose to pick on, and then take off to the basement to drink. He claimed the kids drove him away, but never tried to discipline them, only yelled and complained.

Faye worked most mornings with a fashion agency helping the models with their clothes and makeup, and then returned home in the afternoon, after school. She loved her work and came home happy to her family.

Francine reported the first time was a few weeks after Easter when she thought her mother appeared different to her. Her parents were out on the back patio when her mother walked toward her, and she immediately knew she was not balancing properly when she walked. Her eyes looked funny. Francine gasped aloud, making it obvious she did not like what she saw. Faye straightened up when Francine ran to her room and Faye followed to tuck her in bed. She could tell by her mother's voice that something was different and she smelled different. Francine asked her if she had been drinking, but she called her foolish and left.

Once again, Ruth saw the grand Tudor house show other signs of neglect: wilting plants, layers of dust on tables and floors, piles of dirty towels in corners, laundry draped on chairs.

"Gram, I get so choked up that I can hardly talk to Mom. It is a nightmare. We have always been so close," Francine blurted out, holding onto her dog, Tony. "And now, I feel sick inside. I love my Mom. What is happening to her?" Ruth hugged the little girl, affectionately, and explained it was her mother's sickness and she would work it all out, somehow, she promised. Ruth climbed up the magnificent winding staircase to the second-floor bedroom, finding her daughter asleep. Faye's expensive dress showed wrinkles, spots and disarrangement. Her heavy make-up had soiled the pillows and bedspread.

What has caused this terrible evil to return? Ruth admitted having been oblivious to the possibility that anything could possibly be wrong. What else could her daughter want? She had a beautiful home, children and everything money could buy. Unaware her daughter lived with verbal and mental abuse, rejection and criticism, she wept, slipping down beside the bed. How wrong she had been. The sounds of sobbing awakened Faye, who slowly opened her eyes.

The crying stopped. Faye could see her evening attire and realized her state. Ruth felt her daughter's anguish, when she did not speak, and handed Faye a glass of water from the littered bedside table. They faced one another, each trying to find the right words.

"I won't go. I will not walk away, Faye. I'm going downstairs to find you something to eat, and some coffee, and then we will talk. Go and make yourself presentable, and for God's sake have some answers. We are going straight to AA." Then, Ruth left the bedroom.

After Faye showered and dressed, she appeared more like herself in a stylish plaid shirt tucked into the tiny waist of her navy flannel slacks. Ruth examined Faye more carefully, as she entered the kitchen, sitting down to toast, jam, and strong coffee. Large dark rings encircled her red eyes.

They sat sipping the strong coffee in silence when Ruth announced she knew Todd had been bringing alcohol into the house ever since Ben Cox moved away. AA told her if she felt good about herself, she would not become depressed and feel the need to drink. Alcohol did not give her the strength and courage she believed it did, and the false image created soon disappears, causing depression. Dr. Turner should be notified.

Faye sat motionless, unable to communicate. Ruth whispered kindly to her daughter. "Alcohol is nothing but a drug that makes you feel continually useless whenever you think you cannot cope. They call it a spirit, but it actually is the energy of evil spirits. The demon controls your thoughts and actions. Your addiction is your weakness."

Moments passed and Ruth announced a plan, they were taking a trip to visit her sister in Vancouver and would leave immediately, at the end of the week. All she wanted to do was to take Faye away from the dreadful atmosphere, to talk it out.

At that exact moment, Todd charged into the house, harshly slamming the door behind him and carrying the familiar brown liquor bag from LCBO.

Ruth explained, between interruptions that she had heard from Faye's sister, Emily, in Vancouver, who was ill and needed them to help out. She would not say how long their stay would be, but promised that a housekeeper would come to stay with the children. Todd was suspicious, but Ruth was very persuasive and convincing as her desperation gave her the courage to lie, in the hopes of saving her daughter, once again. Todd hesitated, taken off guard by their unexpected plans.

Ruth explained to Francine and Leonard that all would be well and that she would be away with their Mother for a few weeks. They were not to worry.

Francine regressed during the following weeks, showing symptoms of withdrawal and resentment as she became openly contemptuous of her father. Leonard argued and rebelled at every opportunity. They longed desperately for the family relationship that Faye had lovingly created.

Francine's uneasiness grew more constant as Todd invited his drinking friends into the home and the drunken brawls became unsettling when she witnessed scenes more disturbing than she cared to admit.

Ruth returned to Toronto, explaining that Emily needed Faye's assistance a little longer. No one could convince him of the hurt and damage he was causing his family by simply being an alcoholic with a closed mind. His belligerent attitude and need for alcohol was his weakness which had destroyed the family, but he was not about to change, nor did he want to.

Faye phoned Francine regularly. She thought her mother sounded stronger, much more like her old self, and she missed her dearly. Francine felt in her heart she would be fine, and all would be well again when she arrived back home.

Late one evening, the following week, Ruth sat taking her tea in the living room of her modest apartment. She opened the envelope she had found in the day's mail. Drawing a deep breath, she reads Emily's letter.

Dear Mom,

Things are not good.

After Faye had heard of my own difficulties of three miscarriages and numerous bouts of depression, she began to talk openly about herself. Apparently, ever since Faye's time at the recovery clinic, she felt she had closed the door on her other life. She suffered through Todd's verbal, mental and emotional abuse as the children grew and made more demands on her. She became depressed, lonely. Todd underwent financial hardships, borrowed against the house, lost construction jobs, and drank away what little money they had saved. She needed a husband. This feeling of being pushed aside became intolerable. Meanwhile, Todd started bringing alcohol into the house along with his drinking friends, knowing that she could not cope with it or them. Once Faye started working, she gained self-esteem and began to feel good about herself and her family. Then, at work, a few men made passes and she was flattered because any kind of affection filled the void that she could not fill at home. Eventually, she became interested in one of the buyers from an international couturier who was infatuated with her for a long time, but since he too was married, they knew it would never work. They fought against their attraction by never seeing each other on a regular basis, but their love grew, and that was the cause of her emotional turmoil.

Although her children mean the world to her, she neglected her own personal feelings for several years, which caught up with her. It has been a terrible time and she knew there were no solutions. We must remember, Faye wasn't yet 20 when she married. She has decided to stay with Todd and her children, and will need all the support she can get. Pray for her, Mom. She really needs it.   *Love, Emily*

Chapter 14
Fatal Outcome

Fall - 1964

Another Hurricane Hazel developed with constant wind and rain filling muddy streets and overflowing ditches. A young man dragged a limp body through the front doors of the Harrison home when a shot rang out. Leonard pulled his mother's body along the hallway despite the sounds of violent cursing and banging from the floor below. Francine appeared from the hall closet where she had been hiding with her dog, Tony. Faye's face was pale, her body bone-thin. Although frightened, Francine helped her brother hoist the body up the long winding staircase to the bedrooms. Anguished moments passed as they lifted her onto Leonard's bed, and then he went to find dry towels. They began undressing the unconscious body.

"She passed out over at the Bonds' house last night. Dad left her there. Look, look at the bruises all over her arms and legs. Beaten again," Leonard observed.

"Maybe, she just fell. Leonard, she is going stiff - do you think? I mean, is she dying?" Francine cried through her tears. Leonard removed the shoes, and then the stockings. He too noticed the change in body temperature.

"This happened once before when she blacked out, something like a seizure or an epileptic fit. I'll call the hospital and have an ambulance come right away."

Francine stood shaking, frightened not only by the sounds of gunfire coming from the basement below, but by the horror on her brother's bed. She continued undressing the cold body.

Leonard returned. "They're on the way. I tried calling Gram, but no answer; cannot figure out where they are in this storm. Here, Frannie, wrap my sweater over her. We'll do the best with what we've got."

The two teenagers managed to get Faye undressed, dried off and dressed again before the ambulance arrived. The large cuts, scars and injuries gave the impression she had fallen down a flight of stairs. She looked like a neglected street person. Nauseated by the sight of her matted and stringy hair left unkempt for days, they detected the smell of alcohol, mixed with cheap perfume and perspiration.

Nervously speaking with the ambulance drivers, Leonard watched as they moved the body onto the stretcher. Francine overheard comments that her mother might go into convulsions as she noticed that not only was her skin changing color, but also, it was rapidly getting colder. One attendant remarked that she might have had a stroke. Tears streamed down the cheeks of the two teenagers.

The siren screeched into the wet night as the kids turned from the doorway to see Todd standing in the back hall.

"You bastard! You no good bastard! You have killed her this time! If we ever see her alive again, it will be a bloody miracle," Francine lashed out, trying to wipe the tears from her bloodshot eyes. His cursing fired back as she noticed the gun in his hand. Leonard showed no emotion, no tears, no anger or fear – he just stared at his drunken father holding a revolver at his side, which he had witnessed several times before.

"Shut your fuckin' mouth, you little bitch! You don't know what you're talking about," Todd yelled as he walked toward them.

"Lay a goddamn hand on her, and I'll kill you," Leonard gritted through his teeth. Todd weaved to the side and grabbed the wall for support.

"Who the fuck do you think you are? No good cocksuckers, causing trouble." Todd slurred, dropping the gun. The once powerful man slumped down to reach it.

"There was nothing the matter with your mother that couldn't be handled. You two caused all the trouble. Arguing, fighting, never doing what you were told, causing her problem after problem - why you....

"What the hell are you blubbering about?" screamed Francine. "Did we ever throw booze at her? Did we FORCE her to drink? Did we BEAT her up? You no good lousy drunk - you did it all! You tormented her, slapped her around like a piece of dirt from the gutter. YOUR WIFE!" she screamed. "There just wasn't enough of her for all of us, was there? You had to destroy her totally. You wanted her all to yourself. She couldn't handle the liquor, so you beat her when she stumbled, kicked her, and yes, raped her!"

"What the fuck are you mouthing off about, bitch? Little whore," he blurted out, vengefully.

136

"Many times I listened to you swear at her, slap her and force yourself on her despite her cries. I will never forget it. NEVER!" she cried, trying to pull away from Leonard's grip. Grabbing an umbrella that was leaning in the corner of the hallway, she swung out at her father, swearing at him all the while. Todd picked up a letter opener from the hall table and flung it, missing Francine's head by a fraction but catching a chunk of her hair and pinning it to the wall. He leaped at her.

Leonard threw her to the side, grabbing at his father's shoulders, awkwardly knocking him to the ground. Todd swung out, hitting Leonard on the jaw, forcing him to stumble backward. Screams, curses, and blood spouted from Francine's swollen lips. Todd rallied, shouting obscenities, when Frannie kicked at his stomach so hard that her shoe flew off. She pounded him, screaming hysterically.

"Liar! You no good drunken, useless liar! You were never decent to any of us. You were never a father to us; you forced her into a hell, a goddamn nightmare of a life, taking us all down with you. If she was touched by anyone, it was your godforsaken drunken friends - bums! The bums you brought into our home." Frannie dropped to the floor, unsure of her whereabouts, remembering the love and affection she had received from her mother, before alcohol, which was now nothing more than a distant memory. Leonard grabbed his sister by the collar, yanked her to her feet and pushed her out into the thunderous storm. They ran away into the cold night realizing their nightmare was real as they yearned for the lost comfort of a happy home.

Hours later, the two of them got off a bus near their grandparent's apartment. Desperate to protect themselves from the blistering winds, they slowly walked up the steps and pressed the buzzer for B.M. Reynolds, 101. A few seconds later, they heard the rough grumble of their grandfather's voice, and then he released the lock at the entrance. He stood at the door by the time they reached the end of the hallway. His index finger went to his lip, indicating quiet.

"Your Gram's sleeping now," he smiled. They went into the small kitchen where he closed the door and plugged in the kettle. He waited for them to speak. Leonard wiped his brow and took off his wet sweater.

"I'm never going back there, Gramps. I hate him. He's really done it this time." For the second time, tears seeped from his gray-blue eyes as his grandfather listened patiently to their story. Francine hugged her brother. She sat slumped in a corner chair, confirming by her silence that he told the truth.

"Gramps," he continued. "Mom's drinking ... so many times I've had to go ... I've had to pick her up drunk from places I would rather not talk about. I called the hospital for an ambulance earlier. They came and picked her up again. It's not good." Silence. His grandfather made a pot of tea in his calm manner and put some cookies on a plate in front of them.

"She's committing a slow suicide," the grandfather answered to the saddened faces sitting opposite him. "Alcohol is an addictive suicide drug and don't ever, ever forget that."

"I know we shouldn't have come here. We argued with Dad. He's crazy. He has guns. He fires them, throws knives and almost got Frannie in the head with a letter opener tonight."

"He did what?" exclaimed their Grandpa.

"Drunker than hell," she joined in. No one spoke for several minutes.

"I'd better give your grandparents a call. Your Dad's sister, too. I'll go to the hospital. Frannie, you had better wash the blood off your mouth, put some Zambuck on that cut. Get a little bit of rest and stay here with your Gram. Leonard and I will go to the hospital to see how bad it is this time." The telephone punctuated their conversation. Francine felt a sickness growing inside her that she had never experienced before.

"Yes, yes, doctor. This is Bob Reynolds, Faye's father. Yes. Why, of course. I'll be right there." He hung up the phone, not relaying the message to them. He quickly dialed a number.

"Hello, yes. This is Bob Reynolds. Oh fine, but I do have some very unfortunate news. Faye was taken to emergency tonight; she suffered a stroke and paralyzed along the right side of her body. Yes, yes. That is correct. I don't know. Leonard is here now. We'll go immediately," and he put the receiver down.

Overwhelmed and unable to focus through the constant tears, Francine sobbed as Leonard kissed her cheek, took a last sip from his cup and left the kitchen with his grandfather. She heard the click of the apartment door closing, but she made no effort to move. Dropping her head onto her folded arms resting on the table, she cried inconsolably.

The once beautiful, peaceful home and life that Faye had provided for her children for several years was only a distant memory, and Francine desperately missed those loving days.

She realized two women affected her father, Todd, in his life. He drank because he could not face up to his mother, and Faye could not face up to her husband. A life of fear.

Drifting into a deep sleep as the rain splashed against the window and the wind whistled through the panes howling a blistering storm, Francine unexpectedly matured into a young woman, unaware of her destiny.

PART III
'A Sense of Worth'

Chapter 15
Relationships

Trial etiquette leaves no room for error. One must be calm and alert. I know what to do; now all I have to do is carry their instructions through to completion. I'm prepped on how to act, what to wear, how to do my hair and several other little details.

On Friday morning, while waiting patiently for Peter to arrive back at his townhouse, I nervously check my appearance in the hall mirror, smoothing a piece of long hair back from my face. Within a matter of minutes, I lock up and join Peter in his truck. He extinguishes his cigarette as he watches the road ahead. The sleeves of his plaid shirt are rolled up to his elbows; it is the first time I take notice of his appearance. Peter looks much older than his years as he lives the hard life. He retrieves his sunglasses from the visor and slips them on, looking directly at me.

"Hope you are ready, because I'm as ready as I'll ever be." Peter turns the vehicle into the traffic.

"We'll be fine. I know all about what I am supposed to do, Peter. Relax." I inhale, vigorously.

"It's too bad you have to go through all this bullshit. Both Susan and I think you've come a long way since the sixties. We wouldn't want any of this to come between you and Brad, now." Peter speaks the truth, knowing Bradley is waiting to hear back from me in London.

While wrestling with the thought of messing up, I say as placidly as possible. "Don't worry."

Time is here to learn the name of the man who orchestrated the murder of my fiancé. Newman put out a call to his partner in the contract, and now I am to make the connection and set the stage for the encounter, but I'm unsure of what to expect.

We are less than one hour away from our final visit with Whittmore and Detective Riley, and then I must confront the horror that still haunts me. For the life of me, I am still unsure who the person will be.

Peter relaxes and reminds me of our conversation from the previous evening. We reminisced 'my growing years' he had called them. While he struggled with the day-to-day duties of thoroughbred racing, I wandered from place to place and wrestled with complicated relationships. He was curious to know more.

'It was so long ago,' Peter thought.

November - 1972

I remembered a cold whistling wind of an Ontario winter that blew early, leaving drifting snow covering the ground. Toronto's skyline filled with black and silver towers that embraced a soon-to-be restored Harbourfront complex.

Lifestyles changed with fewer teenage marriages, couples lived together and women launched their careers, postponing the wedding ceremony until after age thirty.

Yorkville Village had matured, groomed into one of the country's finest districts.

Atop the *Fifty-Fourth* floor of the Toronto Dominion Centre, I sat next to a tinted window overlooking the foggy, bustling city while turning the pages of a financial newspaper and sipping my vodka martini. I pricked the olive with the end of my swizzle stick when I noticed a well-groomed man standing at the entrance to the lounge, holding a black leather briefcase. He looked to be in his forties and accompanied a smartly dressed young woman toting a large portfolio. As they glanced around the crowded room, a waiter directed them to the table where I was sitting.

Susan arrived with her friend, Gregory Woodcock. They ordered cocktails and we chatted about their work for a short time. While redesigning several out-of-town government municipal buildings, she consulted with him regularly, maybe too frequently.

"So, you have definitely decided to run for Mayor, Gregory?" I asked.

"Why, Miss Harrison! You have doubts?" he smiled.

"I was thinking along the line of finances. It takes big money to win an election in this city."

"He doesn't have to worry about that. Why ol' Gregory here is loaded and has all the right connections. All he has to do is push the campaign in Rosedale, to his old classmates from Upper Canada College and he'll come through with a hefty bank roll. Not to mention the faulty engine design he caught six years ago for General Motors, saving them several million dollars by stopping production before it would have cost them a bundle. I'm sure they'd return the favor with a small contribution."

"Now dear, let's not get carried away." Gregory tapped Susan's hand with his, coaxing her to drop the subject. "Ladies, would you excuse me for a moment. I must call home before we order dinner." He shifted his chair anxiously.

Susan tossed off her drink in a gulp and set the glass down, asking with somber conviction, "Well? What is it now, Francine Harrison? I can tell by your tone and your look that you don't approve of something."

"Oh Sue! You're messing with a heap of trouble. I thought this thing with Gregory was just one of your whims, but now, for God's sake, you're seen everywhere in public together. What next? You cannot continue like this if he thinks he wants to run seriously. He has family. It is one thing to have an affair, but you are practically his mistress."

"Yeah, well, I intended to talk to you about that. I was considering moving out on my own."

"Grow up, Susan Edwards! You are not fooling around with some boy from Thornhill now. Gregory Woodcock is a financier from an extremely wealthy family. He has three young kids and a very intelligent wife who isn't about to put up with this nonsense when she finds out. What kind of game are you playing? You! You, of all people! Don't you see what is happening?"

"No, Frannie, you've got it all wrong. I don't want anything from him. Well, I do, but not in the way you think. Listen, I know what I'm doing."

"Well, you used to. You used to talk to me, but now you need a warning." I stretched across the table. "Susan. You are no fool! Quit, while the quitting's good!"

Plaintively, Susan assured me not to worry.

"Do you love him, or is this just a… thing?"

"Well, I love who he is, his background, ambition, wealth, brains, professionalism, you know. But, if you are asking, if the situation presents itself, would I marry him, the answer is no."

I drew a deep breath. "So you mean his power is like an aphrodisiac?"

"Humm, something like that," Susan admitted shyly. Gregory returned explaining that his nanny had returned from the doctor's office with his daughter, who had come down with a case of the chicken pox. His sons were stranded at the 'Y' waiting for a ride home. Nonchalantly, he tipped the waiter a hundred dollar bill, asked him to take care of all our needs, and then paid for our meal in advance before escaping into the night.

We left the lounge and stepped into the dining room where we ordered wine and appetizers. A group of young men settled in beside us, chatting loudly about the Canada-Russia hockey series, a topic discussed by most Canadians across the country that winter. Their excitement was contagious as the battle of the blades was turning into a battle of nations.

During dinner, I related my involvement with Travelers Restaurants, working for Regal Oil, giving details of how I had compiled several reports for the company. My portfolio made recommendations to consider and rethink their locations, menus, and themes as the company needed to market a new concept for their highway diners. Stan, my manager, requested a complete overview.

Waiters served our salads and topped up our silver water goblets while I went into monologue and spelled out my ideas for my newfound career.

"Sounds like a lot of work." Susan commented.

"Yes, well that's what a researcher's responsibility is all about in this department." My work had become my life and I was up to the challenge.

Nearing nine o'clock, we took the elevator down to the King Street exit where the howling winds foretold a terrible storm. Wrapped in warm furs and hats, we fought our way across the street to the parking lot where the red Ferrari parked in the back corner. The freezing rain had caused the key to jam in Susan's door.

I let the car idle for several minutes until we became comfortable. The Ferrari had been released from storage on the anniversary of John's death.

***

In early spring, Peter and I drove his pick-up south to Mechanicstown, Ohio to visit John's parents. We felt compelled to see them. John's brother had driven the Ferrari back to the U.S. a couple of months after the death where it sat parked in a heated garage ever since. John's dad urged me to take it as well as John's gambling winnings. I adamantly refused the money because no one was charged with the murder and I didn't need any more attention by taking and spending the money, drawing notice to myself. Peter suggested that they invest or donate it in his name. I did agree to take the car.

That first day in Ohio was traumatic. It had been difficult for me to make the trip as it brought back many memories. Mrs. Mencini needed to reflect. She missed her son and believed that no one ever changed another, saying we all make our own choices and that our expectations are sometimes beyond the realm of possibility for that other person we so dearly love.

I admitted that John and I had little in common, but something always pulled us back together when we separated as if we were soul-mates. Perhaps, we had a guiding spirit over us and once it left, our lives together ended. Maybe, we would have grown apart. I only knew that I didn't want to put myself in that predicament again. She reached out and we embraced. Noticing the engagement ring, she requested that I wear it on my right hand, and move on with my life.

On the last day of our visit, Peter and I drove to the gravesite on the west side of their estate where John lay beneath a large willow tree. We knelt down side-by-side, quietly expressing our thoughts. I shut the door to the past and began coping, hopeful that the pain would finally cease.

***

Revving the engine as it sat in neutral, I shifted gears and crept through the accumulating snow onto King Street and back home where Peter was preparing a tray of hot chocolate. Some days, I thought he lived more with us than on his own. He lit the fireplace, talking excitedly about his day. Larson Farms invited SnoMann to stand stud when he was ready to retire from racing. He had won his last seven outings, all Stake races, and became a notable contender whenever he ran. The strained tendon, which initially occurred at Blue Bonnets Raceway, five years before, would always cause havoc, but Peter was now willing to consider other options for the great stallion.

The discussion turned to Susan. Peter teased her about her relationship with the married Mr. Woodcock; she defended herself saying she knew what she was doing.

"Are you truly considering moving out of here?" I asked, taking a bite from a cream-filled éclair. Sugar was not good for me, but I loved it anyway. She waved her finger at me.

"As a matter of fact, I might be, but not until after the holidays. I'll let you know in plenty of time, ok?" The mention of Christmas reminded me of my own forgotten plans to visit Leonard and Julie. I hadn't arranged a flight to Holland.

Peter poured a second mug of hot chocolate and lit another cigarette while he elaborated on his intentions to spend his winter months racing at Hialeah in Florida. Karen would be riding there, who was now recognized as a noted jockey throughout the country. We had never kept in contact.

"We should all get together when she's back in town," I remarked.

"She's here now," Peter announced. "She's flying off to Florida in another week, so I'll try to arrange something. I read about her in the papers and magazines, but I rarely see her around anymore. Heard she had an apartment in New York, Toronto, and another in California as well as a wardrobe fit for an heiress. Success looks good on her." I nodded, smiling. Another friend who knew what she wanted, and went out there and got it.

As the holidays neared, my primary concern was to finalize my reports to management. This was a big deal for me, as the changes I proposed would prove beneficial to the company. I consulted Stan Taggert, my immediate manager, to review the completed package.

Thursday morning found the previous night's freezing rain had left the roads slushy with reports of an impending ice storm. I arrived early, parking the Ferrari in my allotted spot and then headed for the closest coffee machine. The office filled with the sound of ringing telephones and gossiping employees that broke my train of thought. Stan called me with the time of our meeting with the Planning and Measurements Managers. Smoothing my hair back, I reached inside my purse for my cosmetic mirror and applied fresh lipstick.

The meeting progressed well for almost two hours. My comparison figures were precise and my percentages accurate. Now, for the plan.

Stan spoke. "Francine, you have accurately tracked the current markets' potential, our mistakes, and the cost factors affecting the problem, including the food waste. That has excellent ammunition for any argument, but what about the future? What do you propose as the resolution, the budget etc.? The time factor is important, and so is a well-planned approach." The three managers appeared eager to know my next move. An offending knock at the door disturbed their focus, as Stan responded.

"Excuse me, Mr. Atkinson." A handsome woman in her late forties apologized. "It is almost noon, and you have an appointment in ten minutes."

"Yes, I should have been paying more attention. I wonder if you could call Graydon Courts and tell them to cancel my game and lunch. I'll probably be tied up here for the remainder of the afternoon. Similarly, my other appointments, please rearrange and book them for tomorrow. We're into something that needs our attention."

We proceeded to the cafeteria. Seemingly refreshed, the men cleared their trays, butted their cigarettes and we headed back to the planning room.

We continued as I gave it my best. "As mentioned earlier, we are losing a tremendous amount of the market through high prices and lack of appeal. My proposals are..." I replaced the graph sheet with a new one. "...something along this line. Consumer and purchasing reports indicate a definite savings by, firstly, quantity buying, especially in the food area. That is one of the main areas of concern. Secondly, we have to cut costs by concentrating on a smaller menu, one that will reduce waste, a highly sensitive area with the food and drug departments. I propose we limit our choice of dishes, cut down the list. Again, from previous surveys..." I exhibited a new transparency. "One concludes that travelers don't necessarily want fast food because this is their break from long highway drives and they will wait - if the price and the decor are right. Therefore, we give them both. Marketing indicates the most popular dishes are chicken, burgers, and pasta. For breakfast, we keep the same basics as we already have, but the lunch and dinner menus are drastically cut down to five main choices each and reorganized, adding daily specials. Steak is always a good choice - as long as it isn't too expensive. We also have to develop an entirely new 'fun' image so that they become a destination. We design all the restaurants with the same basic layout, but decorate and use different finishing materials where we offer unique themes for each. One location would reflect a *western theme,* as a corral and with a menu to match. Saddles, bridles, pitchforks on the walls; stalls for booths; barrels for tables; posters. Another restaurant will have a *movie theme* with nostalgic posters from old movies covering the walls. Create a healthy salad bar, a proven instant success on any menu.

"Another of our restaurants becomes a *fantasy world*, done up with cartoon and comic book characters hanging from the ceiling, posters, and brightly colored tables. Our list includes a *fifties theme, animal theme, a literary theme, automobile themes* with hub caps, steering wheels, license plates, paintings and photographs of antique and racing cars on the walls, just like in a garage. The possibilities go on and on as indicated in my proposal. We would create a destination so that travelers would want to try a different restaurant each outing. The menus are to be similar to keep costs down, but the décor would vary creating interest. This concept can be utilized throughout North America.

"The menus would be printed on shaped, cutout folders patterned after the restaurant's theme. For example, a classic car cutout displayed as the cover." I passed around a few samples prepared by the marketing department. We discussed the possibilities for the reduced menus, all following statistics of what was eaten by today's travelers. Marketing would advise them of any changes. The primary concern was to cut the waste, reduce the menu from sixty-five items to fewer than twenty, and purchase the supplies in quantity.

"Show us your costs on these changes." Atkinson requested as I picked up another transparency page comparing the present figures with the prospective ones.

"If we can pump another 25% of that lost 73%-market into our restaurants, we'll increase our sales 66% while we cut our food costs and wastes by 78%. The public will be encouraged to visit a fun place when tired and hungry, making their dining experience a relief, as well as enjoyment. Due to the smaller, limited menu, fresh food will be cheaper

147

and healthier in the end and require less storage. It will reduce costs by cutting the processed quantities stored and the time spent in cold storage. Here's an advertising layout, and here's what we are presently doing and using, and this third page will show you the comparison of our costs and expenditures over a three-year period." I took a deep breath and waited. The numbers would speak for themselves.

Deliberations continued for another hour until finally, a reluctant halt was called, and they agreed to consider and report back. My sense was that they would approve it for executive review within a week. Feeling slighted not to have received a more positive reaction, I swept the materials from my desk and locked up.

Since my recovery, I had put all my energy into doing my job, and doing it well.

Stan's familiar voice echoed through the hallway. He was complimentary in his attempt to promote my ideas. I continued on my way, leaving the building.

Chapter 16
The Pick-Up

Winter - 1972

Blizzard winds hurled freezing rain as I started out from Regal Oil's main lobby into the slippery parking lot. How would I manage the treacherous drive home?

There were many vehicles abandoned on the side of the roadway. It took two hours to get from Don Mills Road to York Mills and Yonge Street. Taking a risk to climb the steep hill heading south on Yonge Street at Hoggs Hollow, I became frightened. The icy pavement caused me to slide, swerve back and forth, and then the car hit the curb. After repeated tries, I left the Ferrari parked in the driveway of an apartment at the base of the hill. My hands felt frozen. In the rearview mirror, I saw several cruisers stationed at the bottom of the hill setting up roadblocks. Climbing cautiously from my vehicle, I slipped and fell as I crossed Yonge Street to the Jolly Miller, an old two-story brick building that had become a landmark.

I entered the dark and smoky tavern filled with the smell of alcohol and loud music, and then shuffled through the crowded room, squeezing up to the bar where the bartender caught my eye.

"What'll it be, lady?"

"Telephones. Where would…" With a glance of his eye, he indicated a doorway leading upstairs. I felt my throbbing bruises as I hurried to find the wall phone that hung directly at the top of the stairs. Extracting my wallet from my overstuffed purse, I searched for change, but found nothing. I swore. A tall, dark-haired man rushing past turned in surprise.

"Something wrong, ma'am?" he asked with an American southern accent.

"Oh!" I startled by his question and embarrassed at my expletive. "Why, I was just looking for some coins and don't seem to have any." I stared directly up at him, seeing John's eyes in his.

"Why, I'm sure I could assist a damsel in distress. Let me just have a peek here. Why yes! I do have change. Here you go. Now, no more nasty talk like that again or I'll have to call the owner," he joked, proceeding down the stairs. I grinned as he left and inserted the money, only to have my call go unanswered.

Quietly slipping back into the lounge, I ordered a glass of Dubonnet and relaxed. When I finished my drink, the American approached, after excusing himself from another table. He disliked seeing a woman unescorted, he teased.

"Here's to a damsel in need of a sand truck." His corny line made me smile.

"Thank you, ah... Mr..."

"Chuck Connors."

"Not the TV star? The Rifleman?"

"No Ma'am. And you? Miss?"

"Francine Harrison." We acknowledged one another by shaking hands. His handshake touched a dormant emotion. It was warm and firm.

"You live far from here, Miss Francine?"

"Not really, just a few miles away near St. Clair Avenue, but I work in Don Mills."

"Kind of going in the reverse direction to the traffic. Most everyone works in the city and lives in the suburbs."

"Yes, I suppose you could say that."

"What do you do? Model?" I blushed, knowing that I rated a mere five on a modeling scale of ten. "No. I'm a marketing analyst for Regal Oil."

"Oh. I understand." Repeatedly nodding, he took a swig from his mug of beer. Compared to John, he was almost fifty pounds heavier and four inches taller. 'Looks and sounds like a rich Texan,' I thought.

"And you? Where are you from? And what's your line of work?" I returned the questions.

"Why ma'am, I actually live across the street at the '4000.' My line of work is big investments. I represent some mighty large companies. I used to play ball for the Green Bay Packers a few years back but had myself one hell of a bad injury during a game, and my daddy, he hauled me off that field faster than a possum goes after grits. My real home is Louisville." He ordered another round and made himself comfortable.

"Very interesting. Tell me, Chuck," I sipped my drink, "what kind of investing? Would you be into land speculating, or what?"

"Well, Ma'am, we're mostly into businesses that are going under. Say a firm puts a high-rise up on King Street, and then during construction they experience strikes, or materials are held up causing delays in finishing, or some other problems where the company becomes indebted. If we like what has been done so far, we put up the finances, and for a percentage, take over the completion."

"Well, I think that would be speculating." He deliberately ignored my statement.

"We believe that Toronto is really going places. There is a lot of Yankee money here now, and probably a lot more to come." Chuck looked over his shoulder, as we chatted, to watch a woman step up to play the piano. The dance floor filled within minutes.

"I must try and call home again. Please excuse me." I climbed the stairs painfully and placed a second call to Susan, but no answer at our flat.

My sudden interest in Chuck caught me off guard. Three years had gone by since John's death, and I never once allowed my feelings to become any stronger than one would feel toward a friend. I waited a moment, watching him at the table, rhythmically moving to the music. I studied his tan corduroy suit, set off by a brown and yellow plaid sports shirt, neatly folded over the collar of the jacket. On his right hand was an engraved onyx, perhaps a family crest. His rugged features showed deep-set brown eyes, golden skin and thick black hair.

Retrieving my coin from the pay phone, I returned to the table.

"I really think I should be going. It's well past nine and I haven't eaten a thing since lunch and, to be frank, I'm beginning to feel the wine go to my head. If you would excuse me, Chuck, I'll be..."

"Oh, please, Miss. Don't run off. We haven't even got to know each other yet. Why, I was hoping to spend a little more time together. I'm sure the weather hasn't got any better. Come, we'll check it out together." Chuck assisted with my coat, and then accompanied me down the stairs to the side entrance. Pushing the heavy steel doors, we felt the howling winds pushing back. The freezing rain had now changed to hail, foretelling a long blizzard. I stepped back inside again.

"Why, Miss Francine, I believe this storm is here to stay for a while. Tell you what. Join me across the street at my place and we'll conjure up a meal fit for a hungry giant. How about it? Join me? This place is getting too rowdy for me, and I'm just as hungry as you are."

My heart skipped a beat, amazed by my own nervousness. Having no intentions of staying in the tavern, I couldn't see myself swept off my feet by this smooth talking American. Chuck recognized my dilemma. He assured me he did not propose to ruin our good friendship, and then patiently awaited my response as the boisterous singing, laughing and smell of smoke grew stronger.

"Well, I suppose it would be all right. Thank you, Chuck. I would appreciate getting something to eat."

We fought our way out into the storm, crossing the street to the gray brick building passed the barricaded road. Chuck gripped my arm as we reached the entrance of *the '4000'*. He swiftly opened the door. A tall slim security guard greeted Chuck by name and unlocked the enclosure leading to the elevator. The mirrored doors reflected my red cheeks and wind-blown hair. Chuck pushed PH button.

"Br-r-r. That's cold enough out there for Eskimos." His smile broadened as he unlocked the ornate, brass-handled door while I knocked the snow from my boots and I stepped inside. He helped me with my coat, hanging it in a spacious mirrored-door closet as I took note of the expensive décor. His worldly treasures included an oriental tapestry that hung on a wall next to the arrangement of brass trays that looked like they might have come from India. Soft gray leather sofas encircled a contemporary acorn fireplace in the center of the room against the black suede walls. Bar Stools constructed from bicycle seats, had pedals rigged on the sides of each. Large cactus plants and scattered silk pillows filled the corners of the eclectic room. I casually reclined in a womb-like black rattan-hanging chair and gazed around the room at the exotic pieces of African art.

He removed his jacket and proceeded to build a fire. Soon heat filled the room and the atmosphere softened with classical background music. Between the overgrown plants, I could see hail and sleet outside as Chuck poured me a glass of wine, and then raised his glass.

"Here's to you, a stranded fair lady. This will comfort you and warm your tummy. I'll just stir us up a little meal." He talked casually about his work and all his worldly travels. I was impressed. By comparison, I felt I had never been anywhere.

Moments later, I heard the banging of pots and pans and his distant muttering. The sounds emanated from the Hollywood-style kitchen, which opened up onto a sunken dining room at the far end of the apartment.

Intrigued, I curiously poked around, catching a glimpse of myself in the hall mirror where I tried to straighten my tangled hair, without much success and refresh my makeup. I went to tie back my hair when I felt his touch on my shoulder.

"Don't. Leave it down," he pleaded, running his hand underneath, loosening the curls. As he walked away, I became aware of feeling drained of any confidence, like a starry-eyed teenager on her first date. Nonchalantly, I returned to the dimly lit room and sat on a cushion close to the fire, entranced by the flickering flames.

Chuck waltzed into the room refilling my glass, and then sat down across from me. He casually propped his feet on the edge of the hearth.

"Cozy?" he whispered, between sips of wine.

I nodded and took a large swallow from the crystal goblet.

"Typical dinner tonight - steaks, salad, and a bit of garlic bread. Suit you ok?"

"Sounds delicious." I was so hungry I could have eaten a horse - well, sort of, I thought.

He chuckled, noticing my nervousness.

"I'll just pop them under the broiler, and we'll dive right in." He stood up and returned to the kitchen. Weakened by the intoxicating influence of too much wine, my eyes closed. I reached out to set my glass down on the unusually shaped glass and iron table, but I missed. The wine spilled all over the floor and the antique Persian carpet. Recovering from my stupor, I jumped and ran to find a towel to wipe up the mess. I carefully placed the goblet onto the table. Somehow, I misjudged and bumped his Orrefors vase and knocked it over. A crack shot across from one corner to the other like a shaft of distant lightning descending a darkened sky.

"Holy shit! What have I done now?" I gasped. With a shaky hand, I picked up the broken glass, looking around in desperation. A large pot caught my eye that held the cactus. I positioned the fragments into it and grabbed several magazines from a wall unit, placing them over the table's marred top. I heard Chuck call from the other room. Taking a last frantic look over the situation, hopeful of having covered my clumsiness, I stepped aside following the aroma of garlic now permeated the apartment. I couldn't decide if it was the odor making me nauseous or the wine. My reddened features veiled in the dim light of the room when I walked into the dining area, stumbling down the single step. I suddenly felt terribly hot, uncomfortable, and desperate to finish the meal without another catastrophe. Chuck served the steaks, well garnished with fried onions and mushrooms on wooden platters with the appropriate steak knives, of course. I winced at the sight of the enormous meal and waited for him to take a seat before starting. He chattered away, but I couldn't concentrate. He seemed to have lots to say.

He topped the wine glasses, once again, from a new bottle, and then offered some warm bread and a large helping of Caesar salad. As the food started to fill my empty stomach, I relaxed, but apparently not enough. Casually, shaking a piece of hair from my face, a thick lock flicked a piece of my salad, and a piece of romaine landed on the wall behind me. Feeling quite the fool, and not as polished as I had first hoped, I stood up and retrieved it, wiping the spot with my napkin. There was no way I could look his way, but I could feel that his expression had changed. He did not refer to the embarrassing incident. Barely able to digest the rest of my food, I heaved a definite sigh of relief when the meal ended.

While he cleared the dishes, he announced that he would serve coffee by the fire.

Watching the snow whip the trees and drift over stalled vehicles below, Chuck returned carrying two large mugs.

"Anything in your coffee, Francine?"

"No, thank you. I take it black." He stoked the fire before getting comfortable, and then reached for a bottle of Remy Martin, placing it on the edge of the table. The perspiration beaded on my brow.

'*Please,*' I mumbled to myself. '*Don't see the crack.*'

He shifted the magazines to the side, still not revealing the damage to the table, and set two liqueur glasses down. Quickly, I spoke to distract his attention.

"My car, I'm... ah... really worried about my car. I didn't actually get it pulled completely off the road."

"Oh, I'm sure it will be safe. It doesn't appear that anyone has got up that hill in hours."

"Yes, I'm sure you're right, but I couldn't bear it if it got hit. My Lord, it would take months to repair and cost a fortune."

"Why, I'm shocked! Why would you be so worried about such a thing? It's only a little storm and no one is using the road. Is it diamond-studded or something?"

"No."

"Well then?"

"It's a Ferrari, and I feel..."

"I beg your pardon? Did you say a Ferrari?"

"Yes," I winced, trying to sound matter-of-fact.

"My God, lady, did you win the lottery or something to have one of those?" Chuck's eyes rounded in surprise as he sipped his liqueur.

"Well, kind of, you might say something like that. I try to take such good care of it, and really would die if it got hit."

"Yes. I think I would too," he responded in amazement. We chatted about our work, and then I began to yawn uncontrollably. I closed my eyes and drifted into a very deep sleep. Chuck retrieved a small but thick quilt from one of the closets, wrapped it around me and carried me into his bedroom. Placing me on the oversized waterbed, he closed the door.

After ten, the following morning, I opened one eye, then the other, taking in the items of the unfamiliar room. I lay motionless, putting the previous evening's incident into perspective, checking my clothes. No sound came from the other end of the apartment. "Chuck?" I whispered. "Chuck, are you here?" There was no reply as I went to fetch my coat. A quick glance through the picture window showed overcast skies and a busy street below. As I turned to open the door, the tall, good-looking gentleman stood at the entrance.

"Good morning, Francine," he greeted. "Now, you weren't about to run out on me were you? Not even without a thank you first? Or leaving your phone number?" He chided, gently taking me by the arm and leading me back into the apartment.

"What time is it, Chuck?"

"Well, let's see," consulting his Rolex, smiling, "I'd say it is almost eleven."

"What! Oh, I must run, get back and change for work; my clothes!" I pointed to my wrinkled outfit.

"Yes, they are a wee bit tattered, but that still doesn't explain why you should rush off." He tossed a set of keys in the air toward me. Recognizing them as my own, I flipped out my hand to catch.

"I brought your car back here. Nice machine," he complimented.

"I must run, honestly. My job is important right at the moment, and I don't have a minute to waste." He grabbed my arm at the elbow.

"Francine, I mean it. I want your phone number, at least." I hesitated, and then stopped.

Taking a pen from the entry table drawer, he handed me an envelope on which to scribble.

"Chuck, I really appreciate all you've done and I enjoyed myself immensely last night. You are more than a perfect host. But..."

"Well, why don't you have some breakfast, or at least coffee before you run off?"

"No, I can't. I have to leave now. Another time." I smiled, and sincerely meant it. Chuck, who seemed to tower over me at that moment, held my shoulders, pulled me into his arms, and kissed me firmly. To my surprise, I responded. Our embrace became more than a goodbye kiss. Confused and flustered by my own emotions, a rush of excitement swept through my veins when he lifted my chin with his forefinger and tenderly swept his lips across mine.

"Until later, so long, precious," Chuck whispered, opening the door for me. I rushed to the elevator and when the door opened, I hesitated and turned for a last look, unknowing how our meeting would affect the lives of others. There's no such thing as a coincidence.

Several long days and nights passed as I concentrated on my project, trying to prepare it precisely for a final executive review. Chuck left the city, leaving word that he would call.

While at work, my patience had worn thin two weeks before my departure to Europe. I decided to find out whether my project was a go or shelved .

Early Thursday morning, I made my way down the narrow hallway to the Executive corridor where I noticed a small gathering outside the VP Sales and Marketing office. Somehow, I felt drawn to the area. A secretary, whom I had gone to night school with, approached me.

"Francine, can you believe this?"

"What? Carol, what is this all about?"

"Stan got a transfer to the U.S. in the new year. He just received a fabulous promotion and a Special Achievement Award for a new concept he presented to the VP of Marketing last week. He will report directly to the VP as National Support Manager with responsibilities for revamping all the company's food chains. I just can't believe it."

Gasping ... couldn't be what I was thinking. He couldn't have...

"Carol, does this have anything to do with proposed changes to the restaurant chain that would convert the whole North American concept into franchised family style restaurants?"

"Exactly. How did you even know? It won't be announced until..." she stopped. "Francine, is this the same project you were working on?"

"Working on?" I stammered, and then I leaned towards my friend, whispering, "Carol, it is my guess that son-of-a-bitch stole my research file, and presented my whole restructuring concept, in fact my whole marketing plan without consulting, discussing or briefing me."

Carol stepped back in awe as my temper flared, wondering what move I would make next.

Precisely at that moment, my boss, Stan, caught sight of me as the small crowd dispersed. His expression confirmed my suspicions. He didn't move. I confronted him in the open corridor. I glared into his small squinty eyes, ready to pounce.

His new position was now public. That gave him the opportunity to nod a sly acknowledgment as if disdaining my agitation. He walked away into his office. Shocked by the double-cross, I followed, demanding an explanation. Deep within, I had to admit that it was useless. His continual spying and his phony helping hand were nothing more than part of his master plan. He used me for uncompensated work to accomplish his ultimate goal. His gain was my loss.

Searching the depths of my despair, I yearned to make contact with the other managers who worked with me, but suddenly, returning to my cubicle, I sensed defeat. Voices came from the doorway.

"Hey. Are you ok?" Carol pulled up a chair. "I had no idea Stan was doing such a thing. I can't believe that he would do this to you."

"Me neither. I am so naive. All my life I have never been able to see what's right in front of my nose." I paused. "I trust too many people. I am so pissed off that I have been conned and manipulated once again! Will I ever learn?"

Carol consoled me. "Confront him again with the facts. Talk to the other managers. Don't give up."

"There's no use. I have already met with him. They don't want to see me whining like some poor sport. Who am I anyway, just a marketing analyst. They were probably all in it together. You know, Carol, this is the last straw. I've spent almost three years working my ass off for this goddamn company; working more overtime than anyone else on this project, and what the hell was it all for?" My voice trailed off.

We stared at one another, and then I straightened up, took out a sheet of letterhead and scribbled down my resignation. Placing it in an envelope, I marked it for the 'Personnel Office'.

"Carol, take care."

"What do you mean? What is that?"

"I quit! Right now! I am going to go home to pack and take an early vacation."

Tossing the envelope into a tray of correspondence, I left the building, never to look back.

Chapter 17
Moving On

Peter's new red and white Ford pick-up pulled up in front of our Victorian house. His rawhide jacket caught in the door as he jumped out from the driver's seat. Rushing through the snow covered walkway, he entered into the midst of a heated argument.

"Ok. Alright already. Hold it!" Peter shouted, turning aside, finding two suitcases placed on the loveseat. Silence. He tossed his jacket over the Boston rocker, and then walked around the room sensing the tension in the air. Opening the fridge, Peter reached for a beer as Susan summed up our discussion. After removing his ball-cap and downing a few gulps, he commented. "How can you turn your back on something you developed, and let some mousy bastard steal it from right under your nose? For the love of God, Frannie, come to your senses and take a good hard look at the situation," Peter pleaded, aware of Susan's sigh.

He appeared puzzled as I showed no fight left, and wasn't even angry anymore. Walking to the closet, retrieving my green leather coat, I placed it over my arm, and then turned to face my best friends.

"I fully intended taking this situation to the Chairman of the Board, but, I didn't." I hesitated, turning away as I spoke. "You see, I felt stabbed from behind and would have to fight a losing battle. Sure, you are right, it's not like me to give up what I rightly felt was mine, but, I don't have a snowball's chance in hell of proving my position. There was no discussion, plans, correspondence. The sneaky son-of-a-bitch knew exactly what he was doing. Now, I want to get away from all this negativity. I've just had it. I mean, honestly, I can't be bothered. It is what it is."

Peter could sense my misery, realizing much more happened than I was willing to admit. He knew it was time for me to leave, fly across the water as if cleansing my spirit. Peter smiled and nodded his approval.

"In fact, I have more than just a trip in mind." Susan met my gaze but said nothing. Instead of getting her own place with Gregory, she could just stay on without me because my trip would be an indefinite one. I had made contact with Leonard and in a few hours, I would be flying out. Both friends stared in utter amazement.

"I don't know what to say," Susan blurted out. "I mean this is all happening so fast. One minute you're on cloud nine and your job is your career, your whole life, and then the next day we're standing here saying goodbye and don't know if or when we will ever see you again. What the hell?"

Peter held me, and then we hugged. Unexpectedly, a harsh bang sounded at our door. No one moved until the second knock. Susan opened it. A tall dark-haired man looked down at a piece of notepaper.

"Hi there, Ma'am. Would you be so kind as to tell me if a Miss Francine Harrison lives in this here building?" The deep southern drawl gave his identity away, and Sue's expression mellowed.

"Why, Chuck. We've spoken several times on the phone." She extended her hand. Peter heard about Chuck from Susan, and now he cast a curious look in his direction waiting for an introduction. The handsome American entered the room as I slipped into the kitchen. Susan made introductions.

Looking at the luggage, Chuck commented. "Is someone going on a trip? Hope I didn't come in and interrupt something."

Peter understood my nervousness. He snickered.

"You know, I have the strangest feeling, honey, that you have been avoiding me." Chuck gazed deeply into my eyes when I entered, grinning boldly. "Now, if you think you are going to get away from me again, you are sadly mistaken. Why, you little scoundrel, you owe me for a cracked tabletop, one dead cactus plant that had been saturated with wine, and a new vase."

"What?" I reacted, innocently. "Who, me?" I grinned.

"Yes, you, Miss Harrison. If you think for a moment that I could be remotely interested in a clumsy, scatterbrained dame like yourself, you've got to be..."

I swung around, surprised by his harshness. "Just a damn minute, buddy," I responded.

"What I was about to say is that you're bloody right I'm interested." He took my hands in his. I blushed, aware of Peter and Susan laughing in the background.

"Listen, Francine, you know that I have been trying to get hold of you," he whispered. "I mean, I have called, and no reply. I go to your work - no Francine Harrison. I get the impression you are giving me the brush-off and I don't like that without an explanation." He paused, and then continued. "Is there something wrong?"

"Why, not at all," I lied. "I'm going on a vacation to Holland to visit my brother and his wife."

"Wonderful. Then, I can expect you'll be back after the holidays?"

"My idea was to take a little longer stay than that," I continued.

"Yes. A little longer," added Susan, knowing that I was not ready for Chuck's assertiveness.

"When does your flight leave?"

"In a couple of hours."

"Well then, that gives us time for a drive and a drink at the airport. Let me assist with your luggage," he commanded. No one seemed to notice my argumentative expression.

Peter came to my side and whispered. "Fran, let's say goodbye here and now. We know you are leaving. It will be better this way." He embraced me tightly. "I love you, take care. Please keep in touch. Remember, we have a history together, eh?" We separated as Chuck patiently watched. No tears of sorrow, as things were happening too fast and I was doing something that I felt I had to. It was now or maybe never. Ready to stand up and take hold of my life, for the first time ever, I drew on inner strength as I was about to venture into the unknown.

I reminded Peter to take special care of SnoMann, for both of us.

Susan approached in tears. We hugged goodbye, realizing we both had changed. She instructed me not to forget those back home.

Turning, I faced Peter. "Here, take care of my baby for me. A good grease and oil change will do it good once in a while." I winked, tossing him the keys to the Ferrari, and then closed the door as Chuck and I left the building.

After a quiet drive to Terminal 1 at Toronto International Airport, I checked my baggage at KLM, allowing time to relax with my escort over a cocktail in the lounge.

"I gather, that by giving up the Ferrari, your trip will be more than a few weeks?" Chuck inquisitively twirled his napkin around his finger.

"Yes, you gathered right. I don't have any definite plans, but a wallet full of traveler's cheques and an unlimited amount of time to visit scores of places. After that, I suppose I will settle and get a job."

"If, by any stretch of the imagination, you would like company during your travels, this fella here sure could use a good long holiday. Perhaps in Spain or the Canary Islands?" he offered openly.

"Sounds like fun!" I replied. "But, I'm not really into that kind of relationship, at least not yet. I'm not saying that I'm waiting for Prince Charming to sweep me off my feet, it's just that being an occasional mistress isn't my thing."

"Well, honey, what makes you so sure that I'm talking about an occasional lover? You know, after you're playing hard to get, I have this growing desire to be with you more and more." He laughed, quietly, touching my hand.

"Listen, Chuck. You are a super person, and extremely handsome. I'd love to go to the Canary Islands with you. It is a tempting proposition and I'm sure you are more than sincere in your intentions. It's just that I need some space. I want to have one hell of a good time without any involvement. You move around a lot with your business, all over the world, I'm sure. You're very experienced, which I am not - not yet anyway. Give me some time, and I'll be your match someday." I giggled.

Chuck grew interested the more I pushed him away. We waited for the departure call. Shortly after ten, my flight was ready to board. We paid the bar bill and he accompanied me to the loading platform. He left me with a passionate kiss, which betrayed his arousal.

"Francine, I really like you and I don't even know you, even though we did spend the night together."

"Don't bother to remind me, thank you."

"Well, I'll remind you once again. I have a tendency to somehow pop up out of the blue, almost anywhere."

"Uh-huh." I laughed.

"That I do. I am all over the world at one time or another. If I can find you, I'll be there some time or another. Just you wait."

"I think I can wait."

"Perhaps one evening in Vienna or Paris, we shall run into one another."

"Perhaps." I turned away to hide my smile. "Listen, Chuck. All kidding aside, I have been through quite a lot over the past few years and right now, all I want is space. I need to get over one ..." I stopped.

"One what?"

"One incident that I haven't been able to handle. I lost someone very dear to me. It is a long story. Perhaps one day in the Canary Islands, when the mystery unravels, we can talk once again over coffee." I turned to leave. "That is if you ever turn up again in my lifetime."

"Well, Miss Harrison, whatever it is that still bothers you, I am sure that you will handle the situation. I just hope your mystery will be solved before our next meeting, and whoever he was, he was a fool to leave you."

"Well, let's just say, he had no choice." I smiled as he touched my hand once again. His body pressed tightly and I responded.

As we parted, he whispered, "Francine, I'll come whenever; just call. Give us a chance." Chuck reached into his overcoat pocket and retrieved a business card, which he scribbled on. "Here, don't lose it. This number will find me wherever I am, and I mean it. When you are ready, I'll be there." He tucked the card into the side pocket of my purse. Caressing my cheek with his hand, he kissed me quickly. For the second time, I turned to leave, and disappeared from view.

The long flight gave me time to contemplate the past three-and-a-half years. I loved my friends and knew we would miss one another, but it was time to de-stress, relax and enjoy time with family. I once read that crossing water was a form of cleansing, so I figured I'd be 100% after the flight.

The plane landed on time and without mishap, followed by a speedy train ride into Central Station in Den Haag. Searching throughout the crowds, I recognized Leonard's curly hair and ran to him with open arms. We had not seen one another since Montreal. As we departed the station, the bright blue skies were almost painful to the naked eye, so I slipped on my dark glasses, chatting rapidly. Leonard led the way to his small green Fiat parked in the distance.

"You certainly travel light for someone who travels indefinitely," he joked.

Leonard handed me a street map to follow as he drove out from the core of the city, which I noted was remarkably clean. He pointed to a particular area on the map. "We live over here; see Westduin Park, just off Van Poot Laan."

Holland's capital city seemed larger than I had imagined as we headed northwest to the suburbs, passing numerous historical landmarks and ancient buildings. Our twenty minute drive took us north off President Kennedy Laan, onto Houtrust, passing a large arena, Houtrusthallen.

I pointed my finger toward a large building. "Oh, that's our hockey arena," he explained. "Raak is our team. Not exactly the caliber of game we grew up with back in Toronto, but it's enjoyable. I'll take you there after the holidays." I nodded.

We passed several low-rise apartments, turning into a crescent of small homes, all with the same color brick and similar in every detail. Leonard steered into the driveway of number sixty-three.

"I really like living up in this neck of the woods because my sailing club is only five minutes away, just off Houtrust Weg."

"Yes. Lots of water around. I never imagined it like this."

The front door was appropriately ornamented with a decorative wreath of holly. I recalled their home in Montreal where they enjoyed setting up for the festivities.

Before Julie arrived home from work, I had unpacked, showered, and taken a short nap.

Dressed in warm jeans and a bulky wool sweater, I joined my family in their living room. My searching glance at Julie brought yet another pleasant surprise. She was pregnant. They had once told me that they weren't planning on having a family, but soon learned they came to accept the idea. Julie explained further over dinner that the expected birth date was the end of April, and pleased that I would be there sharing this time with them. Once again, I thought it was amusing how these weird connections happened in my life. I knew my intuition was stronger than most, but didn't listen to it as often as I should. I was in the right place at the right time.

At the end of January, Leonard and I planned our night to see a hockey game. Julie tired quickly, and by eight o'clock was ready for bed, so she preferred to stay at home.

Arriving at the arena early, I read the billboard that displayed the night's program, featuring the London Lions vs. Raak.

"London?" I questioned, hunting for our seats five rows up from center ice, directly facing the opposing team's bench. He clarified that the players were mostly Canadian and not Brits. The league included teams from Finland, Austria, Luxembourg, the Soviet Union, and also Czech and Swedish teams. Their style of hockey was more like Canadian Junior hockey, very fast and rough; not a lot of finesse or good stick-handling.

We didn't have to wait long before the teams stopped circling the ice and took their places for the playing of the National Anthems, and then the game began.

Nearing the end of the second period of play, the game stopped when three players started pushing with high sticks. At the south end of the rink, an obvious tripping penalty missed by the referee provoked the players into a fight, bringing others off the bench. They swarmed onto the ice as fans leaped to their feet, screaming. The coaches shouted hoarsely from the bench as sticks and gloves littered the ice.

My attention turned to one of the coaches, pacing back and forth, calling the referee names and shaking his fist. He removed his glasses and rubbed his brow while I watched. I became dumbfounded by my discovery. I jumped to my feet along with hundreds of other screaming fans and focused solely on the opposing team's coach. Leonard was too involved in the fight to notice. Whipping his program away, unrolling it, I searched for the list of players' names, frantically turning the pages.

"Leonard, Leonard. Take a look over there ... behind the London Lions' bench! Look! Who is that guy?"

He shot a quick glance toward the players' bench, then back to the fight. "No one I know," he answered.

"Yes it is, look ... look here," I tapped my finger onto the open page of the program.

"Leonard ... Leonard. Damn it! I don't believe it!"

"What? Frannie, what is it? Or, who is it?"

"Coach, the coach is Bradley, you know, BJ Nichols. Can you believe it?" I smiled excitedly, taking a closer look at the man pacing behind the bench across the rink.

"BJ?" Leonard stood up for a better view. Although he did not recognize our old neighbor's facial features, he knew from the overall appearance that the possibility was there. He took back the program.

"Well, I think you could be right. I'll be damned!" he exclaimed.

165

"Boy, that guy is something else! After his injury at the high school track meet, they said he was finished with sports, but he actually found a way back, right there at center ice." I laughed in disbelief.

The fans returned to their seats as the referee untangled players from the fight and awarded penalties. The remainder of the game progressed smoothly. My eyes stayed fixed on my friend from Toronto. I decided that I would try to find him after the game, which ended in a five-all tie with numerous penalties for rough play.

As the fans left their seats, we followed in step to the entrance of the dressing rooms. We spotted several Raak players leaving the stadium. Leonard approached one, asking where the London team had gone. We were directed to the Lido on Zeekant.

We arrived to find a crowd of people celebrating in a darkened room. Leonard directed me to the bar where he asked one of the serving attendants where the hockey players sat. Following instructions, we crossed the dance floor and walked through to the dining area noticing several players seated at a long table against the back wall eating dinner. I scouted each of the players, not spotting the fair-haired man I sought. One of them caught my eye, saying, "Hey there, cutie, if you're looking for a seat, I can certainly share this one." The others snickered at the comment. I blushed, easily pulling back as he reached for me.

"Ah-h, thanks anyway. I'd love to join you all, but I'm a friend of BJ Nichols, and I was looking for him. We were at your game tonight and thought I might catch up with him here."

The player looked puzzled. "Who? BJ? Oh, you must mean Brad." I nodded. "Well, you were right to come here. This is the right place, but not for him. He'll be back at the hotel. He doesn't appreciate the strippers while eating his steak." The team laughed, turning to one another.

"Humm, too bad."

"I can give you the address, and if he's not available, why I'll give you my room number, and..."

"Ah, gee – thanks," I kidded, "but I really am stuck on finding him." I winked, playfully.

Leonard asked, "What's your schedule? Do you play any more games here, or are you leaving right away?"

"Between the middle of December and the end of February we'll have played thirty games in eight countries. We leave here for

Czechoslovakia, Austria, Yugoslavia, Switzerland, and then West Germany - let's see." He pulled a crumpled piece of paper from his pants pocket and smoothed it along the table's edge, reading it. "So, we don't actually leave here until Thursday, with another game on Tuesday. No. No, let me see. We will be playing Monday night, and then leave Tuesday. Right guys?" The player looked for approval.

He gently gripped my arm, pulling me close. "Miss, I tell you what. You come by the arena tomorrow morning. We have an early practice and should finish by eight, and you will see him before he leaves. He has to go to Rotterdam for the weekend to pick up a new player," he smiled, giving my hand a tender squeeze.

Leonard thanked the players for their help, coaxing me to leave.

"Hey Miss, what's your name?" One player shouted as we departed.

"Leonard, thanks for your help. I owe you one," I whispered as we headed home.

Saturday was cold with cloudy skies. Everyone was asleep when I finished my morning brew and started out to the arena.

Finding the main entrance doors locked, I fussed around in an effort to get in, noticing a bus parked at the back. I rushed down the driveway in search of an open door. No such luck. However, as I was about to turn away, a dark figure shuffled up and I walked right into him.

"Well, well, I couldn't think who the guys were talking about. Hey! It's great to see you, Frannie. Ah-h, Frannie." BJ whirled me up into his arms with a warm hug.

We exchanged small talk for a moment as I explained how I found him.

"Come with me and have some breakfast. You look fantastic! I mean it. You get better as the years go by." He smiled, taking my hand as we crossed the busy street to a small restaurant.

I retraced the events leading up to my arrival in Holland as they served a second cup of coffee and we finished our food. He had read about John's murder in the paper and then heard more details from Susan's boyfriend, Kenny, about a year later when he was visiting in London.

Placing brown sugar crystals into his coffee, he stirred, and then offered them to me. "I must admit, I couldn't be happier to see anyone else right now." I accepted the compliment.

A look of wonderment swept across his brow. "Frannie, I know this is really out of the question, but I am going to ask it anyway." BJ turned to look at the clock on the wall as the kitchen helper cleared our plates.

"I have to take the train to Rotterdam in another hour or so, to meet a player coming in from London. He is crossing the channel on the Hoek Van Holland. What I was going to... would you like to come? It would be fun to spend some time together and catch up on the past few years before I have to head off again. I don't expect to be back in London for several weeks. How about it?" He waited patiently for my response. I had to get in touch with my feelings. There was a reason that we had met again. Stuff like this happens for a reason.

I gathered a few belongings without disturbing anyone at the house and left Leonard a note saying - *'Not to worry – going out of town for the night and will be back tomorrow. I am well escorted. See you...'*

The train station was not as crowded as I had remembered. As the sun broke through the scattered cloud patches, we arrived in Rotterdam. I followed him hearing all about the hockey team's need to pick up an up-and-coming star, hopefully, who would be Mark.

I listened to his nervous chatter as he led the way from the station. He was no longer *BJ* in his new profession. Bradley Nichols had a career. We climbed aboard a nearby tram that took us to our *pension,* situated near the Kunsthal museum. He checked the arrival time of Mark's train.

After a quick wash, I rejoined him in the lobby where I found a selection of tourist pamphlets displaying a few spots of interest. I suggested we eat at the harbor restaurant, the Euromast Space Tower, which promised a great view, and then take a walk on the boardwalk.

"In this cold weather? You must be nuts. There won't be any boats around this time of year," he explained. Noticing my disappointment, "Fine. We'll go there... in our snow suits."

Shortly after one-thirty, we ate in the rotating dome, above the city, with a breathtaking view of the canals, parks and buildings. We ordered a Heineken, sausages, sauerkraut and devoured the large servings. It was turning into a great day.

"Tell me, Frannie. What are your plans now? Are you going to settle in Den Haag or move on?" He quaffed his beer.

"I plan to stay here until Julie's delivery and help out for a few of weeks. Probably in June I will take off to do some traveling before I settle into a permanent job. Next week, I begin working at Madurodam with an English translation group, preparing for their spring tours through the miniature city, which opens in mid-March. I love it here. Europe is exciting and very different from North America. I want to see as much of it as I can before I leave."

"Yeah. I think I get your drift," Bradley nodded, wiping his mouth with his serviette. "This will be my last season coaching hockey. It takes so much of my time, and I have to make a commitment to the firm. We have an office opening in London this spring and will need to crack down, organize the place, and search out some proposals as soon as possible. We've done very well, in Birmingham, so far, and can finally say that Dad made a good decision when he made the move here; in fact, we all have done well. Nancy eventually moved overseas and started a small business of her own."

"The university buildings you've designed sound very impressive. I will have to make a point of checking them out when I get to the U.K."

"Do that. I mean, just make sure you come."

"Oh, I will. I'm not terribly bilingual, you know. I cannot stay here forever. I'd be lucky to survive on getting myself to the washroom, literally speaking."

"Yes, I know what you mean. Playing hockey in the Soviet Union was definitely a challenge, really put me in a bind once," he grinned, recalling an embarrassing incident.

"By the way, when you decide to look for a job, consider London and remember me. I'll do my best to help you out, whether you want to work for us or find you something else."

"Thanks, Brad, I'll remember that."

We finished off our lunch with a large piece of black forest cake, and then felt the need for a constitutional around the nearby park. Strolling comfortably, he found a lost ball and bounced it away as we jogged after it. I stumbled as I reached out for it; he landed beside me grabbing my wrists. Our child-like play turned into exhausted gasps. He pinned me to the ground.

"Gotcha now. I win. You'll never be able to get out of this one alive," he teased. He leaned closer, glancing at his watch. "Oh-oh! It's late, gotta run." He smiled, awkwardly, as he brushed the dirt from my clothes. We jogged to the edge of the park to hail a taxi before he drove off to meet Mark.

Following a quick shower, I called the lobby for their assistance in getting my coat cleaned. This took some time because of my poor language skills. They promised to return it by seven o'clock that evening. I flopped across the bed and in a matter of minutes dozed off.

Within a couple of hours, a pounding on the door startled me from a deep sleep. Realizing it was Bradley, I unlocked the door. He glanced over my body, covered in a thin cotton robe, tightly tied at the waist.

"Humm, now that's more like it." He winked. "Mark is waiting for us at the bar. Get yourself dressed and come on down. We will grab a bite to eat in the dining room. Do you think you can manage, or would you like my help?"

"Yeah, right! Out of here."

Within a few minutes, I joined them and we waited for our table. I found Mark quite nervous, and hoped that I wasn't the cause of his uneasiness. During our aperitifs, he excused himself from the table. I commented on his behavior. Bradley explained his nervousness lasted only until he put on a pair of skates. He appeared very shy, but then, he was only eighteen and this trip was a big adventure for him.

The team was in the midst of a European Tour, and not doing particularly well. They were hoping Mark would spark the players to get them going again as the Lions were a scramble team consisting of bits and pieces from other Junior teams back home or NHL farm clubs. Bradley was trying his best to improve the Lions. Mark returned, appearing frustrated.

"Boy, I am going to need a translator, for sure. They just sent me to the telephone and I had asked for the cigarette machine."

Nearing ten, our dinner ended and Mark was the first to leave, requesting an early night. Brad suggested some sightseeing before leaving in the morning. In the lounge, we sipped Jagermeister and danced, feeling comfortable in each other's arms.

"I'll get your coat for you. It's in my room. They delivered it earlier, sometime around six-thirty," Bradley commented as we walked to our rooms.

"And how many guilders is that going to cost me?" I asked when he delivered it.

"Well, I'll tell you what! It's my treat." His arms were quick to move, encircling my waist as he kicked the door shut. I let out a half-scream in surprise before he covered my mouth. He tossed me onto the bed playfully, leaping down beside me. We wrestled, pulling at one another. Arms, legs, and bodies thrashed about as he accepted a wee bite on his ear before we rolled off the bed onto the floor. Pinning me beneath his strong, athletic body, I gasped out of breath, laughing. Without further hesitation, he held me, kissing my neck and then caressed my lips softly with his.

"For someone who looks so sophisticated, you sure do play like a tomboy, you sweet thing." He whispered, carefully dropping down on top of me. He gently stroked my body and slipped his tongue past my lips. I could sense his longing and felt his firmness.

He dropped his arm to my thigh, drawing his hand between my legs, and pinned his hips tight to mine. We rolled to the side, without separation. He undid my blouse feeling me stiffen slightly as he kissed the nape of my neck. Gently caressing my body for several minutes, we relaxed. Feeling his growing desire, longing to respond, I craved the lust and satisfaction I had once known so long ago.

Bradley squeezed tenderly, as his swelling pressed against me and his movement soon became one yearning a night of impulsive lovemaking. I reached for him hungrily, fingering his back, pulling him closer, and responded to the exciting sensation. We peeled away the remnants of what separated us as we closed eyes, wrapping our legs around one another, drifting into a satisfied, relaxing daze.

The warmth of his being spiraled through me as I rhythmically responded to his movements and we accepted the energetic vibration of the kundalini experience. The spiraling twisted energy spun from the base of the spine to the top of my head, enlightening a new dimension, which lasted for the longest moment. An esoteric incident. Bradley lay by my side, relieved of his tension, eyes closed. A slight smile curled his lips as he floated into a gentle slumber. In the midst of the night, he heard me murmur 'Johnny'.

The sun shone through the crack between the heavily draped windows shortly after five am The stirring of my nude body next to his aroused his interest. He leaned my way kissing my bare arm and dropped his head to my navel. I moaned as Bradley stroked my skin and our foreplay progressed, filling us with erotic excitement. Yearning for still more, we united and became aware of our own private ecstasy. It all felt too familiar, as we fulfilled our own personal needs.

We lay in silence. He leaned over, kissing my ear. "It is almost seven and a perfect time for a morning run. That's when I meditate the best. We have time before breakfast." He pulled away from the tattered bedding as I stared into his hazel eyes, and ran my fingers through his wavy fair hair, pulling him closer to me. I kissed his lips sensuously. We parted.

"Brad. I have... so much to say to you, I..." There was an awkward silence.

"Never mind, I know more than you think." He withdrew from my clasp, dressed and left quietly.

Mark enjoyed sightseeing with us before we returned to Den Haag, leaving the remnants of my passionate weekend behind. The young hockey player relaxed, knowing we were his friends, saying I had been there to divert him from the pressures, which followed. I also enjoyed joking with someone nearly ten years my junior. I suddenly felt very mature.

By early evening, we returned to The Hague where the taxi dropped me off at my brother's house. Bradley stepped out for a final embrace and we decided to meet after the game, the following night.

On Monday, a cold, damp and cloudy winter's day, I worked at Muduradam Miniature Village. Following dinner, Julie asked if I would like to help decorate the nursery by choosing wallpaper and paint. We agreed to shop on the weekend. Leonard looked pleased, as he had once worried if Julie might have felt a bit resentful about our close relationship, but from our first meeting in Montreal we became special friends.

I cleared and washed the dishes, and then Leonard and I drove to the arena while Julie looked forward to resting with a good book.

The Raaks had drawn a capacity crowd of nearly 8,000 for the game. During the final period, the game changed, becoming wide open. The rough, hard checks caused numerous penalties. It was close to the halfway mark when they called the Lions for icing the puck. The play returned to the opposite end of the rink. From the face-off, a husky player from the Raaks, number eighteen, gave a blistering wrist shot which went right between the goalie's legs to make a 1-0 game. The spectators cheered wildly for the home team and threw paper cups, programs and things onto the ice, causing a delay in play until the debris cleared.

The Lions came right back and threatened to score as the Raaks went on the defensive with their one-goal lead. As the Lions took possession of the puck, passing it back and forth across center ice, slap shots and rebounds couldn't seem to get it into the net. With only minutes remaining in the game, Mark sidestepped a body-check and got a breakaway from outside the blue line. Dodging defense, escaping an offside play, he back-passed the puck onto the stick of his winger, who slapped it over the shoulder of the opposing goalie, which made it a 1-1 game.

Returning to the coffee shop across the street from the arena, I passed the time until Bradley arrived, full of the evening's game with encouraging comments on Mark's ability on the ice.

By the time we arrived at the hotel where the team registered, it was midnight. The Lions General Manager usually shared his room, but not that night!

Shortly after seven am, a commotion sounded in the hallway as each player took a deliberate rap on our door, or shouted a sly remark. We meandered arm in arm through the lobby, hesitant to say goodbye, before hailing a taxi.

"I'll keep in touch. You are my special girl, you know. We'll just say bye for now and see each other in London." He held me close, surrounding me in his warmth, and then I withdrew.

"I had fun. Good luck, and I'll be watching the papers for your games." As I bent over to climb into a taxi, I heard him whisper, "Nice ass, Frannie."

"Hey, boy! You ain't seen nothing yet."

"You mean there's more? I can hardly wait!" We laughed.

As the taxi pulled away from the curb, I saw him reach into his jacket pocket for his glasses. Experiencing a new kind of desire, a passion for life, I no longer felt intimidated. I remembered that someone from my past had once said 'always have the courage of your own convictions' - somehow thinking they were my Dad's words.

Bradley returned to the hotel and sat with the players already at breakfast. He rubbed his forehead thinking, "Now, how am I going to explain to Frannie that I have been living with someone. But, worse still, how am I going to tell Cheryl?"

Chapter 18
Growing Pains

Spring - 1973

For the fifth time on April 29th, a bouquet arrived at the Harrison household. Leonard enthusiastically ran to get it, beaming with pride as he took the enormous floral arrangement and placed it on the dining room table amongst the others. I called out for him from the nursery.

"Leonard, everything is ready up here now." I marched down the stairs watching my brother pace the floor.

"I guess it's time to go and pick up my little lady, or should I say little ladies? What do you think, Sis? Do I look good?"

"You sure do! And stop pacing; you will be the best-damned father in the whole world. Now, take it easy, I will have things set out and in order for your visitors. You attend to mom and baby." I hugged Leonard, affectionately, and kissed his cheek.

"Yeah, you're absolutely right. I'll be back in no time." He had paused at the doorway before he left. "It's all over. I can't believe I went through the whole delivery with her. What an experience! And, what a beautiful little girl. Do you like her name?"

"Oh, of course, I love it, Martha Faye Harrison is lovely. You picked the best from both families; Faye for Mom and Martha for Julie's Grandma. Now, be off with you," I urged and went to the kitchen to set out the trays for the food we had prepared. I was so excited about being part of the special event.

In less than five minutes, the doorbell rang; two cablegram deliveries. After I signed the register and gave the man his money, I tore them open. The first was from Julie's mother, detailing her flight arrival time and sending them love and best wishes. Apparently, Julie and her mother had never been particularly close, but Leonard explained that her mother insisted she visit for the first month after the delivery.

Placing the telegram next to the phone in their kitchen, so as not to lose it, I realized it was only another couple of days before my own departure as I didn't intend to stay around when the mother-in-law arrived.

I automatically opened the second envelope without seeing my name on it.

"*Miss Francine. Expecting your company to Luxembourg. Arriving Amsterdam Thursday - KLM 791 at 08:45am. Staying at the Hilton. Still trying. Chuck.*

I set it on the table and suddenly felt drained, remembering my trip several weeks earlier, in March, when I made a visit to London.

***

February had been miserable, wet and slushy, keeping everyone in gloomy spirits, yet I had received letters, phone calls and flowers from Bradley making my days much brighter. Routinely checking the newspapers for any report on the hockey games, I decided to take a few days in March to visit London and surprise him at their first home game at the Empire Pool in Wembley. Looking forward to our meeting again, I accepted Leonard's offer of a place to stay in Swiss Cottage.

Traveling via the tube to the arena, where I picked up a Lion's souvenir, it was music to my ears to hear the English language spoken again. I sat a few rows behind the players' bench and the game against the Prague All Stars was Lion's first game on home ice. A rambunctious group of fans filled the arena. When the Lions scored their first goal, I leaped from my seat. Mark caught a glimpse of me cheering as he skated to the bench for a line change. He did a quick double take, smiling.

During intermission, when I walked back from the *loo*, I passed a group chatting near the entrance. An unfamiliar woman's voice called out.

I turned, not recognizing anyone. Then, a woman touched my arm.

"Frannie, Frannie Harrison? How are you?" I stared for a brief moment. "I'm Nancy Nichols."

"My gosh, Nancy. I didn't even recognize you after all these years. Why, I am fine. What about yourself?"

"Doing well, thanks. What brings you to Wembley? I'm working in London and couldn't pass up the opportunity of seeing the Lions' play their opener. You know, being Canadian and all, it just wouldn't be right," she laughed.

"Brad mentioned in one of his letters to Mom that he met you in Europe someplace. Oh, I'm sorry, Frannie. Excuse me. Let me introduce you to Cheryl Patterson." Nancy introduced her friend. We shook hands.

Nancy inquired, "Are you with anyone?"

175

"No." I took a closer look at the attractive brunette standing next to Nancy. "I am staying with my brother in Holland for awhile and remembered Brad had mentioned their playing here in March. I was here visiting and thought it would be great to see them play again," I stuttered, awkwardly.

"Terrific!" Nancy looked up, catching sight of her brother. "Hey Brad!" she called through the crowd, but as I turned in his direction, I saw him abruptly walk the other away.

"Oh, for Pete's sake," Nancy mumbled.

"I hope it wasn't on account of me," said her friend Cheryl. Puzzled, but I didn't inquire as Nancy talked about her antique shop.

"I met Cheryl as a buyer for a jeweler and antique outlet, and in no time at all she became part of the family." The dark-haired English girl blushed.

"She does not mean that literally," Cheryl added. "You see, Bradley and I have lived together for a couple of years." Hearing these words, my eyes widened as I swallowed the last mouthful of my pop, trying not to choke or show my surprise.

"I think we should get back to the game," Nancy announced. "Hope to see you later, Frannie."

"Yeah, for sure," I replied. Stepping back into the rink, I stood at the top of the stairs, gazing vacantly toward the ice. I felt as though my world had just fallen apart. My stomach churned. One part of me wanted to turn and leave, and then another wanted to destroy him in front of his teammates. I became furious.

"Come on, Miss … either go seat yourself or move. You're blocking the way and holding up the line," a fan called, tapping me on the shoulder. I sat down.

The teams returned to the ice, circling in their own ends, as Bradley spoke with the General Manager of the team. Suddenly, I felt embarrassed sitting there. Bradley walked behind the bench and gazed my way, but showed no expression.

The game ended in a four-three win. Mark waved to me with his stick at having scored the winning goal, which I missed. I signaled back to him, showing some enthusiasm when he skated eagerly to the bench as his teammates congratulated him.

When I felt the urge to leave, I startled when Nancy's called. "Hey, where are you going? I hope you didn't think that you could get away without speaking to Brad first." We briefly discussed the game, about which I knew nothing.

Nancy looked closer. I could tell she sensed something when she bluntly asked, "And, just why is it that you are in London, again?"

"Visiting, being a tourist." I glanced down at the program rolled in my fist. At that very moment, a thundering sound of running steps came from behind.

"Frannie, fantastic to see you!" It was Mark. He blurted, excitedly, extending his arm in friendship. "Boy, oh boy, is it ever good to see a familiar face! Mind you, it is not Rotterdam, but London will be just fine. How are you? Have you seen Brad yet? Man, did he ever miss you during that European trip." My eyes widened, hoping the others had not made the connection.

"Ah, Mark! You are so sweet. I'd like you to meet Brad's sister, Nancy, and this is Brad's girlfriend, Cheryl." His face reddened as he shook hands, politely, and asked if they were going to join the players for a bite to eat. A few more uncomfortable moments, and then Bradley appeared. He hesitated. I smiled and ran my fingers across my forehead, partially covering my face, as he slowly descended toward the platform where we had gathered. Wishing I could have just disappeared, my curiosity got the better of me. Cheryl reached out to him as he approached. Mark leaned over and whispered, "Sorry, I really blew that one." I shook my head, indicating not to worry.

"Well, well," Bradley muttered. "A genuine fan club. What a surprising welcome home, eh, Mark?"

"Yeah, you could say that." Cheryl clung to Bradley's arm, telling him sweetly how much she had missed him.

Feeling uncomfortable, Mark and I casually stood by.

"Good game, guys. I am sure glad I made it. Didn't want to miss that first one on home ice. A little weak on defense tonight, but I imagine after all those bus trips you would be," I announced. Mark could see my dilemma and immediately came to my rescue.

"I see that all these ladies are more than enough for you to handle, Brad. Frannie's going to join me for a draught at *Dukes*, right lady? I prefer older women," he teased. Bradley reached for my arm, stepping away from the others.

"Will I see you later?"

"I'm afraid not. However, I am so glad I made your first game back. Like I said, it certainly was an exciting evening." My sarcasm was evident as I brushed by him.

Mark hailed one of London's shiny black cabs that drove us to the pub where several other players enjoyed a bite and a drink. A few comments passed regarding the change in my partners when I ordered a 'light and bitter.' One of the players asked me to join in a game of darts. My efforts were useless; I felt exhausted.

Saying goodnight, they offered to escort me back to the flat in Swiss Cottage where I was staying. I declined, thanking them for their hospitality and reached for my jacket. Mark assisted politely, and then walked me to the door where Bradley confronted us.

"Oh no!" Mark whistled. "This is where I disappear." He backed inside, leaving me in the doorway. The others stretched to peer in our direction.

Staring straight ahead, I was unaware of his touch.

"Frannie, give me five minutes."

"I'm not stupid. You don't need any five minutes!" I snapped, and then continued walking. "You need a goddamn lifetime." I stared directly into his eyes. "I have no hold on you. You do not need to explain anything. You have your life, and I have mine. I just didn't like being made a fool of, or was it my mistake? Was it just a one-night stand that we had?"

Brad closed his eyes, breathing deeply.

"Frannie. You know how I feel about you. That has nothing to do with what I want to say. Damn it, woman, just stop and listen to me!" he retorted.

Several passers-by turned to look. "Frannie, I didn't want it to happen this way. I wanted to handle one thing at a time. I have been away for a few months, and I didn't want to have to tell Cheryl on the phone - or in a letter. I wanted to let her know about us face to face when I got back."

"Yeah, something like how I got it. Face to face!"

"Look, we had lived together on and off for awhile, and I traveled more than half of that time. There was no real commitment between us."

"Well then, what's your problem? There is no commitment between us, either."

"Frannie, I was hoping that we had something special. Something more than any commitment could hold. I have always liked you and something has grown over the years, not a weekend. I know that I don't have to explain my feelings to you, now. I know I handled this wrong, but there was no time, no place for me to explain to either of you. I had no idea that we would hit it off so well. What we had was beyond anything I could have wished for."

"No, there never is time when you've got the bull by the tail. I mean, what was there to explain - one broad in London and another in Europe, both ready to jump whenever you called. Hey, boy, let me tell you something else. Stick it!" and I turned to walk away.

"Frannie, come on! Let's not be hasty. I'm not going to let you just walk out of my life. You mean too much."

"So does blood. And you've got mine boiling," I snapped again. Bradley wore out, he could not win and he knew there was no use trying.

"What do you want from me?" he asked, taking me by the arm.

"Honesty, for a start. You had time to level with me. Ah, what the hell. Why should I waste my breath?"

"Where are you going?" He rushed to my side again.

"Back to The Hague. I'll find a few others around without having to be two-timed by some immature fickle hockey jock!"

"Good God, Frannie, will you settle down? Come on, let's talk rationally."

"Sure, why not? I suppose you want to talk in bed."

"You're the one who suggested it. Not me!" he snorted.

"Come off it! Hey, we are still friends, Bradley Nichols. Just remember, that's all. Listen, I am no fool. I will need your help to get a job in a few months. You'll be a good contact, and you said you'd be setting up in London or is that off?"

"No, it is still on. After this series ends, I take over the London office, but, what I'm trying to say is that I don't want you for an occasional friend. Frannie, give me a break. Please."

"Where? Your arm or your leg, perhaps?"

He grinned. "You've got an answer for everything, right?"

"No. I sure as hell don't, or else I wouldn't have been sitting a few rows behind you tonight." He drew a deep sigh, thinking he had better give me time to cool down.

"Look, this is getting us nowhere. Let me call you tomorrow. Where are you staying?"

"Swiss Cottage." I waved for a taxi, rushing to the curb.

"So… where?" he persisted.

I climbed into the spacious cab, calling back to him. "Lovely way to see London! Alone and in the rain!"

I left London and returned to The Hague. A confused brother walking out from his garage greeted me.

"Short visit, wasn't it?"

"Visit? Who's got time to visit? I was not only greeted by his sister, but by his common-law partner, if you want to call it that." I slammed the cab door, joining him in the house. I brought him up to date.

Julie and Leonard listened to my tale of woe as I sipped on a glass of wine. Leonard checked the clock on the wall explaining they had some other news for me about a person named Chuck Connors who had called three times while I was in London. He was waiting for me to return his call. Julie said he wanted to have dinner when I got back in town and would send a Limo to pick me up. He was staying at the Holiday Inn on Haagse Schouwweg, Leiden.

I fell back onto the sofa, amazed at life's twist of fate. You shut one door and a window of opportunity opens. If there is such a thing as a spirit guide, then someone or some thing was having a field day with my life.

Leaving Chuck a message, I went upstairs, calling down, "I'll be in the tub and then washing my hair if Chuck calls back. Please tell him I will be ready." My brother and sister-in-law shook their heads in confusion.

At ten minutes past eight that evening, Leonard answered the doorbell with a curious wife at his heels. "I just can't wait to meet this one," she whispered.

"Good evening, y'all. I'm Chuck Connors. Is this the residence where I may find a Miss Francine Harrison?"

Julie's eyes widened as she gazed at the tall, well-built Texan standing on her front doorstep.

"Sure is. Come on in. I'm Leonard Harrison, Francine's brother. We spoke earlier on the phone, and this is my wife, Julie."

"Pleased to make your acquaintance."

Moments later, I appeared in a fitted black cocktail dress, gathered at the neck with a wrap-around bodice revealing more than a shapely curve or two. As I walked, the ruffled pleat opened at the side, exposing a slender leg up to the thigh. I wore my hair swept up one side and loosely falling over the opposite shoulder. Chuck was impressed, took my hand, and kissed it. "Pretty as a Southern Belle, Francine, simply lovely." I accepted his compliment as he assisted with my gray mohair cape. Leonard snickered as I turned to leave.

"Think you will be home tonight?" he whispered.

"Damn right!" I returned, sticking my tongue out.

"Chez Eliza on Hooikade," Chuck told the driver after reading a piece of paper, and then placed it back into his vest pocket, "then on to the Playboy Club." They waved as we pulled away in a black limo.

Julie clapped her hands. "That sister of yours is something else. I never saw that dress of hers before. I bet she bought it for London."

"Probably, but tonight will be good for her. She is still very upset."

A lingering, enchanted evening followed.

***

The front door of my brother's home opened. I heard the tiny whimpering of a newborn baby. Their life was about to change for the better. I assisted with Julie's coat, and then prepared a tray for them as we enjoyed God's new creation, sitting altogether. We had an enjoyable evening and the following day some neighbors dropped by to visit baby Martha.

My departure day was approaching. "You know, Frannie, it won't be the same without you, and all your misadventures. We quite enjoyed your little escapades, eh, Julie?"

"Sure did. Why, I never saw so many handsome men in such a short period of time, in all my life," Julie added, yawning.

I showed Leonard the most recent cablegram from Chuck, and then handed it to Julie. "Have a look here; this ought to take the cake."

"How about it, Missy? Are you going to join him? I hear it is an intriguing city, an ancient battleground. You'd love Luxembourg."

"Oh, I'm sure I would… just wondering how long our platonic relationship will last. It won't be much longer," I grinned. "Not if he has his way. Right now, he acts madly in love with me."

"… and that is only because he hasn't got you. Don't let his southern charm sweet-talk you into something you're not ready for. By the way, have you heard anymore from Brad?" Leonard asked.

"Not for awhile. He did send me his address and phone number in London,"

"When the time is right, just make sure you pick the one you love. You know, it will never be the same like you and John had it. That was first love and will never be repeated. Remember and cherish it, but don't waste the rest of your life with memories, either." Julie offered.

"Hell, she isn't eighteen anymore," Leonard commented.

"Well, she isn't thirty yet. There's no rush."

"What if she wants children?"

"So what? Doesn't mean she can't have them later."

"Hold on," I interrupted, laughing at them squabbling over my personal life. "I'm thrilled you both care so much, but I'm not in any position to make that kind of decision, but, of course, I will let you know when I am."

During the night, cries from the newborn quickly sent me to see if Julie needed any assistance, but she told me to go back to bed, where I tossed and turned. This was a new experience for all of us. Baby Martha was in control.

My baggage blocked the front entrance while I hugged my family and kissed baby Martha.

Retrieving a small package from my purse and handing it to Julie, I asked her to put it in Martha's room. She unpacked the picture and smiled, observing the photo of hot-walker standing next to SnoMann from a few years earlier. It had been my favorite photograph.

"Yes, and as she grows, we will make sure she knows all about Aunt Frannie."

"I'll keep in touch and write as soon as I know my forwarding address; most likely London. I'm going to miss you!" We hugged, and then I was off to the train station.

"Well, Leonard, back to our dull little life," Julie teased.

"Dull? How can you say dull? My women could never be dull. But, all the same, we'll just pray Martha's life isn't quite as eventful as her aunt's, just to be on the safe side."

"Yes. Just to be safe." A precious gurgling sounded as the door closed behind them. They would have the day to rest before Julie's mother arrived.

Chapter 19
Contract Killing

Toronto – 1977

As we reach our destination, Whittmore is waiting for Peter and I to arrive. Together, we drink our coffee at a nearby Tim Horton's before we continue our mission. He seems pleasant enough, but I'm sure he is aware of my nervousness. While his mood alters slightly, he bends forward and speaks just above a whisper. I can feel my stomach begin to churn.

"Francine, Peter has helped the police with our investigation for a long time as you are well aware, and kept certain information confidential as we requested. Now, it's time for you to know the name of the person responsible for the death of your fiancé." I begin to tremble. "The person who Newman identified as his contact and who actually contracted the murder of John Mencini was none other than Robert Sharp."

"Oh, my God!" Gasping for breath, I feel faint as I can hardly believe what Whittmore reveals. Uncontrollable emotions rush through me. I experience shock, anger, and then all of a sudden, nothing. No one says a word. The waiter puts the bill on the table, which is swiftly paid.

I need fresh air and want to think for a few minutes, so I leave the room in a hurry. The information is overwhelming.

It takes me longer than a few minutes to regain my composure before Peter and I continue on our way to the racetrack while Whittmore waits to hear the results. We are less than ten miles away from making connection.

"A lot of crap about John is about to surface." Peter explains, breaking the silence. Dumfounded by how he kept the secret from me, I snap back.

"Alright, already! I know! I have heard it over and over. He was not the person I thought he was. I realize that. Don't worry. Nothing will surprise me anymore." I take a very deep breath.

"Don't count on it."

Peter maneuvers his way into the backstretch where several large horse trailers are pulling out. The Woodbine meet ends in three days and the thoroughbreds will move south to their next racetrack. He wheels his truck into the barn area where he stables his horses, and then glances toward me, noticing that I appear extraordinarily calm. He smiles. "The show is on, kid. Ready?"

Peter checks the time and listens for the call to bring the horses to the paddock, and then he equips Bob's horse for the afternoon's race. Nonchalantly, he explains that Marathon Runner has raced too often, only because the owners want to see him run regularly. I notice some nervous tension as Peter continues with his duties checking the stalls to see if the groom topped up the water buckets.

Hearing the call in the distance, "The horses are at the post." I swiftly turn around. "They're off!" The familiar words echo in my mind as it's been years since I heard the call, and feel a sudden nervousness thinking of our days with SnoMann. It is their inbred desire to compete and strive to reach the finish line first. So much history flashes through my mind.

A groom from another stable returned from watching the race.

"Looks like it could have been a dead-heat, Pete. A real close one. Photo finish for sure," he calls out. Peter glances at his watch, nervously. Another groom leads Bob's horse, Marathon Runner, out onto the pavement. Peter takes a rub-rag to wipe dust from the horse's coat, then combs his tail and mane as a new black Lincoln pulls slowly alongside the stable. Peter motions to back away.

Robert Sharp steps from the limo. He looks down toward the ground as he approaches. Showing signs of age, he exudes a certain distinction, no longer resembling the 'Bob Sharp' I once knew when I was a hot-walker.

"How's he doing, Pete?" Sharp indicates the liver-chestnut standing nearby.

"Fine, Sir. He is not as alert as he was the other day, but other than that, he is holding his own."

"Good." Bob walks around the horse, strokes his neck and looks into his eyes.

"I know, old boy, you're over-raced. No animal should have to run as often as you do." Peter watches the man closely, feeling uneasy.

"Everything all right here, boys?" he calls to the grooms before returning to his car. Unexpectedly, he stops. We are face-to-face but standing at a distance. Bob does a double take.

"Oh, my God! Frannie, Little Britches!" He holds out his arms as he walks toward me. I swallow hard, ready to make my entrance. My insides are trembling as I try to calm.

Smiling sweetly, I step forward, with a heavy heart, one of the hardest tasks I am faced with. "Mr. Sharp, how are you?" We hug. "It is such a pleasure to see you after all these years."

"Frannie, you are lovely. Here, let me take a good look. You were a skinny bit-of-a-thing, but how you have developed." He gives me an affectionate hug. "It truly has been a long time." He rubs my hand in his. I force a weak smile.

"You know, I thought I saw you here at the track a few weeks ago with Pete. I saw him driving the Ferrari, but wasn't sure." He hesitates. "It was a *déjà vu* thing."

"You have done miraculous things. I have followed your success in the papers over the years," I lie, smiling.

"Why, thank you. I became involved in other endeavors, but the horses are still my first love, as you well remember." A groom passes, leading the gelding to the track at the call of the third race. "Please, will you join me while I watch this race? Then, if you have time, I'd like to take you to dinner. We have so much to chat about. A lot has happened over the years."

"Yes, it certainly has. I'd love to spend some time with you. I'm staying across the street at the Ascot. Perhaps we can stop in there before dinner while I change into something more suitable, and we could have a drink."

"Sounds like a plan. Come, we'll go over to the Clubhouse." He escorts me around the car and opens the door. Sitting down into the luxurious leather, I smell the aroma of Havanas.

During the next hour, I face frequent interruptions while we make conversation. His popularity is a clear indication of his financial success. While he speaks with one politician, I excuse myself and rush to the ground level to place a *combine* bet on Marathon Runner. Peter is waiting for me.

"Well, what's up?"

"So far, so good. There is no hesitation on his part. I told him I am staying at the Ascot, like we planned. We are heading over there for a drink, soon. I will change clothes, and then we will go for dinner."

"Perfect! Remember, just pace it slowly. See you later." Peter hurries back to the paddock and watches the horses enter for the third race. I return to the Club House.

"Did you place a bet?" Bob inquires, interrupting his own conversation. I confirm as he makes introductions. Our discussion turns to his recent success with his horses.

We watch Marathon Runner as Bob explains how the owners don't care anything for the animal. I agree with whatever he says.

The horses are quick to load in the gate. It is flashback time. My stomach tightens as I take another deep breath watching them break. The pack of seven runs together for almost a quarter of a mile. I see by his cumbersome stride that Marathon Runner is hurting as they head down the backstretch. Still displaying a big heart and natural instinct to race, he runs his hardest even when boxed-in and ends up finishing third.

He limps from the track under the watchful eye of Bob. I figure the freezing wore off. It sickened me to see a horse suffer when I know that his trainer predicted the results. Why Bob would accommodate the owners over the safety and health of the animal was beyond me. There were some things I would never understand, yet, I knew that was how owners became unfaithful. As a watchful trainer heard the rumors about demanding owners, he would approach them directly. The trainer promised better results for them in his barn. I had seen Bob do the same thing to increase his stable. He guaranteed a cost savings to train and house the horses, but then again charged them extra for vet bills, morning workouts, and traveling expenses that never occurred. It's in bad taste for an owner to switch trainers.

Following the race, Bob proudly escorts me through the oak doors of the Paddock Room at the Ascot Hotel, finding a table in a dimly lit corner. The bar is in full view from where we sit. As he orders our drinks in his polished manner, several men pass by acknowledging him, and giving me the once-over, but his full attention focuses on me.

"Alright, tell me how things are going for you."

I sit up tall; straighten my red cashmere blazer and brush down my Levis. My eyes fix on his. "Fine, really. I plan to marry next summer and settle into family life for a change." I explain.

"That's wonderful. Congratulations! We were all worried about you after John's death. You two were so very much in love."

"Yes. It took a long time. Once the truth became apparent, about all the crimes and the lies I'd been told, I wasn't too long realizing that I was better off. Who knows how it would have ended?"

"Frannie, that pleases me. I never thought I would hear you say anything against John. You both were from different sides of the tracks, and that wasn't too hard to see for any of us."

"Yes, you're right. I guess I was a follower and wandered into Yorkville and into his life. Whatever he said or did, I was a believer." I inhale deeply to remain calm. "It's hard to look back now and admit how I trusted someone so much. He withheld a lot from me, I suppose, like several other people."

"Yes, Frannie. Those are very true words. He did mislead us, but truly, there were times when I missed him, desperately. You must understand he was like a. . ."

"I know, Bob. I know how close you were. Just like family - like Karen." I watch his expression immediately change.

"That girl gave us stress. You know, I have never told anyone this, but we were very close when she was a child, which was why I allowed her around the racetrack when she was young. For the life of me, I nearly dropped over when John let her ride SnoMann." He pauses for the longest moment. "Frannie, it shattered my faith in him. He destroyed my marriage, shamed me so, that I've not faced her since that day."

"Bob, no! You couldn't have held a grudge that long." I force a look of bewilderment as it becomes hard to hold my tongue. I want to scream that the only reason he's pissed off is because he never got to cash in on the bet. John had overruled the jockeys who never expected such a betrayal from Bob's stable.

"It wasn't just a grudge, Frannie." Bob finishes his drink, and waves the waiter over to our table to order another double rye and water.

Hesitating a moment, then I ask politely, "Did you read about Karen's wedding in the newspapers awhile back?"

"Yes, I did!" He gazes across the room.

"She is gorgeous and the man she married is a terrific guy. I have known him for a few years and have no doubts, whatsoever, that they'll make a great couple." A slight smile crosses his face. "Honest, Bob. We spent some time together in London and when she left England, he was with her. He's from. . ."

"Yes, I read all about him. Very successful American, but your words suit me fine. I have always admired you and would not doubt what you say.

"I want to ask you something about this trial coming up. I am sure that's the reason you are back in Toronto and I wonder if you're prepared for it?" My stomach quivers as it takes every bit of strength not to leap across the table and strangle the man who murdered the love of my life. I observe him very closely.

"Not a problem, like I said, it was a long time ago. Now that I have heard all the bad, it certainly overshadows any good I thought was in him, especially after listening to you." I lie, again.

"Hated, despised him. John took every bit of love I had for him and destroyed it, and then he used everything I taught him and turned it against me, and..." He stops, stares at me. I sit very still. He rolls his empty glass in the palms of his hands as he glances down at the table. I sense someone approaching as my heart begins to throb. Bobs dark eyes look up.

"Sorry to bother you guys. I was just over at the bar and noticed you in the corner."

"Hi Pete," we say in unison.

"I thought you'd want to know about Marathon."

"Please, excuse me, I'll let you discuss whatever it is you have to, and I'll go change. I won't be long. That is if you don't mind?"

"Certainly, go right ahead. We'll wait," Bob encourages.

Leaving the room, I head toward the lobby, still trembling, to find my denim duffle bag that Peter placed beside the wall phone. I check the time on the clock near the reception desk.

Peter gives details to Bob regarding the crippled thoroughbred lying in its stall too sore to cool out.

"Give him a couple of *butes* at feed time and he'll be on his feet tomorrow. We'll take a closer look at him then."

Peter sits down. "How do you think Frannie is doing?" He tries to ask innocently, rubbing his sweaty palms together beneath the table.

"Beautifully. If truth be told, she has matured and is more sophisticated than when we first met; what ... ten - eleven years ago?"

"You're right about that."

"I am amazed, you know, Frannie wasn't even fazed in the least about this trial. I asked her some questions and she admitted it's been a mistake on her part. You must remember how she used to act, like a star-struck teenager. It made me feel good that she realized that John was nothing more than a bum. So glad to see she has gone ahead and found someone else, although it took her long enough. John would have only destroyed her innocence, turning her into something she's not. It's amazing … all the lives he touched, damaged and even destroyed. We were all affected in some way or another."

Peter agrees, listening to Bob drone on about the past. His heart aches and he can't respond because he loved John like an older brother.

"You're right. He conned me into doing things I would have never even considered," Peter explains with convincing overtones, and then checks his watch, knowing Bob is agitated.

"Bob, I got to take care of Maxwell and his buddies drinking at the bar. We don't want them to race Marathon again for a while. As soon as I take care of their drinks, I will get right back to you." Peter hustles to the bar, leaving Bob tapping his pen on the edge of the ashtray.

A short man, who seems to come out of nowhere, approaches Bob's table. He is wearing an unbelted gray-cloth trench coat with a well-worn hat tilted over one eye. Clean shaven and walking with a slight limp, he pulls out a chair turning it around, taking a seat, straddling it. Bob raises his brow, looking up from the table. He squints into the shadows until he recognizes the person.

"What the fuck are you doing here?" he whispers, leaning across the edge.

"I didn't know you hung around classy spots like this, Bob, or I wouldn't have come here," Newman gloats. "I only wanted to come over and thank you for releasing me."

"Listen, Smoocher, it's only temporary, remember?"

"Oh yeah, I remember. I remember a lot of things."

"Well you ought to just remember one thing more, before you go and think about some crazy ideas about popping off. It is your word against mine and don't forget it."

"No-o-o I won't. Hey, Mr. Sharp, nobody would ever believe me, anyway. I ain't gonna waste my breath. I mean, I was the one who pulled the trigger on that innocent kid."

190

"Bullshit! Don't give me that crap about innocent young boy. You know as well as I do that he was mixed up with the mob, and if you didn't do it, someone else would."

"Yeah, but it was you who comes to me, remember? Not one of your gamblers."

"I remember. I also remember we were both in a drunken stupor for days. After I came back from the States and found out what that bastard had done; screwed up the gamblers biggest bets, stiffed the jockeys, and used my daughter as part of his ploy. Then, he bet mounds of money, not only at the bookies, but through my 'House' account, which he was not to use. John took everything that had taken me years to build and shredded it to pieces. I was lucky you were drinking with me, or I would have probably gone and done it myself. You, Smoocher, were at the wrong place at the wrong time."

There is a pause in the conversation. A waiter interrupts with the drink Bob ordered earlier.

"Yup. John literally pulled the plug on your organization, didn't he? He knew all about your falsifying documents and papers, and all about selling horses that had great racing forms, by stiffing them to innocent buyers. Selling a useless ringer, or unraced horse with matching body markings that never got tattooed. Hey, you even sold Wellington Whiz to three different owners. You see, he was your shadow, Sharp. John only did what you taught him. Fixin' races, shooting-up horses full of drugs, dealing with the heavies, the big gamblers, bookies, riders and the vets. Then, when you sees him out there doing your own tricks successfully, it pisses you off big time. He was doing it innocently. The kid never knew any better because he was only copying his great teacher and added a few new tricks of his own."

"Nah. Don't give me that shit. He turned against me. We were a team, like father and son. He went ahead and. . . ."

"No Sharp! You are wrong! *You* thought you were like father and son, not John. That is why you couldn't take it when some of them drugs were bad. When you weren't in on every front-runner and when he makes a fortune with SnoMann, enough money to leave the track for good, you don't like it. He wants to follow his dream of turnin' dirty old Yorkville into a high-end village of boutiques. John don't just dream big, he took

191

action. He makes it happen, man. Losing him, along with your family was too much. You thought he turned against you, but he didn't. He was …."

"Whatever he was, he was a con, and got what he deserved. And for a lousy ten thousand, you rid me of my most painful burden." Bob grasps his forehead with his palms. "He killed me just as much as I had him killed. Only my pain has never stopped."

"Sharp, you're a leading trainer, a big name in that there financial world, all because of John. You took over his Yorkville deal, or should I say, stole it, making your greatest wealth. And that gave you new connections. I may have sold the racing forms around the track, but I knows everything that was going on, all the time, and everybody involved. Remember, John was my 'in' for the narcotics. And I knew where they were going and what happened after they were bought."

"I was only a middle man; nothing will be pinned on me. I never administered a thing. The vets did it all." Bob offers.

"No, not all. You were the mastermind. You said when to use them, so you could notify the gamblers. But the truth is, you never got to do any of the dirty work."

"Well, isn't that the way it should be? Give the orders. They get their kickback, everyone was happy."

"Yeah, you're just some guy behind the scene when the real trouble starts. Givin' the orders is the real crime, before they ever gets carried out. And, one more thing - how was it you convinced jockeys to go along with your plan of putting a horse on the lead? It was just another one of your ways of getting a sure win."

"Always… because of the gamblers. The jockeys either listened or they would end up in the Humber River, floating face down. The little mafia took charge of the dirty work."

"Probably true. You had them heavies following you to make sure everything happened as planned."

"Well, Smoocher, you had better run along now. Someone might recognize you. Not that I am worried; you see, I am known for helping out the delinquent, the under-dog. It wouldn't seem unusual for me to talk with someone like you. Since you are up for a murder charge against another fellow tracker, someone could really panic if one of these guys got the word that you were here."

"I suppose. Remember Bob, you was drunk when you paid me to kill Mencini, but your words are sober now."

"Off with you."

Newman stands, stares down at the prosperous, well-dressed man. "See you around, Sharp."

"I doubt it."

Newman disappears from the poorly lit lounge, passing Peter and I waiting together in the lobby, tipping his hat in our direction. Peter motions for me to re-enter. The sergeant takes Newman and the recorded tape back into custody.

Horseracing might be the sport of kings, but I am hopeful that this king of sports is going down.

PART IV

'International Intrigue'

Chapter 20
Reunion

Three thoroughbreds shuffle through the mud on their way back to the stable from their morning workout while two men walk ahead. I am following closely as training finishes for the day.

The preliminary hearing scheduled for Monday states Sharp has hired one top lawyer.

Peter and I ponder the possibility, what if he gets off on some technicality? "I hope the bastard hangs!" Peter curses.

"Karma. Watch your words." I respond.

Noticing a half-ton truck pull up between the barns, he grins as a pretty young woman with auburn hair climbs down from the cab. Her beautiful smile overtakes the extra weight she carries.

"Gotta run now, see you later. Thanks for helping out this morning." He gestures a wave goodbye, as he heads toward the redhead. Peter has a new girlfriend.

Watching them drive away, I recall our conversation earlier with the police. They explained how gamblers and bookies waited for the last possible second before placing their bets, known for betting *laundered* monies. To cover himself, investigators found out Sharp paid others to jam the fifty-dollar wicket, which prevented further wagering. He controlled so much, but all his contracts were verbal. He never signed anything.

Bob's lawyer tried to claim drunkenness so that Sharp couldn't be proven guilty, saying '*too drunk to be capable of forming an intent*' to have John killed. Whittmore remarked that drunkenness only affected the mind, and Sharp would be more willing to commit the crime. Whittmore must show that a general intent to murder existed.

Chatting briefly with the grooms, I make my way to the track kitchen for lunch when one of the assistant veterinarians, Stretch, stops me. He needs my assistance as he does dentistry, manually floating or filing the horse's teeth. I hold the filly and calmly rub her nose as he questions me about the upcoming trial. Stretch places a stainless, full mouth speculum into the horse's mouth, and then secures it to the horses head with the attached dental halter. Cranking it open to keep the animal's mouth wide, he begins to rasp the teeth, smoothing the jagged edges, which make it more comfortable to chew and digest food. Stretch explains his connection with Smoocher and rambles on.

I change the subject saying that horses' teeth never stop growing; they lose their baby teeth when they turn three years old. Stretch is hopeful to get information from me, but I am sworn to secrecy and know he is one of Smoocher's inside contacts.

Meeting Peter at his townhouse, he explains that Whittmore called him earlier at the track and wanted to see us right away. By this time, the newspapers have news of Sharp's arrest and are running full page stories relating to the murder, giving personal details about his life and his successes. There will be no pre-trial publicity or there could be an order to exclude the public. This means the papers are not to print evidence and procedure until after the hearing, which could take several days to complete. The case will go forward when the judge feels he has sufficient information for committal to trial.

After a short wait, James Whittmore arrives for our meeting. He first outlines a few procedures and the importance of getting the right judge. He admits that he's satisfied with the one named to sit trial, Judge MacIntosh.

"I want to let you both know that Mr. Sharp's attorney and I have come to an agreement. He will waive the preliminary hearing of evidence on Monday for a copy of our new brief. He feels he can waive evidence and we'll go right to trial." Both attorneys do not want the reports printed, which would affect each of their cases.

The change in plans takes us by surprise, as the trial date will be sooner rather than later.

A nervous excitement stirs within at the thought that the end is close and I will return to London in the near future. I pray for justice but fear the wealthy magnate might escape his penalty. The news is all-good.

Peter and I decide to take a drive and walk the streets of Yorkville Village, no longer like the1960s. We check out the trendy shops, and then try to find a few landmarks from the past. While enjoying dinner at one of the new bistros, Peter reminisces, and then remarks he didn't make it to London, which leads to more questions regarding our friends from high school, Bradley and Susan. He is curious to hear how I teamed up with Karen, as we never did discuss how she met her husband.

"Tell me, Frannie, how did it happen that you ended up in London working for the architect firm with BJ? There is so much I missed. For me, the last seven-eight years have been living, working and breathing racetrack life, but what about you, what happened after you left Holland?"

Right... I recall my time in Europe.

London, UK: September - 1974

A large crowd lined the harbor for the Hovercraft crossing the Channel to Ramsgate, ready to board. I leaned against a nearby post and cleaned my streaky over-sized sunglasses. My faded blue jeans and canvas runners bore many holes and my hair had sun-streaked to a golden color. I was anxious to reach the U.K. following my sixteen-month tour through Europe.

Towns, cities, villages, and campsites drifted through my mind as I recalled several of my visits from Copenhagen to Crete, and from Paris to Vienna. My longest stays had been at a small resort in Zermatt, Switzerland, and St. Moritz where I had learned to ski and lived on cheese fondues. I had stomped grapes in Lyon; hitch-hiked in Milan, and harassed in Rome. I attended operas in Wiesbaden, Vienna and Paris; walked hundreds of miles through galleries from Antwerp to Geneva until my feet blistered. I roamed the ruins of Athens and sunbathed on the nude Greek beaches. I quaffed beer in Heidelberg, watched strippers in Hamburg where I learned what pornography was really all about. Weeks ran into months, viewing the Rhine from Basel to Dusseldorf, traveling with gypsies in Yugoslavia, riding a bike through Belgium with a group of Australians. Now, I looked forward to getting back to some basics - and English.

In early May, I left Amsterdam after spending the day with Chuck, and a very rapturous night in the Hilton. I smiled as I recalled the trip knowing it was not the time to get involved; so bought myself a Europass for the train and said my goodbyes, heading south to Brussels where my travels began. Once, when in Munich, I had grown weary and called Leonard, hearing all the gossip and getting needed encouragement to continue onward. I had spent time with a family in Larissa in central Greece until they planned a move to Malta. Money was getting low and it was time to return to England.

The Captain on the hovercraft announced the landing time and everyone synchronized their watches. It was half-past six when I arrived at Victoria Station. The heavy luggage, which had remained in a Paris locker while traveling Europe, got hauled to the nearest information desk where I located the currency exchange and public telephones. The English dialect was music to my ears.

The address Bradley had given me was 6 Hyde Park Gardens, W2. The driver of my cab headed north on Grosvenor Place through Knightsbridge, twisting and turning in and out of traffic. I felt confused by his traveling on the left side of the road, but within twenty minutes, the cab came to a stop.

"Well, Lassie. Here you are."

Gazing at the posh row-homes lining both sides of the street, I hesitated a moment. "Would you please wait until I see if anyone is at home? It will only take a sec." There was no answer.

Sadly returning to the cab, contemplating the dilemma, the driver drove to the Charles Dickens Hotel, off Bayswater, where I spent the night.

The following morning, I showered and dressed for work in a pair of gray pleated trousers with a navy blazer and hurried through breakfast, and then called Brad's office. Forty-five minutes later, I reached Russell Square Station, walking briskly, remembering the location was near the British Museum. Passing several older buildings, I saw a large white sign above an entranceway that read 'Nichols, Patterson, & Partners, Architects'.

The substantial marble-walled lobby, covered in black and white framed prints of the firm's impressive designs, filled the space. I did not recognize anyone for a moment, then suddenly, a familiar face. The young woman turned around at the reception desk. It was Cheryl! I thought, Patterson, wasn't that her name? The boss's daughter? I began to feel uneasy.

"Cheryl, isn't it? I'm Francine Harrison. I believe we met some time back at Wembley." The young woman's expression changed into a forced smile.

"Well, so it is. What a pleasant surprise." She turned to answer a busy switchboard.

I wondered if I had made another mistake. Before I had time to reconsider, I noticed a couple enter the foyer. The man kept walking, but the woman stopped. It was Bradley's sister, Nancy. She gasped.

"Well, I'll be damned. Where are lost souls found? How are you?" She asked. "This is fantastic, Frannie! You will never know. You really look marvelous. Great tan!"

"Thanks, you too," I replied, sincerely.

"Look, I've got to run, but before I go, I've got to do something. Come on, follow me." Nancy led the way up the old cement stairs to the second floor. She elbowed the office door open, and then left.

I tapped gently, looking into the impressive oak paneled room with its large leaded casement windows overlooking Russell Square. I saw Bradley at the far end, facing an over-sized whiteboard built into a wall unit, contemplating a math problem. He wore lightweight tan slacks and a navy cashmere sweater.

"Yeah, Nancy, so what's your problem? Sometimes you are more of a pain than you are worth having here. I hope you're not going to tell me some idle gossip or that you misplaced another Reddich file," Brad's voice rambled. He turned toward the entrance.

Eyeing the former hockey coach, giving him the once over, he now sported longer hair and a moustache. I could sense a strong attraction. The seconds seemed like minutes before our eyes met. He stepped toward me, paused, and then shook his head.

"Well, ahh, hell! Come on in, Frannie." It was a bit of an awkward moment. He stepped back behind his desk without taking his eyes off me. Casually strolling into the centre of the room, I noticed numerous rolls of plans, files, and magazines covering the large granite-top desk. I removed a pile of literature from a leather chair and sat down without waiting for an invitation.

Still leaning against his desk, Brad smiled. We spoke at once, laughed, and then said nothing.

"Frannie." He leaned forward, whispering, "Where the hell have you been all these months? I have called The Hague faithfully, repeatedly trying to locate you. That brother of yours would not tell me a thing. Not a damn thing!"

Crossing my legs, I tried to appear relaxed. "Well, that's because he didn't know. I wanted to travel and enjoy some peace of mind, so a year ago, I...."

"Of course. I know that, but why so long?" He questioned. "Leonard said you left Amsterdam in May, and wasn't sure if you were coming to London or taking a trip. TRIP?" He raised his voice. "I don't call a year and a half a trip. Whatever possessed you to stay away so long?'

"It was needed. I wanted to see how the rest of the world lived."

"Humm. That's all in the past and you're here, now." He sat on the front edge of the desk, close enough that our knees touched. I stirred slightly, feeling uncomfortable.

"You look good, better than I remember. Put on a little beef, eh?" He smiled. "It suits you. And your hair is longer."

"Thanks. You've made a few changes yourself. Nice, too!" I nodded, smiling.

"Oh, you mean the mustache. I got hit with a golf club, and the scar didn't heal properly. So, this was an alternative for now. Tell me, what are your plans?"

"I am here to take you up on your offer." Brad's expression changed. He stood up.

"Which offer, Frannie? Which one?"

"The one about a place to stay and a job."

"You mean you actually plan to settle down, right here in London? How dull it will be for you, after all that traveling. Are you sure you can handle it?" he replied. I smirked.

"Brad!"

"Yes?" He touched my hand and I felt his tenderness.

"Frannie. I'd do anything in the world for you. Remember what you once said, friends forever. Right?"

He pulled me to my feet and hugged me tightly, kissing my forehead, and then released his grip.

"I've missed you", he added, cautiously, "and I think we should start over. What can I do for you? I can give you a job, but it is a hell of a place. We are so busy, understaffed and overworked, as you can see. It wouldn't be fair to ask you to step into this mess." He sat back.

Glancing around the office, I saw no exaggeration. "In fact, right about now, any job would be better than none. I will take it. Apparently clean-up duty, right?" He laughed at my honestly.

"Let's call it, Office Manager." I smiled.

"Where are you staying?" he asked.

"Dickens, Lancaster Gate."

"Really? Not far from the house."

"I know. I tried to reach you there last night when I arrived, but got no answer."

"Well, I let the girls live there since I have been working out of town lately. I just took another proposal to Antwerp last week and needed to get Nancy out of the antique business to help us out while others were taking holidays. The company is growing."

I gritted my teeth, but knew I had to ask. "And, Cheryl? Or is she here permanently? I noticed the name Patterson listed as a partner in the company."

"Hold it! Just a bloody minute. Don't go jumping the gun again. Patterson is my Mom's brother, William, who is my dad's partner. The name is nothing but a coincidence. And yes, she is working here temporarily, helping us out."

"Convenient, isn't it?" I answered, sarcastically.

"Quite!" he teased, and then winked. "Frannie, there isn't and hasn't been anything between us for a long, long time, before I even met you in The Hague. It is Cheryl that won't let it go. So, stick that in your pipe and smoke it!" He grabbed my knee, shaking it playfully. "Ah-h … you look good," he growled.

"About a place? What do you think? Have you any ideas in mind? I'm getting down to my last pound, and can't afford to stay where I am."

"You can stay at my place with the girls for a few days. They will finish working here at the end of the week, and then you can have the place. It's large enough."

"You mean, stay there with you, that is, whenever you are around?"

"That's the gist of the idea. Like it?"

"I'm not against it, but I would like to take things slowly. Kind of like a fresh start. Let's go nice and easy, you know. Develop gently." I added.

"I suppose you are right. We will just make sure we don't brush shoulders. We can make it work."

"It will be just fine, I'm sure." I responded.

Bradley checked his watch.

"I'd like to spend more time and show you around, but I've got this meeting that I should be attending. It's a partners' meeting and. . ."

"It's ok. I'll go and get myself settled. I'm just dying to get a haircut."

"Look, I'll try to get away early and meet you at the flat. We can grab a bite for dinner. You are right. We'll try and start fresh." He reached across his desk for a particular file. "I'll let Nancy know and she can get you keys. I can't tell you how pleased I am you came back. I worried about you and thought you might have gotten yourself married."

"Honest, Brad. I'm so glad to get my feet back on familiar ground where I can speak the same language and recognize familiar faces. Thanks, I mean it. Thanks for keeping your word." I reached up and kissed his cheek. He squeezed my hands, stopping me at the door.

"Hey, Frannie! Best friends? But, just have to say it ... sure would like to jump into the sack with you, right now!" My eyes widened, releasing his grip.

"God, Nichols!" I snapped, in my old sarcastic way, waving my finger at him, "Just remember, I've got more class in my baby finger than you'll ever have!" and then, I turned to leave.

"Frannie?" he called in return, "Up yours!" I laughed. We had such attitude together.

The wall clock chimed seven-thirty when Nancy and Cheryl arrived. Nancy's friendly chatter made me feel comfortable while Cheryl went directly up to her room.

"We grabbed a bite to eat before coming in. As I am sure you know by now, not much to eat here," explained Nancy, tossing her sweater-coat over the rocker next to the fireplace. "So, what's new since I saw you last? You've obviously had a haircut."

"Did I ever!" My hair was shorter by a good eight inches.

"It looks fine. Talked briefly with Brad and he said you can start work in the morning and that you will be staying here with us. We'll be gone in a few days and Brad is literally not here."

The front door unexpectedly opened and Bradley burst in. Affectionately, he ruffled my hair. "Wow! You really did get it chopped! I like it." He stopped, grinning approvingly. "I thought we were going out to dinner, come on. We'll shower and change and we're off."

"We will, will we?" I met his glance.

Bradley huffed, "Take everything literally, eh?" Cheryl appeared at the top of the stairs, watching us, yet making no comment. Brad skipped up the stairs. "Put a move on it, lady. Reservations are for eight-thirty."

We had a relaxing meal, which consisted of mussel canapés, seafood entrée with all the trimmings, in the Rendezvous Room at the Swiss Centre, a small restaurant in Leicester Square, and we finished with a trifle of liqueurs. There was so much to talk about as we strolled along Pall Mall, through St. James's Square and up to Piccadilly. We had great karma, and I wondered if our relationship would work out someday.

"Our business is booming, but we just can't get ahead of ourselves. One minute we actually are making headway, then strikes come or some dumb catastrophe would set us right back where we started. Dad sent a few of the unfinished jobs down to this office, and they have been a real pain to handle."

"What do you mean?"

"Well, for instance, this school we designed near Churchill won us an 'Award winning design', but then things started to go wrong. The kitchen drains backed up. We had subbed the job out. But, the actual work was completed by another contractor and the whole mess was turning into a court case to decide who actually was responsible. Nothing but problems." He became visibly tense when he spoke of his work, but it was important that I learn all the jargon and names of the architectural firm and its jobs.

"You take it all too personally. Don't you have qualified people working for you to delegate these..."

"Yes, but the problem is that the partners take things for granted. For instance, Uncle Ted had a nervous breakdown some time ago and a few other problems, but he still tries to run his end of the business as if nothing has happened. He just can't cope. Communities are growing so fast with immigration and city expansions. He misses meetings and then I get the unfinished tasks to complete on top of my own. We also have commissioned jobs in Europe which I am excited about, but don't think I will be able to handle."

"What about Associates? Haven't you got anyone to step in, working here or up in Birmingham? Couldn't some of these jobs or problems be solved while you get other things rolling."

"Yes. We don't have enough and I have suggested a number of solutions to the Partners, but they are so set in their ways about doing business, and they don't realize how large this firm is getting. They are leaving many things undone and it will be too late by the time they actually come up with a resolution. Right now, it is a vicious circle. We have over a hundred on staff as it is."

We relaxed comfortably in the back of a cab; the windows glistened like diamonds as the drizzle caught the light of the passing headlights. We drove back to his West End row house.

Brad removed his clothes from one side of the large closet and then made up a bed for himself in the living room, explaining, "For now, anyway."

By the end of November, I was comfortable living and working in London and began making plans to visit The Hague for Christmas when a letter arrived from Leonard. I read it in the living room of the Hyde Park flat.

Julie is thoroughly enjoying the company of Martha as the toddler becomes more active. She does the usual things like crawling, throwing things and playing with her food. I am enclosing a letter for you that arrived on Friday. By the way, Julie and I are looking forward to your Christmas visit, so until then, take care. It has been a long time since we visited.

I forgot, one more thing, Chuck Connors called. I gave him your new phone number as he said he would be in London sometime in the New Year. Hope that was ok. Kind of late now if it wasn't.

I placed the folded letter on the coffee table, took a sip of wine, and then opened my letter from Susan.

Moments later a weary-eyed Bradley stepped through the door, kissed my cheek, tossed his overcoat onto the back of the sofa, and sat down beside me. He yawned and stretched out his arms. "How are you doing?"

"Great. You?" He nodded, pulling me close to him, "Look, I just got a letter from Leonard, who forwarded this one from Susan."

"What does she have to say?" he mumbled between kisses.

"She is apparently on her way to London, or at least making plans to come."

"Huh?" he sat up. "What is this all about?"

"I don't know. Says she is fine and will cable her flight number by the first of the month. No news about any of the guys or her family," I shrugged my shoulders. "I wrote to her from France sending your address."

Bradley took the short letter and read it. "Think everything is alright?"

"Who knows? Maybe she and her politician friend, Gregory, have split. That would be my guess since there is no hint of how long she will be staying."

"You could be right." He went to the icebox for a beer and returned to the rocker across the room. In London, only a Canadian would put a beer in the fridge, I was told.

"I suppose you will want to have some time off and would like her to stay with us?" I nodded, smiling.

"That would be nice."

"And, you also want time off for the Christmas holidays? The company usually closes at that time, so no big deal," he paused. "Listen, I have something to show you," he continued, standing up and reaching for his coat. He withdrew a rolled-up magazine from the pocket.

"Take a good look at the cover of *Elle* fashion magazine. The picture took me by surprise. "I saw it in the lobby of one of my contractors today."

I stared at the cover for only a second. "It's Karen! Karen Sharp!"

"You got it." I turned to the feature article written about the famous woman jockey turned model. The French interview wrote about her successes and recent popularity, and between the two of us, we managed to translate most of the story.

"Wow! Can you believe it? Karen, she's absolutely gorgeous."

"No contradiction there."

We read the magazine article a second time. He pointed out, "See this, it says something about doing a session for *Vogue* at Ascot" He paused. "Wonder if we could find out when. Wouldn't it be great to see her in London?"

"It sure would. I haven't been too faithful a correspondent, have I?"

"No, you never were," he reminded me, and then changed the subject. "How about going to the 'Navi' Pub and getting a bite to eat. I'm starved, and I have a busy day tomorrow. A new client is coming in, or I should say, a possible new client. I have to convince him that N.P.&P are the best choice for his new construction."

"Who and what is it all about?"

"The contract would be for a new recreational center with library, sports complex, and entertainment theatre. Some forty thousand square feet or more, I've heard. Dad called today and said this person would be coming into the office late morning. This could be a terrific chance to design something unique, right here in London."

"Sounds impressive," I grinned.

"You know, I was going to get Kris in on this, but since we've started redistributing the workload and named three new Associates to the firm, I'd like to feel this one out myself. It would be interesting to listen to the man's expectations. Anyway, how about going to get a bite? We don't get to talk much anymore. Everything seems work related." We headed down the road to the neighborhood pub.

We ordered a pint of Light and Bitters and chatted with the locals until a table in the corner became vacant. Along with our plates of chips and haddock, Bradley set a bottle of ketchup down on the edge, commenting that he never did lose his love for the red sauce.

"You're not supposed to put that stuff on English fish and chips." I reached for the malt vinegar.

"Oh, but I love this stuff," he winked, removing the cap. He looked down the neck of the bottle and hit the bottom hard, and then again, this time spraying the ketchup across the table. I jumped up as the blood red sauce splattered into my face, reminding me of another suppressed incident, where such a red spray had put me into a state of shock for several months. I screamed, startling everyone in the pub, alarming Bradley, who came quickly to my aid, wiping the ketchup from my face, trying to calm me. Once people saw what caused the interruption, they returned to their drinking. He knew differently. My whole body began to shake. He held my hand tightly knowing it was no laughing matter. We quietly finished our dinner and left the pub.

"My God, Frannie. I am so sorry. I never realized the depth of your horror. Oh, honey." We hugged and I soon settled.

"Have you ever heard any news from Peter? Hasn't anything been solved?" Bradley nervously rambled on, knowing the murder needed resolving before anything could come of our relationship. I couldn't believe how deep those feelings had buried.

The thrill of living in London was exciting as I set up shop on the third floor using Kris Monroe's tidy room for privacy when he was on site. The employees were friendly. The only tiring aspect was fighting the crowds when traveling to and from work. Once I found myself in the midst of a bomb explosion in the King's Cross tube station. These kinds of incidents became second nature to the natives as the city was threatened, constantly, during the troubled 1970s. I thought things might settle when Margaret Thatcher was elected.

One morning, while concentrating on a section of files in Bradley's office, the large oak door opened and he entered talking with a well-dressed overweight man in his late fifties. I sat unnoticed near the corner.

Bradley offered him a seat. My movement startled him. "Frannie. I didn't see you there. Excuse me." He paused. "Mr. Mallett, I would like to introduce Miss Harrison, one of our key organizers around here." As I stood to shake hands, his gaze traveled down my body.

"I'll just get a few things together and leave you two gentlemen," I offered, packing a few files together.

"No rush, Frannie," Brad interjected. "Just finish up whatever you were doing, and then perhaps you could bring us some coffee. Regular?" Mr. Mallett nodded, not taking his eyes off me.

Half listening to Brad's explanation of his new concept for his client, he simplified the details, which made it a very good learning experience for me.

"The essential idea, we believe, is to identify your building as a sound shelter, which isn't necessarily the priority. We relate the structures function to the environment and will create a symbolic building. The new building should flow with the environment, which I identify on my first site visit. I do not know whether the mass of the buildings will be horizontal, vertical, cellular or transparent. Like any creation, some types of buildings and some sites are better and more exciting than others. A reinforced concrete frame with white marble chippings suits one area over another. It is a fact that the fewer constraints, the more unique a structure can be, so that it doesn't merely repeat a particular type or style.

I honestly feel this design must proceed from the general to the particular. Perhaps, that is why systems fail when applied to building forms for which they are not designed, just like a family of four living in a seven-bedroom mansion, for instance. I like to look at things early, when the scheme becomes anchored to road frontage. I like to promise a unique building, which is a product of time and experience." He paused as I excused myself from the room, leaving Mr. Mallett's concentration with him.

When I returned, I held the tray of coffee and plate of sweets as I listened eagerly to the architect's jargon.

"We will be developing the significant features of the building in relation to its use, just as a school plan must be flexible enough to allow for change in teaching methods, etc. After the war, new schools looked like factories. Now, they want a factory that won't look like a school," he laughed, honestly. "But the style sometimes has to be based on climate and materials, and I feel guided by the functions of structures and building materials. To me, sheet steel, glass, and plastic show no element of scale, and concrete is acceptable only if textured. It is a lost art. Lack of craftsmanship leaves us visually weak." I set the tray down.

"Today, we are given fewer choices of brick and timber, but we are getting a rich variety of synthetic boards, plastic floor tiles, and the like. You see, I need to understand its function, environment and your likes, to find that individual element and to bring it out." A long pause followed.

A strong ray of sun glared off the prism of the casement windows, allowing the room to show its rich wood finishes as the two men turned my way. Bradley walked over next to me. He placed one hand on the tray's edge and with the other took an irresistible pinch from my buttock. An incoherent sound came from my mouth, and the tray tipped ever so slightly, spilling some hot coffee on the desk, splashing the prospective client. I quickly grabbed some nearby tissues. As Mallett stood up, I leaned over, stretching across the desk, offering apologies and assistance. He stared, and then willingly accepted my help, enjoying his view. Bradley giggled silently, admiring my move.

"Oh, please, Mr. Mallett. I cannot tell you how terribly sorry I am. I apologize sincerely. But that isn't going to help your suit." He seemed unconcerned about the suit. My guess was that he could have been a womanizer.

"I'll just be one second and go and get some towels." I turned to leave, whispering, "You stupid ass, I ought to give you one..."

"Yeah? Save it 'til later," Bradley responded in my ear, as I hurried from the room.

Mr. Mallet watched me slip away through the oak doors, proclaiming, "Great body, but a little slow on the reflexes!" He laughed, broadly. I began to think that Bradley knew exactly what he was doing.

Later that evening, before leaving the office, I walked into the front lobby of the old building where the switchboard rang persistently. Hesitating before connecting the old-fashioned posts, I took the message. Bradley walked in accompanied by two of the associate partners and Mr. Patterson.

"Mr. Mallett just called," I announced in a low tone, handing him the memo with the telephone number inscribed on it. "He's anxious to speak to you." Bradley turned to Mr. Patterson,

"I presented our design portfolio on the Universities in Newcastle, Durham and Walsall to Mallett earlier today. He said he would take some time this afternoon to look at our work here in London. He seemed impressed with the Library at Uxbridge, which is what led him to our Birmingham office to talk with Dad. But, I have to remember that both the Morris Group and another firm, recommended from the RIBA Group, are our contenders for his business." Patterson nodded in his distinguished British manner.

"He has apparently arranged mortgage financing with the bank regarding this project," Patterson explained. "I've heard back from the company he set up for this project. He has also acquired a superb site through secret dealings with council. They placed compulsory purchase orders on properties outstanding. Then, he obtained planning permission, leaving them all under the impression that the public would gain the most by accepting the proposal. He is a very experienced and discreet operator and is known to have paid a half million pounds an acre." Bradley whistled in amazement.

I waited. Bradley excused himself as the others walked off, and we sat in the lounge.

"Well?" I asked.

"We want you to consider the position of job coordinator. You will accompany the architects on site, attend council meetings, visit clients and take field trips with the surveyors, engineers, or whatever else is on the go. You'll need to take precise notes regarding the construction, misdemeanors, conflicts, or any unsatisfactory procedures, etc. One of the secretaries will type your reports, and they'll be signed-off by one of the partners. You'll need to keep the activity reports up-to-date and filed, as well as be responsible for recording anything confidential, assisting with project management. The firm is at a size now where everything needs documentation. Too many companies are being sued. Your title will be Architectural Administrative Assistant with double the pay."

"But I haven't taken shorthand since school!"

"So, you relearn it," he tapped my knee. "You'll be expected to sit in on luncheons where many of our discussions take place and mentally note everything of any significance. You'll report to me, but will be on call for the other partners. Just make sure I know what's up so I don't go and make conflicting arrangements that will need your support. You will need assistance once these larger jobs begin. So, what do you think? Are you ready to take on a dedicated career path? We will work together, but you will be your own boss. In some ways, everyone will report to you." Bradley allowed for a couple of weeks to brush up on my secretarial skills.

"Not much time. I'll see what I can do." I stood up to leave, buttoning up my coat.

"Do you like the idea?"

"Sounds great! I love it!" I replied. He turned to leave, adding.

"Oh, by the way, I have concert tickets for Elton John, I got from Mallett. Celebration time." He laughed and reached for the door.

I could not resist the temptation, so I grabbed his ass from behind. He let out an expletive.

"Why you little..." But, when he turned, I was well on my way out of the building, down into Russell Square, and into the snowy night.

"Payback time!"

Chapter 21
Family Matters

Kris Monroe drove his Jaguar around the parking lot of an old brick junior schoolhouse, built in the late seventeen hundreds, where I was taking photographs. Soon to be demolished, the fight for historic preservation had lost to new larger construction. After packing the camera into its case, I climbed into the luxury sedan and Kris drove to the West Midlands. His thick accent was frustrating, making it difficult to take notes at each job site. No sooner would I translate one problem about a job, than the terminology would stump me again.

During our leisurely drive back to London, Kris rambled on softly about the other partners and talked about when he first connected with the firm. I realized his penchant for perfection and trembled at the thought of translating and typing my notes.

Around eight-thirty, I reached the house. Two large duffle bags sat on the floor of the living room, leaning against the couch. Bradley announced we had a visitor; Susan had arrived unexpectedly. I wondered why there had been no response to my recent letter to her.

"Her doctor held up the trip." Bradley motioned quietly for me to sit down.

"What's this? Is something wrong?" I could hear footsteps and turned to see. "Sue? Oh, my God, Sue!" There, standing at the bottom of the stairs was a very pregnant woman in maternity dress. She smiled weakly, appearing ashen and frail. Aware of her blotched skin, greasy hair and large darkened rings beneath her eyes, I gave her a gentle hug. Susan waddled across the room to take a seat.

"It's a long story, but you know the gist of it, Frannie."

"Gregory?"

"Yes."

"I told you," I shook my head, disapproving.

"No, Frannie. It's not what you think." Susan knew what she was doing. You see, she told both Gregory and me that she did not want any commitment from him. Susan knew exactly the position she had put herself in, as she knew what she wanted and it wasn't marriage. Let's say that all she wanted was the 'product' of marriage. Gregory couldn't cope after he found out because she kept it hidden for a long time until he announced he wanted to run provincially in five years. That was no problem for Susan because she was ready to move on. She experienced some pregnancy complications and had to move back home. Susan promised her mother that when she was well enough, she would be on her way. Her doctor wouldn't let her travel, so she lied and said the father would marry her, but he lived in London. Her doctor allowed her to make the trip and gave a referral for her to see a doctor within forty-eight hours of her arrival. Susan took a breath, explaining her position.

"But, why here? Why wouldn't you wait until the baby was born," I protested, "for your own health and the baby's?"

"Well, things were just not that great for me in Toronto as you can well imagine. I was getting short on funds, my family did not approve, and everyone in my neighborhood knew what was going on because they would see Gregory and me coming and going all the time. What else was I to do? Pete suggested writing to you, but I felt you would blow up. I thought the best way to get away was just to do it. Therefore, I did. Frannie, I am happy about what has happened; only it is bothering everyone else." Bradley sat still, finding it hard to comprehend.

"You mean to say, you intentionally went with this guy just to have his kid?" he questioned.

"Not really. That wasn't the way it all started out, but it somehow ended up looking that way." She heaved the weight of her enormous belly relieving the pressure as she took a seat on the sofa.

"What about giving it up? Did you not think about that?" I suggested.

"No way! This is what I want," she stated firmly.

I looked to Bradley, sighing. The mood soured.

"Want a glass of milk?" Bradley offered as he had decided to accept things the way they were. *It is what it is*. He already had experience with this kind of drama from his sister, several years before.

"We don't have any," I answered. "I just don't believe it! Here I am, expecting you to play tourist together and instead I get the arrival of two - in no state to do much of anything!" The situation overwhelmed me.

"Come on, Frannie. It will just be a matter of weeks, and then I'll be on my way."

"Like hell you will. Have you looked at yourself in the mirror lately? Well, in case you haven't, you look pretty bad. You will stay here as we have plenty of room. St. Mary's Hospital isn't far at all, and we'll manage somehow. We will make it as easy for you as possible," I promised. "Look, you had better get to bed. You'll have jet lag for sure. I have to go into the office early and finish some work from today, but I should be back by noon, and then we will get you to that doctor and settle you in. It must be hard, all this walking."

"Another thing, I am supposed to do nothing and keep off my feet so there won't be another incident." I didn't care to ask what that was all about.

"Wonderful! Shall we get a maid?" I kidded. As Susan made her way upstairs, I called, "Hey, Sue, I haven't forgotten all that you did for me a few years back. This is no inconvenience. I owe you one." I turned to face Bradley, who appeared calm compared to me. He poured a couple of drinks, turned on the stereo and cuddled up.

"I will cancel my Christmas trip to Holland. She won't be able to travel anywhere in that condition," I assumed, sadly.

"We'll work something out. I'll stay with her for a while, and then when you get back, I'll run up to Birmingham to see my family. Don't go upsetting your plans now. It'll all work out just fine." Brad ruffled my hair.

The next morning I arrived at the office to complete my work, then taxied back to the row house to get Susan to her two o'clock doctor's appointment. There was a long wait before Dr. Bamford did his examination and gave her a list of instructions.

"What's up?" I questioned as Susan returned to the waiting room.

"The baby is in an inverted position, and if it doesn't turn, I will have a breach birth. He says no reason for alarm, a few weeks to go. I have prescriptions to fill, and he wants me to visit every ten days. My blood pressure is low, and I need a dairy diet as I am drained of calcium. I had three blood tests."

"Wow! You had a lot done for one visit."

"Not really. At least there's no real complications."

"What about finances? How are you going to manage?"

"No problem. I have money to get through this pregnancy, until I am able to get to work again. Between my savings and the money Peter gave me, I'll be fine."

"Is that your intention? To work here?"

"I don't know. I'll have to think about it."

After having her prescriptions filled, we retraced our steps along the wet pavement back to the flat. I wondered how much financial support she got from Gregory.

Over a steaming cup of tea, we talked about our friends back in Canada. I was anxious to hear how Peter was doing.

"Peter hasn't married or anything exciting like that, but he turns thirty in the spring. He likes to keep playing the 'Joe Cool' scene."

"It's funny that none of us married."

"How come you and Brad haven't set anything up? Things look pretty cozy here."

"Give us some time. I don't want to rush into anything."

"It's over five years since ..."

"Right now, I'm more concerned with you and your free spirit lifestyle. Have you ever considered your baby, and how you are going to explain this choice you made?"

I refilled her cup, returning to the dining area.

"Frannie, this is no big deal. It happens all the time these days. I just don't want the hassle of marriage. Not many work out, actually. People's interests and dreams change over the years. There are so many things for us to see and do now. To be honest, I have rarely seen a good relationship last more than fifteen years without one of them having to make significant compromises. It's just not my bag. People grow. Everyone's direction, opinions and needs shift over the years, and not always in the same direction."

"You mean you wouldn't even consider it in the future?"

"One thing at a time. Perhaps, when I'm forty-five. Companionship is important to me. Right now, I have other things that I want to do with my time and I just haven't found anyone."

"Well, maybe you have not been in love? That would account for some changes."

"The sexual thing becomes less exciting after a while, and then people take each other for granted and life become routine. Sometimes, I see couples in restaurants where they don't even have anything to talk about anymore. It is sad. No, thanks! Not for me!" Susan pushed her empty cup to the side. "I'm sure good marriages exist, but not many anymore; too many uncertainties and concessions. I think couples become bored with one another. They grow apart." Susan stretched out her legs but never took her eyes off me as she spoke out about her new beliefs.

I refrained from asking any more questions, knowing that I had no definite opinions one way or the other myself. Tired and feeling stressed, we went to bed shortly after dinner. I worried about her situation, knowing Susan was obviously in poor health.

The flight to Holland went as planned. I had a wonderful holiday with my family and new niece knowing that in another few weeks there would be a new baby in my home. Leonard was flying high as the family patriarch. I gave them a full report on Susan's concept of marriage and her rationale regarding her unborn child. They disapproved, but only because together they found so much enjoyment in their own baby. They thought Susan's way was selfish and that both parents should nurture a child.

Upon returning to London, I was anxious to share my feelings with Bradley, but he had already left for Birmingham. Disappointed, but satisfied that my trip had given me an insight into my own life, I stepped back into the role of helping Susan. She appeared in good spirits even though she still neglected her appearance.

The days were long. I missed Bradley, busy drafting designs for his new project and traveling more than ever. We rarely saw each other. Occupied with work and tending to Susan's needs, February suddenly arrived and the forgotten phone call came.

Chuck Connors was in town, expecting to spend some time together. After a negative reception, he decided to meet at the office.

Unannounced, he walked into the lobby of the historic building where a group of females gathered, overwhelmed by his movie star good looks. His natty pinstriped suit was immaculate and his hair perfectly styled as he announced himself in his thick southern drawl.

Dressed in my business suit with a lacy blouse opened at the neck, I had forgotten how debonair he was, giving him the once-over. The girls whispered as we greeted with a warm southern embrace, causing me to blush. Word would travel far and fast when he took my arm and entered his chauffeur-driven limo that had been waiting at the door.

"It's been a long time since Amsterdam, and a night I have not forgotten. Two years ago." Chuck remarked as I smiled, admiring the man I had tried desperately to avoid.

The driver motored cautiously through the core of the city to Piccadilly Circus. Once parked, we passed through glass swinging doors etched in gold and descended into a tiny restaurant. The crystal sparkled from the ceiling to the tables, with accents of polished silver. The Imari dinnerware sat precisely on impressive Irish linen tablecloths. Overcome by the opulence, a formal waiter seated me and bowed as he departed. The maitre d' called Chuck by name as another placed a splendid bouquet of red roses on the table in a tapered pewter vase, and a cocktail mat of exquisite hand embroidery awaited our magnum of Champagne.

"It doesn't seem to matter what city or country we are in, you still come across with such pomp and grandeur," I whispered as the Waterford glasses were carefully half-filled.

"To the lady of accomplishments." He lifted his glass to toast me.

"And, to the American with know-how." We sipped the champagne.

"Francine. What can I say? You astound me as much as you think I do you. Here I am, in London, with a woman I met in a Toronto tavern, driving a Ferrari. I became obsessed with trying to know you and I end up chasing you all over the world. Isn't it supposed to be the other way around in this day and age? I am the one who travels, remember?" He grinned and I laughed. "No, I'm kidding. You are a classy lady. Wherever you came from, it shows."

"And you are a gentleman with a great deal of money, and it shows," I was quick to return.

"I suppose. Does that impress you?"

"To be honest, yes. It's very flattering seen with a successful man, so handsome and rich. It is too bad you are American."

"What? You don't like us?"

"No, nothing like that. I almost married one, once."

"Well, well! That is the first personal thing you have ever said about yourself since we have been together. I'd like to hear more. That is another thing, you are too secretive, and I don't know much about you."

"Well, it works both ways. I don't know a lot about you, either. Married?

"No, you?

"No."

"Well, then that suits me fine. We can continue," he laughed. The waiter removed the first-course aperitifs and refilled our glasses.

"Can we spend some time together this week, sightseeing? I have a little work to do here, too."

"Well, if we are honest, I have a friend staying with me, and things could be a little complicated," I admitted.

"In what way? I presume you mean you are living with a man."

"Well, that too. But, my friend I was referring to is Susan Edwards."

"Oh yes," he nodded. "Your Toronto roommate. Do you travel in pairs?"

"No," I smiled. "Susan arrived in London a few weeks ago, to my surprise, very pregnant, and about to give birth any day now."

"So, I take it there was trouble back home, or a mistake made some place along the line?"

"Wrong!" I told him Susan's story the best I knew how, bringing him up to date. Our luncheon lingered and was turning into dinner as exquisite as the decor. We dined royally after which we left for the theatre to see the comedy *The Card*.

As the performance ended, our evening continued. We danced into the early hours of the morning at the Mecca Ballroom. I felt pampered by his attention that could no longer be dismissed as a mere flirtation.

"That was a pretty nice evening. Could we do this again? I work at the Park Lane Hotel tomorrow negotiating with my lawyer, but perhaps Saturday could work for you. What do you say?" I agreed. "I think I have more phone numbers under your name than I do all my other business contacts." He chuckled. "It is my intention that we will be able to have a serious conversation before I leave London." He reached, touching my thigh with his hand, placing the other on the back of my neck, and pulling me toward him. I hesitated, and then he withdrew slowly. He clasped my hand before I left. "Now, you listen here, my little Canuck," he announced firmly. "No leaving town this time, ok?"

"Ok," I promised, cautiously stepping from the limo. The large black vehicle pulled out of sight as I unlocked the door and tiptoed up the stairs.

The next morning, when the alarm sounded, Susan was full of questions about the evening.

"I like him a lot, although he is a little flamboyant for my taste. I'm telling you, can he ever show a girl a great time!"

"Does he know about Brad?"

"Not specifically. Not too many know about him, or should I say about 'us'?"

"You're lucky he is away now. When does he get back?"

"I don't know," I answered, honestly. "No one seems to, lately. He is so busy with his designs, working with the quantity surveyors costing out the new recreational centre, that I have hardly had more than a couple of hours with him over the past weeks, as you are well aware."

"I thought it might have been because of my being here. He did tell me once that he thought you needed to, how shall I say it… have more time?" She waddled back into the kitchen, picking up a banana from a wicker basket on the counter.

I hesitated, "Oh really?"

"Uh-huh. He knows you better than you think. Might as well face it, he wants you but only when you are ready. And, you are not."

"I know. I get myself into these damn predicaments, fate or whatever you want to call it, and don't wish to screw up his life or anyone else's. It's about getting myself straight."

"I know. But, what are you waiting for? What are you running from? It's time to get in touch with your true feelings."

"I have dreams. I have needs, but I can only handle one thing at a time. You, on the other hand, have always known what you want, and how to get it. Me? I guess I am more of a follower than a leader. What is my destiny? Not sure. Maybe I don't want more than just the simple things. I certainly have had choices, but maybe haven't picked the right ones."

"Maybe, you need to learn to trust again. You should start a list of your own wants and needs for the next ten years. You do make choices, only you don't consider the outcome."

"Right now, I am not under any pressure or commitment to anyone." I gazed out the window. "I'm going on thirty and I still can't see my way clear from the past. Some days, I wonder if I ever will." I sighed. "Have you heard from Peter at all, lately?"

"No."

"Figures. Me neither."

Another busy morning followed, filled with burdensome meetings. Littered with transcripts that waited editing as two typists were away, I felt bound to my desk trying to catch up.

A call rang through to the drafting office where I was working. Taking the phone, against my better judgment, I felt it would be from Chuck. I spoke in a low voice, "I'm afraid it is difficult to talk at this moment, but I think that would be fine. Of course, please do, thank you. Bye."

"Got a hot date, Fran? Must be the American," echoed a voice from the doorway. It was Kris. I blushed. "Yes, the word is out, Miss Harrison. The British gentlemen just aren't your type."

"Nonsense!" I stammered. "They just don't find me attractive enough to ask me out," I grinned, passing him by.

Later that afternoon, while I was reviewing a few tenders in Kris's office, before sending them out for publishing, another call came through. It was from a neighbor who lived next door to us on Hyde Park Gardens.

"When? Well, is she ok?" I dropped my file of papers. "I'll be right there. I'll leave now."

"What is it?" Kris queried in the midst of a calculation.

"Sue. My friend who has been staying with me has just gone into labor and rushed into the hospital. I have to get there, but the tube is so slow and it is rush hour. I'll never get a cab now. Oh, shit! What am I going to do?" I paced about the office, my mind starting to race in confusion. "I'll get my coat."

"There is also a royal parade for the princess and her husband this afternoon. The crowds will have several streets blocked off. There is only one thing I can think of. Come with me. Let's go! Do you have any other clothes? You know, jeans?"

"Yes, in the locker in the basement. I keep them for site visits, why?"

"Just hurry and go change your clothes."

Moments later, I dashed out excitedly. Kris was pushing Bradley's gold Honda along the driveway. I stopped, paralyzed from fear. After a few calming words, we rode off through the heavy traffic crossing London along roads I never traveled. Kris dropped me off in record time and I went to the appropriate waiting area with several other impatient visitors.

A nurse walked from the 'no admittance' area. We chatted briefly.

"Susan was in painful labor when admitted because of the baby's breach position. Dr. Bamford is in the delivery room now. We are confident that he will be able to get it turned, but if not, and complications arise, then a cesarean will be performed. I'm sorry, it's all I can tell you at this moment. I know you are her only relative here, so we will keep you posted. I'll let her know you have arrived."

At ten o'clock, I saw Susan's doctor walking down the hallway and called out to him for information.

"Yes, Miss Harrison. I am aware of who you are. The baby is turning. I am keeping a watch on her. You should go home and get some sleep. It could take another twenty-four hours or more before it ultimately turns into position. Right now, it is a matter of time. You may see her tomorrow morning. Susan is aware you are standing by, but for now, I recommend that you go home and get some sleep. That is what I am going to do after I take one more look in on her. You do not have to worry. I'm in the hospital at all times." He smiled, reassuring me.

First thing next morning, I called the hospital. No change. I cooked breakfast and called Bradley, leaving a message. Moments later, the phone rang.

"Oh, my gosh, I forgot all about today. You see, I have run into one of those complications I told you about. Susan is in the hospital, in labor." I explained to the caller. "Yes, as a matter of fact, I will be going right over. No, but give me your number and I'll call as soon as I hear something. Yes, of course. Talk to you later." I forgot my promise to Chuck about sightseeing.

As I was leaving for the hospital, the phone rang a second time. Bradley returned my call, saying the phone had been busy on his first attempt. I explained that I had been on the line with a friend and then updated him on Susan's condition.

"Would that be the same friend who came into the building the other day?" I evaded his question.

"He just came to the office to pick me up for dinner, which was all."

"Tell me all about it. Where did you meet this aristocrat? I don't recall hearing about him before."

"In Toronto. I had met him a couple of years ago before I moved to Holland. He drove me to the airport when I left. We were just acquaintances; met in a snowstorm."

"And?"

"And what?"

"You saw him again, perhaps?"

"Yes, he had appointments in The Haag when I was living with Leonard, and we spent some time together, and now he is working in London for a few days."

"Sounds like a persistent type," Brad remarked, "And the truth? A guy just doesn't happen to follow a woman across the ocean for dinner."

"Bradley, he is in the business buying up, investing and consulting real estate tycoons. We enjoyed each other's company, and he likes to get together whenever he is in town and catch up on what's new, have a meal, or whatever."

"Single? Divorced?"

"Single," I snapped back nervously in return. "Listen, I gotta go. I want to visit Susan this morning."

"How do you feel about this guy? Honestly."

I took a very deep breath. "Testing, the big quiz is it? It's nice to wine and dine with a rich, handsome, American. No complaints there."

There was a quiet moment. "Frannie, is there anything else between you and this guy that I should know?"

"There could be, but there isn't."

The sun burned through the clouds for the first time in weeks. Susan gave birth to a nine pound, two ounce baby boy. He was healthy but jaundiced, which kept them in the hospital longer than expected.

Bradley and I visited baby Matthew, who appeared fat, bald and had a good set of lungs, and according to Susan, was worth the wait. Both the pregnancy and the birth drained every bit of her strength, but she was ecstatically happy. On the table by her bed sat vases of flowers from Peter and Bradley and a Paddington Bear from me. Although the hospital expenses were much more than she anticipated, Susan found she had saved enough - just enough - to pay the bills.

Back at the office, I was describing to our receptionist, Florence, Susan's complications when Chuck unexpectedly arrived carrying a large bouquet of orchids. He waltzed into the office like a movie star, leaving the girls speechless and me feeling awkward. Thanking him graciously for the flowers, he planted a big kiss on my cheek. I introduced him to the others standing near and then excused myself to fetch a vase from the basement lounge, passing Brad, Kris, and Mr. Patterson on their way to lunch.

Having found a suitable container, I returned to the lobby using the back staircase. Bradley had waited and stopped me. Suddenly, I felt uneasy.

"Is that your friend in the lobby, sweet-talking our staff and handing out bouquets?" I agreed. "May I ask your plans, or is it none of my business?"

Drawing a deep breath, whispering, "Don't be a jerk. He is a friend of mine. He asked me to show him around the city and spend some time with him before he leaves. It will probably be another two years before I see him again, if ever."

"He acts as if things are more serious than that, or was it one of those one-night affairs that go on and on?"

"Well, if it is, I'll let you know." All of a sudden, he realized that he was over-reacting and backed off, apologetically. I waited a moment before entering the reception area, hoping that he had left the building.

Placing the bouquet on the entry table for everyone's appreciation, I accompanied Chuck to a small Italian restaurant in Bloomsbury, where a few of the office staff were also eating. They did a double take when we entered.

Chuck listened to my excuses regarding my complicated weekend, apologizing for not spending more time together. He wanted to spend a couple of days seeing the city.

I thought for a minute about Bradley, who would be out of town by the end of the week. "Tell you what; I'll take off Thursday afternoon and all day Friday. Will that be enough time?"

"Anytime, anytime at all is better than none. That sounds great. I will have to fly out some time on the weekend, but I haven't confirmed anything yet." He reached for a large bag beside his chair, handing it to me.

"After you told me a little about Susan, I chose some things for the baby or at least the saleswoman did. Have a look."

I wiped my mouth, and then peeked inside. There were sleepers, blankets, rattles, powder, pins, and baby towels. It was so unexpected and his thoughtful gifts aroused a new emotion. I leaned across the table and kissed his forehead.

"Chuck, you're fantastic! This is super! Why would you have done such a wonderful thing?"

"Because she is your friend, so she is a friend of mine, too. I have met her, remember? I hope it is an appropriate gift for a newborn. Don't know a lot about these kinds of things, but I suppose I'll have to come and see the little guy."

"Not bad pickings for a bachelor. She'll love to see you, but her discharge from the hospital isn't for another six days because of complications. You're gone by then, so Thursday will be perfect. I'll meet you at the hospital."

"No. I'll pick you up at the office and we'll go together. I'll also get theatre tickets for Thursday night."

"How about if I make dinner on Friday; we can pick up some groceries and I'll cook something up for us," I added, suddenly surprised by my offer.

"Sounds fabulous. I'm looking forward to it already." We finished our meal and walked back to the office.

On Thursday morning, I arrived before seven to ensure I had everything in order. While hurrying through the hallways carrying several rolls of blueprints under my arms, I bumped into Bradley. He was on his way out of town again. He stopped, setting down his overnight bag down and briefcase.

"I suppose you will be busy this weekend," he coughed, turning to his pocket for a handkerchief. "I have to leave in an hour, to settle... you know all about it. What I really wanted to say Frannie," he took hold of my hands. "I do care for you, and I ..." he hesitated. "You see... I know I have no hold over you; you are a free woman and are going to do whatever you want, anyway. I know all about your past, and had only hoped that someday you could possibly care for me as you once did for John. I love you, Frannie. Please, be careful." He kissed me tenderly, picked up his things and walked on.

Bradley's words were unexpected. I waited, disturbed by his forthrightness. Was he hoping for a commitment from me? I wondered. I thought I wanted the love and security of a family, as I had seen with Leonard, but Susan's situation confused the matter. Somehow, somewhere in the back of my mind, something forbade my admitting to any serious engagement. 'What is it that I can't let go of?' I thought. 'What fear is so deep that it can't be faced?' Someone calling from an open office door interrupted my thoughts.

"Florence said to tell you that Connors is here," Kris relayed the message. I continued on my way with Chuck to the hospital.

Friday morning we walked to Buckingham Palace and watched the changing of the guard in a crowd of a thousand. We bussed on to the Tate Gallery and in the afternoon, and then visited Kensington where I delighted in shopping at *Biba's*, my favorite stop of the day, and later at Harrods. We ended up on Regent Street where Chuck tried to spend his money on extravagant gifts. Flattered, I still refused. I offered, instead, to pick some things out for him. Walking through Soho, stopping for a pint at the pub before heading to Westminster Abbey, we then headed back to Marble Arch where we found a little market to pick up food. All the little details made our days memorable.

As we reached the house, I noticed a storm brewing in the wind as the leaves swirled in clusters, gathering in pockets along the curb's edges. Welcoming a restful evening, for a change, Chuck poured wine as I unpacked the groceries. His appraising eye surveyed the place in minutes, approving the personal touch of family photos and fresh-cut flowers. He longed for a fire and found some kindling in the cellar. I assembled some veal, mushrooms, green peppers, onions and lamb on skewers for the broiler. As I sipped my wine, I prepared a special marinade for them. I was playing a scene unfamiliar to me.

"Well, I still have the knack. How's that for a fire?" he asked, searching approval.

"Not bad at all. Cozy, eh?"

"Just a Boy Scout at heart." He followed me into the kitchen, eyeing the pile of fresh shrimp and chopped vegetables. "This is my specialty. I shall prepare," he motioned.

"You sure like to cook, if memory serves me right."

"Well, don't you go and get so tipsy, you might damage some furniture," he teased back. The Toronto memory of a previous dinner still lingered.

The rain splashed against the window as I set the table. I drew the drapes, and he dimmed the lights.

"Candles, madame?" he called from the kitchen. "And no funny stuff tonight. Keep your food on your plate." I giggled.

The rice and kebabs were ready to cook. Chuck drew back my chair, and then opened a second bottle of Valpolicella. We each had half a dozen large shrimps, done, as he had promised, to perfection, and dipped in a tangy sauce.

"I apologize, Monsieur, they are done to a *T*." I toasted our friendship.

"Francine. Don't doubt my ability to cook." He tasted his food. "I must sound like a broken record, but honestly, I enjoy every minute we spend together. We just can't let this relationship drift apart and not do anything about it." Chuck coaxed.

"Of course, we have a great relationship. I always look forward to your visits, unexpected as they are," I added, sipping my wine, paying close attention to his reactions.

"I won't be traveling so much anymore."

"Really?" Without looking up, he spoke of taking over the company's presidency and would be settling in Dallas for most of his time. He paused, his brown eyes fixed on his goblet.

"Now, tell me, how are you going to handle your women all over the world if you can't make your rounds? Just what are you going to tell them?" I teased.

He rested his chin on his palm. "You tell me, Francine, do you like living in London?" The question caught me off guard.

"Yes, it offers a lot. I have a career and new friends with lots of opportunity to travel. I love the city, the people and the history. I couldn't imagine anywhere else."

A loud splash of rain hit the window. I cleared the dishes and took my time in the kitchen, slowly preparing the rest of the meal. Chuck stoked the fire.

Our conversation during dinner was on the lighter side as we recounted the events of the day. He placed a Mantovani album on the stereo when I served the dessert plates and put the coffee on. Returning to the living room, I saw Chuck stretched out on the sectional in the dark, with the glow from the fire lighting the room. Placing a cushion on the floor, I lay down facing the fire, choosing a travel magazine from the coffee table.

"So, you really do like to travel?"

"Love it; except my next big trip won't be with a knapsack. It will be first class, all the way." Chuck dropped down on the floor behind me, whispering. "Show me what places fascinate you." He extended one arm across my back and rested on his elbow with the other. I scanned through the pages feeling his closeness and warm body.

"Now, look here, Malta. That wouldn't be so commercial. Lots of history."

"Really? The island of the ancient Templars. And where else?"

"Oh, let's see." I flipped through the pages. "The Canary Islands would be my second choice. Have you been?"

"Uh-huh. El Hierro. It's considered the westernmost land in the world; smallest of the Canary Islands with just over 10,000 people while Tenerife has a population of around a million."

"Did you enjoy it?"

"Yes. Many of the larger islands are very commercial, but some of the islands are not so popular but are adventurous. The Canaries are also a good choice."

Chuck leaned over and brushed back a lock of hair, caressing my features. He tenderly kissed the back of my neck, slowly turning my head to face him. Running his tongue along my upper lip, we kissed lightly, then more fully. We lay entwined in the flickering firelight, stroking one another affectionately. In harmony with the soft background music, my pelvis moved rhythmically pressing against him. His sensuous touches increased. We lay together quietly for some time. Firmly holding my breast beneath my sweater, he undid the zipper of my jeans, gently rubbing his hand over the skin and along the inside of my thighs. We eagerly moved as one.

Passionately, we slipped off one another's clothes clinging together and craving the affection of each other's warmth. Fondling his muscular frame, I pulled him closer wrapping my legs around him as the music created a romantic atmosphere.

His hand ran gently up my back. I moved quickly, increasing the moment's sensations. "Easy. Easy baby," he whispered, kissing my nipples as his firmness pressed against me. Caressing one another tenderly, we were overcome by a stimulating desire as our naked bodies pressed into one and we locked into a frenzy, moving in unison with passionate moans trying to hold on to the moment's delirium. Breathing heavily, we inflamed with satisfying fulfillment as we entered a rhythmic orgasm.

The crackling sounds from the fire echoed through the room as we lay in each other's arms; eyes closed, drifting off into the morning dawn.

Beams of warm sunlight sliced through the drapery panels when I awoke from a sound sleep. "Francine," he whispered. "Tell me. What would it take to make you mine?"

My eyes opened. I saw the seriousness of Chuck's expression and the light in his eyes.

"I think you care deeply for me, but I can't be sure you are in love with me. I admit we do everything so well together." He smiled, observing tired eyes.

"Please, give us a try."

I hesitated, and then slowly got to my feet, leaving the room to go upstairs. He followed, showered and dressed, and then returned. Several minutes passed before I reappeared, freshly groomed. He watched, and then reached out. I sat close beside him as he kissed my cheek and held my hand.

"Look, Chuck, I'm not saying last night was a mistake. But, I don't think you actually want me. We play a great game of hide and seek, but we are not of the same kind. I like different things, a different life style. You don't desire anything long term with me and I'm starting to think about a relationship."

"Nonsense. You are wrong," he spoke frankly. "You are everything I have ever wanted, only I couldn't catch you. You are so full of surprises, so exciting."

"No. No Chuck. I am only slightly different from all your other women. The novelty would soon wear off and the real 'me' would not hold your interest. What you need is someone more sophisticated, elegant, and poised. Those things I am not. I know. A woman could not ask for anything more than you could offer. I can tell you that for a fact. Nevertheless, you would be right back on the trail, leaving a little of yourself here and a little there, everywhere. That is not for me."

He shook his head. Again, he did his best to convince me differently until he knew only time would be the answer. Departing, he turned at the doorway. "Once more, what would it take to get you? Come to Malta with me?"

Deep in thought, I grinned. "Oh, let me see now, Malta and an eight-cylinder, four-seater, British racing-green Morgan!" I laughed, loudly, punching at his shoulder, jokingly. He stepped down onto the sidewalk.

"Francine, how about a final farewell dinner at Parsons? An early one, say four-thirty or so. Please?"

I sighed. "You are so persistent, but no way." He pouted. The tall American folded his hands in prayer. "Please."

"Oh, what the hell. Ok. Four-thirty and then you are off?"

"You got it."

Feeling something wonderful, I did love him, but he was not the type I was searching for. My intuition warned this was not a lasting relationship.

Gazing around the room, I decided it was time to prepare for Susan and Matthew's arrival; time to clean house.

Chapter 22

Mistake or Misfortune

A few flowering shrubs invaded the cold, damp London days, pleasing the visiting tourists and Bradley, who enjoyed his early morning jog in Hyde Park.

He stood near his office window one morning, entranced by the traffic below. Pushing his glasses into place, he thought about the changes London was experiencing. Bradley cut his mustache, but not the longer hair. A tap sounded on the door.

"I think that was a waste of time," Kris commented, dragging his weary body to a nearby chair. "I talked with Chandler about our entry for redeveloping the Square and he admitted that our conceptual design would definitely enhance the town, *making it a better place to live*, so he says!"

"Yeah. I think I heard all that before when it became the prize-winning scheme," Brad frowned.

"Well, listen to this one. The County Planning Authority has submitted to the town's urban district council sketch proposals for a rival scheme which will likely be approved."

"That burns my ass." Brad slammed his fist on the desk. "There never was any specific reason given for turning us down and I damn well feel something should be made public." He stared for a moment, and then Bradley shoved a pencil between his teeth, biting in frustration. "This will cost big dollars."

I knocked before entering.

"Come on in. Join our dismal gathering," Kris called. "So, what's new on the Worcester job?"

"You'll never guess."

Bradley rolled his eyes, fearing more bad news.

"Our contractor selected a sub-contractor from Bath to do the masonry work. The client specifically requested LSM colored mortar, recommended for the type of brick we specified to create a smooth appearance. And guess what? They cheapened out and used another product, which did not do the job. We have problems, again. Andersen is up in arms." I flopped myself down beside Kris.

"Oh, wonderful!" We sat in silence, each absorbed with problems.

"Just to change the subject, for a minute, I have a question," I announced. "You know how hard Susan and I have tried to find her a place to stay, right?" Brad nodded. "I'll be damned if I didn't pass by Queen's Park where a couple of large apartment complexes sat empty and boarded up. Mr. Patterson said numerous such places are all over London. I couldn't believe it. What's that all about?"

Kris twisted in my direction. "Did he tell you that there are more than four hundred sites threatened by redevelopment in central London? Speculators buy them and while they await planning permission, they board them up. What they should do is revise the Rent Act, making short term, low rent and terminable leases possible. Then property owners, awaiting redevelopment, would be encouraged to use their properties. Take, for example, a group of buildings near Victoria Station. The owners have been emptying them for at least two years and now sit vacant. They should use them for short-term housing rentals. It is a vicious circle.

"Just around here, the London University in Bloomsbury is ready to demolish what remains of the housing in Woburn Square. Also, right up where you two live, near the Bayswater Terraces in Hyde Park, the Church Commissioners want more terraces, so they will redevelop more in that area. As the flats sell, they will sit empty until the actual developers can get full control, and then submit plans. Here, read this book, *Goodbye London*, and you'll see what I am talking about." He passed a copy taken off the shelf next to him.

Brad commented, "It won't get any better. I'll try and line something up for Susan, perhaps with a family who is looking for a boarder. Maybe find someone who has the time to take care of Matthew. Mr. Patterson knows of an agency that just might be able to give her a hand now that she has a good job as a design consultant for Marks and Spencer."

"Maybe once she gets on her feet, she'll reconsider returning to Canada. This city is no place to raise a kid on your own."

Bradley grinned. "You mean we'll actually be alone, together, after she finds a place?"

"Oh, Brad! You are not funny. I can't help it if the little fella had colic for the past three months. He's better now and she wants to get back on her feet."

"Please, spare me the details. I remember!"

Kris gathered his paraphernalia. "Well, you two unfortunates, I see I'm only getting in the middle of a domestic argument, so I will leave you now. Oh, remember, Brad, tomorrow, Nastase vs Connors, Centre Court at Wimbledon. Be ready, I hate to fight the crowds." He winked.

"For sure," he waved to his partner.

Bradley approached me, smiling. "I have some good news for you."

"What is it?"

"Someone special is in town. Someone you might like to see." My heart leaped. I thought it might be Chuck. I looked the other way.

"What's the face for?" I didn't reply.

"Hey, Frannie! Look at me! It's Karen. Karen Sharp is in London. I read it in The Times, so I called the Inn on the Park and left her a message to call an old friend, leaving your name. I spoke with her briefly and she will try to get a few hours free tomorrow to come over to the house. She sounded quite excited."

I perked right up at the thought of seeing her again.

"Look, I'm off to see Patterson. I won't be in until late." We hugged, and returned to work.

Hours later, Susan and I met for a coffee in Sloane Square on her way back to the house. We talked about Karen's visit.

"You're kidding me!" Susan exclaimed, struggling with her large portfolio, looking overweight and not as well groomed as she had once been.

"Honest, she really is here. Imagine that, a world famous supermodel." There was an awkward silence.

"What's up, Frannie?" Susan questioned.

"It's just that it got me thinking about our time together, working on the racetrack and when I last saw her. It seems like a whole other life." I confessed.

We arrived at the house to find little Matthew waiting in his stroller with his neighborhood sitter. Susan thanked the elderly woman for staying later than usual, and then helped her carry a few groceries back to her place.

Once inside, I picked up rattles and a blanket from the living room floor, and then attended to things in the kitchen as we discussed the idea of taking a drive to the Cotswolds on the weekend.

After Susan ate dinner, she put Matthew to bed and we sipped tea on the front steps, enjoying the last of the summer sunset when the phone rang. I could see the panic on Susan's face when she shouted excitedly that Karen was on her way over. Frantically, we rushed around, cleaning up, dusting and vacuuming. We had just finished when the doorbell rang.

The stunning platinum blond, wearing the latest designer fashions, greeted Susan. I whistled.

"You make me sick! You are even more gorgeous than ever!" We embraced, laughing like teenagers.

"It's been a few years, hasn't it?" Karen replied. "I am so glad we finally found each other. You must know, you really have changed a lot yourself since our days together on the racetrack. You've put on a couple of pounds, and in the right places," Karen complimented. I reintroduced Susan. They had previously met at the dinner following SnoMann's win.

"Come on in and sit down. Where to begin? So much has happened over the past few years - for all of us," I was unable to take my eyes off her. "I can't believe a world-famous cover girl, supermodel – sitting here, in our living room."

Karen laughed, "Yeah, it is a long way from the stable area of Blue Bonnets, right? This place is terrific; I love this part of London."

Susan offered to get us coffee or wine.

"It's Brad's place."

"Well, from my perception of real estate prices in London, he is really doing well and he sounded great on the phone. Is he as good-looking as ever?" Karen smiled and I agreed. Susan was quick to return with some refreshments, including a bottle of Beaujolais, my favorite, and three glasses.

"Great taste, ladies." Karen grinned as the cork popped.

"A toast - to old friendships and new successes," Susan stated, lifting her glass.

"According to the papers, you have certainly done well. Gone right to the top! 'Woman Athlete of the Year' in Canada, a very successful North American jockey, and now one of the world's most photographed women. I just do not believe it! Like Cinderella, from pumpkin to princess," I said, laughing.

Karen casually dropped back onto the couch, slipping her shoes to the side, describing her lifestyle, followed by a lingering pause.

"Let me explain a few things. Not too many people know about this. It hasn't been all sugar and spice."

"What do you mean?" I became intrigued.

She recalled the day when Peter and John ran SnoMann and she got her chance to ride, her first big break. She reminded us that it was a time when no trainers would ever let a female jockey ride their horses, let alone in a Stake race. Proving herself and seizing the opportunity to hit the big time, she received huge press coverage and picked up more mounts. The following year, she rode at Aqueduct where Sports Illustrated interviewed her, which in turn, led to questions on her modeling profession. The cover featured photos of her as a jockey, plus, a picture of when she was runner-up to Miss Toronto. That was her next break. Phone calls, more interviews and her choice of many modeling jobs resulted in the end of her riding days.

"You see, it was the 'jockey' that brought me the big break. I stepped into the modeling industry because they thought I was celebrity material in the world of sports."

"That certainly doesn't sound any less than fantastic," Susan clasped her hands.

"What I wanted to say was, one of the reasons Dad allowed me on the race track as a kid was to exercise and keep trim; positively not to think about riding. He quarreled with Mother constantly, saying it was ok and insisted that it wasn't going to harm my reputation seeing as I was there with my own father. Then, I received my jockey license and rode SnoMann without their knowledge. He had been away for a few weeks at a yearling sale in the U.S. He begged me not to continue, but I couldn't give it up.

"Well, that was the beginning of the end of my parent's marriage too. Mother left him. Everything I did seemed to hurt Dad. Mother could not face the fact that her daughter was a jockey, and said repeatedly that I had lowered my standard of living, rebelling against everything she believed in. She would not listen to anyone who tried to convince her otherwise. First, she lost my brother, and then me. Dad was livid. I had made my decision, but Mother swore never to speak to me again - and hasn't. When my brother died in that motorcycle accident, they put everything, all their hopes and energy, into my life. But, to them, I ended up just another disappointment because it wasn't what they wanted. I am not saying that I have any regrets, but for my family, it has been worse than heartbreak. It has been like another death."

Feeling badly because I had known Karen and her family very well and could see she missed them as her story came as a complete shock. We chatted about happier aspects of her success until the whimper from Matthew opened a door to another tale. Susan attended to the call. She carried him into the room and we fussed over him for a while before she disappeared to feed him.

"I never really knew your friend Sue, but remembered her as very attractive," Karen whispered.

"Yup! She used to be. However, she has always had a mind of her own. She desperately wanted the baby, but the pregnancy took a lot out of her and now she has no interest in anything else but Matthew. He has become her whole life, and I've literally dressed her in clean clothes some days. She does not care one bit about her appearance. I tried persuading her to buy something for her skin, but no way. She refuses to even wear make-up." I shook my head in disappointment.

"I suppose she feels that isn't one of her priorities anymore," Karen commented, "and how about you, Frannie?" I told her my yarn about Europe and coming to London.

"Have you found anyone special?"

"How special?" I teased.

"Stop trying to evade the question. John died a long time ago. Do you have anyone else?"

"Yeah, well I'm working on it," I explained.

"Bradley?" I nodded, and then asked the same question.

"How about you? I would imagine you would have men on both arms, a lover in every port."

Karen straightened. "I suppose you could say that I have never found the right man. Not that I haven't been looking, mind you. I have been busy, traveling, and enjoying the entire ride; like you said - a Cinderella. I suppose that I haven't found a man who is dynamic enough. Lots of photographers and artsy types, fashion executives, mostly married, and the odd diplomat, but not Mr. Right." She paused, taking a deep breath. "Look

Frannie, how about checking out this town, some sightseeing tomorrow? I have an early session at ten-thirty, hopefully, should finish by noon. Could we meet and do something together? Remember Expo? We had a blast that year in Montreal, didn't we?"

"We sure did. Call me when you're free, in case you run late."

Susan re-entered the room. I explained our plans and offered to watch Matthew in the morning while she shopped.

Shortly before midnight, Karen returned to her hotel. I laid awake, rehashing Karen's family situation. Our lives had crossed paths, once again.

Saturday's weather was perfect for touring the fabled historic city. Playing with Matthew while Susan checked out a few rooms for rent and shopped in the market, she promised to return before noon. Shortly after eleven, I received a call from Kris asking me to deliver job estimates to the quantity surveyors, and then wait for their adjustments before returning them to the office for his completion. I explained that I already had plans and tried to convince him to find someone else.

"Frannie, I'd do it myself, but I have these tickets to the match today at Wimbledon and I really don't..." he started explaining.

"Alright, already! I will do it. But I have to wait for Susan to come back. Will you still be in the office?"

"I should be, but if I'm not, I will leave the package in Florence's desk drawer in the lobby with instructions for repricing. Thanks a lot, dear. See you later."

Down went the receiver, furiously. For once I had plans that I did not want interrupted by my job. Storming around the house, I became short-tempered with Matthew, who cried for his bottle. Susan returned minutes before noon, relieving me of my baby-sitting. Explaining the situation, I rushed out the door saying I would return by two.

Just as I had climbed into the back of the cab, a green flash passed by. A sports car cut right in front of us. Its unique antique lines made me smile, and then forgot about it.

Kris had left by the time I arrived at the office. The package was where he said it would be with a lengthy description attached to it. By the time I reached my destination in Chelsea, it was after one o'clock. The building's locked doors presented a further delay, so I knocked persistently until a security guard came and directed me to the office designated on the envelope.

The young man on the phone talked for fifteen minutes. Finally, he took the package with the new pricing structure for the renovation and announced that the required totals were not listed. He gave me a calculator, to work on the thirty-two page report, while he restructured the necessary sections for the price increase. Unaware of the time, two and a half hours had passed before we completed. By the time I returned the package to the office, and then traveled back, I arrived at the house at six o'clock.

I paid my fare, stood on the side of the road and faced a British racing-green Morgan with a large multi-colored ribbon tied in a bow to the zipper of its tonneau cover. My mouth dropped. I blinked repeatedly, disbelieving, and hoped the vision of the roadster would disappear.

The front door opened and Brad marched across the street to confront me, extending a velvet-covered box. His silence matched his stern facial expression. Carefully, he loosened the lid, displaying a set of keys on a gold ring, lying over a folded letter. Slowly, I closed my eyes. He snapped the lid shut and whispered harshly.

"Just what the fuck is going on here?" Fear crept up from the pit of my stomach into my throat, strangling my reply. "I want to know just what the hell this is all about. It does not take too many brains to figure out that this is obviously some kind of *special* gift and I don't have to ask from whom." Bradley spat the words through his teeth.

Susan called from the doorway, but neither of us made any effort to look her way.

"Don't you dare move one inch until I get some answers, woman!" Bradley harshly shouted. Susan approached us, carrying Matthew in her arms.

"Bradley! The phone, it's for you!"

"Take a message! I'm busy, and I'm not leaving here until I get some friggin' answers!"

"Listen! It's Mr. Patterson."

"So! Take a message, will you?" he fumed.

"Damn it, no! Go answer it yourself," Susan bellowed in return. Brad stood his ground for a moment, then threw the package at me, and turned toward the house.

Without warning, Bradley halted in his tracks. He spun awkwardly in the middle of the road, taking a step backward, pointing at me harshly.

"And there's another thing, Miss Harrison. You sure pulled off a hell of a snow job on Chuckie and me. What was it? Were you afraid of having to make a commitment to one of us? Is that why you backed off? That goddamn affair between you and Mencini really screwed things for you, didn't it? I don't know if you will ever know the difference between infatuation and real love. When will you get over it? He conned you, and you still can't face it. I don't know if you'll ever get over the whole ordeal or not, but I'm telling you one thing, you're no good to anyone until you do. I only wish to hell there was some way you could clear your head." His tone softened. "You're still running, aren't you, Frannie, either from the truth or the unknown. You know, if you have not heard anything by now, after all these years, you might as well face it. You are not ever going to hear the truth about the murder. He's dead. He's gone!"

Susan hollered at him again. He returned to the house. She ran up next to me.

"I don't have a clue as to what is going on here, but I'm here to tell you that after you left this afternoon, 'this' car pulls up, and guess who is the driver? Right! Chuck. I told him that you were working, and while we were talking, along comes Karen looking spiffy as ever. It was like a magnetic attraction between the two. I served them some tea, we chatted for a while, and then right there before my very eyes, they started getting pretty friendly. After three, they decided that they were not wasting good weather by sitting around, so they left, driving off together. Honestly, it was like a scene from a romantic movie. Bingo, they fell into one another's trance."

"So, what then?"

"Well, he left this box on the hall table. It was around five when Brad comes back from tennis and saw that car. I told him some story that he didn't believe, and he stomped around calling you every name in the book. You see, he opened the envelope and saw two airline tickets for Malta."

"Oh, shit, no!" I gasped, covering my face. Susan nodded. "I can't face him. Not now. I got to get the hell out of here and think this thing through."

Leaving the area with tears running down my cheeks, Susan tried calling, but I was already out of reach. "I forgot to tell you. You got a letter from Peter."

Stumbling into Hyde Park, I walked aimlessly, buying a hot dog near the Serpentine. Feeling shaken up, I tried to put things into perspective wondering if Bradley spoke the truth.

Down a winding flower path and onto the boardwalk, through Kensington Gardens, across to Marlborough Gate, until there came a bench where I sat watching the spouting fountains. Believing I'd lost Bradley's trust, I desperately made excuses, but knew none existed, and slowly made my way back to face the consequences.

Was Chuck just another devil with a pretty face? Had all the good-looking guys in my life been like that? Am I continually being the fool manipulated by every man... my father, my fiancé, boyfriends, my previous boss... everyone but my brother?

The Morgan remained parked with the ribbon blowing in the breeze. Drawing a deep breath, as the cool night air settled in, I slowly turned the front door handle and entered.

"Thank you for keeping your promise, Frannie," Chuck spoke, "I hope my gift is exactly as you wished."

My stomach tightened as I brushed the loose hair from my face, waiting for someone to speak, because I was not able to utter a syllable.

Karen stood next to Chuck. She turned, "And, thank you for our fabulous day, Frannie. Chuck and I both feel you are the perfect matchmaker."

Susan sat in the corner, smiling and trying not to laugh.

Brad, obviously inebriated, tilted his glass downing half the drink and falling into the closest chair.

"Sit down, kid, before your knees give out," he ordered. Confused, I stepped toward the fireplace and sat near the hearth.

"I don't get any of this bull. It sounds like a scam to me," Bradley continued, "but, the tickets to Malta? Why the fuck is your name and Frannie's on them?" he swore, slurring his words.

Chuck approached me, holding my shoulders firmly. "We made a deal, a long time ago. She would find me the perfect woman, and I'd give her whatever she wanted. I knew she loved cars. I mean any woman driving a Ferrari has to be a little unusual and so the Morgan was part of it.

237

Francine said she found the perfect girl for me, so I came right away. And, the tickets were in her name, because I didn't happen to know the name of the woman she would find for me."

Brad was pissed. "Bullshit! So, how would you know anything about Karen? I mean, she just arrived and even Frannie didn't know anything about it?"

"Well, it only took a quick phone call after they spent last evening together, right Francine?" Chuck responded. Brad turned away, unbelieving.

"Well, now you have another automobile to go with your collection of gifts from the men in your life. I suppose the motorcycle would never sit well alongside either of them, eh?" The dimly lit room fell silent. Karen approached Chuck, "I think it is time for us to leave, if we want to make the club. It's after ten."

"Yes, I almost forgot. Anyone care to join us over on Regent Street?" No one replied. The couple hugged, held hands and strolled out, bidding goodbye to all.

Susan retreated to her room while I retrieved a can of soda from the kitchen, listening to Bradley mumble. "This will take me a goddamn long time to figure out. Don't bug me." Within a minute, he had fallen into a deep unconscious sleep and I quickly turned out the lights and went to my room. My head ached. Within no time, Susan tapped on the door.

"What happened?" I asked, retrieving my PJs from the closet.

"You know, it was the strangest thing. Bradley started hitting the bottle right after you left, and I could not say anything. About half an hour before you got back here, Karen and Chuck returned, and they strolled in, all starry-eyed and lovey-dovey. Brad did a double take, and then started to cross-examine him, putting Chuck on the spot. But, that guy is too smooth. Ol' Chuck conned him and Karen right along and I thought at first neither of them would question the whole thing. That is until Bradley started to mouth off and went to get more to drink; one right after another. He was so pissed off, I can't tell you." Susan's tone softened. "You know, I think Karen fell for the whole setup. She thinks the world of you, and when Chuck turned up unannounced and sweet-talked her with his southern ways into spending the day with him, well, let me tell you, she was definitely enjoying it. That guy really has a way with words, doesn't he?"

I couldn't help but smile. "A way with women is more like it."

Hesitating, only a beat, before exclaiming, "God, I pray I haven't lost Brad. I really do love him. I guess I always have."

"Well, only time will tell. This will be hard for him because he saw Chuck around enough that he knew something going on between you two. If he can accept this con job, you will be fine. If he doesn't, I think you're finished. You should have heard him! I think he would have done something dumb. He was livid."

Tossing all night, realizing in my heart I was glad Chuck and Karen had met. They actually were perfect together. Once again, there it was, that serendipity stuff; funny how these coincidences keep coming up.

In the morning, Bradley had left for Birmingham before I came downstairs. The days became weeks, and then turned into months.

In October, Kris found a flat in Maida Vale that Susan could afford. An older couple provided her with a separate section of their house and the woman assisted Susan with Matthew. Delighted with the arrangement, she enjoyed having her own place as we had lived under the same roof for almost a year.

One evening, while Susan and I walked with Matthew, laughing at his excited chatter that we could not understand, we heard a car honk from behind us. Turning to see the green Morgan pull up beside us, the retro roadster turned the heads of many as Bradley sat at the wheel. We had not spoken much, other than what was necessary during work, as he had cooled considerably.

"I decided that you shouldn't have this in storage, it is yours to enjoy. Since you decided to keep it, thought it was time to take this machine for a spin. How about it? Want to go for a drive?" Susan and I glared at one another as my surprise became obvious. She nodded.

"Go ahead. Now is your chance. Take it for a spin and find out just where you stand."

"Right!" Quickly climbing into the vintage roadster, I slid down into the leather seats stretching out my legs and strapping my seatbelt. We spun off heading through the city with the wind blowing and knotting my hair. Crossing the Putney Bridge, taking the A205 over to the A4, we headed west. I shouted over the roar of the engine as he changed gears, "Where are we going?"

"Back to the days of Jane Austen."

"Where?"

"To the Roman City of Aquae Sulis."

"Oh." He caught a glimpse of my blank expression.

"Bath, dummy," he smiled, touching my hand.

We drove late into the night, stopping at a roadside Inn. Without a word of affection, I quietly went to my room. After a hearty breakfast, we drove on, and were not long before reaching the ancient Roman city. The skies were bright and the temperature cool. Bradley stopped the car next to the Avon where we had a perfect view of the river.

"Look at that view! There is one magnificent piece of architecture for you. That ancient bridge that crosses the River Avon, built by Robert Adam, and named after Sir William Pulteney is one of my favorite sights in all of England." Bradley leaned against the iron fence, appreciative of its work and beauty. I looked closely, intrigued by its structure and admired the colorful landscape along the river's edge.

"Yes, I can see why. It's such a splendid, beautiful view that reminds me very much of the Ponte Vecchio." We hugged.

"Frannie," he whispered. I looked into his eyes. "Will you marry me?"

Surprised by the unexpected, my mouth dropped open, my stomach tightened and my heart began to beat faster. Staring, without responding, my world suddenly brightened.

"Huh? What did... ? Why, yes, of course, I will." Taken completely by surprise, I leaped into his arms, embracing him tightly. Tears filled my eyes with joy. I would remember that moment forever because I barely remembered the rest of our weekend.

On our return trip to London, we found another surprise. We entered the house grubby and windblown from our long drive. Susan called from the kitchen.

"Hey guys, thanks for letting me know you were leaving for the weekend. See if I consider you on my next overnight," she laughed. I rushed to her side, revealing our news as we poured drinks in celebration. Bradley decided to delay calling his family until the following day. "When are you going to set a date?" Susan asked.

We looked at one another. "Umm, we don't know," we replied.

"We need to pick out an engagement ring, I think." Bradley took my hand in his.

"Geez, I almost forgot to tell you the reason why I'm here." Susan jumped up from her chair.

"What is it? You look like you were just struck by lightning." Bradley reached for his drink.

"A phone call, yesterday, for you Frannie; it was the Canadian Consulate."

Puzzled, I shrugged my shoulders. "I have all my papers in order; visa and passport. What else could they want?"

"The man who called asked me if you still resided at this address and I told him you did. Then, he wanted to speak to you, and I said you were away."

"Yeah, yeah. So?" I implored her.

"He had all these questions and I was afraid to say anything." Susan stood in front of us seated on the sectional. She gestured with her hands tightly fisted.

"It seems that someone from the embassy here wants to give you some notification of trial." I sobered. "They have charged a man with the murder of John Mencini and they want, or are requesting, your return to Toronto. Something about a preliminary hearing."

My heart started racing and I felt dizzy. Bradley and I held one another, realizing I had broken a cardinal rule; never bring your *past* to the *present*, because it will dominate your *future*.

PART V

'Trial by Jury'

Chapter 23
Toronto - 1977

Time is approaching... the trial is about to begin.

The months we spent apart ended when Bradley flew to Toronto. We needed a holiday as the time with lawyers, police and investigators wore me down.

Bradley takes a few days to make the necessary arrangements for our trip as the winter winds blow, causing hazardous conditions with heavy rains. Damaged hydro lines, broken branches and trees littered the streets. We are glad to leave the city for sunnier skies in Nassau.

The Bahamas are just what we need. We land in Providence and take a taxi, in the hot sun, to the Nassau Beach Hotel. Our waterfront room is breathtaking with a corner view of the ocean. In no time at all, we toss our clothes aside, put on our bathing suits, and race to the beach to catch the last of the day's sun before dinner. Our week holiday goes by fast as we enjoy the beauty of basking on the sun-filled island, relaxing with the slow pace of the natives, taking long walks, sipping exotic rum punches and dancing to the steel drums. I especially take pleasure in shopping in the markets for straw bags and hats during the daytime, and then gambling at the casino at night. The colorful gaiety of the cabaret is mesmerizing, but on the other hand, Bradley prefers the exquisite gourmet dinners and romantic evenings on the beach.

As we take our last walk along the roadway, we notice the ruins of an abandoned racetrack. Although the course is knee deep in sand, broken railings surround its remains and debris. We observe a few thoroughbreds bathing in the ocean waters and imagine various scenarios, leaving much of the rest to our imagination. A dilapidated sun-blistered grandstand traces a partial outline in the distance. The government closed it down unexpectedly with no further discussion.

Time always flies by when having fun, and before we know it, I am packing our bags. Following a long flight back to New York, we change airlines and fly to Europe to visit Leonard for a week. Our PanAm 747 leaves on schedule.

The welcoming open-arms of little Martha immediately takes a liking to Bradley, and prepares us for an enjoyable visit.

We relive many memories the night we return to watch a Raak hockey game, but our special time together passes much too quickly. The evening before our departure, Martha falls asleep on my lap while the family talks together. Leonard places his arm around Julie. "It won't be long now and you'll be free of it all Frannie, and you can move on with your own personal plans."

"Thanks, we love being here. And, to think that this little doll is now three. I can't believe it." I caress Martha's forehead.

"Well, believe this; our next baby is due around Thanksgiving!"

"You're kidding me! Why didn't you say something?"

"Just confirmed it this afternoon," Leonard grins, holding Julie's hand.

"Congratulations! This calls for a celebration," I agree as Leonard opens the brandy and Julie sips her glass of water. We end our visit on a happy note, good times together.

Being appreciative for all Bradley's support and arranging for Nancy to fill in as my replacement at the office, I begin to anticipate the upcoming trial during my eight-hour flight back to Toronto as Bradley returns to London. Little do we know our separation would feel like an eternity.

Back in true form, I am spending most of my time in preliminary testimonies before the upcoming trial. I carefully collect my thoughts. Dropping in to visit Susan's parents and my Aunt every week, I am grateful for their hospitality and support as Peter and I struggle with the complications concerning Susan and the Edwards' grandson, Matthew. I show them the few snapshots I carry, and then, gradually, we feel their disapproving opinions mellow. Their distress and worries aimed at Susan's lack of morals had developed a great distance between them.

I decide stay at the Edward's home for the duration of the trial as Peter has his girlfriend move in to his townhouse.

The weeks and months of preparation pass slowly, and then finally, Whittmore declares it is now time. While conversing in his office, he recaps and clarifies that following the jury selection, he will present his opening arguments, stressing how he will establish guilt. The defense will then present arguments telling the jury how they intend to prove Robert Sharp's innocence, or try to establish insufficient evidence for conviction.

"First, we set the scene of the murder by calling Sergeant Warren, and then the pathologist. There will also be someone to testify from the Center of Forensic Sciences to identify the firearm. And then, it will be your time to take the stand." Crown attorney James Whittmore explains.

"Will his daughter Karen testify?" I ask, sitting in his office where we discuss the particulars.

"Yes. She will have to answer questions about their relationship as well as the connection between John and her father." I think the trial should last at least two months by the number of witnesses.

Karen would testify, but have the support of her husband, Chuck Conners. After their meeting in London, their involvement flourished and when news of their engagement arrived, I was still living there.

Whittmore and I rehash the questions they will ask of me, explaining that at the beginning, it's the Judge's order to have all witnesses removed from sitting in on the trial until their testimonies are given. Whittmore suggests that I wear something dark and limit any jewelry as he wants me very natural looking.

The phone rings. It is Reagan, his son.
"I'm sorry Francine, I am running late and have to go to Power Squadron class with my son, so if you don't have any further questions, I'll have...."
I understand, leaving his office shortly after six.

Snowstorm.
Rushing into the courthouse late, I locate the information table where I scan the trial lists posted along the twelve-foot counter. Courtroom sixteen in the Supreme Court, names the trial *Regina vs Sharp*. Taking the escalator up

four flights, I discover the impressive wooden double-doors where a constable waits, wearing a navy blazer with a nametag pinned to his lapel.

"Excuse me. Are you a witness for this case?" he asks, politely.

"Yes, I am." I respond.

"Please, come with me. I'll take you to the *witness room*."

We pass several lawyers in their black robes, as crowds of people step off the escalator from the floor above.

Noticing my look of concern, the constable describes the first group taken into the courtroom and called out by name, perhaps, chosen or not, for jury duty. After selecting the twelve, the remainder of the group return to the *enclosure room*, to wait until a different case begins.

Entering the witness room, I anxiously ask where the prisoner is. The constable describes his arrival. "First thing this morning, the handcuffed accused comes from the Don Jail to a *holding-cell* downstairs. After half an hour, the guards transfer him to the *tank*, a room found directly in back of the courtroom where he waits until the trial begins."

An elderly man approaches, dressed in formal attire: pin striped trousers and a jacket with tails. My inquisitive glance warrants an explanation.

"Yes, this gentleman is properly dressed. He is the *deputy* and escorts the judge from his chambers to the bench." The constable closes the door behind him as he proceeds with his duties.

The courthouse and its people are unfamiliar to most residents of the city and I wonder about it. Gazing at the traffic below, I see how Toronto is maturing and suffering growing pains as the city vibrates with an effervescent energy.

Snow continues to fall; I glance at my watch showing twelve-forty. Sergeant Warner enters and we shake hands.

"Terrible day, isn't it?" He sits down. "They've just recessed for lunch. Once selected, the Crown will address the jury. I expect you will testify the day after tomorrow." I concur.

It actually takes three days to select the jury.

Chapter 24
Courtroom Drama

Arriving promptly, I return to the witness room. An hour passes before the constable enters. "Miss Harrison, come this way, please." I retrieve my purse and follow him into courtroom sixteen.

Judge MacIntosh sits at the bench before a mammoth dark marble wall that holds a large replica of the British Coat of Arms with the inscription, *Dieu et mon droit*. The Judge is wearing a red banner over his black gown. I can see the back of Robert Sharp's head in the prisoners' dock as the jurors turn in my direction. My heart pounds heavily as I step closer to the front of the room.

Whittmore concludes addressing the Judge concerning the exhibits. I spot the familiar maps on an easel close to the jury as I pass the podium. Walking by the table where Whittmore's binder lies open, I carefully step into the witness box, clear my dry throat as the Registrant approaches and asks for my full name.

"Francine Mabelle Harrison," I reply, following with a short dry cough. Then, he spells it. He hands me the Bible, which I hold in my right hand as they request me to 'swear in'. He backs away and Whittmore stands beside the podium. He asks my age and address.

"Tell us, Miss Harrison, where did you meet the deceased?"

"We met at a track and field meet in Aurora, in the spring of 1965."

"Did you start dating after that?"

"Yes, we lived in the same neighborhood."

"Which was?"

"Yorkville Village."

"So, you had known John Mencini for a few years before the murder?"

"Yes. We were engaged at the time."

"Where were you and your fiancé on the day of the murder?"

"I was with John, at the racetrack." My voice starts to quiver. Whittmore turns, facing the jurors. "Would you please explain which racetrack and what you were doing on that particular day? Do you know the date?"

"Yes, it was June third, 1969. John and I had been together most of the day, hanging around the stable with some friends, and talking about our plans for the wedding. I remember it was after four because John said that he would do chores that afternoon, and we were running late. We had been staying at the Skyline Hotel when we returned to the track."

"Which racetrack?"

"Woodbine, off Rexdale Boulevard." Whittmore nods to continue. I catch sight of Sharp from the corner of my eye. He is showing no emotion.

"We parked the car in the lot outside the stable entrance." He walks up to the maps beside me.

"This is a chart of the general area in question. Does it match your recollection?" I move over to examine the markings. I pause and then carefully identify it for the jury.

"Now, would you indicate to the jury, please, with this ruler, where you had parked the car."

I step down carefully, taking the ruler and point to the location. "John parked his car here. It was his usual parking spot if it was vacant. We got out of the car and were walking this way." I indicate the area.

"So you were walking toward the stable gate entrance, in an easterly direction?"

"Yes."

"Then, what?"

"I was on his right side. We showed our passes to the security guard, and then walked into the barn area. We heard someone call out his name."

"So, not just anyone could enter the stable area. You had to show some identification." Whittmore slides a pencil behind his ear. "Was this person shouting?"

"Yes. He shouted his name, John. John Roberts."

"You said his name ... "

"Yes, well, he was using an assumed name when I first met him and then he went back to using his own name."

"So, you recognized the call directed at Mencini?"

"Yes. He yelled something else, not quite sure, exactly… something about his name change. Then I heard the shot." I close my eyes, as the painful emotion overwhelms me. "I screamed, because I was suddenly covered with a horrific spray of blood."

"Will you please tell the court where he was hit?" Whittmore asks firmly, as he paces by the twelve chosen jurors.

"I think in the side of the head … or neck, yes, in the neck."

"Show the jury, please." I indicate the left side of my neck, a few inches below the jaw. Whittmore repeats the area of the wound for the jury.

"Can you describe what you thought the gun looked like?"

The defense counsel objects, noting that the size of the gun was an assumption. Whittmore asks permission to have the registrar place several guns on the table. He retrieves them from under his desk.

"Miss Harrison, would you please pick one similar to the weapon used." I step down from the stand, and walk before the bench, studying the weapons. Picking a small gun, it fit in my hand without its being obscure.

"This would be about the size, but I wouldn't know what kind it was or if this could be it."

"Now, assume for a moment that you take this, and point it at me. Yes, that's right. Since he was in the car, was he facing out the driver's side window?"

"Yes."

"You may return to the stand." He continues with his questioning. "Did you hear the shot when the gun pointed at John and if so, how many shots were fired?"

"Yes, I heard it. I believe only one shot."

"What happened when he was hit?"

Filling with emotion, I cover my face. Whittmore pauses, walking back to the podium, giving me time to regain my composure. I try to swallow the pain, and then take a drink of water. "Uh, well." I attempt to speak, holding back tears. "He jumped back, choking and then went down."

The jury turns from me to the prosecutor. He walks over to the map. Tears blur my vision as I envision the pulsing spray of blood splatter across my face.

"Now, you and the victim were near the gate – here - and the car was about how far away?"

"I suppose it was about fifty or sixty feet away." He points out an approximate spot on the map for the jury.

"Did you see what happened to the gun?"

"No."

"What did you do next?"

Perspiration beads on my brow, reminding me of the day when blood dripped down my cheeks.

"I called for help as I tried to assist John when he fell, but the blood was spurting out in all directions. His face and clothes were covered." Tears trickle, and then stream down my cheeks. There is a deliberate pause as Whittmore refers to his notes. The Judge asks if I care to continue as I wipe my face with the back of my hand. Breathing deeply, I continue.

"I'm ok," I stutter, trying to compose myself, thinking I'm not finished with my grieving, as deep scars still need to mend.

A moment later, Whittmore recognizes I am ready to continue. He comes up to the stand. "Did anyone come to assist you?"

"Yes, the security guard. He heard the shot too. He, or someone, called the ambulance that's always on the track, and it was there in minutes."

"Approximately, how long would you say?"

"I am sure it took no longer than four or five minutes."

"And then what happened?"

"They worked on him for a several minutes and got him on the stretcher and into the back of the ambulance. I went with them to the hospital." Someone places a box of tissues nearby.

"Was he alive at the racetrack?"

"Yes. They took his pulse and said they had to rush."

Slowly I return to the podium where he motions with his hand, "Did you see anyone you could identify? You said you were standing about here, not too far from the guard's hut, when this happened." Whittmore retraces his steps to the easel.

"Yes." I twist, facing the map. "When the man had first yelled out John's name, I stooped over and could see him in the car, with the gun pointed at us . . ."

"Could you describe this man?' he persists.

"He was, perhaps, middle-aged, and balding."

"Could you identify him, if you saw him again?"

"Yes."

"Tell us, could you identify the car?"

"Yes. I heard the tires squeal as it pulled away. It was a station wagon, but I wouldn't know the model or the year."

"What about the color?"

"No. I know it was a dark color with woodgrain sides. That is all I remember but if I ever saw it again, I would be able to identify it."

"Show us the direction which the car was driving."

"It left through this entrance." The Judge leans over and asks me to speak up for everyone to hear. I swallow and inhale deeply.

The Crown repeats the direction for the jury.

"What time of day was this?"

"Probably a little after five-thirty. I would think it took us around half an hour to get there from the hotel in all the traffic."

Whittmore walks to a table positioned in front of the bench to retrieve a photograph, which is the same one I identified for the police.

"Do you recognize this man?"

"Yes. He is the same man I saw in the station wagon, holding the gun. He shot John Mencini." The soft rumble that echoes throughout the courtroom lasts several minutes.

Placing the picture in the hands of the registrar, Whittmore requests, "With M'Lord's permission, I would like this photo submitted as Exhibit Two."

The defense counsel approaches, views it, and then without objection he returns to his seat. The Registrar takes it, hands it to the Judge, identifies it with the necessary markings, and then shows it to the jury.

"Do you know the accused, Miss Harrison?"

"Yes."

"Would you tell the court how you know him, and perhaps, when you first met?"

"I met him in the early spring, 1966. I had gone to the racetrack one morning when I wanted to get a job as a 'hot-walker'."

"What is a 'hot-walker'?" Whittmore interrupts.

"It is someone who walks the racehorses after a workout or when they have raced, to cool them down, before they return to their stall," I smile, nervously.

"Walking hot horses? Continue ..."

"Well, John had known Bob Sharp long before I arrived. Actually, Peter Edwards introduced us. Bob gave me a job with his stable."

"Were the accused and the deceased friends?"

"Yes. They were very close."

"What makes you think so?"

"Because Bob convinced John to take his trainer's license and he helped him all he could. They had a close relationship, right up until the latter months."

"Did they argue?"

"Never, in the beginning. They were very compatible, but towards the end, they were constantly bickering. John had his own ideas of how he wanted to run his small stable, and their opinions differed about several things."

The crown attorney turns to his desk, for some papers, and looking at the clock comments on the time. "M'Lord, my questions will be extensive, may I suggest that it would be a good time to break?"

The Judge agrees, and they escort the jury out of the courtroom. While I stand there, the Judge then directs me to return in fifteen minutes. Two constables take the handcuffed prisoner away. The Registrar stands, calling 'order', and adjourns court. Everyone in the room stands as the deputy guides the Judge out a back door. Then, as everyone else leaves, the courtroom buzzes with chatter. I step down, knowing the worst is yet to come, and meet Peter for a coffee.

"How's it going?" Peter is anxious as he can't attend court until after he testifies.

"They have hardly started. They ask one question and they pause, and it slowly drags on. Whittmore has more questions for me and I have yet to be cross-examined. If it continues to go like this, I'll be the only witness on the stand this week." I describe the tedious questioning for the jury's clear understanding; he notices my nervousness.

"What did Sharp do?"

"Not much. He sits in the prisoners dock in his silk suit, wearing an innocent expression. No emotion or compassion."

"Were many from the press there?" Peter asks as he fidgets with something in his pocket.

"I couldn't really say. When I am on that stand, I don't see or hear much of anything else. I am too nervous. I have a hard time focusing on what I have to say."

"Well, it will soon be over. I will be in your shoes soon enough."

"Tell you one thing, the crowded gallery has people coming and going the whole time I gave testimony."

Once back inside the room, everyone takes his place. The deputy calls 'Order', and everyone stands, again he escorts the Judge to his seat. After the prisoner returns, the guard uncuffed his wrists, and then the jury arrives and I take the stand.

Whittmore asks for specific details about the relationship between Mencini and Sharp; their disagreements, arguments, and when the relationship became strained. Questioning continues for hours, until court adjourns.

Testimonies resume early the following morning.

"In your opinion, Miss Harrison, did Mencini show bad taste when he named Karen Sharp, the accused's daughter, to ride the racehorse, SnoMann?"

"Not that I knew of. Karen commented that she thought her Dad would have been proud of the way she rode the race. I didn't hear any negative talk. I would say no, it was not done in bad taste."

"Was there any blame directed at anyone in particular?"

"Bob blamed John for it all, saying that John knew how he felt toward his daughter's riding, and that John had let her ride SnoMann anyway, to get back at him, when he was out of town."

"Did you hear them speak to one another after the race was won?"

"No."

"To the best of your knowledge, Miss Harrison, was there ever a relationship between John Mencini and Miss Sharp?"

I blink, taken by surprise.

"Why, no. Not that I was ever aware of."

"In your opinion, did John ever provoke the accused in any way?" In his casual way, Whittmore keeps his eye on the jurors' reactions, as he moves back and forth during questioning.

"They had their differences and disagreements over certain training methods. John would go ahead and do things his own way."

"Did you know of any drugs that would have caused arguments?"

"Not specifically. Just rumors. He didn't mention them to me."

"In your personal relationship with the victim, did he ever pressure you?"

"No."

Did he ever want you to move in with him?"

"Yes."

"You spent a lot of time together in Montreal, correct?" He strolls up to where I am sitting.

"Yes. I was living with my brother and his wife."

"Did you feel that John was popular and well liked in his profession by others?

"Yes. Very much, by both young and old alike."

"Did you ever meet his family?"

"Yes. I stayed with them in Ohio on a couple of occasions. They lived on a large farm, in Mechanicstown. I found his parents very pleasant and they seemed to care deeply for their boys."

Gathering his binder, he questions, "Would you tell the court when that would have been?" And then I continue with his slow form of detailing for the remainder of the day until Whittmore smiles and announces. "No further questions, Your Honor."

I am exhausted and leave the courthouse depleted of any energy as I take a cab to the Edward's home where a hot dinner waits and a warm bed.

Day three, once again I take the witness stand.

The Judge scribbles several notes before he calls on the Defense.

A much younger man stands, nodding to the bench, and then approaches the podium with a thick file of notes. He continues questioning with reference to each event, covering the day of the murder, and then cross-examines my personal relationship with John. This process takes another two days. He wants to see if my story changes at all.

"From my understanding, Miss Harrison, it appears that you noticed no real problems between the accused and the victim. The only real disagreements were hearsay or rumors as you put it. Did you know ahead of time about this race which John was going to place a large amount of money on a horse called SnoMann?"

"Yes." I think he repeats himself, again.

"To your knowledge, were any drugs involved?"

"No."

"Tell us, who knew about such a bet?"

"Myself, Peter Edwards, Karen Sharp and Raymond Cooper knew about the race. I don't know of anyone else who knew he was going to turn him loose."

"Are you indicating that John did not try to win races with the horse before?"

"No, he was going to turn him loose for the win after SnoMann had recovered from an injury. This took time because John felt he would be stronger and ..." I feel myself fumbling.

"In fact, Miss Harrison, isn't it true they stiffed the horse a number of times and John was upset when his jockey didn't ride that day? Isn't it true that John Mencini was going to do anything he could do to make sure of the win, no matter what or who stood in his way?" he shouts.

I tremble at such an outburst, which cause the crowd in the gallery to chatter.

"Objection. The Defense is badgering the witness," Whittmore interrupts. The rumble in the courtroom subsides.

"Tell us, Miss Harrison, was John Mencini involved in drug dealing before you first met him?"

"Yes, I believe he was."

"Would you please tell the court, to the best of your knowledge, to what extent was his connection?"

"Well, he peddled some hash."

"Miss Harrison, was he known to use them?"

"Not regularly."

"Then, what involvement was there?"

"He, ah, brought them across the border."

"Brought what?"

"I couldn't say, exactly."

"But, you did know he was trafficking in illegal drugs; that is, bringing them into the country?"

"Yes," I whisper. Again, the Judge directs me to speak up.

"To whom did he give or sell these drugs?"

"I don't know exactly. Just contacts he had made before we met. There was never any mention of them when I was around."

"Were there any contacts in Yorkville? Or just at the racetrack?"

"I don't know."

"Whose idea was it that you should work on the racetrack?"

"John's."

"Why did you? Were you involved in drugs? Was John an easy source?" I tense up. This is getting insane.

"Miss Harrison, you apparently had no background in training horses."

"They convinced me it would be a good place to make easy money without long hours, and not have to work too hard." Several smile from the jury.

"Who were *they*?"

"Peter Edwards and John Mencini."

"Were they friends of yours when you hung out in Yorkville?"

"Yes, we lived together."

"Did you have any other friends in Yorkville?"

"No. Just acquaintances."

The Defense Counsel steps to the side of the podium and becomes aware of the time, he directs his address to the Judge for a dismissal until the next day. The continuous, repetitive questioning is exhausting.

On my sixth day on the stand, I am flushed, my skin blotches from nerves, and I am growing weary from the constant pressure of examination. For hours during the morning and again after lunch, the lawyers rehash my relationship with John, Bob, and Karen. I watch the self-assured younger attorney more closely as he speaks very distinctly. I study his polished mannerisms, obviously a private school boy by the way he carries himself and his vocabulary. He reminds me of a performer on stage, forcing his smile, and then speaking abruptly.

'Will this ever end?' I think. It is bad enough that I am not sleeping… for weeks.

"Now, we have established that your fiancé, John Mencini, involved himself in drug trafficking; with whom we don't know. And, that he trained a racehorse SnoMann that he wouldn't let run to its potential until the day he named Karen Sharp to ride it, which was when her father was conveniently out of town. Am I correct?"

"He named Raymond Cooper to ride SnoMann, but the jockey took a spill in an earlier race and went down, so John had to find another jockey.

He named Karen to ride as his second choice, rather than scratch the horse from the race."

"Miss Harrison, it says on the *Overnight* sheet, which I have in my hand, that *no boy* listed under the name of the jockey who would ride, so there wasn't anyone named to ride the horse... he just happened to name the accused's daughter. Humm, very convenient." He pauses again, and then refers to his notes. "Did you ever wonder why there was a need for him to push drugs?"

"Yes."

"Did you ever talk to him about it?"

"On several occasions."

"Tell us, what did he say?"

"He mostly avoided the subject. I didn't get a straight answer other than he needed the money."

"Money? I see. He had an obsession with making a great deal of money." The defense counsel continues to interrogate my connection to the drug scene. He queries my past as he pauses several times during the lengthy drawn-out examination.

"Am I to understand, Miss Harrison that you moved into a house in Yorkville in the late fall of 1966, a couple of years after your mother died? You lived and worked with this man for a few years knowing his attachment to illegal drugs, bad dealings on the racetrack, and a reputation of being a 'pusher'. Also, knowing he conned many of his friends into getting involved with him, you never questioned him more than a few times about his excessive finances? You knew these things and yet did not pursue it, even though you were getting married? Had you no intention of learning the truth? Were you so naive that you would walk into a marriage blinded by the fact that your fiancé had a reputation for criminal activities?"

The Judge interrupts, asking the Defense to put only one question to me, the witness, at a time.

"No further questions, M'Lord."

Hurrying, I step down from the stand as the Crown Counsel requests an adjournment at four forty-five pm. With more than a week of testifying, I rush from the courthouse in a daze and mindlessly drive through the snowed-in traffic, impatient to return to the Edwards' home where I immediately slip into my room in tears.

I sleep fitfully throughout the night.

Chapter 25
The Witness Box

Distressed by the trivia of the trial, Mrs. Edwards and I recapture the events over a glass of Chianti. The wisdom and patience she offers is just what I need and by the following Monday my view of the trial is less confusing.

Detective Riley phones outlining the happenings for the upcoming week. I am recuperating and my concentration is limited.

The court will call the racetrack security guard to testify and describe the scene as he sees it, identifying the automobile and the specific time of the killing. The arresting police officer will be the next witness for the Crown, who describes in detail the events leading to 'Smoocher' Newman's arrest in Fort Erie, submitting the gun for evidence and the car's ownership papers. A person from the Firearm Division of the Centre of Forensic Sciences will identify the gun and the bullets proving that it is the same one in John's murder. I feel some relief by the news, knowing my weak testimony was lacking strong points. Peter and I keep continue to keep in touch daily as he is to take the witness stand at the end of the third week.

The national newspapers cover the trial as well as the news wire, while Bradley keeps up-to-date with the proceedings by reading international newspapers and having regular communication with us. Whenever I am anxious, his calming nature helps.

After a few days of rest, I begin to feel stronger and decide to return to the courthouse ready to hear testimonies.

Detective Riley provides me with the details of the testimony of the Firearms Specialist from the Centre of Forensic Sciences and Dr. Holmes, who is the qualified medical doctor and pathologist, licensed to practice in the Province of Ontario. He carried out the examination on June 3, 1969, performing an autopsy six hours after death.

Whittmore requested information regarding the time of the operation, the height, weight, and age of the victim and a description of any external markings, which indicated violence, and finally a description of the area where the shot entered. Dr. Holmes precisely described the ammunition fragments found, and how the bullet entered and left the neck. He observed that John would have lived only a few minutes after the fatal shot and named the cause of death explicitly. Following his accurate testimony, the Defense Counsel announced "No questions." when asked to cross-examine.

I am sitting comfortably two rows from the front when Whittmore calls Peter to take the stand on Thursday afternoon. The constable repeats the call retrieving him from the witness room. The balance of the day's testimony is establishing Peter's relationship with John in regards to their personal background.

On day two, I return to the same seat. Whittmore focuses on John's relationship with Robert Sharp.

"And so, Mr. Edwards, you were, in fact, the victim's closest friend knowing intimately about his drug trafficking, the way he treated his horses and friends, and some of his personal habits. Am I correct?" Whittmore questions as he walked in front of the jury, keeping their attention. Peter appears tranquil and full of determination as I watch from the gallery, knowing exactly how he feels and what he is going through, emotionally. I begin to fidget, nervously.

"Yes."

"Tell us about the relationship between the accused and John Mencini."

"Well, in my opinion, they had grown very close over the years they worked together. Bob treated him very good. In fact, like a son."

"Like a son? So you mean he indicated his affection for the victim?"

"Yes. His favoritism was well known. You rarely saw one without the other, whether discussing business; eating, watching the races. Bob was helping John get his trainer's license, stuff like that."

"Did you feel that Mr. Sharp knew about John's involvement in drugs?"

"Sure."

"How?"

"Well, they would experiment together on a horse."

"Go on. . ."

"John got whatever drugs that Bob wanted, and then they would ...."

258

"So, they worked together on these experiments." Whittmore concludes.

"Yes."

"Where did John get these drugs?"

"I don't know, exactly," Peter lies.

"How could they get away with it? I mean, it is illegal to drug a racehorse."

"It was usually done during a morning breeze, which is a workout, not in a race."

"So, as an employee of Mr. Sharp, you don't feel that he used anything during a race?"

"No. He did use stuff like painkillers for a horse with a sore leg or horses that were tied-up with colic. For horses that tied-up in the morning, they were given vitamin B-1 with a little liquid *bute* then pump mineral oil into their stomach."

"Were these drugs legal?"

"Not all of them. . ."

"Did you ever administer any drug to any of Sharp's horses?"

"Yes."

"When?"

"A few times after a race for relief of pain."

"Shouldn't this have been done by a veterinarian?"

Peter shrugs his shoulders, the Judge directs him to speak up. "I suppose."

"Then, Mr. Sharp had certain drugs in his possession that were illegal to administer, let alone possess. Tell us, were there any arguments between the two men, concerning the use of these drugs?"

"Not until John began training, then their relationship became strained. Up to that point, they were pretty friendly and congenial. On several occasions, John would go ahead and do things without consulting Bob."

"Go ahead and do what?"

"Well, entering a horse in a race, or forgetting to get a drug Bob requested - like a hop."

"A hop?"

"Yeah, you know, a stimulant, an upper." The jury appears more attentive, now.

"What else did you notice about their relationship, as it began to show signs of strain?"

"Quarreling. They would argue about betting. There were several big-wheel gamblers coming around the barn looking for hot tips. After having one of their disagreements, John would go and stuff hundreds at the jockey to pull the horse, to make him finish out of the money, and then tell the bookies not to place the large bet. They would split the gamblers money held back 50-50. This made Bob look bad."

"Why would he do that?"

"Because he wanted the big bettors for his contacts, so he could be the one to make them money, and then include them in a syndicate he was planning to form. They both used to do this."

"Tell us what that syndicate was about."

"Mencini had always wanted to purchase enough real estate in Yorkville to do some renovations and build an exclusive mall. Back then, he needed twenty million dollars for this. He planned to do it by first getting the gamblers on his side, and then cash-in on a huge bet with the horse, SnoMann, so he could finance most of the construction himself."

"In your opinion, why wouldn't he have consulted Mr. Sharp, and include him in his plans?"

"I honestly think he had planned to, but John knew he would not get the odds he needed if too many knew about the race. He began to feel that Bob was smothering him and wanted to do his own big thing."

"And you believe that is what got Mencini's back up?"

"Probably one of the reasons."

"What others?'

"Well, Bob did his own thing behind John's back. He would take John's drugs and peddle them to the vets for extra cash. They would administer them to different horses for other trainers."

"What drugs? Hop?"

"No. Strictly pain killers, butes, *Phenylbutazone* which is a large white tablet."

I watch Whittmore closely as he leisurely walks back to his table to review his binder, turning the pages and pausing to rub his chin. I think his lack of expression is his best asset. A true poker face.

While I observe the proceedings, I am learning how naive I have been. Trapped in a web of lies, I need to step outside the box.

"Were there any other drugs that you knew about, that the accused used?"

"On occasion, methedrine, heroin, ritalin. . ."

"Those were administered to the racehorses?"

"Yes."

"By whom? Himself, the vet or John?"

"Well, I didn't actually see John inject any of those drugs."

"So, what you are telling the Court is that there was a conspiracy between the two men. A relationship so close that you and others saw them almost as father and son. Then, suddenly, this hostility formed, each of them began doing things and not telling each other?"

"Objection," calls the young Defense Council. "M'Lord, my Friend is leading the witness."

"Sustained," the Judge responds and Whittmore apologizes.

The Counsel for the Crown continues to spend time having Peter cite specific incidents where the relationship began to breakdown. The day ends with a tired looking jury leaving the courtroom.

Peter returns for his third day on the stand, appearing pale. We have not spoken, but I know exactly how he feels and I sympathize. While he attends the trial, he replaces his racetrack clothes with a well-tailored gray suit. He looks mature.

The prosecutor persists in his questioning to create an image of the victim's and the accused's personalities. Nearing four o'clock, the Counsel for the Defense stands up to cross-examine. He commences by repeating the evidence going back to Yorkville days. He continues in developing a picture of three individual hippies on drugs, who lived together in the village.

"Wasn't it true, Mr. Edwards that you had grown fond of Miss Harrison and over the years felt disgusted and jealous with the way John treated her?"

Peter flashes a look of disgust at the Defense Counsel's insinuations.

"Is it not true, that you, yourself, hated the drug scene and felt that Francine Harrison's involvement with John Mencini and the drug scene was really against her beliefs? She apparently had no training or background around horses, so why would she be working in a place where trained individuals were sought after?"

The Judge interrupts, "Counsel will ask one question at a time."

"Were you not jealous of the relationship between John and Mr. Sharp for their closeness and his favoritism?" His voice lowers.

"No!" A look of shock crosses Peters face. "To all your questions."

The courtroom stills as the minutes slip by, and then adjournment is called. Both Peter and I have no idea where things are heading or what the jurors think. Our opinions are those of confusion.

The press snaps pictures and prints them in the morning paper, along with old racetrack photos of the three of us together on the day SnoMann won, *The Yorkville Trio.*

On day four of Peter's testimony, the Defense team return to probe Peter's youth and his relationship with his parents and all those around the racetrack including Newman. He is definitely trying to create an image that is far from the truth.

"Is it not true, Mr. Edwards, following John Mencini's murder, you just happened to take over where he left off - by getting your own trainer's license, and working as assistant trainer for Larson Stables?" He pauses, waiting for a reply, pacing before the jury.

"Please, tell the court, Mr. Edwards, did you train Mr. Sharp's horses after John's murder?"

"Yes, I was his assistant."

"And weren't you the one who caused friction between them? Did you not play the peeping-tom game, snooping around, telling each of them what the other was doing?"

"No. Certainly not. You are way off track."

"Mr. Edwards, were you not in love with Francine Harrison and wanted John's girl, and his job? Wouldn't you do anything to get it?"

I don't believe what I am hearing. This is getting to sound ridiculous, or is it? He needs to plant the seed in the jurors' minds.

"No. She's my cousin's girlfriend. We've known each other for years. I care for her, but only as a friend, absolutely nothing more."

"Really?" He then goes on, requesting Peter to confirm all findings in regards to the police investigation and identify their exhibits. He ends with no further questions.

Court adjourns at four o'clock. Overwhelmed at the turn of events, Peter and I wonder where this case is going. We are speechless, and then spend hours talking it out.

Once again, James Whittmore calls Constable Ryan, who states his number of years with the force, and particular departments where he has worked. He cites a date that Peter Edwards had turned in a piece of paper found in the tack room at Sharp's stable which listed drugs and named specific veterinarians. Constable Ryan explains that a handwriting expert has analyzed the contents, testifying to its authenticity proving it is an original document written in the same hand as the accused.

Whittmore follows through with his list of witnesses, calling the handwriting expert and a fingerprint expert. Testimony is then given from a drug analyst who reads from his reports. All of these witnesses give evidence on the drug findings in the bandages, confirming the officer's testimony. Another day in court adjourned at five after five.

The mood lightens considerably when we visit Susan's parent's home. Mrs. Edwards received a short letter in a birthday card from Susan, who still lived in London. I've not received any word from her since I returned to Toronto, other than little updates on Matthew. Bradley never mentions very much about her when we talked on the phone, and Peter hasn't heard from her either, which made no sense to us.

Several weeks pass before Alexander 'Smoocher' Newman testifies, but first, Whittmore calls the owner of the get-away car, the wood paneled station wagon. Shirley Marten took the stand and briefly explained her relationship with Smoocher and the events that led to offering him the car on the day of the murder. The Defense Counsel cross examined her heavily around the fact that if she had known him well enough to be lending him the car so frequently, why did she neglect to ask where the money came from for the replacement car, if he was so broke.

The next two witnesses for the Crown are both jockeys. The first to testify is Raymond Cooper who talks about his years riding for Mencini.

He detailed the events of the day when Karen rode SnoMann. First, he spoke about when he had to 'test' the horse and find out its true potential by using a crop fixed with a tiny battery-switch that would shock the horse each time he hit him during morning workouts. Other times, jockeys had been instructed to break bad from the gate, or 'hold' a horse during the race, which usually meant another horse was on the lead. Cooper confessed that when it became necessary for a trainer to pay some of the jockeys to

263

guarantee his own horse a one-two spot on the board, it was for the trainer's 'friends' placing bets. The lawyers went after every bit of information they could get from him as he informed the jury how jockeys boxed in other horses, or *stiffed* them so Sharp's horse won. Then, he affirmed how Sharp made illegal bets for the jockeys through his own betting house or bookie. His testimony covered the better part of the day.

The Defense Counsel stressed that it wasn't unusual for trainers to have jockeys perform necessary tricks-of-the-trade so they could ascertain their horses ability by 'giving it a race' to see if it was capable of handling a certain track condition, or a particular distance. These were normal training tactics. He proved that other trainers requested similar tasks. Conclusion was that Sharp did no more, no less, than other trainers did.

"M'Lord, the Crown calls Alexander Newman to the stand." Within minutes, a man in his late fifties enters and shuffles between the two constables, who assist him from the holding cell, immediately above and behind the courtroom. The registrar asks him his full name and places his hand on the Bible, having him swear that what he is about to say is the truth. Whittmore takes his place behind the podium, inquiring as to the man's age and place of birth.

Peter straightens in his seat, looking a bit pale as he observes the jury.

At this moment, I am overwhelmed with emotion as the two men responsible for the murder of my fiancé sit only feet away from me.

"Were you recently tried and found guilty of second degree murder for the killing of John Mencini?"

"Yup."

"Would you please tell the court for what reason you committed this crime?"

"I was hired to."

"By whom?"

"Robert Sharp." A soft chatter rippled through the courtroom for several minutes.

"Do you agree with the testimony from others that the shooting of John Mencini was on June 3rd, 1969?"

"Yeah."

"Are you known around the circuit as 'Smoocher'?"

"Yup."

"When was this name given to you?"

"Back in the fifties. I come to the racetrack after the Korean War. The trainers used to say I *smooched* everything from cigarettes to toilet paper; that I would kiss-ass to get information; so the name stuck." A smile crosses the face of some jurors.

"Did you have a job at the racetrack?"

"I sold the Daily Racing Forms around the stable area and at the grandstand during the races."

"So you were employed?"

"Yah."

"When did you first become acquainted with the accused?"

"Sometime in the late fifties, at Old Woodbine, this is now Greenwood Racetrack. He was much younger, with two little kids and about four or five horses."

"Did you become friends?"

"No more than I was with any of the other guys around the track. I knew them all pretty good."

"What else do you remember about him in those days?"

"Well, they lived in a trailer, out there on Derry West someplace. His kids came to the races with Mollie, his woman. They seemed a happy family."

"Did he ever call on you for any favors?" Whittmore strolls away from the podium.

"Like I said, no more than others, if they needed anything I was to find out where to get it. You know, a good price on bridles, liniment, any kind of bargains going around. Sometimes he asks me to keep watch on his horses if one of them was racing, nothing out of the ordinary."

"Over the years, did you come to know each other better?" Whittmore lingers, walking to his desk and referring to something with his junior.

"He was from a family who showed hunters and jumpers, but he always wanted to race thoroughbreds, himself. Some guy he knew also wanted to get into the sport, so they was partners at first. He did real good and soon he was winning a few races with not such good stock; the word got around that he was pretty talented. I knew an owner that wasn't too happy with the stable he was with. He wants more personal attention than what he gets from this trainer. He was lookin' for a change. I told the guy about Sharp. I guess that was his first break. They talked and got together and hit it off. At the next meet in Fort Erie I think it was, about a year before new Woodbine opened, he moved his horses into Sharp's stable. That give him something like another three horses, but was a lot better class of horse. They run really good for him. Sharp used to spend hours trainin', groomin' them horses like his own pets. They grazed around the grassy areas of the barnyard and he pampers them. He'd keep their legs wrapped so they don't cut themselves in the stall, takes good care and don't run them too often."

"You thought he was a good trainer?"

"Yup, a great one."

"Did you see any changes as the years passed?"

"He got hooked up with different clients who liked to gamble and demanded results."

"When would this have been?" Whittmore confronts the jury, looking at each individually as Peter and I listen closely; he rests his hand on my knee.

"In the early sixties. There was a lot of changes after his son was killed in a motorcycle accident."

"Were you friends all this time?"

"Like I said, we know each other, talked all the time. He mostly wanted to know the gossip around the track. Paid me for these tips on what was going on, and what was new. These new owners were pressuring him for more wins and their horse was sore. Sharp wanted to know what to do because they was going to go elsewhere and find another trainer. He had been freezing the leg before races, but hadn't been getting results. Back then, he was getting something like twelve dollars a day to train a horse and these three guys had five horses. He didn't want to lose them, and was getting a little desperate."

"What did he do?"

"Well, he had a damn good racing record. He was doing really good for a small stable. I could see him changing over the years with the pressure, like I says, especially after his son died. He was pretty irritable. Lots of sadness in that family. It was around the fall of 1964 that I introduced him to John Mencini. He needed wins and I knew Mencini could get them for him."

"And?"

"Well, they hit it right off and became close friends."

"How did you know John Mencini?"

"He was doing odd jobs around the track, working with different stables just about that time. Rumor had it, he used to peddle *weed* but I don't know that for a fact. I tells him if he wanted to make anything of himself on the track it wasn't weed he should be peddling. And he takes it from there. The next thing I knows, he gets some contacts to find stuff, and was getting just about anything anyone was wanting, or at least said he could. Mencini worked around the track, galloping in the morning, taking horses to the post in the afternoon; all the shit jobs, but he hung around the Larson stable the most."

"So you were, in fact, a go-between for everyone?"

The Defense Counsel interrupts, asking the witness to move forward a little because he could not see him behind his Lordship's dais. This is Counsel's way to break the focus of the jury.

"Yes," Newman continues, "I just watched and listened. I suppose I was the track gossip. Knew it all. Saw it all."

"In your opinion, did they use a lot of drugs?"

"I wouldn't know. I knew one of the vets was interested in making some kind of deal with John. But Sharp intervened and sets this pattern thing up whereby he's the contact to get all the vets their drugs, in exchange for information about who was gonna be using them, and when. They organized a ring."

"Was Mencini informed of this arrangement?"

"No. No way."

"So, in your opinion, the accused was bleeding John for the drugs, and then making his own deals on the side?"

"I couldn't say for sure, but something like that was happening."

"So you feel gamblers were approaching Mr. Sharp?"

"I was told that he needed to produce 'sure' wins. He had to cover himself at both ends. It became a line of payoffs, each covering for the other, down the line. Sharp gets the stuff, lets the vet know, who in turn, covered for him by switching the winning horse's urine sample, and so the drugs don't show in the testing. These gamblers, or should I say the gangsters, was happy and so was everyone else."

"And Mencini didn't know about this?"

"Not at first. Then, he goes behind Sharp's back to the gamblers, telling them about some other horse that was going to win a particular race. John told them to save their money, and not bet on Sharp's horse. What he did was pay off the jockeys. It was a substantial amount of money to make sure that Sharp's horse don't hit the board. This only had to happen a couple of times. It don't take long for the big betters to lose respect for Sharp. Behind his back, John was taking over. Stiffing races didn't happen often, but when it did, big bucks were involved and if the jockey's didn't go along, they would end up injured."

Newman pauses, taking a long drink of water. Judge MacIntosh writes down a few more notes, as the attorneys pace their questions, keeping a close eye on the jury. He notes the time, and requests adjournment.

That same evening, after Peter and I discuss Smoocher's testimony, we decide to phone Bradley, revealing all the ups and downs from the trial that we find frustrating, and then I wonder if there is a hidden truth to be uncovered?

The following morning, testimony continues.

"Mr. Newman, could you tell the court your personal opinion of the accused and the deceased?"

"Sharp trusted John, and don't want to lose his contact, or his clients. For awhile there, they seems to have things goin' pretty good together."

"When would this have been?" Whittmore inquires.

"Probably around 1968."

Whittmore refers to his notes and there is another pause, which lasts several minutes. Then, he questions the type of drugs and where they came from.

The jury observes the witness closely. I keep my eye on Sharp who still shows little expression. Whittmore requests specific details for all the incidents that involve the victim, wanting times and dates.

Another long day ends. I marvel how the jurors stay in focus.

On the front page of all the national newspapers, the trial dominates the space. One day we think we have it sewn up, and the next day, we sense Robert Sharp is going to get away with it all. My phone bills are increasing by the day with calls back and forth to London and The Hague. No one can believe the slow process, which is taking months.

Smoocher returns to the witness stand once again for testimony.

"Would you say you knew one of the men better than the other?"

"Mr. Sharp, I knows him for almost twenty years. Yes." Their relationship is discussed in detail.

"Mz. Sharp knew she was a good rider and very capable. All she needed was the chance to prove herself, but I has no idea where she gets the idea that John would allow her to ride."

The questioning turns back to Mencini and Sharp.

"Once again, when did you feel that things were changing for the worse?"

"Well, Sharp did get shit drugs once, in the early spring of 1969. This started a big hassle between them. John denied he had anything to do with it, which was probably true."

Whittmore wants specifics as his testimony continues and the subject of the killing comes up. Newman is in his fourth day on the witness stand.

"And tell us about the day that John's horse, SnoMann, raced. Was Mr. Sharp not informed of his plans?" queries the Crown.

"No, he's away, in the States."

"Why?"

"He told me that John and him had picked out a couple of yearlings from a US Sale book. They thought it might be worth going down and looking at them, so that was what he does. It was three days after SnoMann's race when Sharp gets back to the track. He was furious. I was coming back from picking up a load of papers in the barn area. He don't see me, so I goes over, and he was cursin' mad. I never seen him that mad before."

"What was he mad at?"

"At that point, I didn't know. Anyway, he turns to me, ya see, and what? What the hell is you talking about? I only came by to give you today's racing form, Bob.' And he goes off in a tantrum, swearin' that I was as much behind it all as the other bastards. I keeps telling him - no way. Then, the stuff came out about Karen riding and I swears to him I doesn't know about nothing. Then, he says he finds his best horse that was to race this one day, plugged full of tranquilizers and I tells him again that I don't know nothing about that either. He keeps at me, you see - and he don't let up. We go to my tack-room that I stays in. He is still fighting mad.

269

. .but he gets into the booze and really starts drinking, and he tells me things about his wife Mollie leaving him because of what Karen has done, blaming Mencini for the whole mess, and he moaned and groaned, on and on. He was losing everything. He was drinkin' like a crazy man.

"We kept hitting the booze pretty good, and he complained about this and that; John had no right to do him in. Says he didn't deserve what John did and he cried out his story, the madder he got."

He stops again for a drink of water. Mesmerized, the jury watches Newman.

"We drank ourselves into a drunken stupor. Then, slept. The next day, he don't even leave the room, said he had no reason and sent me out for more booze. This time, as the day goes by he starts saying that John tricked him into going to the sale. It was nothing more than a plot, and that the whole setup was planned so that he would be out of his way. 'Just another one of his tricks' he was sayin' … *'I'll kill the bastard'*. Then he got raging mad, cussing and threatening, sayin' John took away his credibility, ruined his family, made him out to be the bandit, and was only concerned with himself. Never really cared for anyone else. He cried, and then he passes out.

"It got even worse and when he woke, he starts to knock things over. He stumbles on a box and falls into the rollaway I had, bumping the mattress, and then this gun that I have falls to the floor."

Whittmore approaches the registrar, picks up the gun previously identified by the police, and submits it as evidence.

"The gun to which you are referring … is this it?"

"Yeah, that's it." He takes it in his hand, looks it over and then returns it.

"Go on." Whittmore turns his back to him and approaches his table, examining a few papers.

"He is pretty bleary-eyed and he grabs it, cursing and swearing, saying that was what he needed. He'd finish the fucking bastard off himself. So, we starts rumbling a bit, as I tries to get this thing away from him cause he says he gonna shoot someone, and I doesn't want it to be me. Anyway, he falls. We both did, and the gun fell. I grabs it and puts it away fast. He starts blubbering again, going over and over all the things that he did for that boy. *Why, Why?* he keeps sayin', *did he do me in? Why did*

John destroy everything I worked for? He lost his good horses, family, says he was set-up, and then he passes out.

"Only this time, I was gettin' pretty upset. I sees what has happened to him over the twenty years I know this man, and I tries to help him. I want him to sleep it off, so I go out and gets some coffee, and ran into a few guys along the way. Anyway, I was a few hours before I gets back. When I does, he's roaring drunk, sittin' there on the side of the bed. He says, '*Smooch, I'm not gonna let this bastard get away with it. He's waiting for me, I know it. I know he is waiting for me to come around; and goddamn only knows what he's got for me, now. I want you to do it!*' He tosses me the gun, and he tells me he will give me ten thousand dollars to do him in and another ten thousand when done. He goes and gives me this can, like an old coffee can with a rubber lid, and there was the roll of money. I didn't even count it. I think I was still hung-over too. So, he starts pleading with me, crying and says '*I mean it. I got nothing now, and I wants John out of the way. He's trouble for everyone. He's ruining everyone's life - Pete, his girlfriend, Frannie, the owner's, Karen, everyone he ever met'.* He says that John was only out for himself. I cried for this guy. So I did it." He covers his face, sobbing. The courtroom fills with the sounds of whispers, and then quiets, so you could hear a pin drop.

Whittmore requests a recess.

My insides twist tight as Peter and I leave the area and go for a coffee. I am completely drained from the proceedings, and we both wonder how Whittmore remains alert and on top of the case, as if the show must go on. The rest of the world is slipping by without our noticing while the trial dominates our life. The stress is unimaginable.

Once again, Newman returns to the witness stand. Whittmore firms up his questioning, being direct, yet cautious. He walks from his desk back to the podium, waiting. His eyes show no emotion, no expression. The room settles down and Peter and I remain in our seats, not wanting to miss a word. Once again, he holds my cold hand; in fact, the room is much cooler, today.

"Mr. Newman, we have pictures that show you in two different appearances. One, here, as the tracker and this other one, the way you are now, clean-shaven. It's difficult to see much of a resemblance." He passes two photographs to the witness. The Judge looks at them, and then sends them through the jury.

"Well, I didn't see any need to get spruced up, unless I was going out to see ..."

"See your lady? Would this lady friend be the same one that worked in the track kitchen?"

"Yes, Shirley."

"And was it her station wagon that you used to borrow?"

"Yes."

"Well, if I am correct, you had some cleaning-up to do, if you were on a drinking binge with Mr. Sharp; to, all of a sudden, regain your senses enough to do what you did. Am I correct?"

Newman mumbles something.

"Tell us what you did when you left Mr. Sharp."

"I goes and showers, changes and visits Shirley, borrowing her car. I used to do that often. We had known each other for years, so she never suspected anything. I waits for a couple of hours outside the entrance until most everyone has gone, 'til I sees the red sports car come. Then, I follows it."

"We have heard from Miss Harrison that you called out his name. Why did you call to him, 'Roberts'?" Whittmore turns towards the jury.

"That was the name I had always known him by, since the beginning. I never paid much attention to names. I just calls him John."

"Weren't you afraid someone might recognize you?"

"Didn't care much then. I knew the place would be quiet at that time of day."

"Where did you go when you left the track?"

"I gave the car to a couple of guys heading out to Fort Erie, to the new meet. Told them there was some problems with it, and they could have it cheap, so they grabbed it. I guess they sold it before the summer ended, because I never saw it around the track. I bought another car for Shirley and told her I had an accident in her wagon. She never questioned. Believed whatever I told her. She always did."

"When did you get back to see Mr. Sharp?"

"The following day. He was at his farm."

"The hostility had been building up between them for months, would you say?"

"Easy."

"So, this wasn't just a spur of the moment thing?" Whittmore leans towards the witness.

"Well, I guess it was like the last straw. Sharp don't take any more of the cheating and double-crossing."

"What happened then?"

"He stays there for a few weeks and then he came around. Pretty down, depressed. But, it was only a few weeks, and he gets right back to his old self, starting all over, from scratch. Everyone thought his pain was over Mencini's death."

"Did you see the police question him?"

"Sure. But, he plays it up real good; like he lost another son. Everyone would have agreed with that. I mean no one would have suspected him. They thought it was gamblers, or drug dealers."

Questioning continues, taking into account their relationship, and rehashing how the changes took place. Another hour passes.

"Were drugs still used around the track?"

"Yes. I would give him the contacts that John had used who were on the other side of the border. Within a year, Bob was right back in there winning big races. Got the confidence of the gamblers back. He takes over the syndicate John started and went ahead with the Yorkville development. One thing just rolled after another."

Whittmore lets a few moments lapse. The jury appears restless. I am beginning to recognize their habits as some sit with hands folded, legs crossed, and others are head scratchers, nose rubbers, ceiling gazers and so forth. I begin to wonder how they can concentrate on such long proceedings. They vary in age, outfits, hairstyles and mannerisms. Three of the twelve persons never wear a watch.

Questioning persists up to the day of Newman's release, to assist the police in getting a confession from the accused. Whittmore produces a copy of the tape from his table. Facing the Judge, he comments. "We'll have to ask for the Jury to be excused." I straighten in my seat, anxious to see and hear the results. Within a few minutes, the conversations resume.

"M'Lord, I have here a copy of a tape made on October 25th, 1977, that the Crown feels reveals substantial evidence that will clear up any discrepancies or inconsistencies."

The placing of the body pack on Newman was then explained. The Judge questions the man in the witness box.

"Was this tape made between yourself and the accused, Robert Sharp?"

"Yes," he agrees.

The Registrar proceeds to place a recorder onto the counter, and the Crown asks the witness to explain the details of making the tape.

"The day of the taping, Miss Harrison goes to the racetrack. She meets with Mr. Sharp later, and then they goes to the Ascot Hotel. They hadn't seen each other in several years. He's at the hotel with her having a drink, and Pete Edwards turns up. She leaves him and Pete talks with Sharp. They spend a few moments bringing up the subject of Mencini, because of Mz Harrison being back in town for the trial. Then, Pete leaves, and I comes into the room and that is when this here tape was made."

"Approximately, what time of day would this have been?"

"Oh-h, late afternoon. It was around five o'clock when I left the hotel."

They play the tape.

The Defense Counsel concentrates on a number of parts he regards as inadmissible, and then he and the Crown argue, politely. The decision is left for the Judge, who calls for an adjournment delaying his opinion until morning.

The trial gets underway shortly after ten-thirty. The Judge's decision is to leave the tape uncut, and play it for the jury. Newman returns to the witness stand. The trial resumes.

Whittmore recaps the details for the jury's benefit. They play the tape and Whittmore retires. The Judge calls for the Defense to cross-examine.

Defense Counsel approaches the podium briskly, opening his black binder to a marked page. He slowly paces back and forth, slithering like endangered species in front of the jury, not taking his eyes from the floor. I watch him, as he creates drama, an air of suspense throughout the room. Pausing, he runs his hand through his thick brown curly hair. His authoritative manner captures everyone's attention each time he cross-examines a witness. Speaking firmly with an overpowering self-assurance, he turns to Newman, asking him, with the slightest hint of sarcasm, about his contacts with the accused.

He mocks the man in the witness box. Picturing him as a bum, he recounts his past to the jury. The Counsel's quick tongue and clever rephrasing traps Newman. His technique lies in speaking slowly, lingering between details to make sure the jury hears, and remembers. Again, time is spent repeating every minute fact leading up to the murder, claiming that Newman begged Sharp for the money to kill Mencini; that it was his encouragement and his idea which planted the thoughts into Sharp's head during their drinking hours together.

"But, Mr. Newman, am I to understand that we have already heard police testimony describing your arrest because of another shooting incident, involving the same gun; this being key evidence which led them to prove the Mencini murder, pin-pointing it directly to you?"

"Yes," he mutters.

"Is it not true that you received a reduced sentence, with early parole, for your statement to the police, regarding Robert Sharp?"

"Well, I was tried and. . ."

"Yes," Defense Counsel sharply interrupts. "Mr. Newman, they found you guilty of a lesser charge. You did, in fact, kill John Mencini, am I correct?"

"Yes, but Robert Sharp hired me. I did it for money. Sharp paid me. It was a contract."

"And, if he paid you to go after the Prime Minister, would you have killed him too?" He returns quickly to the podium.

"Mr. Newman," continues the Attorney. "Wasn't it enough that you killed the boy, got a reduced sentence out of it? Now, what do you think you can accomplish by taking Sharp's name, which has no connection to any type of offense, whatsoever, and implicate it with this crime?"

"Objection, M'Lord," the Crown intervenes, "My Friend is questioning on assumption."

The Counselors debate the point until the Judge interrupts. The young skillful attorney for the Defense goes back to his questioning.

"To your knowledge, was Mr. Sharp drinking that day in the hotel?"

"Yes, he had a drink in the hotel."

"Was he drunk?"

"No."

"But, he had been drinking. You said he had been drinking with Miss Harrison, and perhaps with Peter Edwards before you arrived on the scene. Who knows if he had anything to drink at the clubhouse before he arrived at the hotel? So, to the best of your knowledge, you don't really have any idea how much he had to drink or even if he was drinking doubles?"

"No."

"Isn't it a coincidence that on both occasions, the day of the killing, and the day of this taping, that Mr. Sharp had been under the influence of alcohol?" Counsel pauses, leaving the thought with the jury. He consults with his colleague at his desk.

"No further questions." Another day ends.

The trial is approaching its third month and the days are beginning to really drag on and on, as if they were being paid by the week.

As the Crown complete their list of witnesses, Judge MacIntosh checks his notes and directs the Defense Counsel to call any witnesses.

"Karen Connors to the stand, please," announces the constable, after hearing the counselor's call.

The doors at the back of the courtroom open, and the famous publicized model, whose face has recently graced the cover of *Vogue* magazine, enters the courtroom. Karen is wearing a basic black and white linen outfit, enhanced by a stunning fashionable hat that she wears tilted to one side. All heads turn watching her gracefully approach the stand. While repeating the oath, Karen sees her father and becomes visibly upset, with Counsel going to her side offering some words of comfort. Moments pass. When she regains her composure, the room settles. I realize that it's the first time I have seen her since London when she and Chuck were first introduced.

Questioning begins with her recollection of her childhood, and the years spent with her father and family, up to the time of the death of her brother, specifically referring to her father's behavior patterns. Her emotions are well controlled during the two-hour discussion until the matter of her riding comes up.

"You see, my father allowed me as much involvement as I wanted at the racetrack as long as it was within our own stable. He encouraged me to ride and gallop our horses from a young age and he often commented on how well I did."

"Did your father ever express any concern regarding the other women jockeys … as it was becoming more common at that time?"

"Yes, he did. But, he never said anything derogatory about it; just that he thought women were better around racehorses and had a gentler touch. He never expressed any opinion about using a woman to ride any of his horses."

"So, in fact, he never used a female jockey?"

"There weren't any women racing on the Ontario circuit at that time, that is, not until I started riding. Then, another woman arrived in Toronto from Montreal."

"Before you decided to ride, was this ever discussed with him?"

"I knew he didn't want me taking any part in the racetrack activities at all, outside of our own stable."

"Why did you deliberately take your jockey exams behind his back, if you knew it was going to cause aggravation and trouble?"

"It wasn't like that. I really felt that I could do well. If I did my best and succeeded then I felt I was doing no harm."

"But, it didn't happen that way," the Defense intervenes. Karen explains the slowdown in her modeling profession. "It was going to take a long time to achieve my dream of becoming a supermodel."

"So, you decided to give it up and try riding by taking the opportunity on SnoMann?"

"Yes. I went to John and begged him to let me ride. It was when the *overnights* came out, and SnoMann had *no boy* named on him." She explained the day she approached John and Peter to ride.

"Did you hesitate, knowing your father's feeling about the subject?"

"No. After I rode the race, I truly believed my father would come around. I was sure he would be proud of the ride, but ..." she pauses. Karen focuses on her father sitting in the center of the room, tears in the corners of his eyes. She grasps the edge of the railing on the stand, begins to tremble, and grits her teeth to hold back her pain. The Defense Counsel draws near.

"Why? Why did you take the mount?"

"Because I knew in my heart that I could win the race. I wanted to prove it to him, to myself. All I had to do was convince John, and I knew if I did well, I would get the press that would lead to my success. Just as my father was known for his successes, I wanted mine, too."

"So, your success was important?"

"Yes."

"What happened when your father returned from his trip, a few days later?"

"He turned his back on me, too. It didn't matter what I said, he insisted John talked me into riding SnoMann. Blamed John for taking on something I never would have done if he'd been there to stop us. He said his trip had been a setup, and then began cursing John and accusing him of all sorts of things. I couldn't believe the hurt and hostility. He was furious. He told me, *'I'll make him pay for this Karen, so help me. That guy has taken the best thing he ever had and twisted it into something destructive. As far as you're concerned, don't ever show your face around me again, until you stop riding.'* He got up and walked out, convinced John and I had planned it all along."

A slight commotion ripples through the courtroom as reporters leave, and people chatter. Testimony continues as Karen describes the way she saw the Mencini-Sharp relationship during the meet in Montreal, when John got his trainer's license. They thrash out the subject of drugs used on the horses. Karen explains how she remembered gamblers hanging around the stable, driving fancy Cadillacs and Lincolns, and then recalled boisterous fights when John and Robert Sharp began drifting apart. Her testimony covered her father's connections with the gamblers, drugs, and illegal betting.

"And tell the court, Mrs. Connors, in your opinion, was your father influencing John, or was your father influenced by him?" Counsel directs.

"The way I saw it, John did have drug connections, but didn't know a lot about horse racing when he first arrived." She cleared her throat. "You see, my father was an excellent horseman. He did very well with his small stable. When John arrived on the scene, it was a time when Dads horses were not producing and were getting a little sore. It was like John was his lifesaver. He took him, and made him into exactly what he needed. John learned the tricks of the trade, and began using them himself. This was the time they began quarreling. Maybe, it was John who changed my Dad, convincing him that the way to win was with drugs. I'll never know."

Again, a slight murmur fills the room, as Defense Counsel converse with his colleague. The Judge taps his gavel, calling Whittmore to cross-examine the witness.

In his usual rugged fashion, Whittmore takes over as he retraces steps leading up to Karen's modeling career from the day she first rode

SnoMann to victory. Whenever he wanted to stress particular points to the jury, he paused so that the witness's reply lingered in their minds. By the cleverness of his tactics, statements given by a witness seemed inadequate.

He leaves the podium, approaching the model in the witness stand.

"Mrs. Connors, did you deliberately approach John to ride the stallion because you knew he would be your only chance to ride, become a successful jockey, and make a name for yourself in your father's absence?"

"I knew that I could…," she hesitates.

"Is it not true that you didn't care what your father or mother thought about your riding, since you already knew how they really felt? You could prove yourself only in your father's absence as this was the only way to achieve the success that you sought. Is this not true? Did you have anything to do with setting up your father's trip to the yearling sale in the U.S.in May, 1969?"

"No. But I thought he would change his mind if I proved myself."

"Yes. You mentioned that. Now, Mrs. Connors, your success was more important than your parents' marriage. The opportunity presented itself beautifully, since everyone was already aware of the trouble brewing between John and your father. You knew he would blame John, but you thought you would be forgiven on the grounds of his persuading you. But it backfired, didn't it?"

The Judge interrupts, directing the Crown from straying. Whittmore carries on, returning to the podium, referring to the brief.

"As we have heard, your riding enhanced your modeling career by providing the agencies with a publicized name, attracting public interest and increasing their readership. This ultimately led to your stint in London, where you met your husband." Whittmore rubs his chin in thought. He reviews his notes and pauses a moment before speaking.

"Is it not true, that similar to your career ambitions, you found someone in London that you fancied and perhaps set out to get, no matter who was in your way, or got hurt?"

"I don't understand," Karen frowns.

"Your husband, Mrs. Connors, wasn't he dating one of your best friends at the time you first met?"

"Objection, M'Lord. This question has no bearing whatsoever on this case and my Friend persists …" The Counselors debate.

"No further questions."

Chapter 26

Final Testimony

The infamous trial continues to make headlines across the nation through media coverage, everywhere. Peter and I sense our lives are at a standstill as he continues to attend to his racehorses before court.

There were a few times we made special visits to see SnoMann, to try and make sense of the court proceedings, feeling closer to the way of life we had once lived. SnoMann was almost twelve and had sired over twenty foals. It seemed to me that London was so very far away, as my job and my life in Britain was a distant certainty.

The Defense Counsel pushes back his chair, facing the Judge, to remark that his next witness is Max Westgate, who takes the stand. This person, unknown to us, explains his current position as president of a large computer firm who sits on the boards of eleven different companies. The Defense asks him to describe his first acquaintance with the accused, outlining both professional and personal relationships.

He recalled the years they had known one another in their youth when Sharp had hitchhiked into the city every day, from a farm near Oshawa, to attend St. Michael's School, where they first met. He remembered when Sharp quit his education returning to his family's farm to race horses. Years later, they reacquainted at a business party in Mississauga. Sharp's successes at the racetrack provided him with the funds he invested in one of Westgate's developments. Their friendship and business dealings developed from there. The Counselor encouraged more testimony regarding Sharp's good deeds, community works and sponsorships to establish his knowledge of the accused, an honorable citizen.

From all appearances, they were close friends, as he talked about their dealings together.

The prosecutor takes to the podium.

"During all the times you were together, was there ever any mention of the victim, John Mencini, during these meetings." Whittmore questions for the Crown.

"Never."

"Is it not true that you were one of the main contributors to Yorkville Enterprises', the redevelopment of the block of land situated just east of Avenue Road, near Cumberland?"

"I did invest in that development scheme."

"Did you not know about the organization and development of Yorkville Enterprises beforehand?"

"Only the information Robert made available in his portfolio for investors to view. The syndicate appeared to have been his creation. He presented it to several individuals who I had suggested to take part in the organization." The man straightens his tie.

"But you never heard the name, or met the person, John Mencini or John Roberts?"

"No."

"No further questions."

The Judge finishes scribbling notes, and then nods to the Defense Counsel to continue. He calls his next witness to the stand, Mr. Robert Sharp.

A light hum fills the room as two constables on either side of the prisoner's dock unfasten the side panel, so he can exit and enter the witness stand. Peter and I exchange glances, holding our breath, unprepared for his testimony.

Robert Sharp takes the oath, given by the registrar. The court reporter coughs as the room turns remarkably still. This unexpected call for the accused makes Peter and I wonder where this will lead.

Leaning against the side of the podium, facing the jury, Counsel asks the accused, "How old are you, Mr. Sharp?"

"I am fifty-four."

"Where were you born?"

"Oshawa, Ontario."

"When did you meet your wife?"

"After I left school, and returned to Oshawa. I was working for National Stud Farm and she was the family's Nanny who came from England."

281

"How long before you married?"

"About two years."

"You had two children?"

"Yes, a boy Larson and my daughter, Karen."

"Your son died?"

"Yes, when he was seventeen in a motorcycle accident."

The questioning continues in this manner for over two hours, creating the image of a gentle loving family man who had worked hard at his profession.

At this time, I lean back and briefly gaze at Chuck and Karen sitting together on the opposite side of the gallery. She appears awestruck focusing on the routine questioning that lasts the rest of the day, and then continues at ten-thirty the next morning. I think it's funny how Chuck, a person who endeavored to always get the best deal possible, found Karen, a very successful, beautiful woman who also did what she had to, to get what she wanted. Little did he know he would be sitting in a Toronto courtroom with the media chasing after them every minute of the day. Could it be more than he bargained for? It definitely wasn't the best publicity.

The discussion begins with Yorkville.

"You mean all three of these kids came from Yorkville to work for you?"

"Yes."

"Were they trouble makers - hippies?"

"No. I never thought of them like that. Just kids with lots of enthusiasm wanting to make a few bucks." He describes my relationship with John and how he saw it develop, and then talks of my relationship with Karen.

"Then, your daughter and Miss Harrison became close friends?"

"Yes, they roomed together when we raced in Montreal. They got along fine and shared a few interests together."

His testimony persists in the same vein and then describes his trip to the horse sale in the US and return to Toronto.

"My daughter, Karen, met me at the airport. I was heartbroken. Really! Those kids had gone and done this behind my back. Three youngsters that I took in and gave jobs ruined everything I had built over the years. Karen changed, too. She told me if I didn't like her riding -

tough! I felt they influenced her over the years. After I heard about the race, my wife left me, and then faced with a carload of gamblers at my barn, ready to kill me. They said I double-crossed them for the last time, and they meant it! It was too much. I was provoked beyond reason.

"Wandering down the shed divested, Alex Newman came along finding me out of my mind with grief." Robert Sharp stops, gripping the edge of the witness box. The jury sits attentively, not missing a word. For some unknown reason, I begin to shake and Peter rubs my shoulder as our eyes meet.

The accused recounts his version of the drinking incident and the days that followed, and the killing. He testifies for two days.

Without moving from my seat, the room empties, and then I stand to leave. Hearing Whittmore call my name, still showing no strain, he invites me to coffee. I am confused by Sharps pitiful yet convincing testimony.

"My feelings are that the jury thinks this guy is peaches and cream. I can see it. I am sitting in the exact same position, and know because I was there, working with Bob for many years. He will con them just as the bunch of us were conned," I shiver. "He is a master in manipulation."

"Francine, relax." Whittmore cautions while he sips from his paper cup. "The case is not over, yet. I have some things to say too, remember. Now, tell me. Tell me about John's family."

I disclose everything I know, including my trips south as I am hoping to shed light on John's background as he questions me.

Back in court, the prisoner returns to the dock and uncuffed, waiting for the cross-examination. The jury settles and we begin once again.

James Whittmore takes a mechanical pencil from the back of his ear and places it upon his papers, reaching for the folder from an assisting constable sitting at his table. A serious crease forms across his brow, as he clears his throat.

"Mr. Sharp. I would like you to tell the court about the day when you first met John. Do you remember where the meeting took place?"

"Humm.. I'd say it was winter 1964. I was sitting outside my barn on a bale of hay, reading my Condition book when ol' Smoocher came down the shed with someone, introducing him as John Roberts. We talked for a while, and he told me he was looking for some work, and had been around the racetrack for a few months. I said I could use some extra help and I'd be willing to give him a try. He showed experience around the horses. He wore his hair almost to his shoulders then and was pretty scruffy, but had a kind face. He wasn't the typical hippie I had met from Yorkville."

"So, in fact, you took to him right away?"

"Yeah, I guess I did."

"Did Newman tell you that John dealt in drugs?"

"No. He said something about he may be more of a help to my stable than I knew, something along those lines. I did not understand what he meant at the time. I wanted to know more about him, and where he was staying. John told me, upfront, that he was an American living in Canada, skipping out on the Vietnam War."

"So, he didn't lie? You knew why he was in Toronto?"

"Yes."

"What was his speech like? Did you think he was on drugs?"

"No. Once I talked to him, I knew he was ok. He was well spoken. I thought he must have been well educated."

"Oh, really? Then, he didn't come across as a dropout or drug pusher?"

"No. Not at all. I thought he showed ambition and was eager to learn, and make something of himself."

"Then, perhaps, Mr. Sharp, it wasn't he who encouraged the use of drugs. It was your idea, once you found out that he had connections to get the supplies you were looking for. Wouldn't you say that sounds a little more reasonable? I mean, here we have a kid, running away, trying to find a job. A draft dodger hiding, unlikely wanted to draw any attention to himself. He finds a friend who gives him a job and will teach him the ropes, if he cooperates with him."

"No. The kid had the stuff."

"Perhaps, Mr. Sharp. Perhaps he did have the contacts, but he was not experienced using drugs around the horses. He probably did not even think about selling it at all. He was just looking for a place to hide out and since the racetrack circuit is a moving business, it was a great cover. Did he ever speak of his family to you?"

"Sometimes, he did mention a brother, and his parents in Ohio, but nothing particular."

"Did John look anything like your son?"

"No."

"So, it was a friendship that grew because he was about the same age as your son would have been – in his mid-twenties. Tell us, Mr. Sharp, did John Mencini learn quickly around the horses."

"Yes he did. Proved himself very well. He was a hard worker and eager to learn."

The Crown Attorney moves closer to the bench, eyeing the witness.

"Mr. Sharp. The young woman Miss Harrison engaged to John, did she seem the typical hippie or into taking drugs? I mean, was she smoking weed, acting foul-mouthed, you know, a tough kid who hung around the racetrack?"

"No. Not at all. She was a cute skinny kid, scared of the horses. She made us laugh with her nervousness. I used to call her Little Britches."

"So, she didn't seem to fit into the scene either. She and John were well suited?"

"No, they weren't! She was naive. She didn't have a clue what John was into, or the type of person he really was."

"What do you mean, Mr. Sharp? In your opinion, what was he into? Do you mean other women?"

"No. I mean he was over his head dealing in drugs. I am sure she knew about his involvement, but did not know to what extent. I think she did try to block it out of her mind. She loved him and love is blind. It would have ruined her image of him. She was a good kid about five years younger than John. She and Karen were a lot alike back then."

"So, you feel that he turned them around? They didn't have a mind of their own? He brainwashed them?"

"Sure he did." *Great,* I think, *no mind of our own.* I look over to where Karen sits snuggled up to Chuck. Ours eyes lock, momentarily. With one arm wrapped around her shoulder, all of a sudden, I miss Bradley. Where was he when I needed him?

"Mr. Sharp, who turned him around? Who turned John Mencini from the innocent draft dodger, scared and running, into a drug-pushing con that learned the tricks of the trade, using them to his own advantage? Tell us, Mr. Sharp, who taught this young boy the ways of the racetrack?" As he speaks, Whittmore faces the jury, throwing up his hands to them and raising his tone. Then he pauses, leaving the thought with them. He flips through some pages before facing the accused in the witness stand.

"Mr. Sharp, we have heard testimony that you were a devoted family man. You must have talked about them a great deal." He pauses. "If it's true that you and John Mencini were so close that he was mistaken for your son, then why didn't you ever speak of him to your personal friends or your acquaintances?"

"I don't understand."

"Mr. Sharp, I am saying that this close relationship should have made you speak well of him around your close friends, like Mr. Westgate and others we have heard from over the past several weeks. He was a friend of yours since high school, and yet, he had never heard of John Mencini." Whittmore waits, without raising his head from his papers.

"I … ah, don't know. Lots of my friends didn't know the ins and outs of the racetrack, so it was not talked about."

"You have just said that John caught on quickly to the things you taught him around the racetrack. Wasn't it true, that he learned so quickly that he started experimenting on his own?" Whittmore clears his throat. "Did this all begin at the time they bought SnoMann? Or was it when he won his big race?" A long silence fills the courtroom as he let the jury consider his question. Sharp does not reply.

"If this relationship had been as strong as you say, then why did he turn on you, if in fact, he actually did? What could have happened to make him lose respect for you?"

The accused shrugs his shoulders. The Judge directs him to answer while the Crown Attorney Whittmore gives a wondering look toward the jury as they sit especially intent on every word.

"Perhaps, Mr. Sharp, he suddenly realized he had been your cover. John Mencini finally got the bigger picture about the gamblers, your tactics, and then finally saw himself as just another one of your patsies, carrying out your orders. Is that not the reason he was waiting to make his large bet on SnoMann, so that he could leave the racetrack?"

"No… no way."

"Mr. Sharp, I think the truth is that John Mencini came into your stable on a day when you were desperate. You needed wins. Newman knew what you needed and took John to your stable. He was a gullible kid, drifting about, when he joined your employment. He eventually followed your every command. You gave him confidence, conned him into getting drugs for the vets and yourself, and whatever else you wished." He hesitates, turning once again towards the jury, and then revisits the podium, pausing to refer to his notes.

"The kid was trouble, I'm telling you, from the beginning, only I didn't know it," Sharp exclaims.

Peter sits next to me, rubbing his hands nervously along his thighs, and then loosens his collar. I observe a change taking place as he listens to testimony.

"I say, John found out you were double-crossing him behind his back and presumably it hurt him because he thought so much of you. He realized you were using him, dealing with drugs behind his back for the money, contacts, or whatever, without his knowledge, he began to rebel. Rightly so, or perhaps you bribed him? Yes, perhaps telling him to produce or you would turn him into the authorities for dodging the draft. You had him scared." Whittmore halts, leaning over the edge of the podium, sneering at the accused. There is another long lingering silence.

"He didn't do you in, you did yourself in. You made sure the boy wasn't going to squeal on you. So, Mr. Sharp, you paid someone to finish him off, because, in fact, he was going to turn you in."

No response. Once again, a soft chatter sounds throughout the room, and then settles. I cannot believe how hot the room suddenly gets as I sense a feeling of riding a roller coaster. The trial takes many twists and turns.

"You rid yourself of what you created."

"Objection. Your Honor, my Friend is working on assumption and leading the witness," the Defense Counsel argues.

Whittmore retires without any further questions as noise rumbles throughout the space. The Judge orders quiet in the courtroom before he adjourns.

My mind is whirling from all the testimony, finding it difficult to concentrate on anything else for more than a few moments without returning to the events of the trial. Something is still missing, I can feel it. Is there still a strong negative force blocking me from moving on with my life?

While Bradley is working hard in London, I am struggling to conquer my past demons so we can have a happy future. He articulates a confidence that is reassuring as he keeps me up-to-date on his work, the office, gossip and the latest happenings with Matthew and Susan.

I am thinking a lot about London, again, so one evening I place an overseas call.

"That's great your job is taking a turn for the good. Is there anything else new?"

"Well, Frannie, it's been weeks now, and I. . ."

"What has been weeks now?" I think I lost my job to another. Why wouldn't it be, I am still in Toronto and it's been a year since I left.

"Susan. I promised her quite awhile ago that I would not tell you until the trial ended, but I really think you have got to know, and the time is right, now."

"What about her? Is anything the matter with Matthew?"

"No." There is a serious tone in his voice. "A lump formed in her left breast not long after you left London. She went for her routine check-up and that's when they diagnosed it. This set her back, and she could not cope with the possibility of surgery. After hearing all about it, I thought she should talk it over with you, that maybe… " He pauses. "However, Susan would have no way of it and made me promise not to mention it to a soul. So, she waited and waited, until finally she decided to go ahead with the surgery because of Matthew, and the doctors worrying. The operation was last Thursday. And, Frannie, she's ok. They removed it, and it was not cancerous. She will be fine, but she has had a tough nine months."

"Bradley," I cry. "I can just imagine, that's awful! I mean, I am genuinely glad that everything turned out fine, but don't ever keep anything from me again. You know how close we have been since she moved to London, and Susan and I have been friends since before high school. Damn! Everything happens at once." Devastated by his news, I beg him to give me all the specific details.

Obviously, Susan needed me and yet she chose not to talk because of my own trauma, which was nothing in comparison. Known for being stubborn, Susan made it difficult for others to reach out and help. *What's happening?* I begin to feel lonely and melancholy.

Later that same evening, Peter and I recount the story of Susan's operation. We both agree that the best approach is to tell her parents of her surgery and be able to comfort them in their suffering. They decide to fly to London, regretting the wasted years, to help with her treatment.

Chapter 27
Summations

Monday, the courthouse fills with more than its usual exuberance as hundreds of spectators linger throughout the hallways and on the street to hear final arguments and the jury's verdict.

Tension rises as a flashing light beams '*In Session*' above the oak doors. The chatter ends as the attorneys organize their papers, preparing their closing arguments. At ten-fifteen, the deputy arrives and the trial resumes.

The podium, a few feet from the witness box, faces the jury who appear alert and ready for summations, as everyone watch from the gallery. The Defense Counsel is the first to present his closing arguments because he called witnesses. He walks up to the podium, bowing to his Lordship, and then turns to face the jury.

The Defense Attorney opens his arguments by focusing on how the lack of evidence against the accused supports 'not guilty'. He emphasizes that the Crown is grasping. His details and explanations last over two hours.

"… and you have heard assumptions and circumstantial evidence about the victim's background. I show you living proof of a well-respected honorable man, who has done nothing, committed no crime, not even a traffic ticket, in his fifty-plus years. He lived no differently than others. He serves his community well; he is hard working, has a good reputation among friends and business partners, and was a faithful, sincere family man. All before the Yorkville boy, John Mencini, came into his life. Yes, before and after his appearance, this man was a sound, substantial being. Mencini was shown, proven, and identified as a con, a manipulator who presented himself as a naive draft dodger, with a hand in several drug connections. If he had the connections for the kind of drugs mentioned, he was no mere good boy from the upper crust. He was in over his head before he ever came to the racetrack. Moreover, it was Mr. Sharp's misfortune to have met the boy.

"The sorrowful days before the killing Mr. Sharp rampaged in anger and drunkenness, which clouded his mind. No one, no one at all, can be ascertained to be in his right mind during a three-day drinking binge. He had lost his family and his reputation. The work he loved became twisted and he felt that his only self-defense was to put Mencini out of his life, forever. In the heat of passion, self-preservation and desperation to save his honor, property and family, Robert Sharp was provoked beyond reason, to pay for the killing of John Mencini." Counsel lowers his voice.

"The drugs, they are a fact of the racetrack. Animals suffer, so they ease their pain. Someone could have planted the harmful drugs in his barn. The years John Mencini and Robert Sharp spent together are history. They fell into each other's ways, with Mencini knowing the ropes more than the experienced race-tracker. We have heard testimonies that John Mencini was too smart to use the drugs that he pushed. However, he knew exactly where and how to push them. He knew where to go and what to get when he set someone up. I do not think that this sounds like an innocent young man. He saw a good opportunity with Mr. Sharp and I say, Mencini used it to his full advantage and financial gain.

"I submit, ladies and gentlemen of the jury, that Robert Sharp is not guilty and that Alexander Newman, who committed the murder has been proven guilty. There was no intent to kill him on Sharp's part. Perhaps, like any of us who have lost everything to someone else, we want to hurt him or her to cover our own sorrow. I say the killer has been convicted, and Robert Sharp is not guilty because, if he were guilty, he would have used the weapon himself when he found it in the first place. Yes, if the thought and the intent actually existed, Robert Sharp would have taken the gun and committed the killing himself."

After taking his seat, a long pause lasts more than ten minutes before the Judge calls upon the Crown to present his closing statement.

Whittmore comes into view, running his fingers through his coarse graying hair and walks to the podium, eyeing each of the jurors. Peter grasps my hand as we both look at Karen, and then to each other. Chuck sits next to his wife, supportive as always. I admit that it was their destiny to meet in London. They are a nice looking couple.

"Members of the Jury, it is now my responsibility to address you on behalf of the Crown in this case. The time is approaching when you will retire to consider your verdict, having heard all the evidence and instructed as to the Law, by his Lordship."

My palms are sweating once again as I listen to Whittmore, who doesn't take his eyes off the jurors while he speaks his closing arguments. It is a long detailed speech.

"...and the first offense is the charge against Robert Sharp of murder. Culpable homicide is murder when the person means to cause his death - the slayer intends the death of his victim. Now, we have heard considerable testimony from several witnesses, who each explained that Robert Sharp had a motive, to get even and be rid of him. He told his own daughter he was going to 'get him for this,' and that 'he was going to pay'. Then Alexander Newman revealed Robert Sharp's plan to do him in. We heard the actual words of the accused telling us, yes telling us on tape, that if it wasn't done for him, he would have killed John Mencini, himself. The proof is beyond dispute." He carefully leans closer toward the jury.

"We have here a distinguished, prominent, successful man of society who once was nothing more than a good horseman. He experienced a tiny taste of success when introduced to a superior class of horse, which won bigger purses and gave him recognition." His tone changes. "We must examine this growth carefully. We must see each stage as it actually occurred." Whittmore briefly goes into detail recapping his life.

"... and now, we're told that he financially reached a slight peak when he began to run into a few difficulties because his horses were not performing as well as he thought they should be. Once he had tasted success, he did not want to lose it. No, he didn't want to be an ordinary trainer, but he was running into trouble. His need to succeed had already started to form and become an obsession. Once he began to lose his success the young victim, John Mencini, came into his life." Whittmore continues to keep eye contact with each juror as he deliberates.

"Now, John had absolutely no knowledge whatsoever of the racetrack, remember? He was just drifting, escaping the draft, innocent to the ways and means of this man. There was word, mind you that he did have drug contacts, but the drugs involved were those used in the village of Yorkville. Drugs like hash, weed, some speed, or whatever the kids of that time used. It was for easy cash, survival money. We heard testimony that his dealings had stopped. Now, he met up with Mr. Sharp through the contact Newman, known as Smoocher. He learns directly from Newman that he knows of a connection that could make him money. His friends, now you have seen them and heard their testimonies, do not seem like the wild, drugged up hippies or flower children of the sixties. Mr. Sharp did not think of them as such, or he would not have hired them. John Mencini became attached to this man as his friends had, and they grew fond of Mr. Sharp. But, you must also remember that Robert Sharp had experience with the ways of the racetrack. He failed to render assistance to the boy, whereby he could just as easily have put him on the straight path. Instead, he allowed a dangerous situation to exist." Another lingering pause.

"Once again, you have heard several testimonies as to their closeness; a closeness that developed over a few years. A father and son relationship, we heard. At least it appeared as such. But, a closeness like that doesn't go unnoticed, or unmentioned. Yet Mr. Sharp never did mention the boy to his personal acquaintances. We heard testimony from one of Mr. Sharp's closest friends, who frequently dined with his family, and never, over that period of five years, heard him mention the John Mencini name. Odd isn't it? Why had he kept him a secret? Unless, the victim, John Mencini, had not really meant anything at all. Perhaps, he was Mr. Sharp's *front* for getting him what he needed so that he could be a big-wheel, without dirtying his own hands.

"Now, the learned Counsel for the Defense indicates that the accused was provoked, but how could he be? The young man only practiced what his master had taught him instead of getting him to clean up his act." Once again, Whittmore looks at each one of the jurors. "Did John Mencini really change his daughter's mind? Did he actually conspire with Karen to ride the horse, SnoMann, in the race that changed all their lives, which seemed the final turning point between the two men. It appears obvious that Karen Sharp was a woman who had a mind of her own, begging the victim for the mount. Yes, there were, perhaps, events leading up to the race that had nothing to do with John Mencini. Mr. Sharp created his own jealousy. The young man had helped create his success and now had become interference. Mr. Sharp certainly did not protect himself or his family, according to testimony we heard. From all appearances, the damage had already been done. Yes, done by his own doing; greed, self-destructiveness. The ego can take a man that one step too far." Silence fills the room. "The idea of murder had not been an accident, an emotional outburst, because it was conceived, talked about, intended, and then done.

Indeed, Alexander Newman pulled the trigger for his own reasons, the money, but remember, Robert Sharp had paid him $20,000. to do it, and that made him as guilty as Newman!" He drops his glance to the floor and then waits and points to the Defense.

"They claim drunkenness, a state of being too drunk to be capable of forming intent to kill. However, he was sober enough to hand over a considerable amount of money... but, too intoxicated to be guilty of murder? Come now! Was his drinking such that he gave in more readily to the violent passion?" He lowers his tone. "We have heard testimony proving he used drugs which cause cruelty to animals and of a conspiracy to traffic in narcotics." Again, the Crown details the witnesses' testimony, proving his claim.

"It's known that 'organized crime' gets revenue from encouraging gambling, and those involved put Mr. Sharp on the spot demanding to get their bets placed, and to win, but he could just as easily, in the beginning, denied them and returned to his small successful stable. The temptation to be in the 'limelight' was too great. Through a conspiracy and fraudulent actions, he pursued an unlawful objective. The trafficking of narcotics, the cruelty to animals, the illegal betting, the defrauding of the public by bribery of the jockeys, have all been proven. He became a master of these offenses," Whittmore points to the accused, a distinguished looking man sitting in the prisoner's dock, and then he faces the jury.

"It is time for you, the men and women of the jury, to wipe the slate clean. Look beyond the successes, back to June 3, 1969, when another ultimatum placed before him. Mr. Sharp wanted all the power, all the authority and did not like having his toes stepped upon by the one he had so carefully molded. When John Mencini began to make plans and investments to leave the racetrack, he believed he would be a tremendous success. He did not include Robert Sharp in the syndicate. Robert Sharp would lose his connections for a winning stable. Eventually, after Mencini's death, Robert Sharp took the business over as his own, revealing yet again the man's lust for power. Greed. Was this Robert Sharp's plan all along?" There is another very long silence. "The evidence you have heard over the past months, can lead to only one conclusion - a verdict of guilty of murder."

The jurors are still. Some appear confused, others reluctant; an older woman closes her eyes while another, lost in concentration, focuses on the ceiling; a middle-aged man rubs his chin, his eyes blank, and others hold their heads defiantly.

The room echoes a light chatter as the two hundred plus spectators watch patiently from all areas of the gallery. I am devoid of any energy.

Judge MacIntosh takes several minutes making notes, pausing every so often to refer to a book. Both attorneys wait at their tables. The jury remains still and thoughtful. They know their time has come. The Constable at the entrance way refuses to let anyone enter or leave. The minutes slip away, slowly.

The Judge, at last, organizes his papers, straightens his red banner, taps his gavel, and leans over his dais directing his instructions to the jury before they retire to the *deliberation room*. He instructs them as to their duty, explaining the law distinguishing murder from manslaughter and applying the law to the case.

"We have reviewed the evidence, both circumstantial and direct. You must remember that the Crown must satisfy you that Mr. Sharp, the accused, caused this death beyond a reasonable doubt." He further explains how they must reach a unanimous decision in their verdict of 'guilty' or 'not guilty'. The Judge explains the basis for their decision, telling them how they should go about it. His cautious manner in the presentation is effective in preventing any challenge of an appeal for a wrongly instructed jury.

I look from the Judge to the jury as he directs them to choose a foreman who will preside over their deliberation. The jury panel of twelve listens with watchful and attentive eyes as the Judge clarifies. It is now time to make their final decision and depart the courtroom. The handcuffed prisoner leaves and the trial temporarily adjourns.

The winds blow hard, and the crowds awaiting the verdict stay indoors. Gradually, the hours pass.

The death of my first love flashes before me. Life is but a journey and the journey is all about how we react to each circumstance. London seems so very far away right now.

At nine pm, the day ends with the rumor that the jurors were escorted to the hotel. It's time for all to leave.

Friday morning, Peter and I arrive at the same time as Karen and Chuck, who are swarmed by media people. We group ourselves in a corner of one of the consulting rooms and exchange condolences. Karen and I hug, understanding each other's loss and the strenuous tension of another day. Chuck and Peter chat as our anxiety over the final verdict keeps the four of us in close contact.

If Sharp is found guilty, the Judge sentences the accused after hearing arguments concerning his character and previous record from both the Crown and Defense counsels. Whittmore had explained previously what determines the Judge's sentence. Depending on the circumstances, he would consider such facts as, the nature of the offense, public pressures, his own prejudices, the convicted person's character, and his age. Since he committed several offenses, the sentencing would be lengthy. The Judge, however, would award only one, because he was being tried for one, murder.

I am suffering a second day of waiting. Peter notices the morning paper carries headlines of the murder trial that shocks Toronto communities with our pictures on the front page. One of the photos was of SnoMann with John, me, Peter and Karen in the saddle, standing in the winner's circle. Peter picks up a copy. We do not say anything, just remember another time. We decide to drive the Ferrari downtown 'for luck'.

Later in the day, the constable outside the courtroom calls, *'in session'*, and things begin to happen. It takes only a matter of minutes before everyone settles in his respective place. The jury returns from the deliberation room at three forty-five. Silence prevails. Their expressions were blank.

The Judge nods to the registrar to proceed. He stands, turns and addresses the jury.

"Members of the Jury, have you agreed upon your verdict? How say you? Do you find the prisoner 'guilty' or 'not guilty'?"

The foreman stands at the end of the jury box. He announces, "We find the accused guilty as charged."

The room explodes with cries, cheers, and mixed emotions. Several members of the press jump from their seats in the gallery as the verdict echoes throughout the room and spectators call out their approval or disapproval. Karen screams hysterically as Chuck wraps his arms around her tightly. For her, there is no family left.

Peter slumps forward, releasing all tension. My hands cover my face as mournful, yet satisfied tears flow uncontrollably. The tightness in my chest and the lump in my throat lift for the first time in years. "YES, for the love of John, thank God!" We embrace.

The Judge places his pen down, once again tapping his gavel. The Defense Counsel stands, asking that the jury be polled. Each juror rises and announces 'guilty' in response to the registrar's question.

The accused remains in the dock staring at the floor in shock. The registrar records the verdict. The Judge dismisses the jury and turns to the accused.

"Stand up, Mr. Sharp. Do you have anything to say, before I pass sentence?"

After a moment, he shakes his head.

"I sentence you to imprisonment for life."

Once again, loud chatter fills the room. The Judge calls "Order. Remove the prisoner." Robert Sharp is once again handcuffed, and taken out. The court adjourns.

My vision blurs slightly as I watch Chuck, Karen and Peter disappear amongst the crowd, followed by several members of the Press. I want to reach out to Karen, but can't find the strength to fight the crowds. Wondering what their future will hold, I remain in my seat until the last of the spectators leave, and then approach Whittmore. He looks my way.

"Thank you. Thank you very much. I had my doubts, but now know why you are one of the best in the country." We embrace, and then shake hands. Soon, it will be time to celebrate.

Leaving through the large oak doors to the marble corridor for the last time, I pass the Crown Attorney's office where I experience the satisfaction of justice done as the case concludes. The reporting journalists, calling their respective newspapers, occupy all the phones. Taking a final look around, I stroll through the lobby of the main entrance, overhearing several opinions.

Wrapping myself in a navy trench coat, I belt the waist, stepping out into sunny skies, and then inhale vigorously the fresh air, slowly treading forward. Two robins resting on a concrete buttress are next to me beside the walkway. 'A sign of new beginnings,' I whisper.

"Excuse me, Miss Harrison." A familiar voice calls from behind. I turn to see James Whittmore cross the concrete courtyard. "Listen, I almost forgot." He hands over a folded paper as his robe flaps with the gentle breeze. I open the letter, and read aloud.

"To the lady in the red Ferrari. I've found your 1937 Packard convertible. It isn't in as good a shape as your machine, but I'll tell you what, I'll have it restored for you if you consider it an even trade. How about it?" signed Reagan.

Looking up at Whittmore, seeing his soft green eyes, I smile. "Your son, of course." He nods.

Withdrawing a set of keys from my gray leather purse, I state, "Here, I wouldn't enjoy it anymore, anyway. I will explain it all to Peter and he'll take care of the rest for him. Thanks again. You have really cleared the air for me, more than you could ever know. My life has real meaning, now."

He shakes my hand, "Until next time, Francine. And... let it not be in court."

Turning to leave, he calls again. "There is just one thing..." He steps to my side. "Something I'd like your opinion on, Francine. A while back, you made a remark how Peter thought that Sharp pulled a real snow-job on the bunch of you." I remember. "What I would like to know is... which one is the 'Snow Man'?"

A look of puzzlement wrinkles my brow for a moment, and then I grin.

Whittmore repeats himself. "Who? Was it John Mencini? You have heard numerous weeks of testimony regarding the two men. Now, in all honesty, you tell me. The real con artist. Who was it?"

A faint smile crosses my lips. I confess. "Me."

His eyes query my remark. He shakes his head, not understanding.

"You see, Mr. Whittmore, it was I who snowed them into claiming SnoMann." His expression mellows as he pats my shoulder.

"I think you have crossed boundaries now."

"Pardon? I don't ...."

"Broke the barriers - no longer surrounded by that negative energy field." Whittmore flashes a broad smile, shaking hands.

I continue walking to the corner of University Avenue when a taxi pulls up and the door swings open. Another familiar voice cries out.

Overwhelmed at the sight of Bradley stepping out, I dash into his open arms as he propels me to the taxi, saying, "Toronto International, please."

Once
I stood in solitude
Against the wind of night,
Confessing all my Satan's past
With eager thought for light.
The pain of knowing I had been misjudged
And graven marks were etched,
Upon my heart of earnest trust,
Once, too young
Caressed.

HOT - WALKER Life on the Fast Track
sports crime romance novel

***

Mallory Neeve Wilkins Books

House of the Caduceus (mystery)
Hot-Walker Life on the Fast Track (sports crime)
Ancient Secrets for a Healthy Home (feng shui - vaastu)
Fun Schway, the North American way (feng shui reference)
Graveyard Autos (photography)
The Laundry Art Book (photography)

About the Author

Originally from Toronto, Mallory Wilkins currently lives on the Pacific west coast writing novels and non fiction, designing interiors and enjoying photography. She worked in the design/build industry specializing in Feng Shui Interior Design as a professional member of the Canadian, American and International Interior Design Associations.

www.ingramcontent.com/pod-product-compliance
Lightning Source LLC
Chambersburg PA
CBHW031111030726
47496CB00002BA/487